A FEMINIST MANIFESTO

A FEMINIST MANIFESTO

THE MARRIAGE WARS

BOOK TWO

MELISSA GOWDY BALDWIN

For information about rights, permissions, or bulk purchases, please contact the author at hello@melissagowdybaldwin.com.
Cover design by Dan Aguilar
Editor: Hannah Sol Marie
First Edition: November 2025

ISBN: 978-1-969712-00-5 (paperback); 978-1-969712-00-12 (hardback); 978-1-969712-02-9 (epub)
Library of Congress Control Number: 2025922086 (paperback); 2025923114 (hardback)

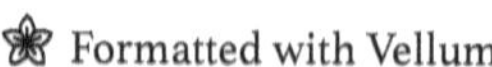 Formatted with Vellum

To the women who make the courageous choices, even when they're the hardest ones.
To the children who discover light in the darkest of places.
And to the friends and family who never let you forget your strength.

CONTENT CONSIDERATIONS:

Gun Violence
Language
Sexual Content
Sexual Assault

"We must raise our daughters differently. We must also raise our sons differently."
Chimamanda Ngozi Adichie

Dear Reader,

Thank you for coming back to the Nation and holding Olivia's hand as her world becomes more dismantled. As I write this, I'm again listening to T-Swift's "Dear Reader", a small nod to the me that wrote the first installment of The Marriage Wars Trilogy. A person I see in pictures, recognizing only small parts of *the me who didn't leave.*

Like my first book, this one found a way to be a mirror of a life I didn't know I was living until it was almost done. As I look back on the last ten or more years and how much of that was written in book one, I can only smile and say thank you for the fires I've walked through.

There are parts of book one I don't remember writing, just like parts of this book too. Writing is a powerful tool to process trauma, grief, loss, and anger. When my world turned upside down over three years ago, I did the only thing I knew–I wrote my way out. I wanted this book to be done so much sooner, but that wasn't the grand plan. I had to sit in the grief and anger and fear and impulsive behavior in order to fully come out alive on the other side.

And I did. And Olivia does too. As heroines do.

Buckle up—this book is messy, flawed, graphic. Olivia is a mess. She's grief-stricken about her children, overwhelmed by truth, and impulsive AF. In this book we see the light and the arc we all wished for her in book one, but was not meant to start to unfold until now. Our girl is finally free to step into who she was always meant to be: *the me that leaves.*

#everyonelovesjude fans will want more of him, but he ended up not being a big part of Olivia's world in this book. I struggled with his silence. There were times I tried to put him in a scene with Olivia because I wanted them to reconnect; it just didn't work. Like so many ideas of mine, I was on the treadmill when his novella hit me. We love our girl, but goodness do we love Jude too. So with that said, he deserves his own HEA in the most Jude way. Plus we also all need more of those pool scenes–he's too hot to let him not have his own story told.

If you want to enhance your reading experience, the playlist for *AFM* is at the end of the book with section breakdowns, QR code, and the list of songs. The chapter sections give hints at the overall story arc, just FYI.

Okay my readers! Grab a glass of wine, your best bubbly, or mocktail, and happy reading.

Always,

Melissa

Remember that all heroines find their way, even if it's a hot burning pile of garbage on its way.

MARRIAGE EDICTS

FEBRUARY 14, 2030

TO: All citizens under the newly formed Nation and any persons who want to freely participate in The Nation

WHEREAS, the people of the state want to change the genetic future of our dire circumstances; and

WHEREAS, the U.S. Government can no longer secure viability of population health; and

WHEREAS, humanity is morally corrupt and in social decline;

NOW, THEREFORE, notwithstanding previous laws under the former State of California Constitution, I hereby issue the following EDICTS for any citizen desiring to marry under Nation law and participate in a truer and healthier future for humanity:

Edict 1:
Both citizens must be citizens of the Nation.

Edict 2:

Both citizens must only be within one tier of each other in the five-tier class system.

Edict 3:

Both citizens must have certified functioning reproductive organs and no prior health conditions.

Edict 4:

Both citizens must be heterosexual or two females only for population growth.

Edict 5:

Both citizens must be within the prescribed skin-tone rating set by the Nation.

Edict 6:

Both citizens must share either monotheistic, polytheistic, or atheistic religious beliefs.

Edict 7:

Both citizens must agree to have children within the first two years of marriage.

Edict 8:

Both citizens must share an educational status approved by Pre-License Board.

Edict 9:

Both citizens must complete the Pre-License Board DNA test to promote genetic diversity and population health.

Edict 10:

Both citizens must agree to be implanted with the Nation

microchip prior to the marriage ceremony to monitor genetic abnormalities, physical and mental health, reproduction, and location. After a child reaches age one, parents must consent to chips being implanted into the child.

Like THE GUBERNATORIAL TERM EDICT, these EDICTS have no expiry date and are effective immediately unless otherwise modified by Nation Governors.

A.T. Valentin
    West Nation Governor Valentin

THE NATION MARRIAGE SYSTEM

Social Class Tiers
One-Bronze
Two-Silver
Three-Gold
Four-Elite Platinum
Five-Upper Elite Platinum

First Five Years of Marriage Requirements
1-Establish permanent place of residence within tier guidelines.
2-First child conceived or born.
3-Second child conceived or born.
4-Consistent home routine in place with active involvement in the community.
5-Mother may return to work with approval; continue with home routine and community.

The Nation Marriage Reward System (MRS)

Year 1-4 Anniversary: Couples may choose from MRS Menu.
Year 5 Anniversary: Both members may use their private

Challenge Pass for one night or select an option from the Nation Bonus Menu.

Year 6 Anniversary: Couples may choose from MRS Menu.

Year 7 Anniversary: Both members may use their private Challenge Pass for two nights or select two options from the Nation Bonus Menu.

Year 8 and 9 Anniversary: Couples may choose from MRS Menu.

Year 10 Anniversary: Both members may use their private Challenge Pass for three nights or select three options from the Nation Bonus Menu.

Year 11-14 Anniversary: Couples may select two options from MRS Menu each year + $15,000 each.

Year 15 Anniversary: Both members may either use their private Challenge Pass for one week or select three options from the Nation Bonus Menu AND complete a Tier Status Increase Application.

Year 16-19 Anniversary: Couples may select two options from MRS Menu each year + $25,000 each.

Year 20 Anniversary: Couples may choose their own Challenge Pass time and location. Couples will also receive an automatic Tier Status Increase and one Nation Bonus for each child they have produced that has survived to year 20.

Year 20+ Anniversary: Citizens may choose to stay married or qualify to void marriage contract if: 1) their children are over age 18, 2) they are still able to reproduce and would like to change partners, and 3) they have reached tier-five. Should couples stay married, MRS bonuses can be selected at the discretion of each member.

1

OLIVIA

Sunshine rays warmed my skin as I sat watching them run barefoot, laughing through golden fields that shimmered like something out of one of their children's books. I was with them again, Rose and Lucas. We were reunited–the three of us back together the way it was supposed to be.

They called out to me, arms open, voices light and whimsical, and my chest ached with a joy so full it felt like sorrow—like this wasn't real. I looked around. The sky was too blue. The grass they ran through didn't bend when it met their feet. They cast no shadows on the ground. My voice called to them, but they kept running. I reached out my arms, but couldn't touch their hands.

Somewhere far off, I heard a clock ticking—too loud, too steady. I scanned the scene and I thought I saw *him*, standing at the edge of the horizon watching us. He sneered, crossing his arms as he folded into the only shadows that his darkness created.

I turned away, clinging to the warmth, to their laughter, to the hope that their hands would find mine–a lie I was telling myself. I didn't care if it was real. I wanted the lie. I wanted them to be with me here, now, without him. I called, but my voice made no sound. How was this possible? Was I being silenced, again? I called one more time, a small voice lost among the thunderclouds rolling in and the sun being stolen from the sky. I screamed, just as the thunder shook the sky–they heard me. Just as their hands were about to touch mine, my body jolted forward, ripping Rose and Lucas from me again. I awoke with my heart pounding, arms still outstretched, clutching nothing but the air in the Resistance SUV.

"What the fuck, Ethan?" My head shot back and hit the headrest.

"Sorry, a coyote ran out in front of us," Ethan's tentative reply made me question his story.

The silence that had lulled me to sleep resumed its seat in between Ethan and me as we drove past towering oaks and the tender green manzanita bushes. Every second felt like a spark, another tiny fire waiting to consume the entire convoy. I clutched the edge of my seat, digging my nails into the leather, grasping for what, I didn't know. I worked hard to tighten the anger in my body, forcing it into hiding so I wouldn't explode. My children weren't here. They were only in my dreams now. They were still there–back in the Nation with Thomas–because Ethan had left them.

He promised.

He promised we would be together. All of us. Not a fraction of what I knew to be.

The thought of that night at the airport hit me again like a blow to the chest, sharp and unforgiving. His words laced in a fool's confidence, declaring he would be going back to get Rose and Lucas. That they were safe from Thomas, from the Nation, from a world without me.

Now the miles between my children and me felt like a betrayal, a choice I didn't make but had to live with. A consequence of the love I held in my heart for Ethan for the last ten years. My penance. My payment. My penalty.

"You lied to me." The words seethed through teeth, my voice low and raw. I refused to cry in front of him, if I could help it. He wouldn't get that from me. Never again.

He stayed quiet, eyes on the road, and jaw tight as he drove us back to the entrance of the Cameron Park Lake compound. When he finally spoke, his voice was icy. "It was the only way. You know that. One day you will understand."

"Don't you dare tell me what I will know or do in the future." I whipped my head around glaring at him. "You promised me. And I left everything because of that promise."

He adjusted his hands, and his shoulders stiffened. We had reached the entrance, and he stopped the car, then turned to me. There was something in his eyes I couldn't place–regret maybe, or guilt?

"It was the only way once Thomas found us. If I had gone to get them or sent anyone else from my team, we'd all be dead or worse, captured and stuck in the Nation. You know that. He was going to kill me. He was ready to kill you, too. Or have you forgotten about that moment you stood on the tarmac, blood dripping down your arm? Blood seeping out of my body as you loaded me into the plane...the moment we both thought I was never coming back...to you."

I looked away, refusing to betray myself as a small amount of tears welled in my eyes. There was a time when Ethan's death would have been one of the worst things that could ever happen to me. But that was before–before I knew the heavier loss of having my children taken away from me.

I laughed bitterly and turned back to him, fire in my eyes. "That's easy for you to say. You still get everything you wanted. Me. Your kids with Samara and Laura. Your rebellion."

He flinched, just barely, but it wasn't enough to make me stop. I wanted him to feel the pain of a mother who'd lost the only things that gave her life meaning. I wanted him to feel the anger boiling up inside me over and over again, day after day, while we waited for the right moment to bring them back to me.

"You said you loved me. That was a lie. If you loved me, how could you do that? You knew they mean more to me than anything in this world." I paused, waiting to give the final blow. "Even you."

His eyes were dark and steady while his grip on the steering wheel tightened again. "I love you, Olivia. I have always, and will always, love you. But love doesn't survive if we're dead. I had to choose. I chose us."

"I wouldn't have made the same decision if you had given me the chance." I looked out the window as a temporary refuge until we got to the compound.

I thought I had escaped the Nation, but I hadn't. I only traded one prison for another. The Resistance, the Nation—there was no difference. They both kept me, and my children, caged until I forced a way out.

Ethan stopped outside the compound gate waiting for it to open and let the convoy back in. I looked in the mirror and watched it close behind us. The world outside blurred into nothing again. The only thing I knew for certain was this: whatever lay ahead, it wouldn't be freedom. Not without my children. Not without Rose and Lucas.

Once inside the compound, Ethan parked inside one of the hangars used to store vehicles, instead of the airplanes it housed years earlier. Samara waved and walked to my door, opening it while other rebels headed to the remaining vehicles to unload the supplies we picked up in Placerville, a town twenty minutes east of us.

"Were you able to get everything?" she asked me.

"Yeah, all good," Ethan interjected before I could reply.

She looked at me, cocking her head slightly, and I rolled my eyes. She reached for my hand and helped me out. "You okay?"

"No, but that's nothing new, right?"

It had been six weeks, nearly June now, since I had left the Challenge Center, and my children, in the Nation. The Cameron Park Airport I had to call my temporary home, stood as an additional base of operations for the Resistance. We had spent six long weeks trying to figure out how to infiltrate the Nation with no luck. My children were still being held by my husband, Thomas, trapped in the Nation's grip. Dark shadows stretched in every direction, and no light we held could cut through them.

Thomas, my husband of ten years, was the Director of the Nation. The Center. The red cage that pressed against me every waking day of my life for the last ten years. I never owned my body. My children never belonged to me. I never had control over my choices. Everything was his from the moment he bumped into me and spilled coffee on my dress. The day he killed my father. The day he took Ethan, the love of my life, away from me. The day Samara's children were fathered by Ethan. The day he found a way for Ethan and Jude to become lovers. The day he told me I would never see my children again.

My heart ached. They weren't here...with me. They were lost. To the Nation. To Thomas.

Samara sensed where I had gone. "Hey, we're going to find them. We're going to get them back." She pulled me in, hugging the body that had changed—leaner now, tougher. "I promise."

It had been six weeks since Samara and I had talked and began our friendship. Even though I hated her for having something of Ethan's, she was the only person I felt like I could trust-I could tell she would always give me the truth, even when it hurt. She was also a mother and knew the stronghold our children had on us. There was no me without them, and I knew she and Laura felt the same way about their girls.

Samara released me and I looked out toward the lake through the barbed wire fence and shuddered. Another sharp reminder of the new cage I willingly just drove back into. The airport compound was large and covered ten acres, not including the lake. Hangars lined the east side of the airport while permanent and make-shift houses lined the west. A giant hangar in the middle had formerly been converted into a lodge, complete with an industrial-sized kitchen, cafeteria, temporary boarding rooms, multiple social rooms, and the war room. If it wasn't the Nation holding its grips on me, it was the rebellion, led by Ethan and his group of supporters.

Ethan underestimated Thomas's ability, especially when it came to what Thomas valued most–his children. They meant the world to him. They symbolized everything he couldn't have as a child: security, love, a home. I pitied Thomas and his childhood, but not enough to lose sight of the strengths he possessed. His resilience, determination, and ambition to rise in the Nation was admirable to everyone, even to me on the days I hated him most. He fought for a life he wanted and would do anything to preserve it.

"C'mon, let's get something to eat before the meeting." Samara brought me back to the present. "Ethan, you and the guys got this?"

"Yep." Ethan looked at me. "Olivia, give me a minute, please?"

Samara eyed me and I nodded. "I'll see you at dinner."

"Thanks." My arms crossed and my stance was solid. "What do you want, Ethan?"

He walked around the front of the SUV, then leaned against the hood. "I know I will never fully earn your forgiveness. And maybe I don't really ever deserve it for leaving Lucas and Rose behind. But I hope that one day you will believe in me again, like you did before all of this." He moved closer, put his hand on my arm, and lowered his eyes. "I love you, Olivia Embers. I have always loved you. And I always will. Nothing will ever change that. Time, space, or..." He paused and looked down, "even people will never change that. It's you, Liv. It's you yesterday, today, tomorrow, forever. No one can ever replace you. Just like I know no one can ever replace me." He dropped his hand and walked to the back of the car where others had started to unload the supplies.

Olivia Embers.

My name.

A name that burned Olivia Smith to the ground.

A name that would eventually burn Thomas and the Nation to the ground too.

I looked out toward the lake once more, the bright sun looming over us, eventually making its way behind the foothill horizon. My children were just beyond it, waiting for me to come find them and bring them home. Tonight, in the planning meeting, I would make damn sure that I was going to be part of the team doing just that.

2

OLIVIA

Before meeting Samara for dinner, I stopped by my room and changed. I thought about the upcoming planning meeting, and how I'd tell them flat out: if they were going after my children, I was going too. Ethan would argue against it because he would claim it wasn't safe. Other people at the table would argue too, but I knew Samara would back me and in the end, there would be no mission without me. What anyone else said didn't matter.

The community dining hall was at the end of the main hallway, just past the war room. Dinner was served to everyone at the same time each night. Although food was available upon request, most of the people ate together, much like when we were growing up. I realized early on that if I missed dinner, it felt more like missing a key strategy session. Most days I just wanted to grab a roll or something portable to take back to my room, but I forced myself to perform the part expected of me: the one who got out. The one who survived. The one who knows the Director the best. All the roles I desperately wanted to shed, but couldn't because I needed to sacrifice, once again, for my children.

When would I stop sacrificing? Was it something innate in me, like my love for them, or was it something conditioned? Only in the past few weeks had I started to unravel the different versions of myself: the me before the compound, the me during the compound, the me with Ethan, and the me with Thomas. They were all pieces of who I'd been, but even they were becoming strangers to me. Why did I submit so often to Thomas? Why did I follow Ethan's orders to leave the children and board the plane? Where was my autonomy in all of it?

My complacency made me successful in the Nation, and a martyr for the Resistance. Would I ever untangle from both and figure out who I was? Who I wanted to be? Would I ever find my way back to the girl I remembered before Elysium? Did she question authority or had she always complied? Was she ever real or just another piece in an unfair game with men? Too many questions, and no room in my head for answers. Like everything else that didn't involve my children, they'd have to wait.

I stood in line, grabbed a plate of food, and scanned the hall for Laura, Samara, and their daughters. Laura sat with their girls in a corner near a window, Samara just to the side. I scanned the room, finding Jude with Chris, Brandon, and Tyler, Jude's eyes never meeting mine. Other families shared the long community table, telling stories about their day. Dr. and Mrs. Conrad sat close together at the far end, taking bites from each other's plates. My mother and sister sat at the communal table, backs to me.

"Hi Olivia," Laura said.

"Hi Laura, girls." I softened my voice and then sat down.

As I picked around my plate and listened to the girls argue over who could go further around the lake without stopping, I looked to the adults again. Pockets of companionship every-where. A forehead softly kissed. A hooked arm into another to help pull bodies closer. A smile that speaks not just happiness, but a deep love unscathed by the passage of time. Unscathed from heartbreak and the Nation.

What was this love? How did it get found in the unlikeliest of ways, but never in the realm that I existed in? I wanted to believe that Ethan would choose me and I would choose him at the end of this too. That Ethan wouldn't choose Jude–that he was done with him. But, if I couldn't heal from Ethan's betrayal, would I find myself back in Jude's arms? Was our connection at the Center actually real, or just another false reality under the Nation's dark veil? Even if it was Jude at the end of this, would he choose me over Ethan? Why was I even wondering about being chosen at all–what did that mean? And why did some quiet part of me want it? Maybe the real question was whether I could be brave enough to find peace in the freedom of living uncaged, untouched by any man, from this point on.

My thoughts wandered back to Thomas, a pervasive occurrence I struggled to control. I often tried to untangle each new thread from the web of our last ten years, which made it hard for me to decipher what was real and what was spun. Thomas's dragline silk framed the lifeline of every new web he chose to weave. Were the children part of the prey he captured or was it just me? Was he keeping me encased in silk, blinding me with beauty, as a means to immobilize my senses until he was ready to make his final move? A tightly spun parcel of death, hanging like forgotten fruit on his ambitious climb to power, money, and control over the world he wanted.

I struggled with the thought that I was nothing more than a transaction to him, and that he chose me because of my value in the Nation. I knew now that he had chosen me for my genetic and reproductive abilities, and wondered what part of my forged tier papers put me in his crosshairs. The small part of me that wanted to be loved had to be quieted and reminded that he never loved me. He loved the idea of me. The idea of the Nation dream I brought because of my climb in tier status, my genetic ability, and my unfortunate naivete that allowed his power to be exerted over me for ten long years.

I sacrificed, like so many other women, in vain. Under false pretenses. Under a veil of socially prescribed gender roles that kept us tethered to something we didn't know wasn't for us until it was too late. Under the conditioning that brought many of us to one form of death or another. He won so many times and I willingly let him. I never contested, questioned or fought back with enough strength to make a change. I never allowed myself to take the blindfold off until it was too late. Not until the final night at the Center. When fear turned into excitement–and with it, the possibility that I could finally be free, living with my children and Ethan.

Thomas never loved me, for me. He loved money. Power. Control. Something, I realized, I could never compete with. My value would never replace the value of those things. I would never be enough for him and because of this, a dark part of me wondered if I would ever be enough for any man.

For so long, Ethan would have been enough for me, but he failed me. He failed Rose and Lucas. How could I recover from that?

"Olivia?" Samara tapped my shoulder. "I'm sorry, I didn't mean to startle you. You okay?"

"Yeah. I was just somewhere else."

She squeezed my hand. "You're going to be okay, remember that."

"Thank you." I leaned into her shoulder and Laura reached her hand to me too.

"Samara's right, Olivia. I've known a lot of women in my life and you are one of the strongest ones I've seen. I don't think we've seen what you're fully capable of yet either. Don't let Ethan," Laura looked around the room, "or any person in this room, let you think anything different, okay?"

I nodded. "Thanks. I'll try not to."

"Are you ready to go?" Samara added. "The Conrads and everyone else just left for the war room."

"Yeah, I'm ready." I looked at Laura and the girls and said a quick goodbye.

I stepped into the room just as everyone sat down around a large wood table. Dr. Conrad sat at the head, with Ethan and Mrs. Conrad on either side. Morgan, our tech expert, Samara and I settled in while Jude, Chris, Brandon, and Tyler filled in the other seats talking quietly. In the empty chair next to me, a woman I didn't recognize sat down.

"Olivia? My name is Vivian, but everyone calls me Viv. I hear you're the missing piece for taking down the Nation, is that true?"

"Viv, she's one of the pieces, yes," Ethan said, not letting me answer.

"Apparently some people think I'm a missing piece, but really, I'm just here to get my kids back. If that somehow helps the Rebellion in the process, great."

"Noted," Vivian said. "Ethan, Dr. Conrad, good to see you again."

"Just get in, Viv?" Dr. Conrad asked

"Yeah, there was an issue getting out of South Borough, but I handled it. I sent the intel to you earlier–Morgan, did you get it?"

"Yeah. There's a lot of data to go through so it's going to take me time." Morgan turned to Dr. Conrad and Ethan, "Once it's ready, I'll send it to you right away."

"Thanks, Morgan." Ethan said.

"Okay, are we ready to get started?" Dr. Conrad asked and then took a remote to dim the lights. Since my time on the compound, Dr. Conrad ran the meetings and appeared to handle logistics for the Resistance. Ethan was still the face of it all, and I learned the Conrads and the other rebels had worked on the Center explosion for months, waiting for the right moment to execute their plan. A holographic map of downtown Sacramento appeared in the middle of the table, floating ominously in front of me. "Olivia is a key piece of what we need to do in order to infiltrate the Nation and remove Thomas and Jeffrey from power. She knows the ins and outs of the Nation world, like Ethan and Samara. However, her access to the upper tier gives us an advantage."

I didn't think I could be much help and honestly, I didn't want to be. I just wanted my kids back. But if this group wanted to believe I was important, I would let them.

"We know the Nation has increased its security and surveillance since the Center bombing. Intelligence suggests that Thomas has the children staying close to their school, most likely in one of the delegate buildings, making it difficult to intercept a convoy on their way back to the home. Intel suggests that they are still attending school, but are under heavy guard. There is another child, a boy, who has been with Rose and Lucas."

Photos of the children rotated above the table. A tan-skinned boy in a Bridges to the Nation uniform stood next to Rose and Lucas. My heart ached seeing the two of them together. Tears almost betrayed me, but I shoved them back down, just as I saw Ethan's wounded eyes leave mine. The boy was familiar to me even though I had only seen him for a moment at the Career Day Ceremony.

"His name is Cooper." A small crumb of information to show my value.

"Do you know him?" Dr. Conrad asked.

Samara shifted in her seat, Ethan and others turned toward me waiting for my answer.

"He was at the Career Ceremony and he's Thomas's intern. He could be valuable too if we want to add kidnapping to our plan." I laughed with no response from anyone.

"She's right, Dr. Conrad, the boy is Thomas's intern,"

Samara said, trying to keep the bridge from burning between Dr. Conrad and me.

"He's been with the kids in almost all the photos we've received," Dr. Conrad said.

I paused trying to make sense of why he would be with the children. I recalled the school assigning older students to younger ones after Career Day, so Cooper's presence with Lucas and Rose made sense to a point.

"Is he only with them at school or other places too?" I asked.

"So far just at school."

Thomas must have arranged for Cooper to be Rose's big brother since he already trusted him. It was strategic.

"Well, it's either because Cooper is his intern or it could be because he's been assigned to Rose through the big brother-big sister program that BTN has. They have older students mentor younger ones after Career Day. Usually it's gender specific, but I bet Thomas had Cooper assigned because he wanted someone with Rose that he already knew and trusted."

"Or someone he could control," Ethan's snide comment sliced through the room. He looked at me, then quickly to his father.

"Like you can even talk, Ethan." I spat, surprising even myself.

"What's that supposed to mean, Olivia?"

"Well, we wouldn't be at this table, in this situation had you made a different choice. This is because of you. You're just as controlling as him."

His face sunk and I knew, even for me, that it was a low blow, but I refused to show it.

"Let's try to focus on what's in front of us, rather than what's behind," Dr. Conrad and his professorial diplomacy kicked in. "Right now, we know Rose and Lucas are safe, but heavily guarded. Intel suggests their routine changes on a three-day cycle and it would be best for us to schedule the mission on the last day. Our plan right now is to use the people we still have inside the school to give us access to the kids when the guards change shifts mid-day."

"Are these people you have inside good enough to do this right the first time?" I looked at Ethan then back to Dr. Conrad.

"Olivia, you need to understand that we've been planning everything for a long time. We had contingency plans in case we couldn't get you and the children out the first time. Our new people are confident about the plan and the resistance continues to grow. Taking down something like the Nation requires a lot of planning and man-power to make it happen." His condescending tone irritated me.

"Why were my children and I part of the plan? I'm not naive enough to believe it's because of Ethan's feelings for me."

"My son's love for you is real, Olivia. His devotion to you comes first. His devotion to the rebellion is second."

I rolled my eyes.

"We've recently discovered more resistor states and we think we can get them to help us overthrow Valentin, Jeffrey, and Thomas. They've been trying to help people trapped in the Nation escape. Ethan releasing the list was the first step in getting the information out about what Thomas and the other leaders have been doing all these years. We knew numbers were growing, but not to this level–had we known, we would have gotten you and Ethan out sooner."

Gotten me and Ethan out sooner? I looked around the table at the eyes sympathetically glued to me. It reminded me of when a woman finds out her husband has been having an affair and everyone knows but her. She's always the last to know and a layer of humiliation coupled with complete distrust of those closest to her settles in.

Dr. Conrad started to speak, and Mrs. Conrad squeezed his arm.

"Olivia," her voice soothed through suspicious speech. "This was not the plan all along. We knew early on, before the mandates and edicts, that Thomas, Jeffrey, and Governor Valentin could take it this far–the kidnappings, killings, but we didn't think they would. We didn't think they had as much support, but we were wrong. We assumed they would take over and tried to prepare for it as best as possible. At Elysium, we included what we thought was best, in all our academics. We tried to structure activities around skills that could help you be a better candidate in the Nation as an ally for us–for the uprising we knew would be coming. We just didn't anticipate it would last this long or that so many people would support the Nation as it continued to control people's lives. When Ethan was recruited by the Nation during school, we knew it was the opportunity for us to learn more about how it worked from the inside." Mrs. Conrad paused, looked at Ethan and Dr. Conrad. "Olivia, your mother and father were part of our group from the beginning. I know Ethan explained to you how your father died...but you should know that it broke your mother to betray you. You had to marry Thomas, Olivia. Once we knew Ethan had been–"

"Hold on." I stood up, my eyes focused on Mrs. Conrad. "You knew Ethan was taken?"

"Yes."

"And you did nothing to get him out of there? To get him back? To get him back to me?" My voice pitched before cracking.

"We decided that once he was taken it was for the greater good. We could monitor the situation and learn how the Centers work. Ethan only learned about us after he and Samara..." She looked at Ethan, his gaze met the floor. "Your father's death was unfortunate, but also an opportunity for us. That's how your mother came to terms with it." Mrs. Conrad said matter-of-factly.

"I don't understand. What does my father's death have to do with any of this? Thomas killed him, right?"

"Your mother knew that Thomas was involved with your father's death."

"Right, like recently, how I just found out too?"

"No, Olivia. She knew then. We all knew then."

"She would never–" The lump in my throat clawed its way up. I couldn't process the information.

"I know, Olivia. Under normal circumstances, your mother would never have done what she did. But it was a sacrifice. One she also made for everyone else–for the Resistance. Just like you did for the last ten years, but without really knowing how far your sacrifice reached."

She stood up and walked toward me, while her eyes stayed locked in place. Her body reached mine, hesitance heard in the space between. Mrs. Conrad reached out her arms and pulled me in. Her smell was the same, after all these years. Pink jasmine. My mind rewound to a kaleidoscope of moments on the property just fifteen minutes from here. Christmas, me wrapped in a blanket next to her while Ethan wandered off. Suture lessons during her wilderness medicine class that inspired me to become a nurse. The long drawn out hug when Ethan and I left the compound with forged papers and her words, "Remember where you come from, Olivia. Don't get lost down there," echoing behind.

My tense body melted into hers. She felt like home in ways I'd almost forgotten. For just a moment, the girl I used to be stirred within the shell of the woman I'd become. That girl was warm with a soft innocence, still wanting to believe in the goodness of people. But then I remembered there is no true good or evil, only the will of the strong, and the power they wield to take what they want.

I pulled away.

"You're just as bad as they are. Substituting one veil of

power for another. What makes you right? What makes them wrong? What makes them right and you wrong? It's all the same–two groups fighting for power and control over people's lives."

"Not quite correct, Olivia." Mrs. Conrad spoke softly.

"No, Mrs. Conrad, it is *quite correct*." I paused and reclaimed my armor. "It doesn't matter to me anymore what you want with this rebellion. The only thing that matters is getting my children back so we can leave this place forever. When they're back, I'm gone. So, tell me your next plan and I will let you know if it's something that will work with what I want to do."

I couldn't believe I had been on the compound for this long and no one, not even Samara, had told me about Ethan, about my mother and her knowledge about my father's death. What other information were they keeping from me? What lies were they continuing to feed me to keep me in line?

Ethan looked down ashamed again at yet another betrayal. I needed to focus, to come up with a plan, to put myself back into the story that ended with my arms wrapped around my children, escaping this god-forsaken place.

Mrs. Conrad rejoined the table, squeezing Ethan's shoulder before taking her seat. Ethan refused to look at me, but glanced quickly at Samara, who nodded back at him.

"Okay, everyone. Are we ready to go over the plan?" Dr. Conrad's voice took center stage, pulling us back together.

"Yes." The one-word answer—spoken in unison—that probably got us, and so many others, here in the first place.

3

ETHAN

Olivia sat across the table from me, her eyes refusing to meet mine. Even with the hollow cheeks and dark circles under her eyes, her face was still beautiful to me. Her dark hair had soft streaks of amber from the daily sun she exposed herself to when she walked laps around the lake. Her lips, soft pink and familiar, made me ache for mine to be on them. She was speaking, but I couldn't hear the words leaving those perfect lips. Lips I knew. Lips I loved. Lips I wished I could have whenever I wanted.

But that wasn't my reality. She had belonged to Thomas for the last ten years. Those lips were on his every single day. Those lips were on her children's–the children I didn't save. The children that weren't ours. The children she was talking about right now?

"It doesn't matter to me anymore what you want with this rebellion. The only thing that matters is getting my children back so we can leave this place forever. When they're back, I'm gone. So, tell me your next plan and I will let you know if it's something that will work with what I want to do." Her voice resolute against the biggest mistake I had ever made in my entire life.

She planned to leave when we got the children back. She planned to leave Thomas and the Nation. She planned to leave...me.

I deserved it. And whatever else she had coming my way.

"Thank you, Olivia, for your honesty and willingness to hear what we have in place to get your children back." My father resumed as the calm, assertive alpha in all situations. "Viv, will you share it with Olivia and the rest of the group, please?"

"Sure thing, Dr. Conrad." He slid the HoloTab across the table to Viv and she tapped the screen illuminating a map of Central. Yellow marks showed the children's school and the Challenge Center on the map, and the 3D picture made me feel like I was in front of the Capitol Mall.

"We know the children are on a three-day rotation with body guards, schedule, and key resets, which means we only have three days to plan and execute their rescue. Our insiders will tell us the reset codes and the plan once we tell them we are ready. Like mentioned earlier, surveillance and security are more intense since your escape. Thomas and Jeffrey are trying to keep a certain narrative in the Nation news about the Rebellion so eyes will be everywhere, including regular citizens. Thomas has the Holo feeds focusing on Ethan as the symbol of Resistance more than anyone else, so we need to make sure Ethan stays masked. Even though Samara was part of the escape, there has been nothing about her in the feeds, so we're still in good shape overall. For now, Thomas is keeping your departure," she looked at Liv, "quiet which gives us more flexibility."

Olivia shifted slightly in her chair, a sign of guilt that only someone like me, a person who loved her for twenty years, would be able to see. But to the untrained eye, she stood solid in place, pretending she had it all under control–I knew her better though. She was barely holding it together and she needed me, just like I needed her.

"We are going to send two teams to the school. We've already made it through as security and tier-two workers at the Bridge to the Nation, so it won't be difficult to blend in. The most difficult part will be getting the children away from the regular security detail."

"What's the plan for that?" Olivia interrupted.

Vivian looked at me and then at my father.

"Although, at first we didn't think it was a good idea for you to be part of the rescue, we think it could actually work to our advantage because the children will see you and want to come to you."

"Absolutely not, dad!" I roared.

"Son, it's not your decision," my father replied calmly.

"He's right, Ethan. It's my decision and no one else's." Olivia's eyes narrowed.

I turned to Vivian for support. "You can't agree to this, right?" She said nothing.

"Explain to me why you think it's not a good idea." Olivia's tone was sharp and on the edge of cutting someone.

Vivian paused and with a poker faced bluntness. "You're too much of a liability, Olivia. Regardless of how much you have trained with Samara, when it comes down to it, your emotional regulation might cost us this mission."

Olivia didn't reply right away, which I knew meant the fire was coming in ways most of the people at this table did not know about. When she was younger, Liv could be formidable if provoked. Most people underestimated her, because her kindness contained the fire that constantly burned just below the surface. When we lived at Elysium, I experienced her wrath only once and I knew I never wanted to feel it again. If only I'd thought our escape through just a little bit more, we wouldn't be at this table–with her fire smoldering beneath the surface, aimed at me.

"I think what you see as a liability, *Vivian*, and anyone else who shares this sentiment, is actually an asset. None of you have any reason to rescue Rose and Lucas. You have no ties. No connection. No need to get them, except that you believe they will help me focus more on the rebellion you somehow think I will take part in once they're back in my arms. I'm going to be more than clear here right now. I don't give a fuck about your rebellion. This place and all of you," she looked at me, "could burn along with Thomas, and I wouldn't think twice about it. The only thing that matters is my children and getting them back. Every. Single. One of you. Are just pieces that help me achieve that goal."

Everyone except Samara and I shifted at the table, believing the front she displayed in such fortitude. But I knew her all too well. She was a force to be reckoned with, but she was also gray. Never explicitly choosing one side over the other unless there was a logical *and* emotional reason. This was why teams, when we were younger, always wanted her to join their side. Why she excelled in her nursing career. Why her friends sought her out. Why Jude fell for her. She accepted everyone and everything for what they were without hesitation and with a full, loving heart. Sure, she had fire, but it only lit on rare occasions and was usually quickly put out.

"Right. I understand that is your position, Olivia. We all respect your choice to leave once we get the children back, although we do hope you change your mind when you realize how much more is at stake for so many other people trapped by the Nation," Vivian added.

Olivia's face softened and her curiosity was piqued. "What else is at stake except two groups of people fighting over power?"

Vivian smiled. "It's probably not the time, but there's a lot more going on than you really know, Olivia." Her tone was snide, not a good move.

"Oh, *Vivian*, I am sure there is always a lot more going on with you than anyone knows." She looked at me, "And I am sure there is with you too, Ethan."

Shots fired again. Another flesh wound from the woman I loved more than life itself.

"Right. Okay. Well, let's move forward, shall we?" Viv stayed calm as she changed the holographic feed floating in the middle of the table.

Once Viv finished going over the plan, Liv asked a few more questions and we left the war room. Olivia and Samara turned to walk together back toward her room—and I knew this would be my chance to talk to her.

I needed to get Olivia alone again. I finally convinced her to go with me to get supplies, but the conservation didn't go how I had expected when she woke up from whatever dream she was having. If I could just get her alone, somewhere, again, I could make her see me. Make her talk to me again. We could have it out and yell and cuss and cry. Then find solace in each other's bodies and come back together. I knew if I could just get her alone she would finally see and understand I'm her only option to get her children back. I'm her only hope to give her the chance to leave this place and start over...with me.

4

———

OLIVIA

After the meeting, Samara and I made our way back to my room. I was overwhelmed by what I'd learned about Ethan, my mother, my father. I couldn't believe any of it was true. Or that everyone had known and said nothing.

"Did you know about everything, Samara, and not tell me?"

"I knew, Olivia."

"Why didn't you tell me?"

"Because I was told not to. One of the hardest parts about being a leader is having information that you can't share, even when you want to. I'm sorry that I couldn't say anything."

"I've been here for six weeks, Samara! What else aren't you telling me?"

She looked down and drew in a deep breath. "Olivia, I'm sorry. You need to understand–at the time, Dr. Conrad, your mother, Ethan, all believed it was best to keep it from you until you absolutely had to know. With everything that happened at the Center, then losing your children and realizing who Thomas really is. It was just too much. They didn't think it would be helpful for your recovery, or for getting the kids back."

Of course they lied. They thought they were protecting me, but in reality it was just control. Another crack in my armor that folded into a sharp edge and tucked beneath my skin like all the others. At some point I wouldn't even flinch anymore. My heart wouldn't race, my stomach wouldn't drop–because it was all expected. Like watching a movie I had already seen a hundred times, waiting for a plot twist that would never come. I couldn't really cry or scream anymore. At some point I would just start to nod, like I was checking a box on my to-do list of betrayals.

I would have to find a way to disconnect while staying connected enough to access the power inside of me that would help me find the children and eliminate Thomas from our lives. I could be here, but not here, and then later deal with the consequences. I had time to face that in the long run, but today, there was only time to focus on the plan, push my feelings deep down and throw away the key.

"If there's anything else, tell me now so I know exactly what situation I'm in. So I know more about Thomas and the Nation and how I have played a role in it for the last ten years. A bigger role than I ever knew. Everyone just keeps thinking that I am this weak person who will crumble at anything 'Thomas' or 'Nation', but it isn't true. I am stronger than all of you think I am."

"Olivia," she took my hands into hers. "I know that and at some point others here will know that too."

"Is there more?"

"With men in power, there is always more, Olivia. You should start learning that now so later we can actually do something about it."

"How can I trust you again?" My voice whispered.

"Because I am on your side and anything I do is because of

that. I was rooting for you long before you walked into the Challenge Center. I've seen you, Olivia, over the years–what he did to you, what you're capable of, and what you're not capable of. If I'm keeping something from you it's because I have to. At some point, you will do the same thing to me, no matter how close we get. For now, focus on the kids and what life you want after you get them back."

"What other things are there that people aren't telling me?"

"With the way things have been surfacing, I'm guessing you and I have pieces to a puzzle that we can't quite put together yet. Leaking the documents was the first step in exposing the Nation, but I know there's more. I know Thomas had layers to him that no one knew about. He was good at giving individuals just enough information, but never sharing everything with just one person. Take Cooper for example, I knew he was Thomas's intern, but why he's with Rose right now, I couldn't say for certain. You think he may be assigned to Rose as the big brother, but we don't know that. More pieces to whatever world he's been running–at some point we will have to connect them and even then, it may not be the full picture."

"Yeah, for another day, I guess, huh?"

Samara sighed. "For another day. I'm going to get some tea before bed, do you want anything?"

"I'm good, thanks."

She walked back to the dining hall and I turned for my room.

"Olivia, can we please talk?" My mother stood, shoulders slumped forward, posture shrunken into the small space she occupied outside my door.

She had aged even more since the first night I saw her on the compound. Her hair grayed, almost completely. Wrinkles thick within the sides of her eyes. Weight lost, making her body a shell, holding a soul I no longer recognized.

"What do you want?"

"Olivia, I need to talk to you…about everything."

"You heard what happened in the meeting? That I know you knew about dad?"

"Yes." She said solidly. "You need to know, to understand why I did what I did, so we can move past this and be a family again."

"Move past this? You're joking, right? You knew Thomas killed dad. Despite knowing this, you let me marry that monster. Have kids with him. Build a life with him!" I yelled.

"It's not that simple, Olivia."

"Go ahead and explain, because it seems pretty simple to me. A man you didn't know is involved with your husband's death, takes your daughter's fiancé and locks him up. Then dates your daughter, gets her pregnant, and marries her–all because of some fucked up Nation plan."

"Watch your language, Olivia."

My blood boiled. "And you complied. You went along with it and chose to be part of *his* plan, trapping me and the children in a world we would have never escaped had it not been for Ethan and Samara."

"You need to know that what I did was for you. For Jessica. For a future I knew was impossible once your father died."

"He died because of Thomas! How do you not see that? How do you not understand that what you did played right into his hand? You gave him what he wanted. Keys to a world that all of us would be stuck in for the rest of our lives."

"I did it for you! Because that's what mothers do. We sacrifice. We look at all our options and then, with our children in mind, make the best decision. What would give you the most chances for a better life. The most opportunities. The best life." She quickly rambled through tears.

"Do you hear yourself right now? You think that the best life for me was to marry an evil man and have children with him? He killed people, mother. How can you still defend him? How can you defend yourself?"

Her voice lowered and slowed. "That's the thing I thought you'd understand. Mothers give life...and then slowly give up their own, day by day, trying to give their children what they never had. I gave up my life for you. For Jessica. That's what good mothers do."

"Don't be a martyr, for God's sake. You chose to keep this from me. From Jessica. You chose to keep me in a cage for ten years when you knew I was struggling. When you knew something was wrong. When you knew I was married to a sociopath. You knew and still let me have children with him. Build a life with him. Live in a numb existence away from the one person I actually loved and who actually loved me."

Her voice raised as if to scold me. "If you don't understand the sacrifices we make for our children then you never will. This is our job. Our duty. Our charge in life. The moment we see the pink double lines, our lives no longer belong to us. They belong to them. It's been that way since the dawn of time and won't change just because society does. Mothers lose their lives so their children can breathe."

"That's where you're wrong. Children lose their lives when their mothers can't breathe."

"Had you known about all of this, about Thomas, about the Nation, would you have left? Would you have tried to find Ethan earlier? Would you have tried to escape? And then how far would you have gotten without him? The money. The connections. The power." She paused. "You wouldn't have gotten anywhere, Olivia. You and the children would be destitute and end up in a tier-one encampment begging on the side of the road for someone's tier-four or tier-five mother to pay pity on you. You had a good life. The children had a good life. Jessica had a good life and gets to live because of what I did. What I sacrificed so all of you could live. You should be thanking me, Olivia. You and everyone else should be thanking me."

Who was this woman? We should be thanking her? For ruining a life that I would have actually loved? Nope.

"In what world would I ever thank you for not giving me a choice? You know what, Mother, had I known about this from the beginning, it wouldn't have even happened. Had I found out sooner, I would have left with the children and tried to make it on my own in a sanctuary state."

"No you wouldn't. You couldn't back then. You had nothing except forged tier-two papers and a nursing job. Once the Nation learned about the forgeries, you would have been out without your children and his power and money. You won't admit it, but part of you was drawn to his world. Once Ethan was out of the picture, that shininess blinded you, and I am grateful that it did. I may have lost my husband, but I kept my children and now have grandchildren because of my sacrifice. The means justify the end no matter how much I miss your father."

Her words stung and my venom was the only thing protecting me now. "You're a lunatic. And when I get the children back, you won't have anything to do with them. They're mine and they will know exactly who you are and what you did."

Was she right? Did I marry Thomas only because the story I was living, was a world without Ethan? And that I couldn't reconcile a life without him, so I did what I was trained to do— marry another man who wanted me. Once I got pregnant with Rose, I knew there was no turning back. That the Nation world was too confining for me to be anything other than a mother to its children. To its values. To its system. I was bound by laws and rules and mandates that I didn't have the power or resources to push back against.

So I complied.

Like so many other women.

Who wanted to.

Who had to.

Day after day after day. Even if I shared my feelings about being trapped or uncertain about things between Thomas and me, no one would have listened. No one would have helped me. No one would have given me a way out with my children.

Everyone loved Thomas. Everyone believed in the Nation. Everyone believed in the story I created for them. I kept their chapters intact because a different book wouldn't give them the fairy tale story they wanted to read.

And I complied and stayed for the money, the trips, the affluence. All sweet pills that made my bitter existence momentarily better. If I could just look forward to the next vacation with the children, then their smiles would serve as a remedy. If I could just look the part—wear the new yoga pants, improve my practice—maybe that would be enough. If I could just taste the newest sip of champagne from a bottle tier-twos didn't have access to, that would validate and reward me for my sacrifice.

Because I earned it.

I deserved it.

For my sacrifice.

At that moment I looked at my mother. She was broken long before the Nation entered our lives. She was part of the United States and the rules women had to follow under its reign. She followed the once American Dream, complying when opportunities opened for her in the sciences, when for most women, that was still an uphill battle. Walking away from a career she fought for in order for Jessica and me to not live in a world that took away our rights as women. Living with a secret that weathered her body beyond any storm I could have forecasted.

Perhaps she and I were parts of the same narrative, but on different pages? Had her storyline of sacrifice been the same as mine, but just with different characters, scenes, and endings? Had we been reading chapters moving toward the same ending–just with a different title?

My eyes betrayed me to yet another person I was trying to keep at a distance.

"Oh, Olivia, please. I see it. I see it in you. Can you...please, can you forgive me?" She cried.

But I wouldn't be giving her that today. I felt a snap in my spine, awakening the breath in my chest.

"No."

"What? No? Did you say no?"

"No, mother. I can't forgive you. Because even though I now understand what we have in common as mothers, we still have something different. I would sacrifice so much for Rose and Lucas. You gave me up. I would burn the world before I'd do that to my children. Give my life for theirs. But I would never knowingly let them walk into hell holding the hand of the devil."

She collapsed to the floor, shoulders shaking as she cried alone on the floor. I felt nothing.

I looked up and saw Samara at the end of the hall. Her eyes showed pity for my mother, but I knew that pity was also for me.

"Rebecca, can I help you up?" She walked toward us and set her tea down. Samara's ability to hold both strength and kindness was something I wasn't sure I had.

"Thank you, Samara."

"It's no problem, Rebecca. Can I take you back to your room?"

"No, it's okay. I'm going to take a walk."

"This late? Let's at least have one of the guys follow you."

"Thank you. Yes. That's a great idea. Thank you again, *Samara*." My mother's emphasis on Samara's name was a classic go-to passive aggressive move for her.

"How much did you hear?" I asked.

"All of it. Are you okay?"

"Yeah. It's just ridiculous. She thinks what she did was right and there's nothing that could ever make what she did right. I would just, never, do that."

Samara waited to reply, creating a longer pause than what I was comfortable with. "Olivia, what your mother did was horrible on so many levels. She lied to you. Betrayed you and your trust. Put you in an impossible situation. She made choices that impacted multiple people, including your children."

"Right? Who does that? I mean–I just would never do that." I said indignantly.

"I wouldn't go so far as to say that, Olivia."

I could feel the heat rise in my body. "What's that supposed to mean?"

"We don't actually know what we are capable of until we are met with very hard choices. Your mom chose her children, just like you are choosing yours. When the time comes and you have a gun against Thomas's head, holding not only his life, but also Rose and Lucas's in your hand too, I wonder what you are going to do."

"I'm going to kill him, Samara. There is no other way." The thought of Thomas's death gave me new air.

"How is that different from what your mother did? She was given a choice. An impossible choice of saying goodbye to the man she loved and committed her life to in order to save the children she also loved."

"It's not the same. Thomas is evil. My father wasn't."

"I'm just saying...we don't know what we are truly capable of until we are met with two wrongs and we have to choose one of them in order to be slightly more right."

Was she correct? Would the moral compass in my heart cause me to pause and rethink taking Thomas's life? Or would the logic in my mind maintain its stronghold because a world without him was better for everyone else? I would be sacrificing a world without their father for Rose and Lucas either way—whether he lived or died, Thomas wouldn't be a part of their lives.

"It's been a long day. I'm going to get some sleep. See you at breakfast?" I needed her to leave so I could retreat into my room.

"Yes, of course. Then off to training." She smiled, gave me a hug, and said, "Goodnight Olivia. Sleep well."

5

OLIVIA

Before heading to bed, a shower would be my only reprieve from what happened today. Between the dream I had about the children and Thomas, the planning meeting and what I learned, and finally, the conversation with my mother, I needed an escape.

The compound had a combination of technology that was similar to the Nation life I lived–like voice automation, sensor lights, and tablets. One of the first things I did when I got here was create playlists on my tablet. Some were for workouts, one for when I needed to feel the weight of missing my children, and others to remind me of a time that felt long gone. The music selection was extensive because Morgan made sure premium services were paid for on all the apps. She, as well as other leadership, knew the power music had in cultivating communities and providing a sense of normalcy. She also always had one earbud in and was working on a new piece of tech where an implant behind the ear could serve as a listening device at all times. She was brilliant and I was glad to have her on our side.

I opened the app, selected the Counting Crows playlist, and

stepped into the shower. The songs played softly in the background–songs from a time when I still recognized myself, when I was becoming the person I thought I wanted to be. Lyrics that taught me how to feel something deeper than just a string of words tied together with a guitar. Voices that called to me in every chapter of my life until the moment I lost it all.

I cried in the shower, the only place where my tears could go unnoticed, becoming part of the water that soothed my body. How could my mother have known about Thomas and my father and still let me go through with the wedding? How could Ethan's parents know about his capture and still keep us apart? The years we lost to battles our parents were fighting left us trapped in a war that we would never win. I could have had the life I wanted with Ethan, if the doors had just opened a different way, and we'd been brave enough to walk through them.

I stepped out of the shower and wrapped my towel around my body and combed through my tangled hair. Familiar fingertips tiptoed across the ivory keys, pulling "Colorblind" into the room and letting the Counting Crows soothe my pain.

I caught a reflection in the steamed bathroom mirror.

"What the fuck, Ethan?" I yelled.

"I'm sorry, you didn't respond when I knocked. I was worried, so I–"

"Broke into my room?"

"No, I wanted to make sure you were okay."

"Well, clearly I am. So no need to be here." I put the thought of my unwritten life with him out of my mind and placed my armor back on.

"Olivia, please. Please let me explain. Give me a chance."

"You had your chance and like I said earlier, you chose yourself. Not me. Not them. You."

He walked toward me just as the words danced through the room.

"I can't go any longer without feeling," his hand brushed the sides of my arms, "You. Please, Liv. I am begging you." His body closed in and he towered over me. His mouth kissed the top of my head and my body tensed. He released me slightly, moved his hands up my arms and into the back of my wet hair, pulling me back in again. The tension released and I relaxed into him. Ethan, who was my always and forever. The ghost I would see even in my dreams. The person I was supposed to build a life with.

"I can't, Ethan. It's gone. We're done. I just can't." My body fought my mind.

"I know, Liv. I know. We aren't gone though. Just lost, temporarily. I'm so sorry. If I could go back in time, I would." His hands tangled in my hair, pressing on the parts that made me melt into him. "I wouldn't even let us go to the Nation. We would be somewhere else now. You, me, the baby. Let me fix this. Liv. You know I can fix it. Please trust me. Please let me...let me be with you." He whispered warmly in my ear.

His lips touched my forehead, then moved slowly down my face, his fingers staying tangled in my hair.

"Please, Liv, please." His lips hovered above mine, warmth I knew all too well filled my chest. Ethan's tongue parted my mouth as his hands cupped my face. I could feel him harden against my body and I remembered him.

Us.

A knowing that doesn't fade over time, but stays buried waiting to be woken.

I needed to escape the reality of the four walls closing in on me, while a mournful voice sang in the background. My arms released the towel, letting it drop to the floor. A toned body and soft breasts on display for the once love of my life. I couldn't hold back any longer. My hands tangled into the hem of his shirt, softly at first, until the heat within me remembered what it was like to be lit.

The world had separated our bodies for too long—disconnecting us from the most primal human need. All I wanted was him and the escape I knew he could give me. I wanted to be back in the dream, not the nightmare. I pulled him urgently to my bed, pawing his cotton shirt between my fingers, desperate to release him from his clothes. Within seconds his clothing painted the floor and Ethan's brown skin stood as a contrast against my olive. My nails dragged down his back marking his oak tree tattoo. He growled and bit into the side of my neck, marking me in return. His tongue coated my skin, wetting every part of me even more, making me almost unravel before he even entered. He trailed down my belly to my center forcing his tongue in between my legs.

I called out, "Ethan." Pulling at the sheets and moaning into my room, my back arched and electricity spread through my body.

I needed him. And only him right now.

The urgency I felt for him to be inside of me swept over.

"I need you inside me. Ethan. I need you." I whispered breathlessly.

He smiled, dark eyes heavy with want, and it didn't matter what was said moments earlier.

I took his length into my hand, spread my legs, and cried out as I forced him all the way inside with a deep want. Ethan pulled my body up on top of his, calloused fingertips pressing hard against my back, pushing himself deeper inside of me until my belly ached.

I ran my fingers over the soft resistance of his coarse hair, like tracing a memory into his scalp, pulling his body even closer to mine. He wrapped his arms around me combining the browns and whites of newly summer-kissed skin. Our emotions were driven by something raw, something rough and burning just beneath the surface unable to be contained any longer. In a quick moment, he unbound us and flipped me over to my stomach. I lifted my body to meet his as he grabbed my hips and entered me again, more desperate this time. The bed muffled my moans as he pressed my face against the pillows. My breath, punished for wanting more. He quickened, driving deeper inside me, making me cry into echoes unheard. The pain from his depth made me feel alive and dead at the same time. His assault left no part of me untouched, and I knew the sheets would be spattered with a crimson hue when we were done.

Ethan growled and cried out, "Fuck, Liv" as the last piano note of the song slowly faded like curtains closing on a scene performed for an empty audience.

He pulled out, staining my sheets a newly tinted red. I sat back against his body, spilling a future we would never have because the Nation took that away from us when he signed his contract. I shifted to find my breath in a room that felt suffocating. I didn't turn around, and his hands never moved to touch me with the tenderness I needed in that moment. Our silence was oxygen to the room and we both knew what had just happened.

We fucked for the first time in our life. It was not love that was shared between us, nor was it a reconciliation of something almost lost.

I pulled at the sheet and wrapped it around myself. Ethan's naked body shifted to the side, tentatively teetering on the bed. He grasped for the comforter and covered himself with it, our bodies moving away from each other, lost in this unfamiliar feeling between us. Was it shame that lingered here?

Ethan reached for my hand and I recoiled. I scanned my body. Sore in the right and wrong places. Reminding me of the balance between love and hate. My breath returned. My heartbeat slowed. But then I felt it. The cold, breathless weight of the grief I kept myself in every day since I arrived here. An air hunger that no escape could satisfy. And like so many times before, when reality screamed at me, I gave in and let the grief cascade out of my body.

"Liv?" Ethan's voice panicked. "Did I hurt you?"

I didn't reply. I couldn't.

My children, the two people who made my heart whole, were God knows where, without me. The life I had known for ten years wasn't real. I was part of a war I never knew was happening just below the surface. The loss of it all clung to me. Even with all his darkness, Thomas had given me stability and shielded me from this reality.

Only tears and constricted sips of air in between crying would lead right now—no words or thoughts or phrases. Just grief and its weight taking me to the bottom of a lake I wasn't sure I would make it out of.

"Baby, I'm sorry. I know that was...rough. So much rougher than...before. I don't know what happened. I just...needed you and I needed to be inside of you...connected...like we used to be...so close...so in love...so together." He brushed my face, wiping away evidence of my pain.

"Time And Time Again" started to play as he lifted and pulled my body into his, letting me cry until there was nothing left. No water, no breath, no life. I was gone. A ghost lost amongst the chords.

I lifted my eyes to him. He studied my face, looking for some hint, some silent verdict that would tell him whether he was the one to blame.

He had always been my life preserver. The hand that pulled me out of the pit. The light that drew me away from the dark. And I had been all those things to him, too, when he needed it. But tonight, I couldn't bring my arms to reach for the circle that might pull me out of the cold water of my grief. I was going to let myself let go. How could I be anything with Ethan anymore? How could I be anything without my children? How could I be anything without Thomas? Despite his wickedness, I remained connected to him in ways others couldn't comprehend. Songs that play on repeat in moments when fingers refuse to interrupt playlists.

"Is it only Counting Crows on here"

"Yeah for the most part."

"Songs from the playlist after the baby..." his fingers brushed through my hair as he kissed my forehead again.

"Yeah, songs after the baby."

After the fetal transfer and my recovery, I had spiraled slowly into a numb nothingness. Between healing from the procedure, losing our baby, and the hormonal shift, I couldn't pick myself back up. Every time I listened to the playlist, it tore me wide open and at the same time, numbed me just enough to take it. Losing our child felt like nothing I had ever experienced. I thought the baby was our only chance at a new beginning. Something real that we could hold onto and move away from the Nation world. But Ethan wanted...needed more. He wanted to prove to the world that he could be part of the Nation. That he was good enough to be chosen. Real enough. Strong enough.

I listened to the playlist on repeat for weeks—opening me up and stitching me back together in the same breath. I couldn't eat. I would fall asleep, tear soaked cheeks, waking up to what I thought was hours later, but was far less than that. I couldn't remember what I had done during the day, who I had talked to, if anyone at all. I tried alcohol to see if that could help me forget about the baby and my potential sterility. It only amplified the memory loss and pain, which then led to anxiety the next day and a blanket of shame.

I was broken, unrepairable and wasting away.

Like so many other times before, Ethan stood as the mast to my ship. He would stand with me on the deck and hold my hand and tell me that we will get through the storm together.

That I wasn't alone. The loss was felt by him, too, and maybe he could feel my loss deeper than his own.

This is why I loved him with the depth of my soul. He was my mirror, and when our bodies touched, everything transferred between us unspoken. Tonight was the same. But at the same time, it felt different. I wasn't the Olivia from then, but I couldn't place that difference yet. I couldn't acknowledge the widening gap between adolescent love and adult reality. At some point I would understand though, that some loves are meant to stay behind, because they aren't built to grow up with you no matter how much you want them to.

"Liv?"

"Yeah?"

"Did I hurt you? Do you need to see the doctor?"

"No...I'm okay."

"I don't know what happened. I just...it's been so long...and I...needed all of you...as mine...It won't happen again, I promise."

I didn't engage. I played the shell game, coated in denial and avoidance. I shrunk myself, something I didn't remember doing with Ethan, but the last ten years conditioned me into this person. Someone I didn't fully realize existed until my entire world was taken away from me.

"It's just the grief from everything. I keep replaying the last night and the explosion and the tarmac. I need you to know that I'm not okay right now. I don't know when or if I will ever be. I'm not even sure if there is still love for you. I can't give you what you want right now. And you should know...I don't know if I ever will be able to again. Something's changed."

I searched his face. His eyes watered slightly. He nodded, but I knew he would hold out hope for me until his last breath. "Olivia, I need to know you're okay."

"I am fine and I will be fine." My words clipped.

"What about Thomas? How do you plan to escape him? His power? His resources?"

Without hesitation and in the cool deep voice I knew was developing within me, I replied, "I'm going to kill him. He won't be a problem for me or the children ever again. I don't know how or when, but he can't be alive if I am."

"I don't think you understand what that means. How that will affect you, the kids. Liv, taking a life isn't easy."

"Nothing in this is easy. I am prepared to do whatever it takes to make my life worth living again. Even if that means starting fresh, on my own, free from everyone, including you."

I could wish that my life had turned out differently than it was today. I could have had a life with the man sitting on my bed surrounded by children and love. But that wasn't my reality. In front of me was a man that chose himself over my children. The weight of his actions had finally caught up with the consequences that would keep us apart. He chose me over my children...something no mother would ever do. A man like him would never understand the bond between a mother and her children. A bond that chooses their lives over hers...every... single...time. A part of me died on the tarmac that night, when I boarded the plan with Ethan's wounded body. The part of us that had a moment of hope for a future together died that night too. As I settled into the new compound, it became clearer every day that Ethan was my stepping stone to the new life I deserved. What was in store for us, didn't matter to me anymore. What mattered was only what he could offer me to bring my children home.

"I understand." He kissed my forehead and released my body. He got up and found his mess of clothes on the floor and got dressed. I sat up slightly, watching him and the body I had once loved cover itself from me. At that moment, I told myself it would be the last time I ever saw his body like that again.

"I love you, Olivia. I have always loved you and I will always love you. I know I messed up. And I hope that at some point you'll forgive me. I will get Rose and Lucas back to you. I promise. Until then, I am here for whatever you need, whenever you need it. If that means you need me to show you how to train differently, or you want me in your bed. I am here for you. And only *you*." Ethan turned, opened the door, and walked out, closing the curtains on a scene that wouldn't have another act.

6

ETHAN

I left Olivia's room, uncertain about our future. I hurt her, probably more than anyone ever had. And that's saying something, considering Thomas was a total prick. I knew I needed to keep my feelings for Jude in check–compartmentalize them because she was back in my life. Even though he had kept me from going crazy during the last five years, she was my goal, my life. He served his purpose for me just like I did for him. Similar to how other men bond during wars or missions. It was like that with Cody, when I was in Brazil. He served his purpose when I struggled to stay focused on the mission we were tasked with. I needed someone to live for when I was down there. So did he.

Jude was no different. We found ourselves in each other's arms because we needed to survive the Center. I needed to survive the videos and do something about it when I saw her naked body—day after day—on the screens in my room.

It wasn't until Jude that I could feel again. At first, the feelings were faint, uncertain, but I grew to love him in a way I never expected. His soft blue eyes were delicate, waiting for someone to tell him he was special. That he had meaning. That he was seen.

His hands would trail up my tattoo and my back in a way that could bring me to my knees, and oftentimes did. His lips, soft and ready for mine and anything else I asked of him.

The connection between us couldn't be undone no matter how hard I tried. I loved him in a space of my heart that would stay like a painting on a wall. Beautiful to look at and appreciate. Adding to the room it hung in. Providing a glimpse of a time that was captured in hues of blue, green, and white. But when I left the room, it stayed on the wall.

Jude would stay on the wall, and I knew at some point I would need to make sure nothing happened between us again. Olivia was my focus. Even though she said she was done, I knew she just needed time.

Thomas was a special kind of fuck–the best kind of torturer. I knew his time with Jeffrey helped turn him into the sadistic prick he was today, but I still found myself shocked at what he was capable of.

Early on in my commitment, he had screens installed throughout the attendant quarters, streaming images of citizens in their homes. Sometimes it would be of families, sometimes of single men, sometimes of women. We would watch them like our own private reality television shows–following family conflicts, joys, celebrations, and lives, as if to replace our own prison-cell existence with something real.

Around year five he added a new streaming channel, one that brought Olivia to our screens.

I was walking to the mess hall, saying my morning hellos to other attendants, when I heard a voice that was like an echo in my heart. I looked up at the screen above Jude's and my table and saw her brown hair blowing in the wind, standing at the edge of a boat surrounded by crystal-blue water.

Her body was tanned and tucked in a perfect bright coral

bikini with a white linen long-sleeved shirt. A camel fedora with a black ribbon sat upon her head and oversized black sunglasses shielded her eyes from the sun, but also from the camera she didn't know was filming her.

I froze, enraptured by her beauty. My eyes glided over each part of her body. One I had memorized in no time when we first became intimate as adolescents. She was perfect. She was my Olivia. Her body turned, revealing a small scar just below her belly button. A scar from our baby? From her new children? Samara had kept me updated every once in a while about Olivia, but only necessary information. Five years had passed since I signed my life away to the Nation, when I last saw her.

On the screen, Olivia was looking out into the distance, lost among the water. I wondered what she was thinking about. Who she was looking at, if anyone at all. If Thomas was nearby or if he had left her alone. If she was thinking of me. If she ever thought of me. I wondered how different our lives would have been if I would have just left when she asked me to. If our baby would be alive. If our family would have joined us in a sanctuary state.

But there wasn't time to think like this. I made a choice when I had no others to make. I joined the Center and slowly ascended the ranks so I could eventually topple the Nation. Samara was part of my plan. Once she learned what Thomas was doing, even with the privileges she gained from me fathering her and Laura's children, her loyalty stayed with me, not to Thomas or the Nation.

Samara wanted everyone to be free to marry who they wanted to. She and Laura had the right to marry because they were a commodity to the Nation. Their bodies served a greater purpose than two men being partnered. There was no point to men being together other than sexual pleasure; that was the Nation's view. But I, and so many other men, knew it was more. It was partnership, being seen, being loved in a way that women couldn't. I loved Olivia with every part of my body, but when Jude and I met, and spent so much time together, my love grew for him, too.

If we were outside the Challenge Center walls, I wouldn't be able to be with him, even if I wanted to. I would be just like the other men that used their challenge passes and fuck men like Jude and me. Trying to remember a full life where bodies like ours made men feel alive, unlike the females they were forced to lay next to every night. They loved their children, but wanted to share with a male partner, rather than their female ones they were bound to in the Nation life.

One pass user told me how he and his wife were both gay. Her family wouldn't allow her to marry a woman, even if it was okay by Nation standards. They chose to marry and lived a half-life together. I asked him if they ever slept with people outside their Challenge Passes. His body stiffened and his voice became solid. "Never. We couldn't risk this life, even if it wasn't fully our own."

The government designed the system to keep people separated from their true selves, preserving an outdated idea of what it meant to be American, even after the Nation's takeover years ago. Threads from the American dream still found themselves in the fabric of Nation ideals and would never be completely undone, no matter how much time spanned between the then and now.

When Jude and I were first together, it wasn't like the other men Thomas paired me with. It was as if he knew Jude and I would have a special connection. As if he finally found a male attendant who could figure out the combination to my needs. And Jude did. It was after a few nights when Jude and I started spending time together outside of Challenge Pass selections. I had my own room because I was the lead attendant. Jude was having a rough time with his roommate, so one night, he came to my room and asked to crash on the floor.

After hours of talking about our lives, he crawled into bed with me, and we spent the rest of the night entangled. Searching for a depth we hadn't had with anyone else. Jude and I met each other exactly where we needed to and I quickly became addicted to him. My jealousy flared on nights when he was chosen by someone loyal to the Nation. The sex between us was amazing, but it was more than just that. We had a connection like no other, not even like mine with Brian. It was being together that kept us alive until the day Olivia walked into the Challenge Center and changed everything.

My night with Olivia, I was so angry with her. For choosing Thomas. For not trying to find me. For building a life with him. Even though I knew everything that happened. That he manipulated it all. That my parents were part of all of it too and I agreed to it. I didn't think it would take this long. I thought she would wait for me, but no, she accepted my absence as a death and willingly walked to her own. Even with everything that happened between her and Thomas, her and Jude, and her and me, I still loved her. Beyond the love I could have for anyone else, even Jude.

When my two worlds collided, I did what any soldier would have done. I stayed focused on the task, got the job done, and moved forward with what was logical. What made sense was Olivia—our history, our love for each other, and a future we could have together. I had loved her since I was a boy and on the off chance our child made the transfer, there was a piece of us in the Nation world; two halves making a beautiful whole. Jude and I couldn't be anything outside the Center. That was a temporary love. Something that couldn't be repeated, even if a part of me wanted it to.

Every time we passed in the hallway. The quick redirected glances we exchanged around the tables in the dining hall. The smell of citrus and bergamot lingering in the hallways like a ghost's calling card. All things there wasn't time for. Not here.

Not now. My focus had to be on Olivia and proving that I could be the man she wanted and needed. I would prove that to her by getting her children back. I would rise up and take the Nation down. I would be the leader, the man, the hero.

I would get Olivia back. Right my wrongs. Take the Nation down and start a life with her outside of here, just like she wanted. I would beat Thomas and win the life I worked hard to get before he stole it from me. If I could just get her back, everything would be better.

My body collided with someone in the hallway.

"Oh, sorry Mrs. Embers. I wasn't paying attention to where I was walking. It's a little late for you to be out. Is everything okay?"

"Yes. Everything's okay. I just...I'm looking for something."

Her eyes were puffy as they searched the hallway for anyone else.

"Anything I can help you with?"

"No. Have you talked to Olivia?"

"Yes. Earlier."

"How was she doing?"

I thought back to her naked body wrapped in sheets. "She was fine."

"She knows about you...her father."

"I know. She found out during the meeting. It's just going to take time. Try to imagine what it must feel like."

"What it must feel like! Please, I know what it was like. When they took her father from me. When I had to choose her and her sister over him. My world disappeared. He was my life. I knew I could live without my children once they had grown and potentially left. But their father? How could I ever live a life without him? He was everything to me just like she is everything to you, but the two of you won't ever be the same once she learns all of it."

"Rebecca, we told her everything tonight."

"I bet it wasn't everything." She mumbled under her breath.

I paused. "Mrs. Embers, do you know something else? We need to know...we have a right to know."

Rebecca scoffed. "Oh, I bet you think you have a right to know. Funny thing about that though," she paused for a moment, and as if her mind left for a moment, then returned, "No one has any rights here. To anything. Or to anyone. The sooner you and Olivia learn that, the better off the two of you will be."

"Our plan is to have the kids back soon. I promise."

"I don't need your promises. I know it will be over soon. I don't need you or anyone else on this compound to tell me that. If you see Olivia again before you go, will you let her know I love her? That I always loved her. I tried to tell her earlier, but she just wouldn't listen. I chose her and her sister, like a good mother does."

"Of course."

Rebecca left for the dining hall, but her words stayed with me. She was part of the group with my mother and father early on, but at what point could she have learned information that my parents didn't know?

The next morning, instead of going to the training room, I went to the library to see if Jessica was there. If there was anyone that might have known what was going on with Rebecca, it was her. As I suspected, Jessica was in the library, reading a book, just as her sister used to when we were children. At Elysium, teenage life's social nuances preoccupied Jessica too much for her to be found with a book. Today, after years of cancer treatment and being forced to slow down, books had become her best friend.

I knocked on the opened door as I entered so I wouldn't startle her.

"Jessica?"

"Hey Ethan. What are you doing here? I'm pretty sure you stopped reading years ago."

"Ha. Ha. Hilarious, Jess."

We had a give and take relationship like best cousins, who would share gossip among families when we got caught up at the kid's table on Thanksgiving.

"What? You can't tell me you've read a single book this year. From what I understand, you've been pretty busy with all your 'Nation takeover' BS." Jessica loved to air-quote, especially when she was making fun of me. An endearing quality that got us through the first part of her cancer treatments before Thomas took me.

"For the record, I could read in the whorehouse. Of course, they were always only books on sex and how to win clients over." I joked.

Jessica burst out laughing, and I did too.

"Well, of course they were. Seriously, why are you here? Aren't you and my sister supposed to be saving the world right now?" Always in the background, unless it was to showcase the weakness of her body, Jessica lived in a constant state of sarcasm and defensiveness.

"Saving your niece and nephew first. The world comes next." I smiled and winked.

"Right, right. The world is next. Ethan and Olivia take on the world. I'm sure I will see it in a book at some point. Some post-apocalyptic piece about the plight of women, the one man that will save the day, and the happily ever after because that's what all readers want."

"Jaded much today?"

"Jaded much, every day, you know that, Ethan." Her lips pierced to the side and she sank slightly. "Again, why are you here disturbing my very busy compound reading schedule?"

"I ran into your mom on my way back to my place."

"Yeah?"

"Yeah, and she seemed a little off."

"Well, she's always been off. You know that. Once dad died, it just got a little more off."

"I don't know...it's more off than usual. She was talking about the kids. And how 'this will all be over soon.' It just seemed weird."

"Well, it will all be over soon, right?"

"Yeah, I just..."

"Don't look too much into her. She moves to the beat of her own drum. I stopped trying to figure out what she was doing a long time ago. It's too exhausting to follow whatever fresh path she's on."

I paused, "Since everything came out, did she ever mention anything to you about having to choose between you girls and your dad?"

Jessica set her book down. "No, what do you mean?"

"Not sure. It's just, she said, or made it sound like Thomas may have told her to choose between your father or the two of you girls living. Or maybe you, living."

Her eyes scanned the room. "I know Thomas made sure my mom understood Olivia would have to marry him so I could be taken care of." Jessica drew in a breath, "Are you saying there's more to it? Because if that's the case, then it changes a lot, right?"

"I think on some levels, yeah, it does. If Thomas gave your mom an ultimatum and that included your life or your dad's and then wrapped up in all of that was Olivia's life too, then your mom has been dealing with a lot more than we thought. I know our parents had a plan to infiltrate the Nation. And your dad was doing something with that when he died. His death wasn't supposed to be part of the plan, but something must have changed and I think your mother was part of it."

"Does Samara know anything? I mean, she's been privy to everything, right?"

"I'll check, but I'm not sure. If this is actually true, there's more we need to find out. I mean your mom has always been off, but this seems like something more."

"Well, then that's saying something. I'll keep an eye out, but I am sure she'll be fine."

Jessica, Liv, and I made light of Rebecca often, even before Luke died. She was a brilliant scientist, but would sometimes make the most off-the-wall comments that either ostracized people or made them uncomfortable. We came to the conclusion her job, and its isolation throughout the days, just made her a little socially awkward.

"Thanks. I just don't want one more thing that I have to handle."

"Sometimes your control freak tendencies are a lot, Ethan."

I stuck my tongue out at her.

"Yeah, well, those tendencies got us all free from the Nation bullshit, so, you're welcome."

She stood up and bowed sarcastically at me. "Oh, dearest Ethan, thank you so much for being controlling and getting us out of the Nation."

I rolled my eyes, and we both laughed.

"Alright, I need to get everything ready. Good luck with the book."

"Thanks." She paused, "I know things are weird with Olivia. I think she'll come around, but she just needs the kids back. They're the only thing that ever mattered to her once she married Thomas. There were so many times I saw, but didn't see, what Thomas was doing to her. What the marriage was doing to her. But when the kids were around or she was doing something for them...in the flow of motherhood, I could see her. The Olivia I knew when I was younger. The one he, and that marriage, took from her. She just needs time, Ethan."

"Thanks, Jess." My uncertain smile met her eyes before I turned to leave. I wasn't sure she was right. My desire to believe

Jessica battled with the knowledge of my past mistakes at the Challenge Center and my decision to leave her kids with Thomas. I should have chosen them too. But I didn't. She was more important than they were. They had a father. They had a life. They would be fine in the Nation. I saw his love for them, even if he was a piece-of-shit narcissist–those kids weren't part of that abuse. They would be just fine if we left them there and Olivia and I left for a sanctuary state.

But I couldn't do that. She would never leave with just me. I had to prove to her I could be more than Thomas. That I could win both her kids and her back. I would win, leaving Thomas with nothing. His wife and children's hands clasped within mine as we walked away from this corrupt world.

I would win. And Thomas would lose.

7

OLIVIA

I lay in my bed, my skin cool to the touch. The electricity once felt in the afterglow of our love, no longer warmed my veins. It was déjà vu. I remembered this feeling. Cold, numb, vacant. A service performed on yet another birthday or anniversary. I was there, but not there. Here, but not here. Flashbacks of Ethan's body and Thomas's body switched back and forth like competing games on a television. Arms wrapped around me under the blanket of a dark bedroom sky, telling me "I love you," or "You're mine." Two phrases from two men that now made me gasp for air.

It was difficult to untangle my life with Thomas–the memories and idea of who I was, or supposed to be. The distance between my todays and yesterdays with him rolled out like taffy, making me see the nuances of the cage I lived in. I was so afraid to leave because I had built my life, my sister's life, and my mother's life around him and around the Nation. Everything rested on the delicate system–a system that could be undone with the pull of the right pin, bringing it all to the ground. A pin that I had pulled weeks ago, bringing it all down in a landslide that took my children from me.

I stood in the landslide's mud and struggled to break free from yet another cage. The compound's cage. Ethan's cage. A cage without my children.

Memories of our marriage washed ashore in the ocean of my mind, in small waves that caught me off guard–made me question both my current and past reality.

Thomas polished our image like fine silver and I helped him make that polish shine in front of everyone. Even though I didn't know that I was the only one in the dark about who he really was, the polish served its purpose even more because I played into it...into his world. But no one knew what really went on at home...no one ever did, except for Ethan.

Ethan had seen me over the last ten years in minor episodes of my life: *Olivia and Rose, Episode 1, Olivia and Thomas on Vacation, Episode 26, 'Thomas Holds Her Wrists,' Episode 9 and 11,' 'Thomas Drugs Olivia, Episode 7, 8, and 23.'* But I didn't know I was being drugged, so did it really matter? Was it really traumatic if I didn't know it was happening? I remembered the Maldives, but it was my fault–he told me so. But was my memory right? Was it real? Or had I applied the thick veil from today over yesterday?

I could ask Ethan to replay the memories, how he saw them, but would those even be correct? Would it be okay for me to have him relive whatever pain that caused, knowing the entire time he could do nothing?

Stepping away from a cage only highlights how thick the bars were. His words would wrap around my body and squeeze me until I couldn't breathe. His questioning of my decisions would back me into the corner, a pressed body against cool steel bars. His gaslighting made my reality blurry, marred, vacant.

I built not only my life around him, but my sense of self. I lost it all in him, the Nation, and the world I now know wasn't even real. My paper heart burned beneath his flame, only to be remade day after day just to burn again.

And now, I lay in this bed in this in-between space lost in my becoming and who I can never be again. Relearning how to unshrink myself in a space that constantly feels like I should. The fire inside me comes in waves, and I want to burn it all down just as much as I want the fire to finally be extinguished. But I could never put the fire out myself. I would have to walk into the war before me and let fate decide whether that fire burns itself out or continues to burn the Nation down. I couldn't be the one who left the children under my doing. A martyr is more glorified than a selfish mother who went back and forth between wanting to live for her children and wanting to die without them. We can go to war as an act of socially acceptable suicide, but never be understood for taking our own life back home.

"Olivia?" A soft knock at the door brought me back to my body and outside the darkness in my mind.

"Come in." My voice, back in place.

"Are you still awake?" Samara stood at my door.

I rolled over. "Yeah, I am. Come in."

"I saw Ethan leave. Is everything okay?"

I sat up.

"I slept with him." My hands tightened around the edge of the sheet and I pressed against my naked body.

Samara walked in and closed the door, then sat on the bed next to me.

"Are you alright?"

I looked up, tears in my eyes. "No." And then let them flow freely as she pulled me in, stroking my hair.

"It's okay. Shh. It's okay. You're human, Olivia. Remember that, okay? You're human."

"How could I do this? He's the reason I am here without them. He's the reason we have to go back into that hell-hole of a city and possibly see Thomas again. He's the reason we all have to put our lives at risk. And I, what? I fuck him? Reward him? Give into my desire to just..."

"Fuck?"

"Yeah. It was definitely that."

"Olivia, you have been here for weeks now. You've gone through an immense amount of trauma–learning that the last ten years of your life weren't really, well, real. You are in survival mode right now. Part of that is going to make you act without thinking. To act based on what makes you feel good in the moment. And there isn't anything wrong with that." She took my hand. "What you're experiencing right now is completely normal, totally okay, and valid. You are trying to navigate one of the most difficult times in your life, and the world that once was predictable for you, no longer exists. Therefore, your predictable behavior, or the way you see yourself or how you react to the world around you, no longer exists, either."

I thought back to the last couple of months–how I woke up one April morning and used my pass, which put all of this in motion. I found my life raft on unstable waters, which I was responsible for. My survival was of my doing. Whatever my children were experiencing rested on my shoulders too.

Samara noticed a shift in my body and pulled away. She examined my face and as if she had known me my entire life and knew all my tells. "You cannot put the gravity of this all on yourself. They conditioned you, and they conditioned us, to believe in a certain life. And that life found us both in the hands of the Nation. You are not alone. There are people here, and those still left in the city, that are just as trapped and trying to find a way out."

"People here?"

"Yes, people here are still trying to figure out who and where they are. You're not alone, Olivia. You never will be. I promise. And we are going to get the kids back. Your life is going to be different, for so many reasons, one being that Thomas won't be part of it anymore."

She pulled me in for a hug. "And for all of the other pieces that are going to be different, and whatever path you choose, I'll be there. Whether it's here or somewhere else. Whether it's with Ethan, someone else, or no one else. You need to live for yourself now, Olivia, and those two kids. You are going to figure it out as this all unfolds."

There was something comforting in her assuredness about me. That she could be someone who I hated for taking a part of Ethan from me, a jealousy I rarely felt today because her children and her life with Laura were so much bigger than my moments of envy. She was one of the only people in this time of life so far that I could truly say knew me, and there was comfort in it.

"You good?"

"For now, yeah. Thanks."

"Okay. Tomorrow morning I am going to grab you early for some training, and then we'll go over the plan one more time."

"When are we leaving? Did they say?"

"The day after tomorrow."

"I know it's close, but it still feels so far away to me."

"I know, Olivia. I know." She clasped my hands. "In no time you're going to be back here with Lucas and Rose, right here in this room, snuggling them like crazy."

The thought of them in this bed with me in just a couple days lit me from within and I smiled. "I can't wait to have them back home."

"Exactly. Home with mama. You're their home, Olivia. You always will be, no matter where you lay your head."

"Thanks Samara."

"Anytime. Now, get some rest and I'll be here bright and early. I don't want to get the shitty equipment because the guys are there before us."

"Got it. Thank you, Samara."

"You're welcome, Olivia."

After she left I took another quick shower to wash Ethan off me, then got dressed and fell into bed. As I dozed off I couldn't help but think of the children and where they were sleeping tonight. If they had night lights on or what pajamas they were wearing. I wondered if they were listening to beach sounds or rain on the sound app. I pictured them here with me on either side. I could smell them and feel the warmth of their bodies next to me as I played with their hair before they dozed off into their dreamworld. I played with the folds in the sheets, mimicking what I had pictured while lulling myself to sleep and into my world, where I hoped to see them in theirs.

"Wake up, sleepy head! Time to get to that gym before the dumb guys do." Samara's voice was a little too chipper for me today. She tossed the covers off me as she walked out. "I'll grab us some coffee and meet you in the dining hall."

I smiled, eyes half open. When she left, I pulled my workout clothes out of the drawer, gathered my hair back into a tight ponytail, and put on my running shoes. I walked out and Samara nodded in approval, and we left for the gym hangar. When we arrived, Brandon and Tyler were lifting weights. Chris, Brandon's partner, was using one of the two rowing machines and Jude was running on a treadmill among four others. I had never seen Jude in the workout hangar before, though I'd often seen him running around the lake and stopping by a certain tree, leaning over. At first I thought it was asthma or a stiff muscle, but as I observed him over the last several weeks, I realized it was him crying. Usually around his fifth or sixth lap, he would stop hidden by the willow tree and sob. The first time I witnessed it, I was sitting on the bank, trying to hide from the world myself. Tucked away with a window to his pain, whether it was for me or Ethan or both, I would never ask.

Samara started me on a small warm up of a few laps around the hangar, then moved me to the boxing wing where a row of punching bags hung waiting for the punishment we would shortly give them. I wrapped my hands and pulled on my boxing gloves, then walked to the bag Samara was standing behind.

She started a playlist, all-too-familiar to me now. Songs from the 2010s and '20s, ranging from Eminem to the Foo Fighters. When I first started boxing, I was an embarrassment to Sam and to myself. I rarely made consistent contact with the bag and I would slip all over the place because I just couldn't figure out my stance. As the weeks went on, and the fire within me stayed lit, I connected with the bag differently. I pictured Thomas every time I made contact, and every part of my body changed. I had already thinned out since leaving the Nation, but I had now developed muscle that defined my arms and made me look like I could actually take him on.

Between the running schedule and boxing routine, I was in the best shape of my life. It was weird to think about how the Nation had made it so that physical exercise wasn't part of our world anymore. They made it unnecessary for any high level tiers to stay healthy with the Healing Machines and med center treatments. I did yoga, like other mothers, because it gave me a way to get out of the house. Expensive yoga clothes made me feel beautiful too, which helped on the days when I knew Thomas was unhappy with parts of my post-pregnancy body. I reveled in this new body. It belonged to me and I could do anything I wanted to with it.

When we were done with boxing, we headed for the shooting range on the far side of the airport.

"Olivia?"

I heard his voice and it sounded like honey, just like the first time I heard it. Jude.

"What, Jude?" I replied flatly.

"Can I talk to you, please?"

What was with these needy men lately? I looked at Samara and she hesitated because she knew I was trying to keep my distance from him. "It's okay. I'll meet you at the range." She nodded and took off along the path. "What do you want, Jude?"

"I just want to talk. I know we don't have a relationship, or didn't before the Center, and we don't know each other that well. It's just we had a connection, you can't deny it. And even though we aren't friends, I would at least like to be at some point."

"Friends?" My tone was snide at the absurdity behind his words.

"Yes. Friends. Or at least learn how to become them. Ethan means a lot to you and a lot to me too. Had things been different, like I said the last night in the Center–"

"Yeah, well they aren't different, are they?"

"No, I guess they aren't. Just know that when we are out there or back here I only want what's best for everyone–whatever that means."

His ocean-blue eyes looked into mine and I remembered when we first met. When we first kissed. When we found each other under the Nation's eye in a room meant only for sex, not love or friendship or anything else; just sex. Jude and I found something else there, on the chair...in the pool...under a hot Sacramento sky. My body remembered him and warmed, but I didn't need any confusion right now. I needed to focus on my children and train my body to no longer react to men from my past. I had to keep him, just like Ethan, at an arm's distance if I were going to be successful at getting the kids back and killing Thomas.

"I think you also want what's best for you. Jude, you can have him. Ethan's all yours." God, I was awful. I turned around, leaving him standing frozen in place unsure of what just happened. Even though this had never come naturally for me, I knew I would have to be more like this as time went on–guarded and suspicious of everyone's intentions.

I made it to the gun range within a few minutes after leaving Jude. Everyone loved him on the compound–he was a great team player, stayed quiet, and followed orders. The war room team found him helpful too. The children loved to play games with him because he would never tell them no, and Samara liked him too, and secretly wanted me to give him a chance, at least for a friendship. If things were different, maybe I could, but right now, I had to forget about those nights when I felt alive under his touch, and focus on the now.

I got to the range and found Samara.

"Everything okay?"

"Yeah," I picked up my gun and fired off a few rounds. "Jude wants to be friends."

"And you said?"

"Well, pretty much no. I don't have the time or energy for anything other than you and the mission right now. Besides, he still wants Ethan and Ethan still wants him, so they can have each other. I can't do this right now."

"I get it. Just don't close too many doors on your way out, okay?" She set her gun down.

"What's that supposed to mean?"

"I just mean, what you're feeling right now is just that–a feeling. Don't let what you're feeling now, toward him or Ethan, dictate what your future looks like."

Something about her telling me what to do didn't feel right. She was just supportive moments ago, and now this?

Samara sensed my change in mood. "I'm just saying, there's a lot going on right now, and making any long term decisions about who you're friends or not doesn't need to be decided right now."

I turned from her, pulled the trigger, and emptied the magazine. Samara smiled, emptying hers too. "You good?"

"Yeah, I'm good. Let's keep going."

Before the compound I had little to do with guns. I had learned how to shoot shotguns and rifles growing up at Elysium, but we never learned how to use hand guns or anything other than what the adults thought were safe and practical.

I loved having my own gun. It made me feel powerful, like I could take on anything–and that I didn't need a man or anyone else to help me. I thought about the possibility of taking Thomas's life and whether I could do it, as Samara had questioned. There was a part of me that feared the aftermath of his death and its impact on the children. I saw the bigger picture though. My children and I would only be free in a world where he no longer existed. It was my responsibility to make sure that happened, no one else's.

"Here," Samara handed me more rounds as we reloaded.

I got back in stance, opened my eyes, and drew in a deep breath. I pictured what I wanted for my future.

A world without the Nation.

A world without Thomas.

A world with no one controlling me ever again.

I repositioned my hand against the handle, put my finger on the trigger, and found the target in my sights. I took in a breath and when I released it, I heard Samara yell "Yes!" A bullet hole perfectly made in the head of the target.

A bullet meant for Thomas. A bullet meant for the Nation. A bullet meant for the death of my former life.

I was ready.

8

ETHAN

Olivia avoided me and spent most of her time with Samara at the gym or gun range until we were ready to leave. We had a quick pre-operations meeting with the team: Olivia, Samara, Brandon, Vivian, Chris, Tyler, and me. The plan was pretty straight-forward: find Rose and Lucas based on intel and bring them back. Timing would be our biggest concern, but as long as things went according to plan, we'd be back at the lake before dinner.

Our connections made it easy to have people on the inside who gave us access to Lucas and Rose's schedules. Our arrival would coincide with the lunch bell, as that's when Thomas's security detail changed. There was a brief opportunity to set off the fire alarm, clearing the school so we could get Rose and Lucas. Olivia was adamant about being part of this, which made sense on so many levels, except that I didn't want her in harm's way. The children wouldn't willingly go with us, so her being there was key to getting them home. She would get Lucas first, then meet up with Rose at the fire exit, right before everyone filed out to be counted by the teachers. It was going to be a tight timeline, but Olivia insisted she could do it. I knew if it came down to it, I would just go grab Rose myself, even if it was against her will.

Once in Central, I asked Tyler to pull off just outside of Central, off 4th street.

"It looks quiet." Brandon looked at his HoloPhone. "They said things are quiet there too. We're good to go in."

"Okay, let's review this one more time," I began. "Tyler and Chris, you're going to stay here. Chris, be Tyler's and our cover if anyone comes out. Vivian, Brandon, you'll go with me. Brandon will message our contact to have him trip the fire alarms. I'll go to Rose's classroom and wait for Olivia and Samara to show up with Lucas. Once we have both kids, we get to the SUV quickly and go home. It should take ten minutes to get in and get out. We can have up to fifteen with the commotion of the alarm and the transition of guards, but only that. Everyone got it?"

Everyone nodded, and we readied our gear. Brandon messaged his contact waiting for the transition between guards, which was minutes away. I looked at Olivia, a solid force ready to take on the world. Something I had never seen in her and something I hoped to never see again. I wanted my innocent Olivia back, not the militaristic one before me. Once this was over, I was sure I could make things go back to normal. Once she had her kids back, everything would be okay and we could be a family.

The fire alarm went off, and that was our cue to head inside. We came in, guns not drawn, but visible on our sides. I headed left into the school, trying to get through a slew of middle school children. I looked to the right and saw Olivia and Samara head for the younger classrooms. Once outside of Rose's room, I looked at each kid as they filed out, perfectly calm and in line. When the last child left, Rose wasn't there. I looked in the classroom and she wasn't there either. I peered back outside and saw Olivia and Samara running toward me.

Samara had her hand on Lucas's arm and turned to the exit where Tyler was waiting for us. Olivia ran toward me in a panic when she saw Rose wasn't there.

"Where's Rose?" She pushed past me into the classroom. "Ethan, where the fuck is Rose?" She yelled.

"I don't know. She isn't here."

"What do you mean? Your people, they were supposed to be on this! This was supposed to go off with no problems!" she yelled.

"Liv, we will find her. She was probably in the bathroom when the alarm went off. Brandon, Vivian, spread out. If you see her, tell her she's safe, and that she needs to come with you. Say something about Olivia being here. That will get her to leave with you."

We ran out, drawing more attention than we had hoped. A teacher saw our guns and yelled, "Active Shooter!" and mayhem ensued. Children and teachers scattered everywhere, and a once potentially controlled situation now turned into complete chaos.

Olivia stood still, scanning the heads of running children, and then yelled, "There!"

Rose was being grabbed by a boy with brown curls and tan skin, arms around her, ushering her to safety.

"Rose! Rose! It's mom!"

Rose turned around and, almost as if she didn't recognize her own mother, stood there, uncertain what to do. She looked at Olivia's gun and screamed. The young boy pulled her away and Olivia took off running toward both of them.

I followed, running through the crowd of children screaming at the sight of the two of us. Olivia caught up to Rose and the boy, cornering them in a corridor.

"Rose, it's mom. You need to come with me right now. I have Lucas. I'm here to take you with me. Please give me your hand." She pleaded.

"Look, I don't know who you are, lady, but Rose isn't going anywhere with you."

"And who are you?" Olivia seethed through her teeth.

"I'm Cooper, Rose's big brother."

"She doesn't have a big brother."

"Yes, she does, and it's me. Thomas chose me to watch over her, ever since the explosion."

"Of course he did. But here's the thing, *Cooper*, this is my daughter, and she's coming with me."

"Dad told me not to go with you if you ever showed up."

"What?"

"You left us. He said you left us to be with the rebels. That you're dangerous and will hurt us too."

"None of that is true, Rose. None of it. Rose, come with me. I'll explain everything when we get home. But we have to leave now. We are running out of time."

"I'm not going with you. Lucas and I are staying with dad." Rose looked behind me.

A chill went up my spine.

"Of course she's not going with you, Olivia. She knows that home is here. Not with you. She knows how you, and those assholes you're with, have hurt hundreds of people. How you and this piece of shit have been lying to me for years. How you never loved me, Olivia, or the life you had with them."

"Thomas." Olivia turned and pointed her gun at him, just past me.

"Hello, my lovely wife. Oh, you won't shoot me in front of our daughter and her classmate, right? No...you wouldn't do that. You know better than that."

I turned around and walked toward him with my gun drawn.

"You won't either, Conrad. You know the only place for you is in a prison. And shooting me in front of all these witnesses and cameras would surely find you at the end of a needle while we all watch you take your last breath. I'll bring the popcorn."

Thomas's calm demeanor set me on edge. The fine line between calm and insanity made my skin crawl.

"Now, here's what's going to happen. Olivia, you're going to leave with your crew of rebels, leaving Lucas on the front steps of the school. Rose is staying here with Cooper, and I'll go back to living my life with them. Your departure forfeited your rights to the children. You have no rights to this world anymore. You're a traitor to the Nation and if you're caught here again, I will make sure you and everyone else on that compound finds themselves at the end of a Nation rope, needle, or electric chair–really whatever we can come up with to make it worthwhile."

"You sick fuck!" I pointed my gun at his head.

"Intelligent phrases have never been your strong suit, Conrad. Better boots on the ground than a commander at the helm." He pulled out his HoloPhone and showed a mass of security detail coming our way. "I can see the panic, and rightfully so. They will not take you alive. Because you killed one, they have orders to kill you. Of course, once I get Rose and Cooper out of the way. Do you really want to do this, Ethan? Olivia? C'mon. You know the best chance you have is to just leave and forget this world. It's not yours anymore."

Olivia looked at me, tears beginning to form, whether for anger or defeat. I wasn't sure.

"Liv, lower your gun. We need to leave," I said.

"Thomas, they're my children!"

"Yes, and thank you for having them." Thomas never failed to surprise me with his coldness. How could a man ever say anything like this to the mother of his children? He had no rights to them.

"You don't know what you're doing." Olivia's words so

familiar to me. Words she spoke over the years streaming in the background of the Challenge Center televisions.

"I don't care, Olivia." Thomas said indignantly.

"Liv, we need to go." I repeated.

"No! I won't leave her. Not again!" She pleaded, and I watched her heart shatter all over again.

There's no pain like the one a mother feels when the right to be a mother is taken from her. I had a hand in that loss too, but unlike Thomas, I carried the weight of it.

"Olivia, we will figure something out. We have to go now."

I kept my gun raised to Thomas, and moved toward Olivia, grabbing her arm, and pulling her back with me.

"No! No! No! I won't leave her. I can't. Rose, I love you. You don't understand. You don't understand what's going on. I didn't do any of those things. He's lying to you."

She sobbed, as we continued to walk backwards to the door leading us to the hallway and eventually in front of the school.

"Rose! No! I can't leave her, Ethan, I can't!"

"We'll get her back. Rose isn't going anywhere with us right now. Not with Thomas or that boy. We will figure it out, I promise. We have Lucas, we need to go." I turned around and pulled her through the halls, running over the dead body staining the floors red.

Once outside, I could see the security detail running toward us. I opened the car door, pushed Olivia inside, jumped in, and fired my gun at the mass of black suits. Olivia screamed as she searched for Lucas.

"Where's Lucas, Samara?" She screamed.

"My grip...it wasn't strong enough...he ran back into the school, Olivia. I'm so sorry. I tried, but the bodyguards and the other kids got him."

Olivia screamed and tried to jump out.

"Stop it! Stop it, Olivia!" I yelled and grabbed her arm, digging angrily into her flesh. "You're being ridiculous!" I pushed her to the front and placed my body at the door as I closed it.

Olivia collapsed into herself, sobbing uncontrollably.

I scanned the SUV and saw a pool of blood. "Who was hit?"

"Just me boss—a scratch that the machine can fix once we get back." Brandon's breath labored as Chris held him.

His words became a muffled mess amid the gunshots firing at us and Olivia's wailing.

Another failed plan with Olivia and me at the center. How would I ever come back from this with her? How would she ever forgive me for leaving the children behind again?

9

OLIVIA

I couldn't feel or hear anything. I knew I was crying as we drove away from my children once again. If I closed my eyes, maybe I could see them here with me. A world without Thomas and the Nation. A world without Ethan, the consistent fuck-up in my life. I took a breath. I could feel my hatred for him and the empty promises he continued to make and I continued to believe.

I closed my eyes, holding my knees close to my chest, and faded away. I couldn't be here anymore, not without them. I let it take me to the deep, to a place I wasn't sure I would return from, but at this moment, I didn't care. I wanted to be done, so I closed my eyes and faded to memories of my past. Things I knew for certain were real. Maybe if I could remember enough, they would actually be here with me, instead of with Thomas. Maybe if I tried hard enough, I could somehow transport myself out of this mess and be with them.

THERE SHE WAS. My Rose. My sweet daughter, sitting quietly on the couch reading a book while Lucas played with his trains on the table. I'm home with them—when was this? It must have been last year because her hair had grown out from when we had to cut it after Lucas "accidentally" put gum on her pillowcase.

"I was trying to be nice, Mama! I wanted to chew it for her so she didn't have to because her teeth hurt from the dentist. I didn't mean to get it in her hair. Rosey, I'm so sorry. I didn't mean to."

Rose had looked at him and then me, tears welling in her eyes as I tried to cut the sticky pink tangled in her beautiful brown hair.

"She knows that, little bear, but she's still upset about it. It's good you feel bad and you're saying sorry. It's important when we do something to hurt someone else we love, we have to say sorry and mean it."

A feeling pulled me from the memory that I was desperately clinging to as an escape from being in the SUV. Thomas's sorries were never really sorries at all. They were thick with "I'm sorry you feel that way," or "I get the sense that you are reading into something that's just not there." My stomach tightened and I forced myself to ignore him so I could go back and be with my children.

"Mama, will my hair ever grow back?" Rose cried.

"Yes, love. It will and probably faster than you expect it to."

"Will it be long enough to curl next year for the ceremony?"

She was always thinking ahead, planning a future for herself that she felt she had power over. As her mother, I wanted to give her that power, but as a citizen of the Nation, I knew her and I would never have what her brother and father had.

"It will be. I'll see what I can get from the salon. I'm sure they have something to help with this."

"I just want to be beautiful for it."

"Oh my goodness, Rose. You are beautiful. Long hair and pretty clothes isn't what makes you beautiful. It's you. The person you are. The person you're becoming. You love your brother, me, your father," I choked back bile with the word, "and your friends. The way we dress ourselves isn't what makes us beautiful—we are beautiful without that. You are beautiful without that."

"Am I beautiful too, Mama?" Lucas interrupted, always wanting to be part of the conversation.

"Yes, darling. You are beautiful too."

He giggles. "You are too, Mama. Even when you're sad."

I pulled back again. Had they seen it, my sadness? My half-life that I was living when their father was home? I thought I did such a good job at making sure they never knew. I smiled in all the pictures. I stepped away to the bathroom to get a quick cry out before going back to entertain friends and family at birthday parties or dinners. I curated the best photos for the world to see. Surely Lucas didn't know, right?

His hand touched mine, letting me come back to them and the memory that projected on the wall of the SUV, like an old movie.

"Mama, I will be right back." Lucas toddled off and was gone for a few moments, returning with a large smile plastered across his face.

"What are you up to?" I smiled and looked at Rose, her tears subsiding slightly.

"Look! I match you too, Rose." He turned around and a giant mess of pink threaded together around his thin hair.

I think many mothers in this moment would have yelled because of the inconvenience it added to time's ever-escaping mother's schedule. I didn't yell. I smiled and then started to laugh. Rose laughed too and Lucas looked confused.

"Why is it funny? I didn't want Rose to be the only one who

had to have a funny haircut." His eyes started too well with tears.

"Oh honey, it's funny because now mommy has two pink bubblegum babies."

Rose started rolling with laughter, Lucas following quickly after, and then I saw it. The three of us and the tether that would always bring us back together. The kindness and thoughtfulness Lucas showed. The grace and forgiveness Rose showed. The love and openness I showed, and would always show both of them.

The Nation and Thomas could have a lot of things, but this was something they could never touch; monsters could mimic love, but they would never be able to carry it in their bones. Because love demanded a heart, and he traded his away years ago.

My body jostled against the seats, rolling me out of the fetal position I found myself in.

"Where are we?" I asked Samara.

"We're halfway up the hill, just past Folsom."

I looked away from her, staying silent, lost again to the Nation and Ethan's failure.

Once on the compound, I left everyone without saying a word, and went to my room. A blur of faces greeted me as I walked past solemnly. My mother stood crying, she must have heard before we got back. For a brief moment, I thought I saw Jessica, but more than likely she would escape back into her world of books, like she had since she was diagnosed years ago. I never faulted her for not being present with me over the last two months, but a part of me needed her and I didn't feel like I could ever ask.

Once in my room, I stood under the hot water in my

shower, letting it burn my skin, as a penance for being an incompetent mother today. How had I let them go again? What if they thought their father was right? That I didn't love them? He painted me ugly just as I had done to him in the narrative in my own mind. I had to find a way to get them back, but how? His surveillance and security were everywhere, another piece of silk I couldn't escape when I was in the Nation walls. There had to be a way though. I had to find a way.

I crawled into bed, shutting the world out around me until I could figure out what to do next. I cried myself to sleep as the sun pierced through the window reminding me of another failed day in my life.

I awoke to a knock at the door.

"Hold on," I said and then quickly got dressed. When I opened the door, my mother stood waiting for me to invite her in.

"What are you doing here?" My tone was chilled and inpatient.

"I heard what happened. Olivia, I'm so sorry. It's just a setback though."

"You don't know anything, Mom. You need to leave."

"I'm not leaving until you hear what I have to say." She pushed past me and stood by my dresser.

I sat on a chair across from her. "What?"

"There's so much more to this than you understand...than you know." She drew in a deep breath. "When your father died he–"

"You mean, when you let him go to the meeting to be killed?"

"Don't, Olivia." Her voice was sharp. "When your father *was* killed," she choked, "he already had a job inside the Nation and no one knew, but me. He told Dr. Conrad that he was meeting up for an interview, but that wasn't the truth. He stumbled across files in the Nation data system during the first few weeks he was employed."

"There's always a file Mom, with names and dates linked to the Nation." I rolled my eyes.

"Yes there is, but these files included lists of names, dates, and centers with trafficked attendants. He copied the files and was supposed to meet with someone at the Camden to transfer the data. I don't know who it was, but they said they were someone outside the Nation. It didn't make sense because sanctuary states didn't have a lot of support then. I've spent years with this secret, and years trying to figure out who he was meeting with that would want this information."

"We already know people were trafficked. That's not new information, mother."

"The Nation wasn't just trafficking people to be escorts; they were also trafficking people because they needed bodies for experimenting on."

"What do you mean experimenting?"

"I know some details, but your father said that it had something to do with a genetics program that Thomas was working on with offspring and viability."

"Did he ever show you the files?"

"No, but I'm sure Thomas knew your father stole the information and that was why he was killed. Thomas wanted you because of your genetic ability and had to silence your father permanently in order for his program to keep running. Thomas had to silence me too. Your father's death was a reminder of what Thomas was capable of and that he would go to any length to maintain his power in the Nation."

I studied her face to see if she was lying. Was this just another story from another person trying to get me to believe something that wasn't true?

When I was little, I believed all things mythical. Santa Claus, the Easter Bunny, unicorns, dragons, WWE. When one of the mean girls at school told me all of it was a lie, I came home crying. My mother was quiet and brought me over to the couch, sitting me down across from her, just like we were today.

"You know, Olivia, you have one of the greatest gifts people want to have—belief. Sometimes people call it blind belief and think those who have it are naïve and lack intelligence. I don't think that though. I think it's people who have belief that make the biggest impact in the world. Because they see beyond the ugly and sad, and see something more. You have that, Olivia. You see more than what's there and you believe in more than what everyone else can see. It will be your greatest strength, but also your greatest weakness. Parents tell stories to their children to give them hope and believe in something outside of themselves. As people grow up, they naturally lose it. So, yes, that mean girl at school is right. Santa and the Bunny aren't real."

"What about unicorns and dragons?"

"I still don't know for certain about those, if I were being completely honest." A sparkle in her eye flashed and I knew she was telling me the truth.

"And WWE?"

"Oh, that's totally fake, but if it makes you feel better, when I was growing up, I thought it was real too...I was actually in my twenties before I learned it wasn't."

We both laughed and she pulled me in for a hug. "As you grow and get older in age, there are going to be other things you learn that aren't real. Some of them will rock you to your core, while others will just be little leaves in the water that float away. Just remember, it's not so much what you believe about other things, but more so what you believe about yourself and how you want to see the world."

Back in my room, she sat on the corner of my bed with that same look in her eye. She was telling the truth. I stayed silent, unsure of what to do or say. I was exhausted, and didn't know if

I could process one more thing, especially this. Were the centers more than just a place to maintain and regulate the marriage system in the Nation? Did Samara or Ethan know about attendants being experimented on? Who else on the compound knew about this and is this another reason why the Resistance wants the Nation gone?

"Olivia, I know today didn't go the way you wanted it to. My heart breaks for you. Let me help you. I can help with this. When your father and I were trying to find out more about this I helped hi–"

I snapped back to the reality of our mother-daughter relationship as it stood today. "I don't want your help. I don't need your help. You've done quite enough, Mother. I guess I should say thank you for telling me a little bit more of the truth, although I expect there's even more you're keeping from me, because that's your current MO."

"Olivia–please, you're being unfair."

"*I'm* being unfair?" My voice rose. "How about how your secret keeping is unfair? How about how Ethan and Samara and everyone else seemed to know about all these things with the Nation and Thomas, and I didn't? How about how you and I are in a room right now after a failed attempt to get my children back?"

"And my grandchildren, Olivia."

"Don't! Just because you gave birth to me, doesn't give you a right to them anymore. Like I've said before, I'm done with you. No amount of apologies will ever undo what you did. You need to leave."

She stared at me as if resigned to my demands. "There will be a time, Olivia, when you will need me again. It's always that way with mothers and daughters. The ebb and flow of one of the most difficult relationships we were gifted in this lifetime. You are my daughter, just like Rose is yours. Remember this, because what is happening between us isn't unique or new.

This is how women, especially mothers and daughters, pave the way for other women—we bend and break each other until it becomes good."

"I have no idea what you're talking about, Mother. Please leave."

"I will. Just remember this, Olivia. And when you call me, because you will, I'll answer because mothers love their children in the worst of conditions."

She closed the door and I screamed. I would never escape her either. How could this be the life I was living right now? So many people continuing to tell me lies or keeping the truth from me.. If what my mother told me was true, did I have a responsibility to find out more and help those being experimented on? Or was my responsibility only to my children and myself? I knew one thing for sure: I was tired of being told what to do or how to feel. I was done being the supporting actor in their film. Done being the one who goes along with plans that weren't mine. Done being told what to do.

10

OLIVIA

I slammed the door to my room before walking to the dining hall. Families were finishing their meals and I saw Laura and the kids alone.

"Hi Laura, where's Samara?" I asked.

"Hi Olivia. I'm sorry to hear about today." She touched my arm.

"Thank you."

"Samara's in the meeting room for the debrief."

"Without me?" I yelled.

"Sorry. I thought you knew."

"It's okay. I'm not at you. Thanks." I turned quickly away from her and the kids and made my way to the meeting room.

More anger filled my body. Why would they meet without me? Rose and Lucas were my children. Today happened because of them, not me. Were they trying to keep me at a distance for yet another reason that I didn't know about. I knew one thing: I would no longer sit by and let them tell me what was going to happen. I would find a way back to my children and a way out of here.

I needed the Resistance's help. I drew in a calm breath at

the threshold of the door, knowing that I couldn't go in there as hot as I was. This would require acting on my part, but I knew I could do it. I had acted in the best production ever for the last ten years, a few more scenes with the Resistance would be no different. I would find a way to get their help, get my children, and be done with it all.

I opened the door, expressionless. There was a seat open for me at the table.

"How are you?" Ethan whispered.

"Fine." I snapped.

Dr. Conrad cleared his throat. "Good to see you, Olivia, although this meeting may not be what you had hoped for. I checked on Brandon and he appears to be doing fine. The machines will have him ready to go in a day or two. Today was a lot and mistakes were made. I think it's best though to give everyone some time away from it, review the footage, and then come back tomorrow with a new plan. Fresh minds and hearts may make for better planning."

This fucker.

If I were to get what I wanted, I needed to comply one more time.

"What time tomorrow?" My voice stood calm among the storm raging inside of me.

"Morning work?" Dr. Conrad replied.

Everyone responded with nods or soft "okays".

After the room was clear, Samara came up to me. "Want to get a drink before I head back to Laura?"

"Thanks, but no. I'm going to stay here. My mom stopped by and said a few things I want to sit with for a while."

"Anything I can help with?"

"Not yet."

"Okay. I'll see you in the morning."

"Good night."

I sat in the oversized chair staring at the greater Sacramento

Nation map hanging on the wall. I followed Highway 50 from West Borough to Cameron Park—28 miles of divided people struggling to find their small slices of power. I scanned Folsom, then moved to the north, where Granite Bay and Roseville used to be. With the Nation takeover, Granite Bay and Roseville were two of the wealthier red cities that conformed to Nation ideals because it allowed for privilege to still reign among the residents. Many of them were already tier-four or -five just because of where they lived. Had they rebelled or stuck with their more conservative beliefs about marriage and family, citizens would have lost power—something they didn't want. They changed the name, much like they did with the boroughs in Sacramento to Rose Bay, still signifying the wealth and power of the past. In the middle of Rose Bay was a giant red pushpin. I walked toward the map.

Rose Bay Challenge Center.

I didn't know there was another Challenge Center so close to Central. It never came up as an option for me when I accepted my pass. Samara and Ethan never mentioned it either. I needed to talk to Samara and hoped Laura wouldn't mind if I took some of her time.

As I rounded the corner outside Samara and Laura's house, I bumped into Dr. Conrad.

"Oh, sorry, Dr. Conrad."

"It's okay, Olivia. No apology needed. You look like you're in a hurry."

"Yeah, I am. I need to find Samara...or Ethan."

"I saw Ethan outside with Vivian a few minutes ago. I'm pretty sure Samara is with her wife and kids." He peered down at me. "You know, I wasn't trying to brush off what happened today. We have goals with this Resistance, Olivia, and I want you to be part of that so that we can help you get the children back. I know you've said you don't want any part of this and are planning on leaving. I just wonder how many times it may take to try and get Rose and Lucas back if you're not fully on board with what we're trying to do here."

"What are you saying Dr. Conrad?"

"Nothing. Just that, you have a lot to offer us, just like we have a lot to offer you...have offered you. That's all."

Another fucking snake in the grass I would have deal with. *Keep playing the part Dr. Conrad wants you to, Olivia.*

"Got it. Thanks Dr. Conrad, I need to go find Sam."

"Have a good night."

"You too, Dr. Conrad."

When I first got here I saw similarities between him and Ethan. Tonight, it was clearer to me, more than ever, that Ethan was a copy of his father. Their need for control and ambition sickened me. It's funny how much clearer someone or something looks when you take careful steps away from them. Only from a great distance can you clearly see what you are meant to see.

Ethan was like a sailing ship where I stood as a passenger, looking everywhere but there for who he was. It wasn't until I stepped on shore and watched him sail away that he and who he was becoming came clearly into view. He loved me. He loved the idea of me. He loved the idea of an "us" in the past. The me of today included my children and the freedom I sought from all men in my life. How he would cope with this couldn't be my problem right now.

I knocked softly when I arrived at Laura and Samara's house.

"Hi, Olivia." Laura's brown eyes and pixie cut met me.

"Hi Laura. Is Samara free? I need to talk to her."

"Yeah, she's just with the girls. Come in." She opened the door and ushered me in. "Can I get you something to drink? Water, wine, whiskey?"

"Whiskey sounds great. Thanks"

"Of course." Laura left the room, leaving me to find my place on their living room couch.

Laura and I rarely crossed paths. I was almost only training in the hangars or in my room, giving me little time to try and make friends with her. I scanned the room, looking at pictures of the four of them. How they got prints of actual photos was beyond me. We had photos in our house because I insisted on having a few non-digital ones. I wanted something lasting, something a finger swipe couldn't delete. Thomas didn't fight me on it because there was a core piece of him that lived in the past too–never wanting to fully let go of the moments that connected each of us to a time that was long gone, while trying to propel ourselves into the brave new world ahead of us.

Laura returned with a small glass of caramel gold. "Here you are."

"Thank you." I took a large sip.

"I know I said this earlier, but I'm sorry about the kids. You'll get them back. Sam is adamant about it. I know...Ethan is too." I shuddered when his name left her lips. Lips that he knew. A body he knew. And a body she knew too. I put it out of my mind. She saw my thoughts immediately and I looked around the room.

I needed to change the subject. "Your pictures, how did you get them up here?"

"They're great, right? There's a printer in the business office. They make it feel a little bit more homey, I think."

"They do." I took another sip. Laura clasped her hands above crossed knees. "Where was that one taken?" I pointed to a picture of Samara and Laura standing to the side of their girls surrounded by tropical trees and a white sandy beach.

"That was the Maldives. Samara used one reward that year. She bonused so we got to choose a higher tier trip."

"How long ago was that?"

"I think three, maybe four years ago. It was one of our favorite trips. We stayed on a private island in this giant house. The girls loved it. We had a private chef and could take a boat into town. We were in town that day—it's one of my favorite pictures of the girls. It really shows how they have the same eyes...just like..." She paused. "I'm sorry, Olivia. I didn't mean for–"

"It's fine, Laura." Another sip helped drown the anger from a life that was stolen from me, but at the same time, a life that would be without Rose and Lucas. When this was all over I would have to find peace within the two worlds. The one where I have my children, but also find space for the world where Ethan has children without me. It never occurred to me when I was younger that Ethan and I wouldn't have a world together with our children. Here, I am confronted every day with the reminders of how things didn't work out and even though I knew Ethan was no longer my path, it didn't mean the pain just went away. A part of me was still sad that he had children with other women and that we would never have that bond between us.

Samara walked in, cutting the tension creeping up the walls.

"Hi, Olivia."

"Hi, sorry to bug you right now, but I wanted to talk. I have some questions."

"Okay, can Laura stay for this?"

"Yeah, I mean, does she know everything that's been going on?"

"She does. We share everything with each other. No secrets. Never. Not even when I was trying to live two lives. It was really hard on her."

"It was. But we got through it. Like we get through everything." Laura took Samara's hand and kissed it. I looked away.

"So what questions do you have?"

"I was looking at the map in the planning room and saw

there's a Challenge Center in Rose Bay. Did you know about it? I thought there was only Central in this area."

"Yes, I do know about it. Rose Bay is only for the people who live there. They made a deal with the Nation and paid a premium to have it be a private Challenge Center. It's smaller and the attendants are, well, more carefully curated. Their citizens have very specific tastes...and it can be a tough place to work if you don't know what you're getting into when you sign up."

"What kind of tastes?"

"Well, normal stuff like we see at Central. Some fantasy or role playing. But there are a handful of citizens who tend to be more dominant or degrading to the attendants. I've heard they have special rooms with toys, whips, chains, where citizens can do whatever they want to attendants, with or without permission."

"Really, without consent?" Laura asked.

"Honey, attendants consent to anything just by signing their contract. The Director's assistant explains the job to potential tier-ones and -twos, about what they could encounter. Most don't care. They're so desperate for money and a place to stay, they would probably sign away body parts if the price were right."

I thought about what my mother told me about the experiments on attendants and wondered how many of them knew. Was it in their contract under the fine print that no one ever reads? The more I learned about the system I was part of, the angrier and more ashamed I became.

"That's awful." Laura's doe-eyes matched her innocent voice.

"It is awful, but again, all part of the system. A system, we have to remember, that we benefited from too, hon."

Laura turned away and drew in a breath. "I know. But we did it for the girls. For us."

"It doesn't matter why we did what we did, Laura. The fact is, we did it. We participated in a system that did...and still does...terrible things to its less fortunate."

"I just...I know...I just want us to do better next time. I want us to do better for the girls."

"And we will. We will." Samara turned to Laura and kissed the top of her forehead. This was what love looked like. Something I hadn't seen since I was a young girl living downtown with my parents and Jessica. My mom and dad loved each other like this. Conversations that could become, and sometimes would become contentious, stayed in a protected space, not held hostage by individual ego or insecurity, but rather ushered forward into understanding and common ground.

This was the love I searched for my entire life. Where I was today, I had little faith I would find it in any of the men that orbited my world.

"What other questions do you have, Olivia?"

"Is that Center still connected to the Nation?"

"Yeah, as far as I know."

"If it's still connected to the Nation, it would have access to the data system, right? And the surveillance?"

"Yes...but it would be really hard to get in, unless we had someone on the inside." Samara's eyes widened and immediately shook her head. "No, Olivia. No way. Not an option, Olivia. You don't want to be part of...that...world. Trust me. It's not a good idea."

"I get it, but how hard would it be to become an attendant at Rose Bay? Like could I do it?"

"Oh my god, Olivia. Ethan wowuld never approve of it."

"Ethan doesn't have to approve it. This is my life. My children. My world. Not his, not anyone else's. If I get information about the kids and Thomas by me being on the inside, then that's what I am going to do. I don't need anyone to give me permission. I just need their help. Can it be done?"

She hesitated. "Yes. Yes. It can be done. Morgan can do it."

"Perfect."

"I'll talk to her tomorrow before the meeting."

"How fast do you think I can get in?"

Laura squeezed Samara's hand. "Samara, she can't go alone."

Samara searched Laura's face.

"You know she can't go alone. You know Challenge Centers inside and out. The system. Even if it wasn't your Center, you still know everything that could help Olivia get them back just that much sooner."

"But that would mean I would be without you. You would be without me. I don't even know how long it would take. And it would also mean tha–"

Laura stopped her. "I know what it would mean. We've done it before."

"Yeah, but this would be different. I wouldn't be the one choosing. I would be chosen. And *that* Center...we could experience some pretty bad things."

"Couldn't Morgan manipulate the schedule so you're not on it as much?"

"She could. Yes."

"But wouldn't that look suspicious?" I added.

"Depends on how it's done. There were always scheduling errors and client preferences. As long as there were enough regular attendants who looked like me or you for that matter, we could be okay. Rose Bay likes exotics though and that would be something for me to be worried about."

"Samara, it's worth the risk. Remember, it's only our bodies, not our hearts. Just our bodies."

"Says the one who will stay home with the girls, not having to fuck random guys."

"Or girls." I said, before realizing my mistake.

Laura laughed. "Yes, you're right, Olivia. And girls. But

Samara, we *will* be fine. We all have to make sacrifices so we can finally be free from the Nation. If I could go, I would. I just don't have the skill set you have. My skill set is here at home with the children—it always has been."

"I know honey, I know." Samara paused, her mind racing through all the what ifs and the long term implications of her choice. "You're sure you won't be here freaking out about whatever happens inside there?"

"Oh I'll be freaking out, but more about your safety and when you're coming home. Not with the people you sleep with. We can make peace with that when this is all over. Right now, we need to look at the bigger picture."

I sat there watching the two of them navigate a conversation unheard of among couples. A conversation giving permission for others to have access to a body that's supposed to belong to their partner. A conversation about sacrificing for others. A conversation about choosing to leave the ghosts on the battlefield instead of bringing them home to haunt their marriage forever.

"Okay." Samara resigned.

"Okay." Laura echoed.

"Okay?" I questioned, breaking the tension of the gravity of the mission her and I were about to embark on.

"You know, we're going to need to get the rest of the group to approve." Samara added.

"I know."

"Remember, no matter how independent or determined you're feeling right now, we still need them. This is a team, as fucked up as it may seem, they're valuable. They'll be on the outside making sure we stay safe on the inside. We need the resources, and anything that can alert us if something's gone wrong."

I didn't like how Ethan would have a hand in this or his dad, but I knew I had to play a part to get the children back. I would have to play the game, hiding behind the mask I'd worn for ten years.

"When do you think we could leave?"

She laughed. "Sometimes your impulsivity is a lot. But for this, we probably need about a week to get the identities forged, surveillance polished, face recognition infiltrated, mission start and end time."

"What do you mean start and end time? We end when the kids are back with me."

"Yeah for the most part. But we will have to have an absolute stop too. Thomas is powerful and has powerful friends everywhere. If we encounter any of those people and they recognize you or me, it will be over. We need to get this planned out so nothing can go wrong."

"Fine. I just don't want to wait too long. It's already been almost two months without them, and now with the botched rescue attempt...I just don't want him poisoning them anymore than he already has."

"I understand. I'll talk to Morgan first thing tomorrow and then we'll present it to the team."

"Thank you."

"Of course." She looked at Laura, "Now, I don't know about you, but I need to get to bed. Get some rest."

Samara walked me out, gave me a quick hug and reassurance that we were in this together. As I walked away from their house, I couldn't shake the envy I was feeling. Laura and Samara still had their core life here. Even if they weren't in the same home where they'd spent a decade raising the girls, they still had the most important part with them. They still get to watch them grow, and I wanted that, too. I knew going to Rose Bay and its cost would be the key to changing my situation. I would get my kids back, and I would rebuild something of my own.

11

OLIVIA

The next morning, I waited for Samara outside the war room so we could walk in together as a united front. We took our seats at the table as everyone else filtered in, Ethan among them, sulking. I fixed my eyes on the map, trying to find the right words that would make me convincing when it was my turn to speak.

"I hope everyone got to rest last night after such a big day. Let's go ahead and start coming up with ideas for how we will help Olivia get the children back, shall we?" Dr. Conrad looked to me with a gentle reminder of our conversation from the night before.

"I actually have a plan, Dr. Conrad."

"You do? Well, let's hear it." He leaned back in his chair and folded his fingers together with a small smirk easing across his face.

"Samara and I are going to become attendants for the Rose Bay Center."

Jaws around the table dropped just as Ethan slammed his hand on the table and yelled, "Absolutely not!"

"Give her a minute, Ethan." Dr. Conrad leaned forward and

placed his hands on the table. "Tell us more. What made you think about this? How will it work? Have you even thought through those details yet?" His condescension pissed me off.

"Yes, actually. And I've also been thinking about the Resistance and the bigger picture. You've helped me try to get my children back, and I am grateful for that. I also know that there are more things happening than we've been led to believe." I needed to use the information my mother had given me the night before to force their hand, to make them let Samara and me do this.

Samara tilted her head and looked at Ethan. He shrugged his shoulders and peered back at me. "What do you mean, Olivia?" He asked.

"It's been known that some attendants at the centers were trafficked." I looked at Ethan, who nodded, pride shining for what he'd told me when we escaped Central months ago. "However, it's more than just that. Thomas and the Nation are also experimenting on them."

"Experimenting on the attendants? Ethan, do you know about this?" Dr. Conrad asked.

"No, I don't." He said, and looked at Samara. She shook her head too.

"Yes, they are experimenting on the attendants. I'm not sure about the details, but I think I can find the information if I just get back to the Nation."

"How did you find out about this?" Ethan peered at me.

"I just know, Ethan. Help me get to Rose Bay and I'll get you the information that will help boost the Resistance and bring the Nation down that much faster."

"And how will you get more information when you're there, if you're busy fucking citizens?" Ethan sneered.

"I'm sure I'll be able to find some time in between fucking. I mean, *you* were able to find time for yourself," I paused and looked to Jude, "and others, weren't you?"

Jude shifted in his chair and a part of me felt bad that I had just used him for my own gain. He was just a pawn in all of this like I had been. But I refused to be that anymore. I would do and say whatever it took to get Rose and Lucas back, even if it meant lying and burning bridges in the process.

"I'd always suspected there was more to those Centers than we thought. Actually, I'm pretty sure your father thought so too, Olivia. Interesting that you're just now sharing this information with us," Dr. Conrad said.

"I think I just assumed you knew about it." I retorted.

"Right. Of course. Can anyone else corroborate this information, besides her father's suspicion?"

A voice from the doorway came through. "I can." My mother walked in and stood in the back of the room, fidgeting fingers and all.

"Ms. Embers, this is a closed meeting." Vivian snapped.

"Vivian, let's hear her out." Dr. Conrad said.

My mother let out a breath. "Luke had files on him that night, a drive of some sort. He told me he was going to deliver it to someone before his meeting. When I got his personal belongings, the drive wasn't there. They probably destroyed it but Luke said it had lists of names, centers, and lab locations."

Dr. Conrad cleared his throat. "Thank you, Rebecca. I know losing Luke was hard and we appreciate this, but I'm hesitant to believe it."

My mother moved to the center of the room, "Theo, do you remember how you and Lorraine learned about their plans?"

Dr. Conrad shifted uncomfortably.

"Remember how I was the one who told you what had been going on in the labs leading up to the pandemic? How Luke got wind of the mandates and edicts, which gave you the green light to relocate your family and recruit others to Elysium. You and your family wouldn't be here right now if it wasn't for Luke and me. I may not have a seat at the table anymore, but make no mistake, I was one of the people who set it. The foundation, the vision, the work, and the *sacrifice* carries my and Luke's fingerprints, and always will. If I say this is true–it is."

The room was silent at the command of my mother, and a small part of me felt pride. I remembered this woman—the one from before the Nation, who showed up and demanded a seat, as if her presence alone could bend the room to make space for her.

"Thank you, Rebecca. I know you've been under a lot of stress lately and with everything in the past, I jus–"

"I don't need your condescension Theo. Save that for your meetings. The people Thomas and the Nation trafficked were, and probably still are, being tested on and the Resistance needs to do something about it."

Dr. Conrad studied my mother, the exchange between the two of them made me wonder what was held in their past, and how my mother gained power over him at this moment.

"Well, I think in light of the information Olivia and Rebecca gave us, and the plan she and Samara have come up with, we should move to vote. It would give us inside access to the highest level data system that we've been blocked from since Thomas changed protocols."

"Wait, Olivia, you would be going into a Center?" My mother asked.

"Yes."

"Olivia, I know how much you want the children back, but this isn't the way. The things you'd let happen to your body. It's not worth it. There will be another way."

"My body doesn't matter to me...they do. I am nothing without them, but I guess you wouldn't know anything about that. Still choosing yourself over something that truly matters."

"Olivia, you need to stop!" Ethan's mother yelled. "She is your mother, and whether or not you agree with the decisions she's made, you still need to respect her." Lorraine paused. "She sacrificed everything for you. We all did. Even my son!" Her voice cracked and my mother walked over to Mrs. Conrad, placing a hand on her shoulder.

"It's okay, Lorraine. She will understand one day, she's just too close to it right now. She doesn't have them."

"Well, I didn't either and I still showed common decency to others. You're her mother, and she needs to give you the respect you deserve."

"Lorraine, will you come with me? I'd like to leave, but don't want to be alone." My mother asked.

She looked at Dr. Conrad and then Ethan, finally to me. "Yeah, I don't want to be here anymore anyway. I've had enough of this. Whatever you decide to do, my love," she looked back to Dr. Conrad, "I will support. You know that."

On her way out, she refused to meet my eyes, while my mother gave me a slight nod as if to say she had orchestrated all of this.

To break the tension, Samara suggested calling for a vote, to make it more democratic, but the real point was to show Ethan that everyone but him supported the plan. As our friendship had grown, she told me she'd learned a lot about how to manage him when they worked together over the years. He would go along with plans, even if they weren't his own, as long as there was significant support from whoever he was leading. As independent and controlling as he was, she said he still did what the greater good believed in.

Everyone but him voted yes including Jude, to my surprise. We ended the meeting with a new timeline and to-do list with a goal of us entering the Center within the next two weeks. The next few days were spent coordinating with Morgan and the Rose Bay Center. The Resistance had supporters everywhere. Ethan reached out to his area leaders to get Samara and me into the Center, without drawing much attention from Nation surveillance. Our identities were changed and added to the database, including new chips.

Our new names were Sarah King and Lila Ahmad. Morgan installed new chips in our arms that could alter face recognition in cameras at the Center. As long as no one knew who we actually were, all digital footprints of us would be aligned with our new identities. Samara and I knew there were risks, but we figured the odds of someone from Central being at a center in Rose Bay were low. Attendants from Central escaped before the explosion, and citizens from Central wouldn't drive all the way to Rose Bay, even if they could get an appointment. Morgan said she would monitor citizen lists and make sure we weren't on the schedule if they happened to show up. For the most part, we felt good about the plan.

The morning we were scheduled to leave, I walked around the lake after an early morning training session with Samara. I thought about my children, the Center, and how I would navigate between the multiple worlds I was living in. The only thing I was unsure about was my role and ability to become what citizens needed me to be. Could I sleep with people so easily, and without getting attached? Was my body good enough for the Rose Bay Center or would I need to have alterations before they put me on the schedule? What if I encountered someone I didn't want to have sex with? Would I still have to, or could I find a way to get out of it?

Lost in thought, I didn't see Ethan on the last curve of the lake until it was too late to avoid him.

"Liv? Can we talk, please?"

"What do you want?"

"I just...I think you should reconsider. There are so many other options that we can take to get Rose and Lucas back."

"It's not just about them now. It's about the Nation. Information. Trafficking. The experiments. Taking them and

Thomas down from the inside. Were you telling the truth? Did you not know about the experiments?"

"No, I didn't. Not really. I mean there were rumors and always this weird sense of fear when someone wouldn't show for their shift. Samara and I wondered often about what was happening, but we never found anything that made us think he was experimenting on people. We would have released those files too. Attendants just sometimes disappeared and I knew that was one of Thomas's things…making people disappear."

For once, I believed him and found the sincerity in his voice to be real. We were all part of something bigger and more secretive than we ever knew. Regardless of my current feelings for Ethan, I knew he wanted to help figure out the truth behind my mother's revelation too.

"This is the only way we can do anything about it and to help people that the Nation has hurt for years. You know Samara and I are right. We have to go back in. "

He looked down and shook his head. "I don't like it. I just don't like it."

"Yeah, well there are a lot of things I don't like. Haven't liked, but somehow that doesn't change the fact that all those things have happened and continue to happen. We don't live in the life we had before, Ethan. We won't ever live in that life again."

"But we can live in a new life. One where you and I are together, again." His voice was soft, desperate.

I sighed. "I can't think about that right now, Ethan. The only thing that matters at this moment is what Samara and I have to do."

"But you don't have to do it this way. I could go, instead."

"You?" I scoffed. "Everyone knows who you are."

"I could go with you then. Blend in somehow. There are ways to make me look different, you know we can do that."

"And then what, be a distraction to Samara and me? Or try

to keep me from being selected? Or her?" The last words stung on my tongue. Even though he didn't love Samara the way he loved me, he was protective of her and I knew there was a part of him that still held claim to her body, as the mother of his child.

"What are you talking about Olivia? You know I don't have any feelings for her except respect and friendship. We have been with each other since the beginning of this. Since Thomas took me–"

"Yeah, I know that story, Ethan. I don't need to rehash it again. I don't need to hear about you and her and the plans and the kids and all the things that happened when we were apart. I'm moving forward and going to the Rose Bay Center. This is our chance to do it our way. To get in and get as much informa-tion as possible, so I can find the children and leave this place for good."

Silent breaths widened the canvas between us, creating tiny pockets of unhealable pain. We were lost, holding on to past versions of ourselves—the ones we reached for when we awoke in the middle of the night in a darkened room of the nothing-ness that suffocated our lives. The sea cast us out, leaving us adrift on a broken piece of our sunken ship, a wreck destined to remain lost forever. It was what we held tight to when we forgot how to let go. And I could feel myself slowly sliding away, ready to reach out my hand once again, fingertips trailing the edges of the us I knew, and finally releasing it like a blindfold in the wind.

"I understand." He finally said. "I'll see you when you get back." Ethan walked past me continuing to the other side of the lake, solemn and alone.

I wouldn't let him persuade me now. Samara and I had a job to do, and if we did it right, we would only be there for a few weeks before returning to the compound–with the children, and one step closer to leaving for good. I couldn't reveal that to the Resistance because I needed to make sure they knew I was part of them. Of the Resistance, but not in the Resistance.

I finished my walk, grabbed a to-go cup of coffee from the dining hall, and headed to the war room. Everyone was there except Morgan.

"Where's Morgan?" I asked Samara as I sat down.

"She's just finishing up some last minute tech things. She'll be right here. Where's Ethan?"

I rolled my eyes, "Wandering down at the lake contemplating all the things he did wrong."

Samara smirked, "You're terrible, you know that, right?"

"Yep." I laughed dryly.

"Okay," Dr. Conrad sounded as he clapped his hands. "Today's the day. We need to make sure everything goes to plan as much as possible. Samara, you and Olivia have your new identities and chips, correct?"

"Yes."

"And Morgan?"

"Yes, she does too."

"Wait, Morgan's going?"

"Yes," Dr. Conrad answered. "We felt it would be better to have tech on the ground with you, rather than doing everything remotely. This way, if you need anything last minute, she'll be there to assist. She's going to be Rose Bay's new Surveillance Analyst."

Ethan cleared his throat at the back of the room as he walked in and sat down. The small glint in his eyes was innocent to the untrained, but not me. If words could float through the air between just our eyes alone, everyone at the table would have seen what it looks like when fire and air collide. He had gotten his way, partially, by sending her with us. Another way to keep tabs on me, and whatever I was about to do.

"Was anyone going to tell me about this? This whole thing

was my idea. My plan. My decision." The coal-like embers inside of me were relighting.

Ethan spoke. "I was going to tell you this morning."

He was going to tell me this morning? What a lie. I glared at him.

Dr. Conrad, sensing more tension between us and wanting to move on, redirected the conversation. "Okay, let's review the plan one more time, shall we?"

Everyone, except Ethan and I, nodded their heads. Morgan walked in and took her spot at the table.

"Good to see you, Morgan. Are you all ready?"

"Yes. We are good to go."

"Excellent. Okay, so Samara, Morgan, and Olivia will check into Rose Bay at approximately 11:00am, where they will be processed as new attendants. Once inside, you will have orientation and be placed in your quarters. Morgan, please correct me if I'm wrong, but you are set up on the same floor, so you can be in close contact, but not too close where it will draw unwanted attention. Your first day will feel like a lot, but make sure you're paying attention to as much detail as possible when you're walking around. Try to get a sense of which attendants are leads and loyal, and which are on the periphery, so you can use them for information."

My anger flared. This was my idea, I knew exactly what to do when I went in there, even if I had no military experience. And out of any of these dumb fucks, I knew how to do it as quickly as possible.

"Morgan has you off the schedule for the first two nights. After that, you will need to be in the Selection Room. That won't be a problem because Rose Bay clients prefer new attendants, and your account is marked as new. I would expect to be in a room a few nights a week, but not more than that. Most centers prefer their attendants, especially new ones, to have a break to acclimate," Dr. Conrad added.

"Your job is to get intel as soon as possible. With Morgan being there, you will have quicker access to the Nation information systems. Just let her know what you need without others knowing. Befriend a center employee, a loyal lead, or the janitor. Make sure you get into the system so you can find more information that could help us dismantle the Nation."

"Um, and find out where Thomas is keeping the children. This mission is also about them."

"Right. Of course. I'm sorry, Olivia, I just thought that was inferred." His lack of sincerity annoyed me.

"Morgan will be in communication with us everyday, and with her being in the surveillance room she will have access to some of the systems. It's important, however, that we don't draw any attention to her. When you're just getting to know everyone, don't sit together at first. It would be appropriate for you two to become friends or meet because you're both new, but not with Morgan. We will be monitoring the situation and making sure to act if anything changes."

I had forgotten how tactical Dr. Conrad could be. His political science training gave him the academic background I trusted, but the actual hands-on components made me question what experience he actually had.

"When you find the information on the Nation and the children, Morgan will contact us and we will get you out as soon as possible."

"What's the plan to get us out of there?"

He drew in a long breath. "Honestly, Olivia, it depends on what's going on. We have a few ideas in place, but which one will be chosen will depend on the three of you, and if there has been any change with the Nation. If any of you draw unnecessary attention to yourself, that will complicate things, but we will get you and the children out too."

Condescending prick. We knew the stakes were high and part of the plan that I came up with was to blend in as best as possible. I wasn't about to do anything that would jeopardize getting Rose and Lucas back.

"Fine. But remember, Dr. Conrad, I have more at stake than you do in this. You're staying here behind the scenes, while I do whatever it takes to get them back after your son fucked everything up. You can mansplain all you want, but this mission is going to happen because of the three of us, not because of you and your supposed hand on the helm." I knew I should have stayed silent because I needed them, but he pushed me too far.

Mouths dropped around the table, except for Ethan's and Samara's. Small hints of laughter hid behind raised lips while they looked straight at me. Ethan nodded as if to tell me good job, but I didn't want to receive validation from him. The person Dr. Conrad saw me as over ten years ago was not the same person who sat before him at this table now. And the person I was today would not be the same after I returned from Rose Bay. A small part of me, that I forced to hide, feared who that woman was going to be at the end of this, just like I guessed Ethan did too.

Dr. Conrad cleared his throat. "This meeting's over. Everyone knows their role. Good luck."

As we filtered out, Samara hooked her arm into mine and guided me down the hallway away from everyone else.

"That was ballsy of you," She laughed. "It took everything in me to not laugh. Ethan too. Did you see him?"

"Yeah, I saw him. You too." I smiled. "I just don't want to listen to men like that anymore. They just think they know everything. That everyone else is inferior to them. That we can't do things as good as them, or we aren't as smart as them. I'm over it. I know it probably wasn't the best thing to do, but I just can't stay silent anymore."

Samara stopped us and unhooked her arm. "I know, Olivia, and you don't need to. But keep in mind we need them...*you* need them. You're walking a fine line right now and you're going to need to deliver information about what your mom said. Even though you're living a life that is slowly becoming your own for the first time in over ten years, you still have to recognize the politics. I know that with everything going on you haven't had time to properly process all of this. But once we get the kids back and things settle, you'll be able to focus on you and everything that happened. These outbursts, because you know that's what they'll call it."

"And then say something condescending, like 'oh she just said that because she was under stress' or 'oh, don't take what she said seriously, she was in a highly emotional state,'" I whined and air-quoted.

"Exactly. When the world sees us as more than our beautifully emotional selves, the power will shift. Until then, we have to use it to our advantage, and also make people uncomfortable with it. They need to know a fire burns, but that it can also be contained...controlled...so they will still help you and all the other women who are in a similar place. But the more discomfort they feel, the more light gets shined on us being more than the box they consistently put us in. So thank you for today." She pulled me in for a hug.

"She's right, you know."

Samara and I both jumped back, startled.

"Samara, you're right. The way the world sees us. As small and fragile creatures. Like flowers instead of bombs. It's a misstep for so many of them. To underestimate what lies below the surface of every woman in this existence..." My mother's voice stood in the background waiting for us.

"Mother, I don't want to speak to you right now. I have to get ready to leave."

"I only need a few minutes, please."

I looked at Samara, she nodded and gave me a soft squeeze.

"What do you want?" I turned to her.

"Olivia, you need to know that there has always been a

world happening outside of you that I worked hard to keep at a distance. I stepped into that room tonight to make sure you knew where my loyalty lies. It will always be with you and the children. Even though all of these things have happened, my priority has always been you, even with consequences from Thomas."

"And those consequences were?"

"Jessica's life, but you know that. Your life too. Before you would go on trips or out of town he would remind me of the power he had over your life. He would send me news stories of people disappearing or medical anomalies that took the lives of young mothers. I was certain that he had the capability of it because I knew the power he had. I also knew he was cutthroat enough to do something like that without even blinking. You never knew this, but when you were in the Maldives, I brought the children here."

"Wait, to this compound or to Elysium?"

"This one. I needed to talk to the Conrads and figure out if they could help get us out. I knew if I called you throughout the day he wouldn't suspect anything, and Penny was out of town too, so she wouldn't be able to slip or say something to him either. Lucas was feeling terrible that day, but I knew this was the only chance we had to see if Theo and Lorraine could help. It was their doctor that made me take Lucas to the hospital. We were all in the library talking about possible plans to escape, and Lucas's temperature spiked. She said we needed to get back to a Nation ER right away. Luckily, it was night in the Maldives because it gave me time to get back into the Nation perimeter without Thomas tracking us." Her voice was shaky.

My mother and children were here three years ago? I could have gotten out three years ago? Could Ethan have gotten out three years ago too and all of this would have just been a distant memory?

"I called Thomas after we arrived and got checked in. You had to leave the trip early, remember?"

"Yes, I remember. One of the previous nights on that trip he drugged me and I woke up with bruises. Before we got to the hospital he made me cover them up so people wouldn't think anything bad."

"I knew those bruises were from him," she confessed.

"And you did nothing?" Red, hot heat crept up my throat.

"I couldn't do anything, Olivia. You, Jessica, and Ethan would all be dead."

"Ethan?"

"Yes, he was part of the deal." She stopped and drew a long breath in. "I'm sorry, Olivia. Thomas told me to encourage him to go to the meeting. Theo and Lorraine agreed too. It had to be this way, Olivia."

"What? You told Ethan to go to that meeting?"

"Yes."

"Oh my god...this can't be true. You, and his parents led to his imprisonment? To mine?"

"Yes." She hung her head and drew in a long breath. "We knew he needed to join the Nation military, but we also needed him on the inside once your dad died. I can't change anything, and given the same ultimatum, I would do it again. To save you and them. You would do the same thing, Olivia."

"No I wouldn't." I seethed. "I would find another way! I would leave. Anything but let the people I love march their way into the hands of a sociopath."

"You say that now, but a time will come when you will face horrible options. And you will have to choose the least worst one."

I wasn't sure how much more I could take. I was here, but I wasn't. She was a mother, but she wasn't. How could she have led so many of us to our potential deaths? What kind of a person does that?

"Olivia?" She touched my arm and I jumped. "There's something else. You need to know before you go. It's about the boy–"

"I don't want to know anything else. As far as I am concerned, you, just like Ethan and everyone else here will be dead to me the moment I leave with my children for good. I need to go." I turned away from my mother and had one more reason why her and the Resistance would never be a place I could ever call home.

12

———

OLIVIA

Tyler drove Samara, Morgan, and me to three different light rail stations with different arrival times to the Rose Bay station. Once there, Center ADAMs would pick us up individually, to take us to Rose Bay Center for onboarding.

My ADAM arrived shortly after I got off the light rail. As I got in, I flashed back to the first time I'd gone to the Center for my Challenge Pass. The inside looked exactly the same, except it was missing the tray full of pills that I was to take before arriving. Classical music played over the speakers in the short five-minute drive to the Center.

The ADAM pulled into the parking lot and parked where a valet in a traditional hotel would wait for its prestigious guests. I grabbed my bag, packed with a few personal items and some extra clothes for the days I wouldn't be in a selection room, and opened the door. A short Asian man greeted me just as I closed the car door.

"Hello. You must be Sarah King, one of our new attendants. I'm Nick and I'll get you checked in today."

I smiled at him. "Hi. Nice to meet you."

"Let's head this way, please."

We walked through glass sliding doors trimmed with gold filigree and entered a lobby with a concierge desk, a check-in desk, and two separate towers with elevators. To the left of the desks was a bar, its floor-to-ceiling gold pipes and mirrors reflecting bottles of alcohol from all over the world. Small tables with green velvet chairs stood scattered with tall black velvet curtains left open around them, but I imagined they would be closed when guests were inside. The Nation always prioritizing the privacy of the rich.

Nick walked me to the desk, where another Center employee stood behind a computer.

"Sarah, this is Girly, she will help get you checked in and settled in your quarters."

"Thank you." He nodded and went back to his post just inside the sliding glass doors.

"Don't be nervous, my dear," Girly said. "You'll fit right in, and once you get settled and make friends, it'll be like you've always been here." She was a short Filipina woman with bright eyes, long hair, and full lips. She smiled, disarming on purpose, making me feel right at home.

"Thank you. It's nice to be met with such friendly people."

I wondered if she was trafficked too, or if she knew there was more going on in the center than just Challenge Pass sessions.

"We have quite the team here, at Rose Bay. Good people. The right people for this job. You'll see." She smiled again and tapped the keys on the screen. "Let's see...Sarah King, 26 years old, Italian and French genetics, no children, no marriages, tier-two." She looked up. "You're quite beautiful for a tier-two. Your skin is so nice for living on the streets, too." Her eyes narrowed.

"Yeah, I know. I get that a lot. I stayed out of the sun and spent the last of my money, before coming here, at an ELLY salon so I could make a good first impression." I quickly lied.

"I love the ELLY salons. They can make anyone look above their tier status. I'm a tier-three and go before my husband and I leave for our rewards."

"You don't live here? I just thought that since you're..." I could pry a little information out of her.

"Since I'm at the front desk in a service job? I get that a lot too. But no, I was a tier-two when I first started working here–like Nick–but I proved myself invaluable to the Center, and last year they promoted me and my tier status. That's what's great about the Nation, anyone can really work their way up, if they try hard enough and know the right people. All these tier-ones who walk around like zombies and live on the streets begging for food and money just don't have what it takes to move up in the Nation. I can't say I'm complaining though because it would be more competition for people like me and you if ones ever did figure it out. So I say, 'stay right there, tier-ones, and stay away from us.'" She chuckled and went back to the screen.

"I didn't see any tier-ones on my drive from the Light rail. Usually they're all over the place, especially by the station."

"Oh yes, that doesn't happen in Rose Bay. We have a tight security team that 'takes care' of any problems like those you'd see in Central or South. The residents in Rose Bay pay enough money, and follow the Edicts, to maintain a less complicated way of life. I tried living in Central and commuting here which lasted all of about six months before my husband and I were like, 'no way'. Down there, our children's exposure to so many things, coupled with the arrival of tier-ones from the South, proved too much for me. We moved back here and will never leave."

I remembered people like Girly from before the Nation took over and the homeless population had become an issue downtown. Encampments, crime, and open drug use became a hot topic in political debates and city council meetings. A social mar that still continued today, and divided people into the haves and the have-nots with no regard.

"It can be different down there, that's for sure." I validated, with a hope of not giving anything away and remaining neutral so she would continue to check me in.

"You can say that again!" Girly laughed. "Okay, let's get the rest of this set up and I'll go over what happens next. After I add you to our database, you'll receive a bracelet that serves as a monitor for your health and wellness."

Right, my health and wellness.

"It will give you access to all of the common attendant areas and then the specific rooms for your selection nights. You're pretty and young and like I said, your skin is beautiful, so you're probably going to be selected often here. We have a policy where you can request two breaks a month after a five-day stretch of being selected. You just need to let the shift manager know."

"Do I have to take the break?"

"Oooh, eager one. You definitely will be good here with the clients we have. To answer, no, you don't have to take a break. It's your body. You do what you want with it...within reason, of course."

For the first time, I stood in a place where that was the truth. It was my body. I could do whatever I wanted with it. Although I wasn't sure about what clients I would have. I knew that whatever they asked, I had to do, but it was still my body. My mind. My choice being here. I chose to use my body to get the information I needed to get my children back, and remove Thomas and the Nation from power. But I could also just use my body for myself, for my own pleasure. This was my commodity, my power, my way out of the Nation.

Girly finished everything on her screen and then looked up at me. "That's it. Now you're going to walk to the second tower elevators—those are for employees only—and go to the third floor. One of my colleagues will meet you there for medical and uniforms, and then someone else will take you to your room. Floors one and two are administrators only. Three through five are attendant rooms. Floor Six is the attendant common areas, including the dining hall. Seven through nine are citizen rooms, with floor ten reserved for special guests. Hopefully you get on floor five so you're closer to the food."

"Thank you, Girly. Will I see you again?" I wondered if she was like Samara, or if Rose Bay really did things their own way.

"Well, let's see...your commitment is two years, so yes, I would say we will see each other over the next couple years."

Two years. It felt like a weight on my chest. How could anyone commit to a sentence for two years, willingly? My empowerment from a moment ago waned as I thought about the men and women who actually have to do this to survive in the Nation, or for those who were never given the choice. I was here on my own accord and would leave in no time, but the people I would meet over the next few weeks would be here forever, unless I did something about it.

"Well, until then, Girly."

"Until then, Sarah."

I walked to the elevators and hit floor three. I waved my wrist in front of the keypad, the doors closed, and I snaked up to my next stop.

The doors opened to a long, quiet hallway lined with gold and teal abstract paintings and live orchids hanging in pots from the ceiling. There was an eerie silence, unlike other hotels I had stayed in before. A silence different from Central, too. I shivered and continued to walk toward the end of the hall, where I found a row of numbers pointing to the left, and the words "Attendant Station" to the right.

I peered down both hallways. On the left, attendant doors lined the wall, but no one was in sight. To the right stretched a long, blank hallway ending in a single door, gold letters above it with *Attendant Station* and a keypad next to the door handle.

I walked to the door, waved my wrist, and then a green light illuminated. The door clicked open, and I went in. The room resembled a spa, and I wondered if the Nation converted it when they took over this hotel as a Center. White marble floors with gold specks extended from the door to a large floor-to-ceiling window. An ocean scene was playing against the windows, blocking anything from the outside world. A large desk was to the right, covered in live orchids like a living wall. Doors to private rooms were to the left.

A petite platinum blonde woman with fillers and eyelash extensions greeted me. "Hi, you must be Sarah King."

"Yes, I am." I stood up straighter.

"Welcome to your first day at the Center. I'm Lucy. Girly got you checked in and now I get to help you with the medical portion and your clothing. Once we do that, I will take you to your room before my next recruit comes in."

I wondered if it would be Samara, or someone else.

"First, let's do the medical exam. I need you to go into that room, undress, and lay down on the bed. I'll bring the scanner in to see if we need to make any modifications before sending you on your way," Lucy instructed.

"Modifications?"

"Oh, yes. Our clients here have quite particular tastes, and we adjust our attendants based on those tastes."

"What modifications?" I tried to hide my apprehension.

"Our machine removes scars and tattoos; it also removes unwanted hair permanently, if requested. Personally, I would have all my hair removed because it's just more sanitary, but you do what you want. Just know that some clients will send you back if you have more hair than what they prefer."

My heart raced.

"But don't worry. You're pretty and young. You're going to do great. Head on in and I will be there in a sec."

"Okay."

I walked into the room and my initial thoughts from earlier were confirmed, this was the spa for the hotel, but without any of the relaxation. A massage table stood in the middle of the room, brightly illuminated by an orb light that hung from the ceiling. A dresser stood off to the side with a basket for my clothes. A set of gray scrubs lay next to it with a number, 844—my attendant number—painted just above the pocket. I undressed and laid down on the table, no blanket in sight.

"Knock, knock," I startled as Lucy entered. "Don't worry about privacy, honey. I've seen it all and done it all to every attendant that has come in here."

"Is it possible to turn the heater up? It's freezing." My nipples constricted and goosebumps checkered my skin.

"Oh, yeah, no. Sorry, we have to keep it a certain temperature because of the modifications. The machine works better in the cold, unlike me, right?" She zipped up a newly adorned hoodie over her scrubs. "Okay, now I'm going to scan your body with this," she held up a toaster sized machine reminiscent of the one I used at the Center after Jude's bruises. "It will scan your body and from there suggest what modifications to do. Sound good?"

"Sounds good."

"Oh, what's this?" She traced her ungloved thumb over my c-section scar. "Your chart doesn't report any pregnancies."

"That's from an accident. Well, an appendicitis after an accident. I don't like talking about it. I mentioned it in my application and it let me move forward. Is it going to be an issue?"

She grabbed the HoloTab. "Hmmm...I don't see it here, but that's okay. I can review your medical records later. The machine is going to catch everything anyway. However, that scar will need to be removed. Same with these." She traced over my tattoos.

"Why?"

"Our clients don't want to think of you as a mother, or someone who was sick at one point. We give them the illusion of perfection. Of what they're lacking in their marriage and can have here when they use their passes. Tattoos and scars on girls like you ruin that image, so they have to be removed."

I never once thought of my scar as something that flawed my body. It was a reminder of motherhood, of carrying my children inside of me, and taking care of them. Unlike traditional births, this outward sign announced to people that I had children. It showed above bikinis, my underwear, and when I was with Jude and Ethan. It was my reminder of what I was doing here to get my babies back.

The tattoos were reminders too. Those I could replace though...my c-section scar, I couldn't. My eyes began to tear up.

"Sarah, are you okay?"

"Yeah, it's just the tattoos, they mean a lot to me. I didn't realize I would have to give them up."

"Well, once your commitment is over and you've saved all your money from here, you can just go get new ones. And without having this hideous scar to distract from their artistic beauty."

"Right. I can just get new ones." I choked and turned my head away.

"Let's get started then, shall we?" Her chipper voice was like nails on the chalkboard, and I had to bury my anger. She didn't know, and I had to pretend in order to keep it that way.

The scan came back noting my scar and tattoos as immediate removal. It suggested adding fillers to my cheeks and lips, but I declined much to the dismay of the Barbie-faced Center worker. Lucy took the scanner, adjusted the settings, and placed it on my abdomen. Within seconds, a hot, stinging sensation touched my skin, and I smelled burning. She moved it from left to right in slow motion, erasing the last ten years of my life in seconds. Then she moved to my wrist, and the coordinates that had served as a guide on a sea I was cast upon, disappeared. Quiet tears slid down into my ears, warming them.

"I know it hurts right now, but you'll be feeling better in no time. The pain doesn't last that long, which is great because it means you can go to work as soon as tomorrow if you want to."

"Great," I whimpered and closed my eyes.

After Lucy finished removing my tattoos and scar, I got dressed, and she took me to my room. I was on the fifth floor like Girly recommended. She gave me the week's schedule of attendant events, said a quick goodbye, and left me alone in my new cell.

13

OLIVIA

I saw Samara at dinner but said nothing to her. Instead, I sat at a table with attendants who had been at this Center for the last few years. They shared stories ranging from humorous encounters to ones that were more horrid. All agreed about the worst clients that use their passes: couples. When I asked how they allowed that, they replied, "At this center, money buys everything."

The following day, I attended one of the yoga classes Lucy pointed out to me on the schedule. I knew Samara would be there too, morning workouts were part of our routine.

I saw her stretching on the outer side of the room in the back and walked over.

"Is anyone in this spot?" I asked.

"No, it's all yours."

"Thanks. I'm Sarah." I extended my hand to hers and she took it in. If Samara was here now, I wasn't going to wait to casually meet her like Dr. Conrad said. I am immediately relaxed, feeling the warmth of her skin against mine. Home to me in the smallest of ways.

"I'm Lilah. I just got here. You?"

"Same. Last night."

"Me too. The intake was a little intense, huh?"

"Yeah." I responded, carefully casual. "The scanner decided that my tattoos, and a scar from an accident on my abdomen had to be removed."

Her eyes softened. "I'm sorry. That had to be hard for you."

"It was. Thank you."

"They actually added a tattoo for me. The woman inside the intake said it would make me more valuable...because I was exotic and I needed to look more like the part." She lifted her tank, revealing tribal-like lines around the sides of her ribs.

"I'm sorry," I mouthed and squeezed her hand.

"It's okay. It's temporary. All of this is just temporary."

"How is your room? What floor are you on?" I asked.

She shrugged. "Fifth floor and it's fine."

"I'm on the fifth floor, too."

"Morgan, remember?" Samara whispered and continued stretching.

"Right. Have you seen her?" I whispered.

"No, we won't. It would be too much of a risk for us to be seen with her. I'll figure out how to communicate with her, don't worry. Our schedules will be in our HoloTab later today, so let's try to meet up casually for dinner to compare."

"Good idea," I nodded.

"We both need to meet other people and start learning who's who here. Morgan is going to give us both the schematics of the place on our Tabs too in case we need to get out quick. I requested to be on the schedule only one to two times a week. You can do that too."

"I don't want to."

"What? Why?"

"I'm here to get information and if that means I need to be on the schedule a lot, then I will be."

"Sarah," she whispered, "You don't know what they'll do to you here. This place is not like Central."

"They don't know what I will do to them either."

Samara sat back and the sides of her mouth peaked up. "Okay, I see you. Do what you need to do and I'll be here."

The instructor came in, clapped his hands, and said, "Okay, my people, let's get our yoga done today!" Samara and I smirked at each other. This was going to be a long class.

We found each other at dinner later that day and compared schedules. She would not be on until later in the week, and my first night was going to be tomorrow. She and I kept at a distance for the next week, meeting up in common areas 'coincidentally' to not draw any attention to our friendship.

That night, I tossed and turned, restless with anticipation of what the next day might bring. I was to be on the Selection Room floor by 10:00am, dressed in my attendant scrubs. I worried that if I didn't sleep, my face would be puffy. Then I remembered I was at a Center, and puffiness didn't exist here. Especially not in a center like Rose Bay.

The next morning, I found my feet atop the cold floor in the Rose Bay Selection Room. A soft light shone down on my gray scrubs, highlighting my attendant number—844. I didn't know the women standing next to me, but I was thankful Samara was off the schedule because I wasn't sure I'd be able to keep my cover this soon in the game. I looked at the two-way glass where the citizen's HoloTab glowed ever so slightly through a crack in the privacy tint.

The women and I stood silently, as instructed, waiting for him to choose us. But then I realized, maybe it wasn't a *him* at all. If a female citizen chose me, tonight would be my first time. My palms felt sweaty as I rubbed my thumbs against my pants. When I turned my head to see if the other women showed any signs of uncertainty, their lights darkened as mine stayed illuminated.

Someone chose me.

Guards came in and ushered me to another room lined with a wall of clothes and a HoloTab sitting on the vanity.

"Choose three of the outfits here for both day and night. We will have them delivered to the room so you have options to choose from depending on what the citizen wants. Wear this right now." The female assistant handed me a skimpy, backless red dress and a pair of black stiletto heels.

Great, I'm going to play the whore tonight.

"Read his profile and use the ELLY machine to fix your hair and makeup. You have about ten minutes until you need to be up there. Your bracelet will grant you access to the room. It's 935 in the citizen towers. Take the attendant's elevator to floor nine, then wait outside the citizen's door. Questions?"

Yes, I screamed inside my mind, but I replied, "None. Thank you."

It took me five minutes to get dressed and have ELLY finish my hair and makeup. I grabbed the HoloTab and left for the elevator. On my way up, I read his profile to be prepared for whatever was going to come next.

Name: William Henry

Tier Status: Four

Age: 46

Occupation: Sales

Family: Wife, two children, ages 22, 20. His kids are pre-Nation?

Likes: Vodka, touch, kissing, travel, beaches, being behind, soft dominance, conversation.

Dislikes: Weak women, being dominant, tequila, inferior intelligence.

Drink Preference: Vodka chilled, no ice.

Food Preference: Mexican, Italian.

Music: Country, Rock, Mozart.

. . .

I FINISHED as the elevator doors opened and I walked to the door, waiting for William to arrive. As I stood outside room 935, I flashed back to my first night with Jude, and the first time I saw him leaning against the door in his slacks and white button-down shirt. His crystal blue eyes had taken my breath away, and I knew they would be my undoing. I could feel my center warm to his memory, betraying my mind for a moment, because I was nothing to him...Ethan was something to him, but not me. And he was nothing to me too.

The elevator chimed and William walked toward me, slacks, button-down shirt and a smile that could bring any woman to her knees.

"Hi, I'm William." His voice deep, laced with a poison I'd gladly drink tonight as I set myself free from the Resistance and the pain that clung to me since my children were taken.

"Oli-Sarah. I'm Sarah." I brushed my hand against his shirt, instead of shaking his hand, like I had with Jude. I needed to prove I was an expert at this, not an unknown player in the game of seduction.

His fingers traced the side of my arm. "So, it looks like you paid attention to my details."

I thought quickly back to this profile, touch. "Yes. Of course I did." I pulled him closer, almost for a kiss, but restrained to tease out the moment.

His smile gave himself away. I was already making an impression.

"Should we go inside?" I asked, and then waved my bracelet over the keyless entry.

He followed me in, hand on the lower part of my back. I flinched slightly, but he didn't notice. Instead his hand slowly moved down my side and to the outside of my ass where he fingered the edge of my dress up slightly. I could feel everything inside of me come alive again, like it had with Jude, and a small piece of me burned for this stranger.

"Would you like something to drink, William? Vodka, maybe?"

His lips crooked up to the side, "Yes. Thank you. Make sure you have something, too."

I opened the refrigerator and pulled out a cold bottle of vodka, and set it on the counter. I opened the cupboards to see what liquor they had. Tequila, rum, and Maker's Mark, all alcohol that wasn't my first choice. I grabbed two glasses and filled them half full with his chilled vodka. William sat at the counter and I slid his glass across to him, keeping myself on the opposite side, so I could warm up to the idea of what I was about to do, but also to help draw out his desire to touch me.

"So, Sarah, tell me about yourself."

"You know that's not allowed, William." I teased him more and slid my finger across his hand softly.

"Just a little...my profile said I like to talk and I like it first. I won't jump right into it with you. And to be clear, I won't force myself on you either. By the time we finish our drinks and conversation, I will have no need to force myself on you."

And I somehow knew this was true.

"Your confidence is admirable."

He roared. "Beautiful and witty. I hit the jackpot with you."

I raised my glass, "Why thank you. You'll be saying more than that by the time our night is through." Who was this girl? Whoever just entered my body needed to stay. Keep talking the talk, playing whatever part it took to get four stars from this tier-four citizen.

"I sure hope so." He took a sip and settled more into the barstool. "So...about you?"

I needed to lie, but also keep him interested. He was in sales so he could smell bullshit from a mile away, but he could also sell bullshit to a cow. Intellect and wit appealed to him based on his profile, and he likes to travel, so I'd go that route.

"I used to travel often. Before."

"Oh yeah? What was your favorite place?"

I paused. Most of my travel in the last ten years was with Thomas and for our anniversaries. Someone manipulated those anniversaries, and from what I know now, they were violent. So those wouldn't be my favorite. I thumbed through the Rolodex in my mind.

"San Francisco."

"That hardly counts as travel. It's so close to us. But I guess as an attendant, or whatever tier status you held, that makes sense."

Yes, my tier status. Genius Olivia.

"What do you like about it?"

My mind wandered to the Palace of Fine Arts, Japan Town, Ocean Beach and then Land's End.

"It's hard to say, really. I spent time there when I was younger, on and off. Japan Town has the best karaoke bar and markets and food. There's this little origami store that my mom would take me to before the pandemic. I would spend hours there, which drove her crazy, but I loved it. The Palace of Fine Arts, when the sun is setting and there's this glow." I looked away from him into the distance as if my words were repainting the images from my youth on the canvas in front of me. "There's this soft pink-orange on the dome you can only see when the sun has gone down. It's a color that doesn't exist any other time of day—almost like the green flash, but for the Palace. Have you ever seen it?"

"No. I haven't." He took another sip, captivated by me. Little ol' me.

"Well, you should see it when you can. I also love the way the waves crash at Ocean Beach. They're formidable, no matter the time of day. There's a power in them. Something I think on some level I always wanted to harness, but knew I never would."

"Why wouldn't you be able to harness it as you say?"

Think fast, Olivia. "Well, obviously because of my tier status."

"There's that." He took another sip of his drink.

"The water is also freezing, which does not appeal to me at all," I said, smiling. "But it's still a place where I'd take my shoes off and bury my feet in the sand when I went there as an adult."

William's mouth curved. "I'm like that with Maui. My job requires me to travel there a few times a year and the first thing I do is to bury my feet in the sand and get a drink. It just feels right, you know?"

I nodded, the image of him barefoot on a beach slipping a little too easily into my head. "Yeah, I do."

He tilted his head slightly. "Any other places in SF?"

The place that brings me back to a time lost to yesterday. "Land's End. Have you heard of it?"

"Maybe. Where is it?"

"Just by Ocean Beach. The old bath house. It's this gorgeous lookout with a beach, and the burned down baths, and a hiking trail that has the best views of the Golden Gate Bridge."

I thought back to the day Ethan proposed, and for a moment, I could feel the Pacific breeze blow through my hair, and the sting of the newly written vow for a love that would never last.

"I'll have to check it out." William took another sip, then rose from his chair and moved to me. He fingered the side of my dress, pulling me closer to his body. "This dress looks incredible on you, Sarah." He growled below his vodka scented breath. "I'd like to kiss you. Is that okay?"

"Yes," breathless and warming in my center.

His hands palmed through my hair, pulling my face toward his, and then tightened around the hold he had. His tongue was warm and tasted like the expensive vodka he was drinking. My body automatically turned to him, melting into his 6'1 frame. My hands found their way into his hair and I guided him toward me, not as an act, but as a *need*. I wanted this man, and I wanted him to do very bad things to me.

"Sarah, we need to get you out of this dress."

He undid the ties behind and let it fall to the kitchen floor, leaving only my exposed breasts and the black lace thong.

"Take your heels off," he ordered, and I followed. His hands moved around to my back, guiding me into the bedroom, lips continuing to cover my mouth. He wanted me. An ex-Nation wife who was lost in a world of uncertainty. He wanted my perceived attendant's body—post-baby curves and all.

This stranger sparked something new in me. He desired me in a way I had never experienced, not even with Ethan or Jude. His fire fed my air, and I needed him. He fell onto the bed and began kissing every part of me. He started at the side of my neck, working his way down, meticulous and unhurried, testing the limits of my patience for what I needed more than anything: him inside me. The scruff on his chin scratched over my soft olive skin in a way that lit me further up inside. When he reached my belly button, he licked his way to my center, and I almost unraveled before he did anything else.

"Do you want me, Sarah?" Still fully dressed, his eyes looked up to me, face buried between my legs as he removed my underwear.

"Yes."

"How much do you want me?" His tongue circled slowly as I tried to answer.

"Very...much..." My nipples hardened, and I arched my back.

He slid his fingers inside of me and I let out a soft moan. "Do you want this too, Sarah?"

"Mmm...mmm."

His tongue swirled, taking notice of the smallest changes in my reactions. He placed his other hand on my belly and pressed hard down on it while moving his fingers in and out, his tongue serving as the conductor for the piece.

"William…" I moaned.

"Tell me," he growled.

"More, please, more. I…want…"

"What do you want, Sarah?"

"More. Please, more."

"Of what, Sarah?"

"Your tongue. Please."

William buried his tongue inside me, moving his fingers underneath and keeping rhythm with the orchestra my body was performing. The deeper he went, the higher my back arched. My hands pressed into the bed and tugged at the sheets. I couldn't take it any longer.

"William…" I moaned one final time.

"Give it to me, Sarah. Come for me."

And with those three words, my conductor brought me home, electrifying every part of my body. A gush of warmth coated William's face.

"Mmmm…I like that," he said, as he slowed his tongue and fingers to match the slowing of my breath, and relaxation of my body. When my body stilled, he slid his fingers out and wiped his face with the sheet, then moved up to lie next to me. "How was that, Sarah? Good?" He traced his fingers up and down my arm, goosebumps showing him a job well done.

"It was so good. William, so good."

"That's what I want to hear."

My body relaxed into the bed. I could still smell the vodka on his breath and my nipples hardened.

"Uh oh, Sarah. Do you need more of me?" He toyed.

I needed more of him. I craved more of him. It didn't matter to me that I had no connection to this man. I just wanted his body, and he only wanted mine too. Was this what it was like for so many people before the Nation took over? When people were on dating apps or hooking up with random strangers at bars? Was this what I'd missed out on when I committed my life to Ethan at fourteen-years old? This would be my drug of choice. This was the drug I wanted repeatedly until I couldn't live any longer. I wanted this man—whose name I would purposely forget—because I only needed him for his body, nothing more. I had Samara for friendship. I had my children for a feeling of home. And now I had this, an unknown need and desire that could be changed like a pair of shoes.

"Yes, I need more. I want more. I want you." I turned to him.

"How do you want me?"

I was in control? This high level man was going to give me control? For a long time, others have controlled me even when I thought I had control, I didn't. So if William was going to give me control, I was going to harness it.

"On your back. Take your clothes off. I'm going to tie you up." I commanded.

The side of his mouth peaked up, and he undressed slowly. His hands tenderly undid each button of his shirt from the top to the bottom, revealing a chiseled body that set me on fire. He stood up and slowly took off his belt, throwing it to the side of the bed. Then he undid his slacks, tossing them to join their friend on the floor. I could see him pushing through his black athletic boxer briefs, bigger than I expected, and continuing to grow in front of me.

He laid down on the bed and asked, "What do you want me to do next?"

I took his belt from the floor. "Put your arms above your head on the pillow." He complied.

I wrapped his belt loosely around his wrists; his chest slowly lifted up and down. I kissed his wrists, then forearms, then his neck, gliding slowly over to his mouth. He was waiting for me, and the moment I brushed against him, a low growl escaped his throat. I licked my lips and continued kissing him, down his neck, his chest, and the sides of his ribs. My fingers found their way into the sides of his briefs and I played the edges like a newly stringed guitar. I teased them down as I kissed the length of his waist until meeting his aching arousal. An arousal for *me* and what *I* was doing to him.

"Do you like this, William?" I purred.

"Yes. Sarah. I do like it." He could barely contain himself.

"Do you want me to do more, William?"

"Yes, Sarah, I want more."

I thumbed his boxers down his legs and he shook them off, landing on the side of the bed next to us. My mouth continued to explore licking, then kissing, then licking again. His body shook and his abs tightened at the undoing I was giving him. When I finally let him into my mouth, a loud moan escaped with "Oh fuck, Sarah!"

Bigger than I could handle, I stayed closer to the tip, giving him the attention he deserved. I took him deep enough to make me react, but not make a mess, and I pulled him back out again. His moans filled the room, his muscled body heavy with need, like an anchored weight waiting for me to bring it ashore. The sensation became too much for him and his bound hands found their way into my hair, where they pulled and pushed me even more. I could taste the saltiness that was about to fill my mouth, and I stopped.

"Don't stop, please don't stop," he begged.

"Put your hands back where they belong." I scolded.

He complied.

I moved my naked body on top of him, sliding every inch that I could inside of me.

"Oh Sarah, you're so wet for me." His body shuddered and his stomach tightened as I moved up and down on top of him.

Everything in my body became more and more alive with each moment I rode him. My hands pressed against his stomach and eventually found their way to his forearms, where

I pinned him against the bed, driving him even further inside of me. My skin tingled and moans deepened as I knew what was coming for the both of us. I looked down and caught his amber brown eyes. This was it, a connection with a stranger that I thought wouldn't leave an imprint, but it did. Our rhythm found its next beat and there was no stopping.

Electricity jolted from our deepest parts.

I tightened, and he hardened even more as he dove deeper inside of me.

He was as deep as he could get, but I wanted more...knew I could take more.

I was as bound around him as I could be.

And there was no more waiting...wanting...our cries met as our backs arched, pushing our chests together. His bound arms found their way over my head and around my body, tempering our bodies together like chocolate.

I drew in a sharp breath as my stomach clenched, letting the rush flow freely through my body. I deserved this. I deserved him. I deserved the power to give William something that only I could.

He called out, "Oh, fuck!" and we collapsed onto each other. As our breathing slowed in the comedown, still joined, he slid his hands over my head, motioning me to untie him. Once untied, he slowly dragged his fingertips over my arms, making me shudder even more.

"Are you okay?" He whispered.

"Yes," I said, as I placed my head on his chest.

We stayed joined a few moments longer, breathing together in a rhythmic motion. His hands moved to my back, gently stroking in the afterglow of our intimate strangeness. We collided like we had known each other for years, but the false veil between us became more clear as our breath came back to us. He rolled me over, and we separated. An intimacy without context lingered. A closeness that only sharpened the distance between two strangers.

We hadn't learned about childhood best friends, or how we liked our coffee in the morning. We didn't know each other's life stories, and he certainly would never know mine because of the lies I spun to gain power in the Nation. We had touched and connected so deeply, without even brushing the surface. Our ghostlike connection would soon be nothing more than a memory—something to file away, just as I had for ten years of marriage to Thomas. I would forget this man and the way he made my body feel. Until he returned in dreams, in the arms of some future partner, or in the solitude of the shower, when my own fingers brought my release.

William would become a ghost. This would become nothing more than a stepping stone to my new beginning. Regardless of the connection or electricity, William...the Center...the other men or women coming my way, were fleeting and I needed to remember to be here, but not here, in order to survive this.

"That was incredible." William pulled the sheet to cover half of his body.

I needed to play the part.

"It was," I cooed. "Would you like anything else, William?" Like I was a server at a restaurant.

He laughed. "Not right now, thank you though. I'm exhausted. I haven't had a session like this in a long time." He turned and kissed my lips. "You were amazing, Sarah. This is a memory I will be replaying often, to help me make it through my world outside of here."

He turned away, and within moments, quiet snores escaped him. I rinsed off and then came back to bed, finding him spread out and entangled in his sheets like a young boy. As I lay down trying to slow my mind, I replayed his words. Is this what marriage and a life in the Nation came to? Clinging to a fleeting sexual encounter or a rare luxury vacation just to survive the daily pains of committing to one person for the rest of your life? How was this reward system enough for so many people to continue in marriages with people they didn't want to be with? How was it ever going to be enough for me?

I awoke the next morning and left a note, like Jude and Ethan had at the Center with me.

Last night was incredible. Until next time. XOXO, Sarah.

Once back in my room, I showered again and took myself to the edge one more time with the memories from my night with William. Was it supposed to be like this? I wanted this life. It was raw and exciting. I felt alive and good. In fact, I felt good for the first time in ages. Thomas and I always had prescribed sex; love was absent, despite my efforts. There was love with Ethan, but looking back, a sadness lingered like a heavy weight that blanketed us with the unknown when we were teenagers, young adults, and most recently, victims of the Nation. With Jude, there had been something in between. But once I knew about his relationship with Ethan, it felt as if we were only stand-ins for each other's Ethan. The time we shared had never truly been ours at all—it was still Ethan's.

I found Samara and filled her in on the details, making myself hot again at the memory of William. I asked her to have Morgan put me in the Selection Room for the following two weeks. I wanted to experience everything and feel alive and in control again.

"Be careful, Olivia. I don't want you to get so deep in the land of the Lotus Eaters that you lose sight of what we're doing here," Samara warned.

"The goal is to get information, *Samara*. And I know what I'm doing," I snapped.

"I didn't mean to upset you, I'm sorry. I just want to keep you safe so we can get home."

She was just looking out for me, and a deep part of me

knew that. It just felt like one more person trying to tell me what to do, when all I wanted was more of what I had experienced with William. This was my chance to be both things at once: the mother desperate to collect information to find her children, and the woman still aching for desire, for sex with strangers. The juxtaposition was so surreal it almost made me laugh. I could enjoy myself while also getting them home. This was my one chance to experience a life like this. A life I missed out on because of Ethan...Thomas...the Nation.

"I'm sorry. I know you're only looking out for me."

"You and the kids." She looked at me.

"Thank you. I just want to feel this right now. It's the first time I have felt something other than anger or sadness since everything happened." I paused, "It's actually the first time I've felt anything good really, in what seems like a lifetime. I want and need both to do this and get information. I'll be okay. If anything, last night actually helped me. I've never felt so in control before. He gave me power, like freely, without any strings attached, or dishonesty. I didn't have to think about anything other than our own pleasure. It was nice, Samara, to have that moment of escape. To forget because he wasn't anyone who was going to help me get the kids back or find out about the trafficking and experiments. We were just able to... be...and it felt good."

She pulled me in for a hug. "Just be careful, okay?"

"Of course." I squeezed her back.

In the weeks that followed, I packed my schedule and discovered that most citizens only wanted the basics from me and, if anything, wanted me to feel pleasure, something not akin to my time with Thomas. They wanted to see my body react to theirs. They wanted me to scream their name. They wanted me to make them feel desired again. And even when they asked for something out of the norm, I gave it to them, because then I held the power over their body...their desires... their ending.

I never had anything like this when I was younger trying to work toward the Nation goals. Trying out new people, desires, and kinks wasn't in the plan. I was supposed to get married, have children, build a small career, and contribute to society... and I did. I knew my time at this Center would end, and the faster I found the information, the sooner I could be reunited with my children. However, I fully planned to embrace the delights this Center was offering me, and I resigned myself to not feel shame or regret for any of it. I could have both things: my pleasure and my plan.

14

ETHAN

Olivia and Samara had been gone for a couple of weeks. Even though Liv only let us be together once, I clung to every memory. Her body's weight pressed against mine. The way her mouth tasted. The way my fingers found themselves tangled in her soft hair. There was nothing she could do that would ever change the love I felt for her. She could tell me she never wanted to see me again—which I was worried would come once she found her children—and I would still love her with every part of who I was. Everything I did...had done...and would do...is because of her. I needed her and would do anything to make sure she knew how much, until the day I died.

I left my room and walked through the corridor of the main building, hearing snippets of conversation in the background. Smiles and nods greeted me as I crossed people busy at work. When I was younger, I rarely stood out or drew any sort of praise or attention. It wasn't until Olivia saw me, like really saw me, that I felt I could be anything more than what I was. When the Nation asked me to join the military and she encouraged me to go to Brazil, it validated me even more. Looking back, it fit neatly into the Resistance's plans and benefited me too. I became who I am today because of her, and because of the hope of getting back to her after Thomas tore us apart.

I remembered the day she arrived at the compound like it was yesterday. Her brown hair swaying in the very unassuming wind like a pinwheel spinning in secret. Only a shade lighter than mine, her olive skin was flawless for a teenager. She stood solidly awkward with her shorts and Counting Crows T-shirt, hiding so much more that a part of me longed to explore.

I kept a teenage boy's distance from her for the first few weeks she was on the compound, because I feared girls. Between the inconsistent high pitch tones when they were excited or angry or sad or just something I didn't know yet, and the blank stares that stood vacantly in their teenage eyes, I had no idea what to say to them.

But, even within this, Oliva was different. I could see her in colors of red, orange, and yellow, muted by a blanket of cream. She shone underneath the June summer sun, buried beneath her family's luggage, and I desperately wanted to ask if she needed help. My 13-year-old mind, and slender awkwardness, kept me tight to the circle I stood on.

When I finally had a moment with her in the makeshift library, I thought I messed it up with the bookshelf falling. But if anything, I think it made her warm to me faster. I wanted to figure out how to spend every moment with her, and eventually I did. I started reading the Harry Potter series with her, then eventually Twilight, which was painful, but I would never tell her that. We went through Percy Jackson, then moved onto stand-alone books. We read Colson Whitehead, Ashley Winstead, and later, Carley Fortune.

We were going to take on the world together. Live in the Nation together. Build a family together. Once we forged our way into the Nation, she and I worked non-stop to move tiers. My deployment never interfered with my love for her, even though the loneliness found me in Brian's bed. He and I justified the first night as a one-off, and the nights that followed as 'things that happened because we were in Brazil'. It wouldn't continue when we returned, and we wouldn't tell anyone it happened. He missed his girlfriend just as I missed Olivia.

One of the first things I did when I returned was ask Luke, her father, for his blessing to marry Liv. He gave it without hesitation and I proposed to her in San Francisco at Land's End lookout, after I convinced her to get matching tattoos of the coordinates. When I heard her voice in the Selection Room, I knew I had to show her my wrist so she would choose me. It was our tether back to each other that no amount of Nation work could ever take from us. She had finally come back to me, and everything fell into place once she was in my arms. Or so I thought.

As I moved through the last part of the building, I didn't notice Jude walking toward me in the corridor until it was too late and I bumped into him.

"Sorry, man." I pulled my hands up, careful not to touch him even though a part of me wanted to.

"It's okay, Ethan."

We stood, silence painfully stretching between us, unsure of what to do next. Our eyes caught and I could see the pain that permeated those sky-blue eyes that saw who I was in a moment of need. I could feel him, like so many times before. I could feel his need to connect with me. To tell me about his day. His desire to be next to me again, like the nights we shared at the Center.

But I couldn't. I wouldn't. My focus was on Olivia. Her children. The rebellion.

"Ethan," he pleaded.

I couldn't let him...us...be anything more than fellow soldiers in a war against the Nation. Couldn't be anything more than two men who just happened to be assigned to the same Center.

He put his hand on my shoulder. "Ethan, please, just give me a few minutes." He squeezed my shoulder, pulling me into him like an invisible rope attached to my center. "Can we please go somewhere to talk?"

I closed my eyes, hearing the whispers of his words that lulled me to sleep after my nightmares. Nightmares about Brazil. About Thomas. About Olivia.

Olivia.

My love.

My life.

The only reason I still breathe today.

My Olivia.

I snapped out of the trance he had cast upon me. "No! Jude, no!" I yelled, drawing dramatic attention to the two of us.

We both shrunk from embarrassment and I pulled him into a nook in the hallway.

"I am with Olivia now. I am not with you. You need to figure that out."

"You're not with her. I see how she barely gives you the time of day. She doesn't want you, Ethan. She won't want you again. The sooner you realize that, the better off you'll be."

"You're wrong, Jude. She wants me. She loves me. And we will be back together. I was with her right before she left. And it was amazing and exactly how it was supposed to be. She wanted me and I wanted her."

Why was I lying to Jude? It's not like he would ever know what really happened. It's not like it would make a difference to him, anyway. I could take him right now, and it wouldn't matter what was between Olivia and me. I could have him or her if I wanted to.

"And you know what? It was better than anything you and I

ever had. I can't be with you, Jude. The sooner you realize it, the better off you'll be."

The words cut deep, and I could see him move back inside himself, like the morning he found out that Olivia was my Olivia. His night with her, and the moments that followed were the happiest he had ever been and would probably ever be. Then he learned the truth: the girl he thought he had finally found was the very one we had all been waiting for to set the rebellion in motion.

Jude didn't know who he was. Who he wanted. What he wanted. Jude floated through life like a plastic bag, looking for anyone or anything to hold on to. And I floated with him, until I heard Olivia's voice in the Selection Room. I would not be that person for him ever again. I couldn't. Even if there was a small part of me that still cared for him, I wouldn't go back to that time of my life.

I had to move forward.

Lead the Resistance.

Get the love of my life back.

There was no room for the entanglements I held with men like Jude.

"I have to go, Jude."

I left him standing there alone and left for the tech room to check in on Olivia and Samara's progress. I checked in on them often, making sure they were safe. The moment anything changed, I would go to the Center and make whoever hurt them pay for every bruise on either of their bodies.

Morgan was great at giving us access to Rose Bay. She had us tapped into the video system within an hour of getting there. She and Samara found a way to communicate without drawing attention. I started watching footage early on, even though Vivian warned me not to watch it. I didn't expect to see Olivia so soon in the Selection Room or, for that matter, being chosen. I needed to see her with other people. To see what I was missing, doing wrong, and could eventually do right.

Her first night, I left the sound on so I could hear her...hear him...I could be what she wanted, what she needed. He went down on her, making her come first. *I could do that.* I could put her first and learn to make her happy in that way. When she tied him up and teased him, I thought about her doing that to me, and I liked it. *I could let her take control in the bedroom.* But only there. Outside of it, she needed to remember that I was the man: the one who took care of her, handled the problems, went to war. Not her. As I continued to watch her dominate this man, I didn't understand. She wasn't dominant or forceful with anyone. She had her moments when she stood up for things, but it didn't happen often. She wasn't like that at the hospital with patients, not with her children, and certainly not with Thomas. I watched enough episodes of her over the years to see she was the same girl I fell in love with as a teenager.

How could this woman that I was in love with be someone else that I didn't know? How could she want to be with anyone else?

I sat down and tapped into the feed to watch more footage from the week. Men consumed her body like she was water. I tried to figure out how many people she had been with since she arrived. Was it seven or eight so far? The most recent one fucked her against the wall, her small body wrapping around his dark skin.

Even though I wanted to watch her, something inside of me snapped. I stormed out and left for the gun range picturing all the men fucking her as I unleashed a wrath of bullets on the target. A part of me wanted to hunt them down and make them pay for sleeping with her. She was mine, and I didn't want anyone else to have her, especially if she was still trying to figure out what she wanted with me.

Vivian showed up eventually, gun in hand, and we shot

together in the silence of gun powder's death, until she finally said something.

"She chose this, Ethan."

"What?"

She turned to me. "Olivia. She chose to do this. You don't have a right to be angry about this. You also shouldn't be watching the footage. She is a grown woman who can do whatever she wants to, and with, her body. You have no right to that."

I forced my voice low, though my hands shook."I have a right to be angry, so don't say shit like that, Vivian."

"No, you don't. She's not yours to control. She's not yours to be with. You fucked up. And the sooner you realize that's what you're really angry about and that all these outbursts stem from it, the sooner you'll stop being a liability to us all."

"What the fuck are you talking about?" My jaw clenched.

"I saw you—with Jude. Well, heard you. You're not yourself, Ethan. You've got to move past your shit so we can bring the Nation down, like we've been planning for as long as I can remember." She fired a few rounds. "You need to let her go. She's not coming back to you and you know what? She shouldn't."

"Oh, she shouldn't, huh? Why the fuck not?" I yelled at her, placing my gun down.

"Because she's a distraction. To you, and to herself. She needs to heal from the shit that went down in April. The shit that went down in her life the last ten years. You are not going to be able to give that to her. And you...you need fucking therapy, man. You're a mess. You've spent the last ten years under the same control as her. And then you fell in love with Jude. And now you don't know who you are, or who or what you want. People like you are dangerous. I told your dad that if it were up to me, I would take you off the team. But he said he couldn't, because you are the poster child of this whole thing." She waved her arm in a wide arc, as if to encompass the entire Resistance.

I never faulted Vivian for being honest. That candor in her was a quality I loved, particularly when directed at people other than myself, but this was too far.

"Fuck you, Vivian! You don't know what you're talking about. Olivia is fine. She's going to be fine. Once she gets the children back and they settle, then the four of us can settle. Everything will be fine and we will rebuild our life together. Just wait, you'll see." I turned my back to her.

"You're living in a dream world, Ethan, and you need to wake up or you're going to get us all killed." Vivan yelled as I stormed away.

My anger from the last few weeks, months, and years consumed me. Olivia and I would be together. I will raise her children and we will get away from all of this. It was going to happen.

I needed a release. I needed this anger to go somewhere. In a red blur, I knocked on Jude's door. He opened it, searching my face, and I pushed my way through, slamming it behind me. I locked it and began kissing him with a fire that I remembered having with him...Olivia...Brazil.

Jude didn't hesitate. We tore our shirts off, clawing at cream and brown skin, driven by the need burning beneath. I threw him on the bed, pinning his wrists down, just like I saw her do, while I licked down his body until I reached his abdomen. He shuddered under my tongue.

"Ethan," Jude whispered my name in deep, breathless notes. I had forgotten how much I loved hearing my name on his mouth.

"Jude," I growled, and I released his wrists and undid his pants.

In no time, we were a mess of naked bodies frantically pulling for whatever strings we could, without completely undoing each other. My mouth on the curved monolith I knew well, while my hands reached below, fondling the sensitive spot below him. I glided my mouth up and down, licking and kissing him, then swirling my tongue around the tip, making him writhe in pleasure. I sucked, pursing my lips around him, as I moved slowly up and down and then changed to a quickening pace.

His fingertips moved through the low, coarse waves of my hair as my hands scratched up his sides, releasing him from my mouth and flipping him until he was on his knees bent over in front of me.

"What about you? Let me..." He tried to move his body back around, but I wouldn't let him.

"No. I don't need it." I was already hard and ready for him. "I just need this. You. Now." I growled again, and he positioned himself in front of me.

I spit on my hand and rubbed myself before entering the tight space I knew so well. I held tight to his hips and the soft center, remembering how my fingers would trace over it when we were wrapped in each other's arms. He let out a soft moan, spit on his hand, and moved his right hand to himself, stroking up and down as I thrust harder and faster inside of him, digging my nails into his hips.

I remembered this feeling, and my heart beat faster. I loved being inside Jude. I loved the way he smelled and the way his balls slapped against me as I made him mine. He turned his face back to me, constricted by the pure pleasure that I was giving him. I moved my hand to his shoulder forcing myself deeper inside, tearing him from the force of me. He quickened his pace and I could see his body tighten, which made my abs tighten.

I drew in a breath and clenched my jaw.

"Oh my god, Jude!" I growled behind him as I pulled him deeper against my body, catching a glimpse of the solid mass in his hand.

"Ethan. Oh, Ethan. Fuck."

"Jude."

Our cries too loud for the paper-thin walls to contain. Desire too much to hold back. A love too distant to reach.

I couldn't take it any longer. I needed to remind him of what his body did to mine. I needed to fill him with reminders that would follow him for the rest of the day. He convulsed and a fountain rained onto the bed. My release exploded, and, at this moment, we couldn't be anything else, but two people bound to each other in an escaping permanence.

I stayed inside of him as we slowly collapsed on the bed. Small moments still finding their way to release inside of him as I began to soften. I loved Jude and he loved me. In so many ways this would have been something more, but the world I wanted and needed couldn't allow it.

Our breathing slowed and I moved to the side of him. Our hands moving up and down each other's sides to soften the departure that was in front of us. Our come down kept our reality at bay, until it didn't anymore.

He rolled over, exposing himself to me, then grabbed my hand. I instinctively pulled it away.

"Jude."

"Don't say it. Just, please, don't say anything."

"Jude. I can't. This can't happen again."

This would be fleeting. This would need to be contained. This could never happen again. I couldn't be with the man that I loved because I loved a woman more. I got up, grabbed my clothes, leaving him on his bed. An audience outside the paper-thin walls proved unfounded. No one would ever know what happened, except for Jude and me.

We were an episode never watched.

A performance never seen.

A secret left within the four walls of Jude's bedroom.

A secret that needed to stay if I were to get Olivia back.

15

OLIVIA

It had been a few days since I'd last been in the Selection Room. After I showed up with bruises from a rough night, Samara made Morgan take me off the schedule. I was grateful for the break, but still anxious to get back to the Selection Room. When I was finally put back on the schedule, Samara only said to be careful, and that she would see me in the morning.

I finally stepped into the all-too-familiar room, its sterile cement floors and marked spots guiding me to my role. This was my tenth, maybe eleventh time and I knew what to expect, even though I didn't know who was behind the glass. To my right, an Indian girl named Nadia walked in. Her mahogany skin tone was dark and rich, glowing with depth beneath the flickering light above us, still capturing her beauty. She was more beautiful than I was, and if the people behind the glass wanted to brag about being with an exotic, she would surely be selected over me. I settled in, standing perfectly inside the circle next to her, and waited for the next attendant to walk in.

My mind wandered to keep busy, drifting to the times I'd already spent with citizens. I was there, but not there. I felt, but did not feel. It was my new routine. A novocaine for the existence I was living in without my children, my life, my freedom. But at the same time, I could be whoever the citizens wanted. I could make my body my own and make their bodies mine too, like I had with William. I had a power that I never experienced outside the Rose Bay cage. Even though I had no control in the selection process, I had control, for the most part, once the citizens chose me and I became 'Sarah the attendant' in the black slutty dress.

My thoughts were interrupted as the door opened and the next attendant walked in.

Samara.

Her eyes caught mine briefly and something didn't feel right. She shook her head slightly so that only I would notice and I knew right away—we were going to be chosen together. Just like Jude and Ethan were, when Thomas was pulling the strings. He couldn't be doing that here too though, right? Samara and I were both under false names. Our chips were false, and Morgan was able to change everything to align with our new identities. Thomas wouldn't think to look for Samara or me in a Center, this just had to be a coincidence.

Samara moved to her prescribed spot: worn out red-painted footprints inside a newly painted black circle. There was no suspense in this selection. The three of us stood for only a moment before both Samara's light and mine illuminated. Nadia drew in a breath, turned to us both, and mouthed "I'm sorry" as if she knew something too. Had our caged existence aligned us with the instinct of animals? Forcing us to operate on heightened senses and intuition, with our internal alarm screaming of the danger that stood behind the two-way mirror.

It didn't matter. We had been chosen, and we both knew the next steps. As if in robotic fashion, we walked to the changing room, put on the prescribed outfits based on the client's desires, then headed to the hotel room, waiting until the client arrived.

After getting dressed, Samara and I got into the elevator, and began our ascent. She pulled up the HoloTab, looking for the details of our client and showed it to me.

"It's a couple. Have you had this happen yet?"

"No, have you?"

"No, I would have told you." She looked worried, "The Lopes. There's nothing more in the details. This can't be a good sign. Whatever happens, we know this is what we signed up for, and we just have to be brave tonight. We will figure out how to deal with whatever happens later." Samara in full survivor mode was now convincing me or herself, I wasn't sure.

"It's going to be fine. They probably just want one each. We're going to be fine...we have been so far." I tried to calm her fears.

"I just want to get back to Laura." Her voice quivered slightly.

"I know. And we're one step closer to it. I can feel it."

I knew she struggled with being here, with feeling like she was being unfaithful to Laura. Even though Laura had agreed to our leaving, I wondered about the things the two of them would have to work through as their marriage entered the next phase of life beyond the Nation. For me, I had no one to answer to but myself. Sleeping with people, with the small possibility of getting information wasn't easy, but it wasn't difficult either. I would do what I needed to do to get the children back and eventually kill Thomas.

This was a means to an end. My body was a tool to be used to accomplish the goals both the Resistance and I had. I would recover and heal later.

We exited the elevator and stood nervously at the door, waiting for the couple to appear at the elevator entrance. The ding of their arrival made us both jump. We looked at each other.

Samara took a deep breath. "We are going to be fine. It's just another night."

"Right. Just another night."

The couple appeared, walking toward us hand in hand. Their smiles dripped in a power I'd seen before on Thomas, when he thought he held all the cards. An arrogance found in people who thought they were untouchable, and often were, until a secret or story finally brought them down. These people were no different. Once we figured out how to take the Nation down, this couple would fall with the rest of tier-four, finding their place among the masses again, powerless. That thought brought the same arrogant smile to my face, and I directed it at both of them.

"Hello girls, are we ready for some fun tonight?" The male asked, as his wife's eyes narrowed, matching the malicious shift in her lips.

"Yes, we are. Welcome to the Center, Mr. and Mrs. Lope." Samara calmly replied, comporting herself into the customer service agent she knew to be so well. "I'm Lil–"

He cut her off. "No, don't tell us your names. We prefer only numbers. You–523, let us in."

"Of course, please, let's go inside." Samara opened the door, letting the wolves into our 24-hour den.

They walked in and went directly to the bedroom. Samara and I looked at each other, drew in a deep breath, and stepped in. This time felt different, and a part of me knew nothing would be the same after tonight. These two wanted something more than just the two of us. I could feel it.

Samara walked into the bedroom first, and I followed closely behind. Mr. Lope sat next to the bed in a deep red velvet chair, his wife seated beside him in a black one. I hadn't been in this room before–it was darker than the other rooms I'd seen. Black curtains and bedding created a dark landscape broken by pockets of reds, while a large black metal canopy bed stood in the middle of the room. Looking closer, I saw metal chains with leather straps hanging from its corners, not the delicate curtains I'd seen in quaint home advertisements on my HoloTab during my life in the Nation. A curved black leather chair sat a few feet from the foot of the bed, just near the Lope's expensive Italian shoes. A giant red X with chains and cuffs stood in the corner, where a chaise lounge should have been. Whips and leather strips hung on the wall, taking the place of traditional hotel art.

I turned to Samara. She gave nothing away, just a blank, heavy stillness, as if she knew exactly what was about to happen. I looked at the couple, holding hands and sitting leisurely in the dungeon the four of us found ourselves in.

"Well, girls," Mr. Lope began, "we are so happy the two of you were in the room today. My wife and I have been looking forward to a more exotic collection. We've had limited options for the past few months here. When I checked in with the director last week about our monthly visit, he mentioned he had new attendants, since the other center closed down. When we saw the two of you in the Selection Room, there was no other option than to have the two of you tonight."

His wife stayed quiet, looking at us like we were an appetizer for the feast her and her husband were about to enjoy.

"My wife and I have eclectic tastes…needs…that this place provides us with. Have either of you ever been in this room?"

"No." We replied in submissive unison.

His wife smiled. "Excellent. I love first time attendants."

Of course she did.

"Well, then, you are both in for a surprise."

I drew in another breath and stood still, waiting for what laced words left his mouth.

"My wife and I like to watch our attendants. We rarely get involved with them. It's just not our thing. So, tonight, you two are going to perform for us. You're going to start at the St.

Andrew's Cross–that's the X over there, if you didn't know what it was." He gestured to me and Samara, then said, "After we see what you do to her, you two will move to the bed. From there, she," he pointed to Samara, "will chain you until you finish. Then you will do the same to her."

I couldn't breathe. I was lost again. My body was in the grip of another evil man. Controlled and powerless. I hadn't experienced a woman at the Center yet, even though I knew it was a possibility. Now, I would be with someone I knew, and grew to love as a deep friend, and I didn't want to. This couldn't happen. It shouldn't happen. Laura...*oh my god, Laura.* What will she think when she finds out, if she finds out? I felt fine about having sex in the same room as Samara; that, at least, felt safe, manageable, and could be dealt with later. But the two of us, together, and in such a violent way? How would we ever be able to come out of this?

"I'm sorry, I may not understand," I postured. "You don't want to be with either of us?"

"That's correct," Mr. Lope replied. "We want to watch you. We want to watch you do what we tell you to. Sometimes we take part or direct, but we never sleep with attendants."

"Not never, darling," Mrs. Lope corrected.

"Oh, that's right, there were those two girls. Very young and ready to be directed. But we don't see being with attendants as civilized behavior for people in our status. From time to time, we may have sex while we are here, but it's only with each other. Rarely with people like you, unless it's needed."

Had I really lived in a tiered life with others who believed this? Had I internalized the belief that people were beneath me too? That humans of lower status didn't matter? That bodies were expendable, at our will, just because we made more money or held a better position in the system? Bile crept up my throat.

"When would you like us to start?" Samara said in robotic fashion.

Mrs. Lope smiled. "I like her. She'll comply. The other one has a little bit more fire, though. She's the one you'll like, right darling?" Poison honey-dripped words I would remember forever.

"Oh, she's definitely mine." He sneered. Bile made its way into my mouth. "But first, get us two glasses of champagne. It's in the fridge. Once you bring those to us, you will change into the lingerie over there." He pointed to a table next to the St. Andrew's Cross where two black boxes sat dangerously atop the black acrylic table. "You," he pointed to Samara, "go get us the champagne, while she opens the box and puts on her outfit."

Samara complied, quietly resigning herself to his power. There was a mechanical way she responded to him, as if she knew the only way to get through any of this was to just comply. Don't fight back. Don't antagonize. Just do as they say, so one day you can hopefully put it behind you and move forward with some semblance of your life. This was the Samara I was seeing today–not the strong, independent, self-assured one I grew to love over the last couple of months. This was a broken mirror of that woman, one I desperately wanted to piece back together just to have my friend in this moment.

I walked to the table and opened the box on top. Inside lay a two-piece set of red silk lingerie. The thong was delicate, with ornate orchids across the front. The top was a bralette, a bow tied across the front where breasts would eventually fill it—a tie I assumed they expected Samara to undo at some point tonight for their own pleasure.

Samara came back with the champagne-filled glasses, setting them on the table between the couple. She then walked to her box and opened it, revealing another two-piece set. Black lace crisscrossed into a sunburst bra and matching thong, the lace forming two slim lines along each hip with only a small strip of fabric covering the middle.

"Get changed girls."

It became clear that our bodies were not ours tonight. Samara's eyes were blank, as if she had resigned herself to whatever was next. She grabbed my arm pretending to help her balance and mouthed, "for our freedom," and I mouthed back, "for our freedom."

We finished changing, and waited for the next set of directions from Mr. Lope, who adjusted himself as our full images came into view.

"Excellent. Don't you think, my darling?"

"Yes. Absolutely perfect." She cooed in response.

"Attendant 523, get on the cross so she can tie you up. Attendant 844, grab the flogger over there." He pointed to the wall of whips and leather. "Once you have her tied up, you're going to use that."

"What do you mean?" I asked, still not fully aware of what I was about to do.

"Well, you're going to hit her, of course."

"I won't."

"Oh, yes, you will. You have no power here. Do whatever we tell you to do. It's how this works. Remember your place, and the role you play in the system. You're nothing to us. To the Nation. To the others. Nothing except a body for us to use because we've earned this life. We've earned the right to you. Tonight, you need to remember your place if you want to stay here."

If he only knew where my place actually was.

"Do you understand?"

I exerted every ounce of strength into containing the fire, shrinking it to a single candle flame, knowing I had no choice. I complied like so many men and women had done before, and would do, after we had the privilege to leave.

"Yes. I understand."

"Good girl. Now, 523 get on the cross and 844 grab the flogger."

Samara stepped onto the cross and I put the restraints on her ankles and wrists. I latched them closed, careful not to make them too tight. Her back, now fully exposed, came into painful view.

"You're going to start by just sliding the flogger straps over her skin. It's deer leather, the best out there. It's mostly soft and quite the sensation. I am sure both of you will like it. I'll direct when to hit her and with what level of intensity, but at no time do you do anything to her without my or my wife's consent. Do you understand?" He leaned back in his chair, legs crossed, his eyes never leaving me. One hand tapped idly on the armrest, a picture of patience, though the tight curl of his mouth betrayed how much he relished the control.

"Yes." I answered as I stood with my friend's mostly naked body in front of me.

I moved the leather strips around her back, as if painting her skin with some new beauty treatment. Her back arched now and then, depending on where the straps brushed. At the arch of her back, I caught my breath and squeezed my center together–unsure of what I was feeling.

"There it is. I can see it in you 844. You like this." He tilted his head, a thin smile playing on his lips.

I didn't reply. I couldn't reply. I wouldn't reply.

Did I like this? Did I want to see Samara like this under my hands, completely powerless against me? Against him and his wife?

"Yes, you have it. You want this 844. I knew the fire in you would make you the best choice for this role. Now, you need to hit her. Easy at first, give that time. Hit her just below her hip bones...the right side."

So specific. Why?

I hesitated slightly, then moved my arm up and brought the whip down against the right side of her butt. She whimpered. My breath caught and a pool of wetness betrayed me.

"That's right." He replied.

I looked over; both of them were leaning forward, their eagerness fixed on what they would make me do next.

"Now, her left," he commanded.

I complied, but hit just a little bit harder this time. A deeper want filled my belly.

"Mmmm. Yes." He said, as I watched Samara's body shiver. "Now her back, but harder. You need to leave marks."

I complied, again. Leaving red welts against her beautiful tan skin. She whimpered again, but refused to cry.

"Again." He commanded, and I compiled. He whispered something to his wife, and she nodded. He then stood up and moved over to me, standing directly behind my body. "Now you're going to do it with me behind you. And I am going to touch you while you do this. Do you understand?"

"But you don't touch attendants," I begged.

"But I am going to touch you. And my wife is going to watch. Do you understand?" He stood just behind me, close enough that I could feel his breath.

"Yes." I complied again. Bringing my arm up, hitting Samara again, just as his fingers entered me. I let out a soft moan.

He sneered. "You're so wet. I knew you would like this. I just had a feeling...that this would be perfect for you."

I didn't want him to be right. But he was. I did like this. Why? What kind of person did this make me? I was inflicting the same pain and power on someone else that the Nation had once inflicted on me. How could I take pleasure in the very thing I was fighting so hard against??

"Hit her again, 844."

And I did.

"Again," he growled as he slipped his fingers further inside me, his wife watching, locking eyes with him.

I hit her again, harder this time. She cried out, and I recoiled into Mr. Lope.

"No, no, no. You need to keep going. Just because she cries doesn't mean you stop. I tell you when to stop," he whispered in my ear. I heard him undo his pants and let them fall to the floor, realizing too late that the scene we were acting out for his wife was about to change, with or without my consent.

He entered me harshly, bending me over, and pulling my hair. My arm went limp, and the whip felt too heavy to lift back up. He pulled me upright, hair tightly in his hand, and pulled my head back toward his mouth.

"Now, it's your turn to decide when, how much, and how hard. I know what you want to do. I can see it. 844...make her hurt the way you want her to." He thrust deep inside of me, making me cry out. I wasn't sure if it was in pain or pleasure.

I drew my arm back and hit Samara a little harder than before.

"That's it, 844." He continued to thrust in and out of me, pulling my body back toward him and then forward toward Samara's every time I hit her.

"Harder!" He yelled again, pushing harder inside of me. Unsure of who I was becoming, a frenzy took over. I hit her repeatedly, in unison with his painful thrusts, anger filling the ends of each leather strap that painted her back a deep shade, like bruised wine. Each strike stood for something beyond me, and what I thought I was capable of. For the person she got to be with, while I'd been chained to a man I never loved. For the forever connection to Ethan that I would never have. For the unspoken power she held for so long, while the rest of us suffered under the hands of that Nation.

One hit after another. One thrust after another. One grasped section of hair pulled, one after another.

Violence against undeserving bodies. Sexual elation against powerless women. Punishment for crimes uncommitted. All tied together in a dungeon where four souls met under the control of the Nation sky.

I continued to hit Samara until he finished, spilling little wolves down my legs. When Mr. Lope finished with me, he undid Samara from the cross and walked her tired body over to the bed. His wife moved to me and pulled me onto the bed, tying me up, fully exposed to everyone in the room.

"My turn now, darling?" She asked her husband.

"Yes, Mrs. Lope. You've earned it for being such a good girl this month." He took his place back in the chair, then swallowed a hefty sip of the warmed champagne.

Mrs. Lope took the lead with Samara, forcing her to untie the bow on my bralette, then telling Samara to place my breasts in her mouth. The wetness pooled between my legs in a confusing mess of desire and regret for what I had just done to Samara's body. I wondered if she would punish me like I had her, now that the roles had reversed.

Mr. Lope sat in his chair, carefully watching as his wife moved her hands around Samara's naked body. The three of us entangled in perfect sexual femininity—images watched on repeat for years by anyone who had access to the Internet.

"It's time for more, number 523." Mrs. Lope commanded Samara. "Move down her body and place your mouth between her legs. She needs to be cleaned up."

My heart raced, and my body shook. Samara released my breasts from her mouth, looked up at me, and mouthed, "It's okay."

She slowly kissed her way down my body, while Mrs. Lope kneeled behind her, hands moving up and down Samara's thighs. Once in between my legs, Samara placed her mouth on me, kissing just outside. My body writhed under her lips and my wrists tried to release from the restraints.

"Uh, uh, uh," Mrs. Lope said. "You're staying in those. It will make for a better experience, I promise. Number 523, keep doing that, but let's add in your fingers next. I think 844 is ready for you."

She was right. I was ready for Samara. I didn't understand, or know why, but I wanted the release that wasn't offered to me when Mr. Lope forced himself inside me while hitting Samara. I wanted it to be over. For my body to be done with the twisted pleasure from our time with them. I wanted to get some sort of ending, closure, finish so I could eventually put this all behind me.

Samara's tongue made tiny little circles around the center as she slowly entered me with her fingers. I moaned in unexpected pleasure, fighting my body from catching up to my mind. My friend and former enemy was giving me what a man couldn't, just moments earlier. My friend, the mother of Ethan's children, the wife to Laura, a leader in the Resistance, was making me moan in pleasure in front of strangers, in a room designed to cage us in.

She continued to trace circles around the most sensitive part of my body, making me push harder against her, and the shackles around my wrists and ankles. I looked down at her between my legs as my breath continued to increase in speed, making me move to the peak of pleasure I knew with Jude, and Ethan, and the other citizens that had chosen me over the last few weeks. Caught between my own pleasure and the need to push reality aside so I could reach my end, I saw Mrs. Lope grab some sort of belt from behind her and buckle it around her waist. A long phallus-shaped attachment stood in front of the buckle, ready to go. She grabbed Samara's hips, and forced the object inside of her. Samara let out a scream. I caught her eyes briefly, tears beginning to stream down her face as she continued to bury herself between my legs.

I turned briefly toward Mr. Lope, his lower half still naked from before and his hand over his aged manhood, stroking it up and down, teeth biting down on his lips. His eyes transfixed on his wife, hers on his, with every thrust into Samara, with every lick of Samara's tongue.

Like a coiled spring fatigued from being wound too tight, my body silenced my mind and snapped, liquid covering Samara's face, my screams of pleasure filling the deafened room. Mr. Lope was next grunting like the dog he was, spilling himself for the second time tonight over the gray carpet. Samara's screams got lost in a paper cup, with Mrs. Lope finishing the siren's song luring us all to a death that could never be buried.

My body gave way to exhaustion as Samara cleaned herself off and shifted away from Mrs. Lope. Streaks of red slowly crawled down her thighs and onto the bed. Samara silently stood up and undid the buckles around my ankles and wrists. My body collapsed, almost pinning her against the red, violent scene under us. Mrs. Lope left her evidence on the bed, then moved toward her husband, securing herself on top of his lap, apparently still ready for what she wanted next.

"Girls, get out. It's time for my husband and me. His pills only last for another hour."

Samara pulled me up and put my arms around her, helping me off the bed. I looked toward the carpet, trying to feel my feet under me, but they were gone. I remembered this feeling once before, in the Maldives, with Thomas. The night he took my body from me. Only learning recently that it was all recorded. My fear was that this, too, was recorded, but I couldn't focus on that now. I needed to leave this behind. Close the door so Mr. and Mrs. Lope could meet their den's demons alone.

Samara and I found the large chaise lounge, and she pulled the black faux-animal throw over the two of us. Our silence echoed the sadness and confusion that stretched between us.

My mind unwillingly retraced the steps that brought us here. The horror story written in the room next to us. I thought of Ethan and what he would do if he knew what had just happened. I thought of Thomas too, and even though I wanted nothing to do with him, I knew he would punish Mr. Lope if he learned what he'd done to us.

I thought of Laura. And although Samara and Laura shared similar intimacy in the bedroom, I assumed violence wasn't part of their relationship. I couldn't help but wonder what trauma this would impose on Samara. I wondered if it would have been different if a man was fucking her rather than a woman. If the trauma would have been understood or compartmentalized differently because a man, not a woman, had betrayed all the women before her. We were supposed to be banned together, fighting against men and their power. Not enacting the same power over our sex's bodies like men had done for centuries. Mrs. Lope betrayed the two of us, like she had probably done to so many other women before; like her husband taught her years ago, when she agreed to be part of the Nation.

"How are you?" I whispered, pulling the blanket tighter around me.

She shook her head, eyes fixed on nothing. "Not good. You?"

"Not good either. Are you going to be okay?"

"I don't know. You?"

I let out a shaky breath. "Same."

She closed her eyes and buried herself further under the blanket. Our newly familiar naked bodies, warm against each other, found their sleep. But dreams wouldn't help us now. Nightmares would find us long before any gentle dream ever could again.

16

———

OLIVIA

I stirred at the sound of voices in the bedroom. Mr. and Mrs. Lope were awake, preparing for their 24-hour stay to end. Beside me, Samara lay wrapped in a blanket. Sometime in the night, I'd found another one, enough to put a layer of space between our bodies and what had taken place only hours before.

I stood up, careful not to wake Samara, and grabbed a glass of water. As I walked back to the chaise, I heard a name unmistakable to me: "Thomas Smith." My hands shook, and I almost dropped the glass. I set it on the counter and moved to the bedroom doors, listening in.

"Great to hear from you. Oh, no, I'm at Rose Bay. The new collection you've curated. Last night we had some wild ones." Mr. Lope let out a laugh.

I couldn't breathe. Was he going to tell Thomas more about us? I pressed myself closer to the door.

"I picked a white beauty and a real exotic one that were both new to the Center and god...I bet the footage is unreal. My wife really got into it this time too. Yeah, I mean, you know, we usually don't, but there was something different about these two that really got her going and I won't complain about that. I mean, after all, that's why I wanted to join you guys years ago. I knew I would need something to keep this marriage going. Your girls though—one was real fiery, the other more subdued, but did exactly what we told her to. My wife took the more compliant one, you know how she is." He chuckled softly into the receiver, leaning back in his chair as if recounting nothing more serious than last night's dinner.

"Familiar? The exotic one reminded me of someone, but I can't place it. Maybe a girl we've had before? Do you want me to wake them up and look them over again? Yeah, once we are done, I'll go check on them." I heard rustling in their room. "Honey, go back to bed, it's just Thomas. He's just checking in, and needs me to do something for him. Go back to sleep before we have one more round."

I heard a mumbled mix of words that I couldn't make out, and Mr. Lope continued with his phone call. "Yeah, yeah, sure. What do you need? All of the Genetics Project files transferred and erased from the primary system?"

My chest tightened. Genetics Project?

"Where do you want the drop to be? Really? You still livin' there with the kids, with her gone? Oh, that's way better, always one of my favorites."

I leaned forward, straining to hear through the door.

"Why the house then? I can just bring it to you. ... Okay, that makes sense. I'll make sure to go unnoticed. How are the kids doing anyway? Good."

Kids. My throat went dry.

"Yeah, if my wife ever pulled what yours did, she'd be out too. But she's not dumb enough to do that. She knows what she has. Yep, no problem, Thomas. And your code? Hold on. Ready. ... 101610. Got it. How do I get access? Will someone be there to let me in or just check with your neighbor?"

I pressed a hand to my mouth. The prison I'd lived in for

ten years held more of Thomas's secrets that I knew I had to find.

"Got it. I'll message you after the drop off. Maybe today, tomorrow at the latest. And hey, thanks again for hooking us up with more nights this month. My wife and I love the Nation life you've given us. Sounds good. Talk soon."

Mr. Lope set the phone down and went to the bathroom. I scurried back to the chaise lounge and pulled the blanket over me, feigning sleep in case he came out of the room. Instead, I heard him rustle back to bed, and moments later I could hear moans–of pain or pleasure, I couldn't tell coming from their dark cave.

I rolled over to Samara and gently rubbed her arm. "We need to go. Right now."

Her eyes opened slowly, and for a brief moment she looked at ease, until she realized where we were. I could see the night before replay in her mind as she sat up. "What's wrong?"

"I need to tell you something, but not here. We need to get back to our floor." My fingers tightened around the blanket as I leaned closer, my voice low.

"Are they still here?"

Our eyes moved to the door as if on cue for the moans that permeated the room.

"Guess so, huh?" She sneered. Samara picked herself off the lounge and we both got dressed before leaving the Lopes behind–without a note, without thank yous or goodbyes.

We didn't speak on our way back down the elevator and into the Attendant's wing. I walked Samara to her room and followed her in.

"What's going on? What happened?" She asked.

"Lope was talking to Thomas. He was asking questions about who they were with last night and it sounded like Thomas was wondering if it was us. But he couldn't know we're here, right?" I chewed at my lip, looking at Samara for reassurance I didn't feel.

Samara's face turned a pallor gray. "Thomas is like a spider, Olivia. He could know we're here and he's just biding his time before the fatal bite. He's casting his strings out because we've been silent for too long. We may need to get out earlier than we hoped."

"We can't leave yet!" I yelled.

"We may not be safe anymore, Olivia."

"I don't care. We aren't done yet. There's something in my house that we need to find too—a drive that has a bunch of data that Thomas wants erased. It could have the information that we're looking for." My hands balled into fists at my side.

Samara's eyes shifted around the room as she pulled a blanket up over her clothed body.

"I know we need to get this figured out, but I need a moment. It's a lot and if there is a drive, yes, we need to get it, but I just can't right now. I'll message Morgan later, so she knows that security may have been compromised, and then we can go from there." Samara paused, "She's going to tell the compound, Liv. She has to."

"No! She can't. Ethan will come here and make a scene and ruin any other chances we may have to use the info we just got from the Lope. Tell Morgan to keep this quiet until we figure out a plan, between the three of us. Please." My voice cracked.

"Okay, but I am not waiting for long, you understand? This is serious. And if Thomas is starting to suspect we're in the Centers, then there's more going on than we know of, and that can't be good for any of us."

Samara was right, but I needed time to think and figure out our plan. Even if Thomas was starting to suspect we were across Nation lines, we still had time...we had to still have time.

"I just...I'm not ready to leave yet, Samara. We're so close, I can feel it. I know this *is* something. What we've been waiting for."

"I understand." Samara's eyes were vacant, lost among the carousel of memories from the night before.

"Do you want me to leave so you can rest?"

She let out a breath. "Yeah, is that okay?"

"Of course it is."

"I just need a little bit of time. A break."

"Are you going to be okay?" I asked, though my chest tightened looking at her.

"Yes." She collapsed into her bed, pulling the covers over her like a tight cocoon that no one could penetrate, and I walked out, closing the door behind me.

I wanted to handle all of this now, but Samara wasn't in a place where she could take on any more. I tried to keep the memories from the night before at bay–my go-to coping mechanism, a shield I'd worn for ten long years to keep me from feeling the pain of the life I chose to walk through every day. I'd use the shield again, just a simple layer to protect Samara and me until I'd have to take it off and let the pain strike me in the chest. But not today, tomorrow, or even next week. I needed to focus on what Lope said, and how I was going to get that drive.

I walked back to my room like a zombie. As I laid down and tried to fall asleep, I noticed a vacant cobweb in the corner shimmering in the morning light. It swayed in the air when the AC kicked on. I turned away from it, wrapped the blanket around me to protect myself from the new morning chill, and fell asleep. It wasn't until the room began to warm from the afternoon sun, and I became too hot in the blanket, that I awoke. The AC was off and the cobweb's owner had returned to its place.

I slowly sat up, scanning my body for damage from the night before. Purple bracelets adorned my wrists and ankles; reminders of my capture with Mr. and Mrs. Lope. I moved my hand to my thighs, where there were more bruises, this time from Samara's fingers digging into my skin, as she'd tried to cope with Mrs. Lope's assault. I wouldn't tell her about these bruises; she didn't need to know what marks she left. I didn't want to see the marks I left on her either. Before our next selection, both of us would need to go to med bay to make the night with the Lopes disappear from our bodies, but I knew it would never fully disappear from our minds.

I showered and got dressed and left to check on Samara. Even if she was still sleeping, I wanted to make sure she was okay. That we were okay. I walked to her room and knocked softly.

"Hey," Samara's voice sounded strained.

"Hey. Can I come in?"

"Yeah." She crawled back into bed and I sat down on the mess of throw blankets she had at the foot of her bed.

"How are you feeling?" I asked tentatively.

Samara's voice was barely above a whisper. "Not great. You?"

"Sore."

"Same."

I studied her face, wondering if she wanted me to push. "Do you want to talk about it?"

Her eyes filled with tears and she wiped them away as they fell down her face. "You know, it's not like that hasn't happened to me before. I mean, before Laura. When we were immigrating here. The center they held us at...we were there longer because we were Muslim, and after 9/11, they found any excuse to not process people coming from middle eastern countries, even families like ours. Did you know we helped the U.S. Government? With the war. My dad, he was an engineer. He had access to the systems the government wanted to use against enemies...really whoever they were blaming at that moment."

"I didn't know that," I replied, softly acknowledging I was here to listen to her.

"Yeah. We lived a great life back home. I didn't even know anything bad happened outside our compound. My family was with us. We had food, private schooling, and went on vacations all the time. I did not know that there was anything wrong. Our mom did everything she could to shelter us from the world outside the four walls. That's what mothers do, protect their children...until one night my mother woke my sister and me up in a panic. She told us we had to leave. That a car was waiting. That we were in danger. I didn't really even know what that word meant outside of 'don't touch the fire, it's dangerous,' or 'don't drink that water, it's dirty and dangerous.' I don't remember everything from that night, but I remember getting in a car, then in an airplane, then arriving in New York. They immediately took us to a center, where my family spent two months 'being processed.' But really, we were being watched. The government was making sure we weren't like the 'other ones',"

Her tone shifted from the once calm and self-assured Samara I had grown to respect, to one of jade and cynicism.

"We had probably been there for three weeks when the authorities sent my parents to a separate part of the facility, leaving my sister and me alone in our family's dormitory. On one of the last nights before my parents returned, there was a knock at our door. My sister was asleep, so I got up and answered it. It was one of the younger guards assigned to our dormitory wing. He was new, maybe just out of basic training, so like, eighteen or nineteen years old? He asked me about my parents' location, and I told him they were assigned to a different wing. He asked how old I was, then my sister. I told him. He then asked if she was asleep. I told him 'yes.' It happened so fast after that. He forced his way into our room and covered my mouth with his hand. He told me if I made a sound, he would 'kill my bitch sister'."

Samara pulled the blanket tighter around her body, her eyes fixed on the ceiling as if she couldn't bear to look anywhere else.

She continued. "'Understand?' he'd asked. He'd spit at me—'you guys are the reason all my friends are dead.' 'You deserve this.' He threw me down on the bed, face down, then lifted my body up to his. He set his gun down on the mattress next to me, then unbuckled...the rest, well, you can figure out the rest. It didn't last long, maybe a couple of minutes. He left, but it wasn't the last time it happened. It happened numerous times, until my parents got released back to us...so maybe two or three weeks. He was just so angry. Like I had killed his friends or something. By the time they got back, I was so used to the routine of it, he didn't even have to tell me what to do, where to be. I just complied. It was easier, safer for my sister. For me."

Tears filled my eyes. "Samara...I am so sorry."

"Thank you. You, Ethan, and Laura are the only ones who know about this. I don't share it because it's in my past. But last night...sometimes...with things like that. And how it was. It just all came back. Sometimes, it just doesn't matter how much work you've done to process the trauma from your past. Tiny little skeletons still find their way out of your closet, scattering bones like memories across a rug you cleaned up years ago." She shivered, despite the warmth of her blankets.

I reached my hand out to touch her, but she recoiled her body from me.

I withdrew my hand. "Sorry."

"It's okay. This will just take a little while. It's just the way it happened. It brought me back to those nights with the guard. And then with Laura...and you. It's just going to take time."

"Of course it will. And it's okay. And...I am sorry. So sorry for last night. I…" I didn't know what I could say to make it better. To make it all go away.

"Olivia, it's okay. We were put in a terrible situation."

"No, that's not what I meant. I mean, yes, the Lopes are awful and yes, I am sorry. But I am sorry for how far I took it. I…was just…" I hung my head.

She looked at me. "I know when someone's releasing their anger on me, Olivia. I will be okay. We will be okay. For now, I'm going to see if Morgan can remove me from the schedule until we leave. I can't go back in there, Olivia. I am sorry. We can figure out how to get info another way."

"Samara, I…just…I am sorry."

"I know you are. We need to move on, though. And in time, we will. For now, let's just focus on getting out of here as soon as possible. What do you remember about what Mr. Lope said?"

And just like that, the self-assured Samara was back in front and center, taking command where and when she could.

"They were talking about the genetics program, and some data Thomas doesn't want anyone to have. Lope is going to drop it off at my house either today or tomorrow. Thomas must still need the information, or he would have just deleted it himself."

Samara's mind calculated our next moves like a shelter against the trauma from the night before. "We need to let Morgan know and Olivia, she *is* going to need to tell the Resistance. Once they have it, they'll send us a plan, which will hopefully get us out of here sooner than later."

"No, Samara. We aren't waiting for them to send us their plan. I understand you need to send them information, but I am doing this myself. I'm going to get that drive." I responded firmly.

She looked shocked. "No way. It's too dangerous."

"I can do this. I need to do this." I wasn't taking no for an answer.

"How would you even get out of here unnoticed?"

"Morgan can help me."

Samara paused. "This feels impulsive...not thought out at all. This is a huge risk, and if you're caught, Thomas will have you again–right back in the same cage you left months ago."

My chest tightened. It was a risk to go home, but a risk that had to be taken. "Samara, sometimes we have to be impulsive and take risks. We're close to finding out more about what's going on in the Nation, and hopefully it's the final nail in the coffin for them. I need to show the Resistance who they're dealing with. If I can pull this off with little help, then they won't question me anymore. I know I can do this. Morgan can take me off the schedule and make it look like I'm here. I know the neighborhood, we can get the cameras turned off, I can take an ADAM. Get in, get out, and back to the center in just a couple hours. I have to do this, Samara."

She sighed and shook her head. "When is Lope dropping off the drive?"

"By tomorrow at the latest. I can prep with you and you can make sure Morgan makes the tech side work."

Samara's brow furrowed. "It has to be a tight plan, okay?"

"Of course." I said quickly, nodding.

She glanced away. "Are you on the schedule tonight?"

"No, are you?"

She winced. "I am." She shifted in her bed, "I just don't think I can do it...after..."

"I'll do it. Tell Morgan to switch it."

She searched my face. "Are you sure? You've had a rough couple of days, too. Besides, when will we plan?"

"Before then? A little tomorrow too?"

"Maybe another attendant can do it?"

"No, Samara, I can do it. I won't be able to sit still anyway." I pulled her in close to my body. She tensed and shook slightly as my hands wrapped around her. It was like the shudder of an animal who'd been abused for far too long—they recoil, partly out of fear, but mostly because their body remembers the pain a human can inflict. I remembered that...when it would happen...and even though I second guessed if those nights with Thomas were real or not, my body always reminded me they were. It always knew and would give its most protective secrets away if I wanted to listen. But I never did.

I held her softly until her breaths slowed and her body melted into the bed. She wiped away tears every so often, trying her best not to draw attention to her abusers.

The Nation. The Center. The system.

Me.

I rocked her gently. "Samara, I am sorry. So, very, very sorry."

"I know," she whispered, "I know." Her hands unfolded and wrapped around me. "I'm sorry too."

I couldn't hold back anymore and tears streamed down my face, too. We stayed wrapped in each other's arms, crying for what was, for what we couldn't change, and for what we could never forget. In time, she would tell me all was forgiven, because we were at war with the Nation, but I'd know it would be a lie. Forgiveness is not simply unlocked by the words "I'm sorry," nor is it earned through the remorse of the one who caused the pain. True forgiveness demands something far greater—a deep, often invisible, sacrifice. And more often than not, it's the victim who bears that cost. It asks them to carry the weight of grace, to loosen their grip on anger, to release the hope for justice, or an apology that may never come. Forgiveness isn't about forgetting the wound. It's about choosing, again and again, to not let that wound define you. It would be an act of strength, disguised as surrender, if Samara was ever to forgive me for what I did to her in that room. When we returned home, we would have to face what had happened here, and a part of me wondered if we could ever share the same air again, the way we had learned to as mothers after our escape from Central.

"Okay, let's at least take you off the schedule a couple times this week. You need some time too, trust me." Her eyes deepened with the sorrow I worried would linger for months or years to come.

"You'll tell her today?"

"Yeah. Let's get to work." Samara folded the pain into herself like a worn letter, tucked it deep, and turned to strategy letting purpose override wounds already hardening into scars, so we could focus on the next steps, the work, the taking down of the Nation.

When Samara reached out to Morgan about the idea, Morgan said, "I have a guy, Sam, no worries." Bolstering my confidence that I could do this.

We planned for me to sneak out of the back of the Center and walk to an ADAM that Morgan would have waiting. I would be safe in the ADAM to West Borough, with its dark tint protecting me from Nation eyes. Samara said to cover myself as much as possible until I got into my neighborhood, where Morgan would have the cameras temporarily disabled. I could only be in the house for a short time undetected, so as long as I worked fast and didn't attract any attention to myself, I would be back here, and hopefully days away from being reunited with my children.

I would find the drive, give the Resistance what they wanted, and then I would have what I wanted too. Ethan could continue on with his war with the Nation, and I would get rid of Thomas, giving my children and me the freedom we wanted. I could feel it—the weight of him being gone as I walked back to my room to get ready for another night with a citizen. It felt good that we were finally making progress. Nothing would get in our way.

17

OLIVIA

Before going to the Selection Room I visited the med bay to heal my bruises. After an hour, I returned to my room to prepare for another night in the Selection Room. As I showered, my mind drifted like the piano keys in a lullaby, notes floating in the air, building on one another, moving through the motions of the piece just as I moved through washing my body and hair. It was routine now, part of who I had become: a body for others, a vessel for pillaging, a treasure for the hunter.

But also a body I had the power to choose what to do with, except for the other night. I was preparing myself for them just as much as I was preparing myself for me. This was my body. My vessel. My treasure.

The thought of the power I held and would continue to hold, knowing our next plans made warmth fill between my legs. I was at a point with my newly discovered sense of self where I wanted to feel pleasure, with or without someone. While I was married, it was a dirty little secret I kept locked away, because Thomas and the Nation held tight to the pleasure I was allowed to experience.

I learned quickly, after our wedding, that he monitored my health app, and although he said he approved, "It would be more meaningful if we didn't do things like that without each other." I followed the rules, until I discovered that if I ran hard enough on the treadmill, or hit just the right angle in pilates, I could trick the app into thinking I was complying. I had to stay cautious, always, but in those rare moments when I let myself feel, a surge of freedom flooded my body. It was like breaking the surface after being held underwater too long, lungs burning, the air suddenly sweeter than you ever remembered.

I took myself to the edge as the water ran down my back, remembering the power I held now. I could do what I wanted. I was desirable. I was calling my future as soft moans escaped me in a state-sanctioned attendant shower. It didn't matter who chose me tonight, in just a few short days I would be out of here and on my way to the new life that I deserved.

My toes felt cold again against the cement floor. No matter how many times I found myself in this selection room, I would never get used to the cold floor. It was as if whoever was running this place wanted to remind us of our true purpose. No connection, no reality, nothing to write home about. We would share no love with the citizens who chose us. No connection to keep us alive. No happily ever afters. Nothing real.

But it didn't matter to me. I had a purpose here. To be chosen just enough to stay relevant so I could fly under the radar until I could get the flash drive, and my children back, and ultimately put a bullet in Thomas's head so I could start my new life.

The lights illuminated, placing a perfect orchid, surrounded by DNA—the Nation's calling card—shrouding down on me. To my left were two male attendants I didn't recognize, which reminded me that this place was unpredictable, and I didn't know if a man or a woman was behind that glass mirror. I smiled at each of them and then faced forward again, bracing myself to see if my light would stay illuminated or go dark.

I recalled my nights at the Center, where I carefully examined the attendant's profiles, judging them only by what was written in a meticulously crafted list of traits meant to attract me. Tonight, I was on the receiving end again, being assessed for what I could offer, what escape they would take with me. What anger or deep-seated fantasies they would take out on me.

I found solace knowing my time here was temporary, unlike the people next to me. One day I would reclaim the skin I lived in and I wouldn't give it to anyone, ever again, unless I wanted to. I could either show it off, or keep it a secret. I could experience sexual pleasure on my own, or with a partner. It would be mine to keep healthy for me, not for a government system that controlled its citizens. It was becoming mine more and more each day, as I drew closer to leaving this place.

Lost in the freedom's thought I continued to seek, I barely noticed the two lights beside me dimming, until my own stayed lit and my eyes refocused. For a moment, I looked to the mirror and the two-way glass gave way, revealing the top of a shadow.

I followed the routine, and found a black and gold fitted silk jacquard dress in my changing room. The gold thread created a half-moon pattern shaped like bird cages, with a matching threaded gold band around the waist, the plunging neckline waiting to meet its solid lines. Sleeveless and form fitting, I looked in the mirror as soon as I was zipped up.

"This is gorgeous. I've seen nothing like it." I said to myself. My hands rubbed over the fabric and thumbed it through my fingers. "It's a little scratchy...of course."

There was always something with the Nation. The veil of beauty that covered up the marred world underneath. That was my life. The one I left behind. Picture perfect and desired by everyone around me. Underneath, it scratched like this fabric, slowly irritating different parts of my body, but never all at once, just in small pockets, making it bearable for the entire time I had to wear it.

Three-inch black open-toed heels were on the floor. I glanced at my HoloTab–he was six feet tall. Makes sense.

After the ELLY did my hair and make-up, I sat down to read his profile.

Name: Kai Acosta

Tier Status: Four

Age: 35

Ethnicity: Filipino, Scottish, French.

Family: Wife, two children.

Occupation: Analyst Manager

Likes: Dancing, conversation, hiking, travel, foreplay.

Dislikes: Quiet, inferior intelligence.

Drink preference: Whisky Must be scotch or Japanese with that spelling.

Food preference: Mexican, Indian.

Music: Country, Jazz.

I CLOSED the app and left for the elevator, waving my wrist over the panel. The number ten illuminated on the panel, indicating he was a special client. Hopefully he wouldn't be as bad as the Lopes, but I knew I would be able to take it and was ready for another night in the center.

It was hard for me to picture the attendants doing this day after day, year after year. As the elevator came to a stop on floor ten, I took a deep breath. Thinking back to my time with the Lopes, I whispered my mantra under my breath, "Remember why you're here. Remember what you want. You want your children home. You want Thomas dead. You want the Nation destroyed. This is your way out. This body is yours." I took in another long breath as the doors opened and I walked out onto the black and gray, orchid-lined carpet.

I hadn't been on this floor before, but at this point it didn't matter where they had me. I looked at the HoloTab, Room 1010, which was to my right. I could hear the citizen elevator arrive and I quickened my step to stand outside his room ready in a calm but seductive manner, waiting for the citizen to arrive and do whatever he wanted to me.

As I looked up, he was turning the corner and walking into view. Jeans, a tight black T-shirt, and a black leather motorcycle jacket hugged a solid six-foot, tan-skinned, dark-haired man. Clearly, I was overdressed, or he was underdressed and unconcerned. He walked confidently toward me. His smile was aloof, but inviting. His eyes focused, but curious.

I caught my breath.

"Kai? I'm Sarah." As if on cue, I waltzed toward him, pulling us together.

"Yes." He squeezed my body tentatively. He smelled like cedar and sandalwood; familiar, but lost in a sea of memories bound to my Nation life. He pulled away. "I'm Kai Acosta."

"Nice to meet you, Kai Acosta." We paused awkwardly. "Shall we go inside?"

"Yes, of course."

I waved my wrist against the keypad, unlocking a new chapter to the romance story that I was not a part of. I opened the door and walked in first, the sweep of the evening dress I wore filling the space. He followed, then past me, taking his jacket off as he walked toward the floor-to-ceiling glass windows. He set his jacket on a black velvet chair and stood looking at the view.

"This view never gets old." He said, hands on his hips, sincerity in his voice.

"You've been here before?" I closed the door to our room.

He turned around. "Um, yeah. I have. I like this room, so I ask for it every time I come in."

Every time he comes in? I went back to the HoloTab to see if I had missed anything in his profile.

"You won't find any information in there that you're trying to figure out." He smirked, then walked into the kitchen, opening a cupboard above the sink. He pulled out a green bottle with a white label, then opened another cabinet and placed a tumbler glass on the counter. "Want some?" He nodded the bottle to me.

"What is it?"

"Laphroaig. A smokey Scotch whisky."

"No thanks. I prefer a Japanese whisky."

"Oooh, fancy girl. And how does one...like you...get access to something like that?"

Shit. Think fast, Olivia.

"A citizen had it once."

"Right. Of course." His voice was unconvinced. "Would you like anything else? I can see what's left from my last visit, or I can always order something."

"What do you mean, left? They clean out the rooms every time. And if anyone is calling anything up, it's supposed to be me."

"Yeah, well, I'm going to let you in on a little secret tonight. This is actually my personal room."

"What do you mean?"

"Yeah. No one else uses this room."

"What does one have to do to get your own room at a Center? Assassinate the competition?" I joked.

"Now that would be fun, wouldn't it?" He took a sip of his whisky and moved in my direction, avoiding my question. "This dress is beautiful, Sarah. It frames your body very well." Peaty breath whispered in my ear.

"Thank you." The warmth of his breath against my neck sent shivers down my body, much like Jude's.

He walked back toward the window and I followed him, hoping to speed things up so I could get out of this dress, do whatever he wanted, and go to sleep.

I placed my hand on his back, and he flinched. "Sorry, did that startle you?"

"No, it's just...I'm not here for what you normally do."

Oh god, what kind of sick stuff is this guy going to ask me to do tonight?

"And that is?" I tried to make my voice coy and interested, even though my anxiety screamed inside me, like a teenager song.

"Sarah, let's sit down." He motioned me to the couch, and I sat. "You sure you want nothing to drink? I can get Suntori or the nicer stuff up here for you."

"No, thank you. I'm good." But for how long, I did not know.

"I'll get right to it. I'm not here for what you usually provide other citizens."

"What do you mean?"

"Well, I'm here to actually know more about you. Like, your life, world, and time in the Nation."

Oh my God, does he know who I am or what I'm doing here? Is he friends with Thomas? Is this another trap that I so blindly and dumbly walked into?

"My time in the Nation?"

"Yeah, like how long you've been an attendant? Why did you become one? What are your hopes, dreams, goals in life?"

This guy felt off to me. "And why would you want to know things like that?" I laughed.

His mouth crooked up at the side. "Well, let's just say I have an interest in it. Not just about your story, but other attendants as well." He moved his glass around in the air, motioning to false pretenses around us. "I mean, there has to be a reason for all of this, right?"

"You mean this hotel room?"

He pursed his lips. "Sarah, even though we've just met, you don't strike me as one of the regular attendants I've seen here. Am I right?"

I looked away.

"Of course I am. Almost as if there's something familiar about you. Is that it?"

My poker face was anything but money worthy.

"Almost as if I'm looking at a woman with a polished status, dressed up in just another cheap dress the Nation puts their female attendants in."

I half-smiled and squinted my eyes. "Sounds like you're reaching, and for what reason, I can't quite tell yet. Most citizens here would have me on my back or tied up by now." I paused. "I believe I'll have that drink."

Kai got up and poured me two fingers worth of warm amber liquid. He sat down next to me, and I took a sip, then winced.

"You definitely don't like the peat." Kai laughed. He pulled out his HoloTab, clicked a few buttons, swiped away, and set it down. "There. You should have Suntori in a few minutes."

His take-charge behavior reminded me of Thomas and the entitlement I lived with for years. Kai felt like all the other high-level tier men with power. Confidence bordering on arrogance. He contained the power and access to money given to all men —breadcrumbs women only wish to pick up on their way to their own freedom.

The door chimed.

"That was fast." I said, as I put the glass down on the coffee table.

"Tier-four has its perks." He replied as he went to the door to grab the new whisky. "Want ice?" He took a fresh glass out of the cupboard and opened the freezer.

"Yes. Two, please."

Kai poured a golden amber into the glass and handed it to me before sitting back on the couch. I took a sip and for the first time in a long time I felt calm. Its warmth reminded me of the cold winter nights when Thomas and I would sit in front of our fireplace after the children were asleep. We would talk about our present, but he would mostly ramble on about the future like his hand was reaching out for the green light. I would float in and out of his words, piecing together a life I would be a part of, but not in. I could never have a full world with him, but I was going to make it work because I had nothing else. My life was comfortable, on the outside, like a pair of shoes that everyone admires because they match your dress perfectly while your feet are being marred with blisters that scar repeatedly every time you put them back on.

"How is it?"

"Great. Thank you."

"You're welcome. My mom always said, 'Too much of anything is bad, but too much good whisky is barely enough'."

"Mark Twain actually said that." I took another sip.

"Oh, we have an educated one, huh? That's a first."

"What do you mean?" I stayed distant, alert.

"Sorry, I can see how that came out. It's just that most, actually, if not all, of the attendants I have worked with have had little to no education. The Nation's predatory practices scoop men and women up out of high school or low tiered jobs and wave this carrot in front of them, like what they're doing here is serving their government. They tout it as this contractual sense of pride; doing what's good for the Nation, and tempting them with money. And, don't get me wrong, it is serving the government, but not for any sense of nationalistic nostalgia or community. The people in here—you, them—are pawns to the Nation that make it richer. Attendants are as disposable as anybody else they deem unworthy."

I knew he was right. I'd known this for months now. I couldn't say any of that to Kai, though, because I was his attendant tonight, regardless of my education or higher-tier status.

"I guess I haven't had a lot of time to think about it that way."

His eyes narrowed on me. "I highly doubt that. You have an opinion about this and given your finer taste of whisky there's a bit more to you than you're willing to share. But we all have our secrets we keep. Stories we hold close to our chests to shape a new narrative for others to see...to believe...to read. You actually may be perfect for what I need right now anyway."

"Perfect for what? Like tonight's activities?"

"No. Something else. But first, I need to do something." Kai took his HoloTab and flipped it over. He removed a small cover on the back and removed a chip, setting it on the table. He then pulled another chip out of his pocket, placed it inside the Holo-Tab, then closed it back up. Once the screen illuminated, he typed in his username and password. "Kai Acosta, 101023." The HoloTab replied, "Voice Confirmed."

"HoloTab, close all monitoring systems in room 1010. Engage glass protection." He tapped a few more times on the screen, swiped the last window away, set the HoloTab down, then lifted his glass of Laphroaig for a sip. Setting it aside again, he smiled and said, "Now where were we?"

"Who are you?" My eyes narrowed on him as a small panic set in.

"My name is Kai Acosta, didn't you just hear that?" He laughed.

"Yeah, got that part. But why are you here and how did you get access to the mainframe?" The wheels in my mind started turning and panic set in. Was he part of Thomas's world and did Thomas know I was here? I was careful. Samara and I were so careful, but maybe he figured it out after what Mr. Lope had told him. I tensed and held tight to the glass, in case I needed to use it as a weapon.

Kai noticed the shift in energy. "Hey, hey, hey," his hands tried to touch me, but I recoiled. "You're safe. I'm not going to hurt you, so uncurl those fingers a little bit on the glass." He smiled. "I'm not here for sex like other citizens. I need information to help with a special project I'm working on outside of here. I chose you tonight because it's been awhile since I've heard from a female attendant, and there was something about you. You can trust me. It's okay."

I couldn't trust him. Something felt off, and I wasn't going to end up in another man's web. "I'm not sure I'd be able to help you with anything. I'm new, and I don't have a lot of experience with the Center."

His lip crooked to the side, his eyes catching the soft room lighting. They weren't brown like his profile said, but a deep amber with chestnut speckles, surrounded by a ring of gold. Perfectly familiar to me yet distant, lost in a sea of memories I couldn't search fast enough to place him.

"Have you been to any other centers? It seems like we've met somewhere before."

"No." I got up and went to the kitchen, pulling a glass bottle of water out of the refrigerator. "I've only been here for a short time, like my profile says." Had he seen me on the television with Thomas? Or at an event in Central? Was this Thomas's way of messing with me, pulling me in with his silk-like the prey I was when we were married?

"Hmm...you just seem familiar."

"I guess I just have that kind of face." I took a sip and moved back to the velvet sitting chair, rather than next to him. "If you're not here for sex, then what are you here for?"

"We'll get to that. First, tell me a bit about yourself."

"I would think that by now you know the rules enough to remember I'm not supposed to tell you anything about myself."

"I'm all for rules, and think they have their place, but I've never really been one for rules. It got me in trouble when I was younger...and sometimes, even today."

"Oh yeah? What kind of trouble?"

He took in a long sip. "My dad...wasn't exactly happy with me when I was a kid. He's uh...an important figure in the government, and I disappointed him a lot when I was little. I was never fast enough, smart enough, or polished enough for him to parade me around as his prize—classic father-son tropes. I just always had a different way of looking at things, and those differences were a problem for my father."

"That couldn't have been easy." I thought of my children, and wondered if they felt the same way when we were at Nation events with Thomas.

"Yeah, it wasn't. But in the same way, it strengthened me too." I felt the hint of a past we may have shared.

"Resilient to a greater extent. More independent. More likely to go out on my own." He looked off and swirled his glass. "We all carry the trauma of our past once we leave home. Then we spend a stupid amount of time either trying to avoid it, or trying to undo it. If you end up having kids, you just transfer it to them too." He set his glass down and in a resigned tone said, "That's one reason I don't have kids. Breaking that generational stuff now, instead of later."

"Your profile said you had kids."

"Not true. I'm not married either. I keep some information on there to be more palatable to attendants, and to show that I am doing what the 'Nation wants me to do.'" He laughed.

"Is anything on your profile true?"

"Well, I do like whisky..." he laughed again, helping soften the space between us. "My racial background is true. And, my name, of course." Kai winked at me.

"So not married, no kids, and a crusader for fighting against childhood trauma. Sounds like a classic case of someone avoiding a life they don't think they can have, or one they deserve." I spoke out of turn, the whisky making my mouth braver than my mind.

"Ouch." His eyes narrowed, and I realized I spoke in a way that was far too comfortable.

"Sorry, I shouldn't have said that...as an attendant."

"And if you weren't an attendant, should you have said that?"

I stirred uncomfortably in my chair. "Well, I am an attendant, so there's no use in talking in hypotheticals."

He took another sip. "No, I think we can talk about hypotheticals here. Hypotheticals from an attendant who drinks expensive whisky, has a polished demeanor, and can hold a conversation with a man like me. What did you mean by that, Sarah? Seriously, I actually want to know what you think." His eyes softened again to a golden amber in an effort to disarm me.

"Attendants aren't paid to think. You should know that."

He moved to the edge of the couch, closer to me, his eyes narrowed. "I mean it. What do you mean by what you said? I won't give you a bad review, if that's what you're worried about."

"I'm not worried about that." I would only be here for a little bit longer, once I got the flash drive and moved forward with whatever was next.

"Then what is it?"

"If you really hold this high-tier status, why are you here? If you don't have a family or kids, then why spend your time trying to get information out of people as low as the ones that live in this life?"

"You mean, low ones like you?" His eyes narrowed with a suspicious glimmer.

"Sure. I'm just saying...you seem like someone who has all this power and access and can't find contentment. It sounds like you've been given every opportunity to do well, and have a shiny life, but it's not enough…it will never be enough. Because somewhere deep inside of you, you don't believe in it anyway. You live in plastic because it's easier than being real. You cling to your family trauma as an excuse to not do what you really want to do. You choose to be stuck because you're too afraid to do anything else." Why was I calling him out like this? The whisky…it must be the whisky.

"And you got all of this from the last hour we've been together?"

"Something like that." I took another sip and tapped his glass.

"And what's your experience with any of this?"

"More than you will ever know."

"So you have power and access here? Where you're essentially selling yourself for room and board?"

Kai Acosta, in his arrogance, managed to make me feel even smaller than I did with the Lopes. I withdrew into the chair and moved my legs away from him. Silence lit tiny little fires all over the room, waiting for me to throw my whisky on the floor to let it all burn together.

"Sarah?"

I didn't respond.

"I'm sorry for what I said. I…that's not what I meant. I was just curious. I misspoke, or rather, spoke without thinking. I don't judge you for what you're doing here. I'm here, theoretically as a participant, because I need something from the people here too. I understand how people like you would need a place like this to survive in the Nation."

"What do you mean?"

He set his glass on the table. "I'm not going to sleep with you tonight, Sarah."

"Why not?"

"I never sleep with attendants when I'm here. It's not part of the program, I guess you could say."

"What do you mean?"

"My name really is Kai Acosta, but what I'm about to tell you has to stay in this room. That's why I disabled the voice monitoring system. Is that something you could promise me?"

Now this asshole is asking me for a favor? "Sure," I say curtly.

"I'm a researcher and all of this is part of my research."

I took a large sip, then set my glass down too. "Okay. And what exactly do you research?"

"The Nation." My back stiffened.

"What is there to research about the Nation? It's a system that's worked for years. The people are content with the way it's running, or at least that's what I've seen." I tried to show my feigned support, unsure of what trap was being set.

"It's worked in a certain way, you're right. But people aren't content, Sarah. I've been coming to the Center for a while now. I've talked to attendants to find a way to...help people see there may be another way to live. That there are possibilities outside of the Nation."

"You mean the resistance groups, or sanctuary states?" My tone stayed unassuming.

"You know about the resistance groups?"

"Well, sure. Everyone's heard about them. But they don't work. Won't work. They don't have enough people to even make an impact. They'd never win–not against the people running the Nation." I had to stay in the game and show him I was nobody to him.

"And who runs the Nation?"

"Well...you know, Governor Valentin. His people. The higher up tiers, people like *you*."

"Sarah, can I trust you?"

"Maybe. I guess it just depends what that means to you."

"It means, can I trust you with something that most attendants don't know?" He paused and leaned in. "The attendants that I tell...I eventually get them out."

"Get them out of where?"

"The Center."

I drew a breath in and for a moment believed in the words of a stranger. I needed to start a new life, but not because of my service in the Center. I needed to get the flash drive and find the children. Could this person be part of that new life I was seeking?

"I've learned to keep secrets over the years."

He smiled. "I had a feeling about that. When you stood there tonight in the Selection Room, there was something about you. Your profile too...which led me to want to know more about you. I rarely choose attendants that are new like you."

"Why is that?" A sliver of jealousy coated my voice.

"New attendants are unpredictable, impulsive. Sometimes unreliable too. When I'm here, searching through profiles, I need attendants with a track record, because it's something I can count on. When someone is too new, it makes my job harder. So, even though you're new, there was something else that drew me to you and I just said, 'fuck it,' and hit select."

"Thanks, I guess?"

"Sorry, I didn't mean it to come out that way." Kai reached for me.

"It's fine." I recoiled slightly.

"Like I said, I'm here because of my research. My father...I told you he's an important person in the government. I come here every month to learn more about the Nation. Its systems, its people, its weaknesses."

"But you live in the Nation. How do you not know about it already? You're a tier-four, just like when I–" I stopped and his eyes caught me.

"Just like when you were what?"

"When I was outside of here. You know, a tier-two trying to work her way up."

"Right." He took a sip. "It's hard to find out information when you're in the system. My current status makes it difficult to learn anything that's not polished, because we get the show, but never learn the behind-the-scenes. I thought, when I first gained the status, it would open up the doors for me to see what was really going on in the Nation."

"Did it?"

"Not at all. If anything, it was more like I was a delegate. You know, hiding the dirty dishes in the dishwasher every time I came over."

"They did that in Central before the delegates got there–hid the homeless. Cleaned up the entire downtown area. It was eerie how quiet it was the days before."

"When were you in Central?"

Shit. I needed to stop drinking. I was losing my ability to lie to this man. "I was trying to figure out what center I wanted to be stationed at, so I was downtown before the delegates arrived in April."

"Were you there when the bomb exploded?"

Fuck. Don't say yes, don't say yes. "I was nearby." *Good job.*

"Riiiight, nearby. It must have been crazy, the aftermath. I think they said several delegates and high-level tier citizens died. I think even a few attendants died at the center... but it was strange that the center was nearly empty that night. Were you checking out the Central Center? Was that why you were nearby?"

"I remember little from that time. There was a lot going on with me trying to find a place and all."

"Of course." His whisky was empty, and he got up to get another glass. "Want one?"

"No, thank you. I'm already feeling it enough." I needed to stay focused on him, his work, and what possible help he could be to me. If I had anymore to drink, I would slip over my own words, and from what I observed so far from Kai, that was a trap he easily laid for others. I wouldn't fall prey to it tonight. "Have you stayed at the Central Center before?"

"No, strangely enough. I could never get a booking because of the main desk girl...Sam, or something like that."

"Samara," I corrected.

He lifted his eyebrows. "Right. Excellent memory for remembering little from that time."

"Thanks." I wasn't going to give any more information away. Kai Acosta was setting me up for something, and I needed to stay away from any real details from my life.

"Yeah, so I couldn't get an appointment, which actually worked out because the security at Central is unlike any other center in the Nation."

"How so?"

"Its firewalls were too difficult to get around with my Holo-Tab. When I went for a tour, I did the same thing I did tonight—transferred out the chip to access the external servers so I could turn off monitoring in one of their showrooms. It didn't work. When my father had his team look into it, he saw the firewall was more intricate than anywhere else, so he suggested I find another center to research. After checking out two others, I settled on Rose Bay because their security was nothing. I hacked into the system within a minute of being in the room."

"How did you not get caught?"

"I asked them to leave me so I could feel what it would be like to stay in such a powerful place. My tier status didn't even make them blink. Once I saw I could get in, I asked to see this room, specifically because of the floor plan and location to the exit if anything went sideways. This room has the front door exit and a pull down ladder on the patio. It's the only one in the entire building. When they remodeled this place to make it the center, they had to keep this one ladder attached because of some historical event. Instead of fighting with the historical society, they complied and brushed the whole thing under the rug. You wouldn't even know it was there when you're out on the patio."

"Let me see."

We opened the dark tinted doors and moved onto the balcony. The heat hit our lungs, stealing breath for a moment until we adjusted to the thick smog-filled air. Suburban lights stretched across our view like polka-dotted pants. Each one, tinged with yellow, seemed carefully brushed onto fabric— clothing worn day after day, never fading, as someone stepped in and out of it, leg by leg, again and again. The patio was larger than I expected. It had a large outdoor couch with khaki cush- ions and two tall Italian-blue planters, each with a mini cypress. A long glass wall sat atop the solid black metal guardrail.

"It's right over here, behind the planter." Kai took my hand and pulled me to the opposite side of the balcony. His hand was soft, like a man who had never worked outdoors a day in his life. The strength of his grip, however, told me otherwise. He moved the planter away, and nestled in the corner was a small escape ladder, taking its users ten stories to the parking lot.

"It reminds me of the ladders in San Francisco on the old apartments that face the street."

"Me too. Did you go there a lot before?" A question about my past, but nothing too unsafe or revealing.

"Yeah, in another life, I did. Ocean Beach and Land's End were some of my favorite places to see when I was there." I recalled telling William the same thing. Was this my standard dating go-to story for citizens? Tell them just enough to humanize me, but not too much to make it difficult for them to do what they wanted to me?

"Was it before the Nation took over?"

Careful, Olivia.

"A little before, a little after." I closed my eyes, remembering the waves crashing against the shore at sunset at Land's End. The feel of the breeze and the sight of the seagulls floating like kites in the sky, happy to just be alive. I hadn't been there since Ethan proposed to me, but every part of it still felt as vivid as if it were yesterday. When all of this was over, I'd find my way back there. Take the children there; show them a part of me before their father.

"I've been there a few times and always liked it. My father's orders prevented me from visiting the city for a while because it was pretty sketchy. He never liked it, and at one point when I wanted to go to school in the bay he said it 'wasn't a place for people like you and me.' I think it always put him off because of its liberal politics and how they handled the pandemic stricter than other places. It also didn't help that Governor Valentin was from there. He hates that man with a passion unlike any other." Kai caught himself in a moment of truth that wasn't supposed to be shared. He glanced around, then grabbed my hand and said, "We need to go back inside."

Without hesitation, I complied. I knew that tone, that look, that feeling. This balcony scene was all too familiar to the one in Central with Ethan.

"Sorry about that." He closed the door behind us. "The system's only down inside here. I can't be too careful when it comes to the work I'm doing."

"I understand."

"If you're okay with it, I have a list of questions for attendants that I usually ask. Sometimes, based on their answers, I go off script, but the main point is just to gather more data about the Nation, the centers, and anything else that seems important while we're talking. I won't identify you in any of the records. Does that sound okay?"

"Sure." I didn't care at this point because I was going to be gone, and Sarah King wouldn't change whatever work he was doing anyway.

"If you want out of this life, I can help you with that too."

"Yeah, maybe."

Kai looked at me tentatively. "Also, I should have said this before–you don't have to take part either. Just because we are here together tonight doesn't mean you are required to answer my questions. If you felt coerced or obligated, the data would be unreliable, and I couldn't continue with the project."

"Isn't bribing me with my freedom an issue for gathering sound data?" I smiled.

He laughed, "You are sharp, Sarah. And yes, it skews it, but not enough to where my father and the team think it will impact us in the long-term. We have quantitative data that helps us analyze the qualitative data, and we cross-check anything attendants say against the main Nation system. The smallest pieces of information that I've received so far from other attendants have helped us figure out more about how the Nation runs. Who knows, something you say tonight about your experience could help us too."

The things I know, Kai Acosta.

"It's worth a shot if I can help. I'd like to wait until tomorrow, though, to tell you if I want out of the center or not. Even if you don't think it will skew what I say, I'd still like to have that off the table for now."

His head tilted. "Sure. That works. No pressure tonight, then?"

"Right, no pressure. Ask your questions and see where it goes."

"Perfect. Let's get started then."

"Sounds good." As he opened his HoloTab, I realized I was going to be assessing him, too. Determining whether he could be an ally, someone I could trust in the long road ahead. Trying to sift through his body language, voice, and how comfortable he actually gets with me. Picking up on any clue that reveals something in his Blackhat HoloTab that could help Samara and me get out of here and onto finding the children...eventually taking out Thomas and the Nation in order to claim a life of my own. I took one last sip of the whisky before I settled into my chair to take part in the chess match we were both about to play.

He interviewed me like I was applying for a job. Asking me questions about the daily life of an attendant and a few other questions that seemed to lead somewhere else. Almost as if he was trying to put a bigger puzzle together and somehow I may have a few of the right pieces for him. It was almost midnight when he finished his questions and from what I could tell, I offered him nothing new for whatever project he was working on.

"Sorry, I didn't mean to keep you up so late. I don't sleep a lot, so I sometimes forget about that for other people. If it's okay, I just have one more question."

"It's fine. Had this been a real night, I would have been on call all night anyway. We don't expect much sleep when selected, but we usually have breaks between clients. One more is fine."

"I know you haven't been here long, but in your time, have you seen anyone go missing?"

"What do you mean?"

"Attendants. Have you met an attendant but then they're suddenly gone?"

I thought about my time here and realized I had spent most of it focusing on sleeping with clients. Up until my time with the Lopes, I wasn't making connections with other attendants, or doing what I was supposed to. It was as if I was waiting for something to fall in my lap, instead of pursuing every option to find information to get Rose and Lucas back.

A pang of guilt settled in my stomach.

"No, I haven't. But, I also haven't connected with anyone, really, other than citizens."

"It is another reason why I choose attendants that have been here longer too, but tonight has been helpful, so thank you. Speaking of what you said earlier about having a break between clients...my status allows me to choose you again automatically, if you're up for more questions."

"You can have back-to-back nights with the same attendant?"

"Yeah, but I totally understand if you need a break. I'm sure you're selected often since you're new to the Center."

My body ached at remembering what had happened with Samara. "Thanks, but it's fine. Does that mean you'll be here all day tomorrow, or do you take a break from the room?"

"I usually work, but if you need space, I can go downstairs to the bar. They have a private room for higher tiers where I can go to schmooze it up with other citizens that are here. It actually might be good for networking. But either way if you want me here, cool. If you need a break, that's fine, too."

Samara, Morgan, and I planned for me to leave the Center tomorrow night, but maybe it would be worth staying with Kai an extra night to see if there was anything I could learn from him about the Nation that would ultimately help us dismantle it. "I think it's fine. I may see about going back to my room to grab a few things."

"I can grant you access to leave, even if I've chosen you for another night. Just let me know when you want to be out of the room and I can schedule it through the HoloTab."

"Thank you. I would appreciate that."

"Of course." He started shuffling around the living room and I went to clean up our glasses, remembering my role as the dutiful wife who picks up after parties. "Don't worry about the mess. I'll clean up and sleep out here. Take a bath and enjoy the bed. I'm sure it's been a while since you could sleep in something like this, without someone trying to maul you the whole time."

"Thanks. It has been a while." I walked into the bedroom and closed the door behind me. A bath sounded amazing, but I wasn't ready to remember the life I had when I could enjoy those pleasures. I was a soldier–of sorts–now. I needed to stay on alert and be here in this role. Stepping into an oversized tub with a bubble bath would just confuse my mind and body into thinking she was safe again. It would make her think of champagne and maple syrup and high thread count sheets. Of children laughing in the living room. Of husbands who give false gifts. Of plastic lives lived behind false walls. No, I wouldn't take a bath tonight; I would just go to sleep in the expensive Nation Center bed, looking up at the false night sky that convinced me to sleep.

18

OLIVIA

I awoke, fingers tightened around sweat-soaked sheets, a soft gasp for air. I wasn't a hostage to him anymore. Just a hostage to the room I found myself in to save my children. Gold orchid filigree met my eyes as an afternoon peered through the softly swaying curtains. I sat up and scanned the room until I found Kai sitting in the chair, pants and button-up shirt on, whisky in hand.

Something had changed. His eyes pierced mine as they narrowed in on my body. I covered myself instinctively with the sheets. He turned his glass, swirled the caramel liquid, and took a sip.

"What time is it?"

"Afternoon."

"Drinking already?"

"And who are you to judge?" His tone clipped.

"What are you doing here?" My panic was trying to be contained.

He set his glass down and leaned forward, fingers church-steepled together and pressed against his eyebrows.

"I know who *you* are."

My stomach sank. Thomas. It was him this whole time. He carefully wove strands in an intricate pattern, waiting for me to step on the right thread so he could pull me in. I would not go silently. My training kicked in.

"Yeah, and I know who you are. You're Kai, a top tier researcher searching for information, and I am Sarah, an attendant at one of the most exclusive centers in the Nation." I shifted and calmly got out of bed, looking for my clothes casually, a proper feigning in any game of cat and mouse.

"No, *Olivia*, I know who you are."

A quick smile could disarm him. "I think you have me mixed up with someone else. My name is Sarah. How much have you had to drink?" I questioned him, straddling the line between a good and bad attendant.

He stood up and moved toward me. My heart pounded a confession against the fabric of my shirt, but my face held steady, loyal to its secrets. I continued to dress as his body slowly walked closer to me, the edge of the bed our only separation.

"You're Olivia Smith, the Director's wife. Thomas's wife. You're his...the one we've been looking for."

Bile entered my mouth. That phrase 'Thomas's wife' was like sandpaper on a sunburn. Like a cattle brand on my skin. A tattoo never to be removed. I pulled my pants on and took a step back.

"That's an interesting accusation to throw out in a place like this. In a place where an attendant like me could find themselves on the other side of a firing squad for lies when I'm just trying to do my duty and serve the Nation. A life I believe in."

"Cut the bullshit, Olivia!"

His voice startled me. He was so quick to move from calm to anger. The voice monitoring system stayed silent, and when I looked at the cameras, the red blinking light that had become my security blanket over the last several weeks was nowhere to be found. The system was still disarmed and I was now alone with an unpredictable man—who for all I knew was spinning me closer into the Nation's web.

When I was studying to become a nurse, we learned about the human brain's fight-or-flight response during potentially traumatic events. People either fight, and run headfirst into the danger threatening their reality or existence, or they run, taking cover and waiting for someone else to play hero. Or they freeze, leaving the body iced to the ground while their mind steps outside their body for a moment, watching every move unfold before deciding whether to fight or flee.

This was me. Frozen inside another cage. Trapped in quickly-freezing water coming up from under my feet, solidifying as I tried to figure out my next move. I desperately studied his body language to see if he supported Thomas and the Nation, or if there was any hope for me.

"Olivia?" Kai moved in and put his hand on my wrist–a soft gesture to him, an act of war to me.

I quickly returned to my body, and every fighting instinct and piece of training from the compound kicked in. It happened so fast. I grabbed his wrists, wrapping my arms around his, then kicked the side of his leg, crumpling him to the ground, giving me the leverage I needed to overpower his solid six-foot 200lb frame. I slid around him, pinning his arms behind his back with my left, while my right fingertips closed quickly around his throat.

"Stop," he choked. "I'm not them. With...them..."

I pressed tighter, my body's adrenaline serving as my strength, so I could wait for him to take his last sip of air. Once passed out, his body slumped down and relaxed against my body. I shimmied away, letting him fall to the floor, knowing I had very little time before he awoke. I hurried to the window and grabbed the curtain tiebacks. I tied his wrists together as he continued to breathe slowly against the base of the bed. I ran into the living room and took the tiebacks from the sliding door drapes and returned to tie his ankles together. I repositioned him, as best as my small-framed body could, against the bed. Finally, I went back to the kitchen, pulled a knife from the kitchen drawer, and prepared myself for a kill I didn't want, but would carry out if he was linked to my former life. I knew killing Kai would complicate things for Samara and me, inevitably speeding up our timeline and making it so we would have to leave as soon as it was over, but it didn't matter to me—I wasn't going to be taken by this man, or any other one, again.

I dragged the chair toward the bed, putting a few feet between us, and waited for him to wake up. As I waited, I ran through everything I told him the night before, everything he told me. He was a researcher. People in the government knew his dad...but he didn't name the Nation; he said 'the government'. Researchers don't study the Nation. His tier status was unknown to me, and if I had left today, I was sure it would have remained unknown to Samara as well.

Could this be someone else? Something else? Someone potentially helpful to me?

As I was trying to pull away from my naïve optimism, Kai's body jerked, and he took in a gulp of air. That sudden, suffocating panic we all know. The moment of realizing you're trapped, locked in place hit him when he realized his hands and feet were bound.

"You're not going to be able to free yourself, Kai. If that's even your name."

The amber in his eyes barely visible outside the large black pupils.

"My name is Kai. It's Kai Acosta. And everything, mostly, that I told you is true. I am a researcher."

"What kind of research, *Kai Acosta*?"

His shoulders raised as he drew in a breath, then lowered as he spoke. "Olivia, I will not hurt you. None of us are going to hurt you."

"What do you mean, none of us?"

"Will you please untie me? I'd rather explain everything when I am more comfortable."

"No. I've never been comfortable and have had to say and do a lot of things. So, you can sit there and tell me what I want to know, or you can sit there, say nothing, and I will start using this." I rolled the knife handle around in my hand.

"You won't hurt me, Olivia. We all know that. It's not in your nature."

Who was this man? And what could he possibly know about me or my nature?

"You don't know me. Or anything about me."

"Actually, I do. We all do. You're Olivia Smith, formally Olivia Embers. A non-vaccinated member of the Nation. A nurse sworn to help, not harm, others. A mother of two. A friend, a wife, a lover...and apparently, now a somewhat trained fighter who thought she could subdue a man almost twice her size." A smile crept across his face and in an instant, his hands were free. He jumped up, feet still bound, and sat on the foot of the bed, still a distance away from me and the knife.

He undid the ties around his ankles, not looking up at me once.

"See, I told you, you wouldn't hurt me." He walked toward me. "Hand me the knife."

Another spark flared, and my body reacted rising fast, driving the knife toward his chest, only to miss and catch his forearm instead.

"What the fuck, Olivia?!" He grabbed my wrist with one hand and the knife with another, tossing me onto the bed and running into the bathroom.

Had I just stabbed Kai? I looked at the nickel-sized blood droplets on the floor and listened to the water running in the bathroom sink, while Kai mumbled something about women and hysteria. A calm washed over me. I could act when I needed to. When I wanted to. I was capable of the same kind of violence men were capable of in moments like these.

Kai stepped out of the bathroom with a towel wrapped around his forearm, blood on his white button-down shirt.

"Jesus Christ, Olivia. What is wrong with you? You have nothing to worry about with me. I'm not like him. You're safe here. You were safe the moment I saw you in the Selection Room. I had a hunch because you look like her...the one I was supposed to find. And I was lucky..." his rambling dizzied me. "Then when I checked your DNA against the system, I couldn't believe it...how lucky I was, and how it had all paid off...the hours I've spent doing this. My father would finally leave me alone and give me the freedom I want."

"What are you talking about? Who are you, really?"

He sat in the chair, scooting it further away from me. "My name is Kai Acosta. Like I said, none of this was supposed to happen this way. But when I saw you, like I said, I just had a feeling you were Olivia. Of all the places where we've been looking for you, I found you here. No one believed my theory. That you would try to infiltrate through the Centers. I told my father and everyone else it just made sense to me. I couldn't fully explain it...I just had this feeling...like I would find you... eventually."

A familiar softness in his voice reached me. Had I heard those words before? There was a tether from another time that calmed me, though I couldn't make sense of it. The black of his pupils shrank under the amber brown meeting mine, imprinting a history between us we had never learned. I looked away.

He squeezed the towel. "I need to get this taken care of before I tell you anything else. Can you go into the other room and grab the black case for me, please?"

I picked up the black case, but its heaviness threw me off, and it hit the edge of the table. I brought it back to Kai and set it down next to him.

"Can you open it for me, please?"

I obliged, unfastening the black clips, revealing sectioned off devices perfectly organized separately in his luggage.

"Can you grab the square one with the medical symbol on it?"

I pulled it out, examining its almost weightlessness. Several buttons with different icons lined the side next to the power button. On the opposite side was a glass screen with two crossing lines, reminding me of the machine at the Center that I used when Jude bruised my wrists.

"Is this a portable Healing Machine?"

"Yeah. I bring it everywhere with me...I never know when I am going to need it. Can you turn it on and place the glass section over my wound? When I move the towel, the blood is going to come out pretty quick—"

"I am...or was a nurse. I know how wounds work." I snapped.

"Of course. Have you used one of these before?"

"Not on patients." I didn't need him to know where I had used one before, and that I had been the patient. "Hold still." I placed it on his forearm and turned it on. My hand felt the vibration counting down from ten until a bright light flashed, illuminating a circle just outside his arm. The smell of burning flesh reached our noses, and we both turned away at the same time.

"That's always the worst part."

"How often have you used this?"

"Only once on myself. A couple of times on others. You'd think with all the advancements in tech, someone would have got rid of the smell. Beggars can't be choosers, I guess. I'm just glad it's always with me."

I looked down at the case and saw five vials filled with a clear liquid. Next to those was a cylindrical silver tube with a black cap. Finally, below it, was what looked like an old gaming system that my friends and I played with before we left for the compound.

"What is all of this?"

"Things I need when I come to the Center, or am out in the field." He replied nonchalantly while he readjusted himself and put the healing device back in the case, snapping it closed from my prying eyes. He picked it up and walked out of the room, placing it back next to the coffee table. I followed him out and sat in the chair by the window while he took the opposite one, closest to the kitchen.

Silence served us both as we determined our next move. Who was this man? Clearly someone who had his own or at the very least, someone else's agenda. He had resources and access to information that I didn't have, even at the compound. I wasn't sure at what level I could trust him with anything about my world, or with the truth of why I was actually at this center. And what did he know about me, Samara, or the rebellion I was a part of?

He broke the silence first. "I know what you're thinking..."

"Is that so?"

"Yeah. Who is this guy? Why is he here? How does he know who I am?"

"Those would be obvious questions for anyone in a situation like this." My eyes narrowed.

"How much do you remember from before the Nation?"

"What do you mean? I remember what everyone remembers. The pandemic, the United States crumbling when Governor Valentin and his group took over, then people accepting the edicts. I wasn't young enough to be oblivious to what was happening, but not old enough to feel like I needed to be a part of it. We fled downtown when vaccine requirements started, and then tried to get into the Nation once we understood we needed to be part of it in order to have any sort of adult life."

"How did you learn about the U.S. crumbling? Did you watch videos, or talk to anyone who saw or experienced it?"

"I don't understand where you're going with this." My tone shifted. "There were videos, yes. We all saw them. And there were posts everywhere. I'd only recently started using social media because Nats, the then new social media app, was already on my phone when I bought it. I stopped watching the videos after a couple of weeks, because it was too heavy to watch a nation, like the United States, be overthrown by fanatics." I thought back to the violence that spilled on our screens. We couldn't help but watch; looking away took a self-control most of us didn't have.

"The Nat app. Did you keep it on your phone after the Nation took over?"

I cocked my head. "Yeah. We all did. It was just one of those apps, like your calendar, or eventually, HoloPics, that you always have on there. No one deleted that app, and it pre-installed on all new phones, so we didn't need to transfer accounts from our old phones to HoloTabs. We had to use it to be part of everything else."

"Olivia. I need you to understand something. What I am about to tell you is going to come as a shock."

I rolled my eyes. "Kai, with the way the last couple of months have gone, nothing surprises me. If you actually know who I am, you would already know that."

"Okay then. Nothing you know...the Nation, Thomas, the system...is real."

"I know that already. Thomas is the Director, blah, blah, blah. Yeah, old news, Kai."

"No, that's not what I mean. The Nation isn't as big as you think it is. The Nation actually isn't the Nation at all. It's just a small faction of zealots who took over Northern California and blocked out the rest of the United States from access. The United States is very much still running–albeit led by some corrupt people, yes, but also by others like me who believe in freedom and choice for everyone." Kai's eyes widened.

"You're mistaken. I saw videos of the Capitol burning. People pulled senators and congressmen from the building and killed them. I saw the President being bound and executed and the flag burning, being replaced by the orchid symbol that bound us all together and still does today, even in this room." A knot formed in my stomach as my whole body went tight.

We looked at the gold filigree orchids on the wall, serving as our captors.

"I'm sorry, but none of that happened." His eyes and tone softened. "It was all faked." The words echoed in the room like a dropped coin in a well.

It couldn't be true. I blinked quickly thinking back to the takeover, the videos, the way our lives changed.

"AI and some experimental tech out of the Silicon Valley fell into the hands of some very power-hungry, fanatical people. Governor Valentin being one of them. When the presidential primary didn't endorse him, he decided to seize California. He had the connections, resources, and vision. Unfortunately, he couldn't take the entire state, just the north. But once he, Thomas, Jeffrey, and the others put his plan into motion, there was nothing the United States could do to stop it. It was too tenuous, and most senators capitulated because of everything else going on."

"What else was happening? There was nothing on the Nat app except the takeover." My chest tightened.

"Wars, gas prices, post pandemic recovery. Water shortages. It was a mess. Adding a potential civil war on top of everything else just wasn't worth it to the government. They still controlled most of the central valley for agriculture, so they chose to give

Valentin what he wanted, hoping it would pacify him long enough for everything else to settle and for Northern California to eventually return to their hands."

"So, you're telling me the Nation is only in Northern California?"

"Yes."

"Then how do you explain the treaties? The rewards? The ease of travel? The technology? The dignitaries that visit Central? This whole time...it's just been fake?" Why was I being defensive?

"Yeah, basically." His nonchalance felt dismissive.

"You sound ridiculous, you know that, right?"

"Do I? Or does it sound ridiculous that a small group of fanatics could overthrow one of the most powerful nations in the world? And convince several other nations to join too? Think about the economic elements alone. Entire countries changing almost overnight. Things like that just don't happen, Olivia. Revolutions take years in just one country alone. How could it be that quick in several others?"

"Everything we saw said it happened. Videos, articles, posts of people dying. Posts of people signing the edicts. Getting married." I had to know if he was also telling the truth. If my freedom was really only a few hours' drive away this entire time.

"Everything was faked. Falsified news articles, doctored videos, and highly controlled algorithms fooled the people of Northern California into believing a false reality. One that only those outside the Nation knew about."

"But when I went on all of my vacations, everyone was part of the Nation. They had symbols everywhere. They greeted us like we were all part of the same thing."

"All highly contrived scenes that you and everyone else played a role in."

"You're telling me actors were just running in and out of these scenes in my life? People who faked it?"

"Yes, and no. The people greeting you, the people at hotels, on flights, or anything having to do with the reward system, were all insulated by the Nation. You vacationed only within the Nation, with other citizens of the Nation. You flew on Nation-only planes that were given access to airspace because it was just easier to let them have it, then to get involved in yet another war. You had food shipped in from other parts of the country and world because it served some government entity. I am really sorry, Olivia. But your entire world has been fake for a long, long time."

Did my mother know too and was this what she was protecting me from? It couldn't be, because we could have left if this was true. Did anyone on the compound know or were they blinded too?

"Who knows about this? Like, how many people in the Nation know?"

"All the officials. And almost all of the tier-ones–but no one believes them, since they've been branded mentally unstable or drug users, even though many had managed to bypass the firewalls and some never installed the Nat app either. They couldn't get out when the borders closed and had no financial access or means of securing themselves as higher tiers. Some of them complied, married, and took part in middle tier society just so they didn't end up like their friends. Many people have, and continue to, live on the streets. Others committed suicide. Others just disappeared under unusual circumstances. It takes a lot of work in the beginning to manipulate an entire population into believing something that will eventually grant full control and power over them. Then you need to create just enough chaos, every so often, to keep people in line and sustain whatever lie is being spun. People in power have been doing this for centuries, and will continue to do so."

"Prove it." I challenged him.

Kai opened his HoloTab. "Here, look at this." He handed it to me, and images from the last twenty years came into view.

The protests, the borders, the videos of Valentin and Thomas talking to the former President of the United States. Image after image of Thomas with officials from all over the world. Pictures of me at events in Central with captions about our fanatical ways. My image plastered all over next to the orchid symbol, smiling like a woman who is knowingly part of a system oppressing its people.

"What do you know about me? Do you know the people in my world?"

"Your personal world?"

"Yes."

He drew in a deep breath. "I know that you're Thomas's wife and were in a high level tier in the Nation. As far as the people you escaped with, we know they're part of the Resistance, but what they actually know or believe about the Nation is unclear. Because of the firewalls and strict information pipeline, even with my job in the Nation, it's hard to tell who inside these borders knows about the United States. And for those that know what, if any, resources they may have to overthrow the Nation."

"They know about the Sanctuary States, but I think that's it."

"What I am telling you is the truth, Olivia. I promise. I have no reason to lie to you because my father says we need you."

"You need *me*? Is that why you're here? To add me to your evil plans and overthrow the Nation?" I joked.

"Yes."

"You're serious?"

"Yes."

"And you're hoping that somehow I have–"

"Information to help us do just that, maybe more."

"Information about Thomas?"

"Him. Jeffrey. Valentin. You've lived here for a long time—between you, and hopefully others in the Resistance, we can gain a foothold against the Nation and dismantle it once and for all. But we also think that there's something specific about you that he needs."

"What do you mean?"

"Honestly, we think you may have some genetic link to what he and the Nation need for whatever they've been working on since the beginning."

"What are you talking about? Do you know about the files that were released?"

"Yes, and they helped give us a better picture of what Thomas is doing."

"And that is?"

"We're pretty sure he's been trying to manipulate genes within the Nation based on genetic viability. You, for example, were never administered the vaccine that caused thousands of women to become sterile. That, and whatever genetic abilities you already had, make you valuable to him and the Nation. Thomas selected you and this is going to sound terrible, to breed with, because of those reasons. It looks like the Nation has been experimenting with genetic manipulation since before the pandemic."

Was my value to Thomas always about some long term plans he and Jeffrey had for genetic manipulation?

I thought about what Ethan had told me the night in the Central Center about Thomas and Jeffrey. How Jeffrey had kidnapped Thomas as a teenager, because he was young and viable for the virus experiments Jeffrey was running. Instead of Thomas becoming a subject, he became Jeffrey's apprentice. What was the depth of darkness that ran through Thomas and Jeffrey for all these years? There was no other option for me except to believe what my mother had told me. Kai was now offering more pieces to the puzzle too. A puzzle that I somehow fit in without even knowing about it.

"Thomas helped Jeffrey with virus experiments before the Nation took over." I said.

"He helped with vaccines too." Kai said.

"Why now?"

"What do you mean?"

"Why is the U.S. going for the Nation now?"

"It's not a pretty answer, just so you know that."

"Are things ever pretty when so much ugly is involved?"

"My father is the reason this is happening now. He wants a presidential endorsement, and he made some deals behind closed doors. If he can get the Nation dismantled, the party will endorse him and he will essentially have a free ride all the way to the White House."

Of course. Another man slithering into another seated position of power. It didn't matter what name we were under—the Nation, the United States, the Resistance—we were all hostages to someone else's ambition.

My eyes narrowed, and for a moment I wondered if I was being told yet another set of lies. Pieces of what Kai said made sense, but the theatrics the Nation employed in order to stay in power didn't. Sitting before me was the son of a man who wanted one of the highest positions of power in the world, and it just didn't seem real.

"If what you're saying is actually true, what do you get out of this?"

He smiled. "I was waiting for you to ask." He shifted in his seat and leaned forward. "I get my freedom."

"Freedom from what?"

"Not what, who."

"Who do you get freedom from?"

"My father. If I can get him the information he wants, I can finally leave and be who I want to be." A boyish crooked line raised in the right side of his mouth, and he looked off in the distance at what appeared to be some level of hope.

"Why can't you leave now?"

"Let's just say, every move of my life has been planned, orchestrated, or puppeteered by my father. Add his highly public profile to the mix, and I had no chance to be anything but what he wanted–what his constituents expected of the perfect American family. When I give him what he wants, I get to leave it all behind. Go wherever I want. Be whoever I want. Do whatever I want. Disappear even. No strings attached."

It didn't matter who we were or how much power and influence we or our families, or even our nations had, we all answered to someone other than ourselves. I'd answered to my parents growing up. Then Ethan. Then Thomas. The Nation. Children. Career and my sister. The ghost of my father. And now the Resistance.

Today, I sat across from a man I didn't know, and saw that he answered to his own Ethans, Thomases, and ghosts too. We were all bound to someone else's tether. A push and pull until we let go of the rope around our wrists. Rope that leaves burn marks visible to the trained eye, yet ignored by the blindness we were taught to embody. I looked at Kai's wrists, and they were like mine. Frayed from years of being pulled by someone else. I looked down at mine, invisible scars that were slowly disappearing, as I continued to untie the tether to Thomas and the Nation. Untie the Olivia from before from the Olivia after. Untether the Olivia from Ethan, and anyone else who ever tried to orbit my world, tugging at my edges, daring to control me.

Kai wanted the same thing, and though only a few steps behind me, it felt like the chaos that disrupted both our lives had aligned us–two people now standing on the same sidewalk, pushing back against everything that had once led us here, trying to walk away from the power that once ruled us.

"I need to get cleaned up, but if you want to go back to your room, I can give you access."

I had to tell Samara about him and see if she had ever heard of Kai's father, or what was really happening outside this place. I wondered if I could somehow use him to get me that flash drive. If he has all this power as a tier-four, and a spy for the United States, surely he could pull some strings.

"Would you be able to sneak me out of here?"

His eyes narrowed and the corners of his lips tucked up. "You're quite unexpected, Olivia. We all assumed a lot about you–from your story–that you were..."

"Weak? Naïve? Dumb?"

He shifted uncomfortably. "That's not exactly–"

"I would have thought the same thing, too. And sometimes I wonder about it myself. How did I not know? There were signs everywhere, I just refused to read them. Besides, the story I was reading wouldn't let me put it down. I had to stay on script. And I wonder if a small part of me–the part that helped me survive him–knew, and kept me in line."

"That sounds like you don't think you had a choice in what you did."

"I didn't have a choice, and if you read everything about me, you know that too."

He shrugged his shoulders. "I think you did have a choice, Olivia, but you just didn't take it. You didn't want to, because everything around you was easier. Looking away is easier than seeing the car accident in front of you."

"You have no idea what you're talking about."

"Please don't take this the wrong way. I'm just saying that if you paint yourself as this victim of a story that you think you had no say in, then you will be a victim. Look at where you are now. You're in a center, sleeping with citizens and trying to dismantle one of the strongest groups the United States has ever seen. You're not a victim though, right? Olivia, you are the survivor."

A survivor—was this true? Kai had read the same story I had, and through all of this we came to different conclusions about who I was. Had I adopted this victim mentality as a way to make sense of the chaos that I lived in? Had I stayed there too long, letting my agency be stripped over and over again until it just became a habit? Did I need to move from victim to survivor—and if yes, what would that look like?

He got up and leaned against the bathroom door. "You're rewriting it all now anyway. Think about it. Would the Olivia from a few months ago think about taking down the Nation? Was she even capable of that then? No, she wasn't. She let herself be a victim, and she lived in that cycle of victimhood that chained people to the floor. You've started to undo those chains, Olivia. And from what we know about you, you're more than capable of doing more. I pity anyone who gets in your way."

I didn't know what to say.

He smiled. I half-heartedly shifted my mouth in return.

"I won't be long. I can definitely sneak you out of here too, but I want to know what for. Let me shower, and then we'll come up with a plan." He turned into the bathroom, closing the door behind him.

19

OLIVIA

I ate what little food was in the refrigerator while waiting for Kai to finish showering. He came out of the bedroom in workout shorts and no shirt, his body catching me off guard. I drew in a sharp breath before looking away.

He ran his fingers through his dark hair and grabbed his HoloTab before sitting on the couch. "Talk to me about sneaking out of the Center. What's that about?"

"I need to get to my house, in West Borough. I was going to try and sneak out on my own, but if you have all this tech I was thinking it might be better to have your help."

"What's in the house?"

Could I trust this man with something as important as this? He was working against the Nation with the U.S., but did that mean his intentions were altruistic and aligned with mine?

"There's a flash drive. I need to take it back to the Resistance."

"What's on it?"

"I'm not sure, but it has something to do with the genetic program Thomas wants off the servers."

"That doesn't give me much to go on, Olivia. Do you know

what kind of files are on there? What about the genetics program we would find?"

"I don't know."

"Well, that's not a lot for me to go on, Olivia."

"There it is. The 'what's in it for me' mentality. Never mind, I'll figure it out on my own." I snapped.

"No, wait, Olivia. You need to understand that I am here to get information to help remove the Nation from power. I can't just go on a wild goose chase because you need to get something from your house. You don't even know what's on the drive, so why should we go?"

"Thomas. I overheard a citizen on the phone with Thomas. They were discussing data transfers and then they said 'genetics program'. Thomas wanted it all to be removed from the main Nation system and put on a flash drive that would be stored in a safe at my house."

"Why your place?"

"I don't know. He doesn't have the kids there, so maybe it's just less obvious."

Kai pursed his lips and furrowed his brows. "Who was the citizen?"

"A man named Victor Lope."

Kai's eyes widened. "I'll take you to get that flash drive. If it was Victor Lope, then there has to be something valuable on it. Lope is one of the lower-level Nation thugs we've been watching for years. He's been involved in a ton of illegal activity, but since he's not a U.S. citizen we can't do anything about it." Kai turned to his HoloTab, tapped a few times on the screen, then returned to me. "When is the drop going to take place?"

"It either happened last night, or it's happening today. I was with the Lopes the day before you selected me. He said he would have the information transferred, and then take it to my house and drop it off. It's in the safe and I know the code."

"We should go tonight then, after sunset, just to be sure it's there. It will give me and my team more time to plan."

"How will that work exactly?" I asked.

"Well...again, the perks of being a tier-four male. At least here, I can take you off-site. Rose Bay likes to think of it as a test drive in a way."

Of course Kai has that power. People with money–real money–live on the other side of an invisible line, where permission isn't needed. They get to buy silence, rewrite truth, and sleep soundly, while everyone else struggles to survive. Was Kai one of the elite men that manipulated the system too? Or was he someone who used the system other men created to carve out his own freedom–someone living on the other side of the line only because he was forced to, until he could finally join the rest of us?

"What does that mean?" I was disgusted with the way he said it, like I was a car to be test driven.

"Exactly what it sounds like. My status allows me to take attendants off-site. I just have to let Girly know."

"Why would anyone want to take an attendant off site?"

Kai looked at me like I was dumb. "Really, Olivia?"

"Yeah, wouldn't wives or husbands find out if their partner was parading around an attendant in front of everyone else?"

"Most husbands and wives at this level have multiple homes and live double lives. They pay for the privilege of appearing married in the face of the Nation, while avoiding it behind closed doors. They show everyone the perfect family because it helps support the cause. It helps sustain the lie that marriage is one of the best choices a citizen can make. Thomas, Jeffrey, Valentin, they all do the same thing."

"Not Thomas," I said defensively, but I couldn't place why. "He was against infidelity. He never took his Challenge Pass. He wouldn't do that to me, or the children. He believes in this life more than anyone I know."

"Okay, Olivia," Kai's expression softened. "It doesn't matter anyway, let's focus on tonight. I can get the cameras turned off temporarily in your neighborhood without anyone noticing, but you'd have to work fast. Are you sure he and the children aren't there?"

"Positive. When we tried to rescue them a few weeks ago, we found out he's holding them somewhere else."

Kai was mulling something over in his mind, but I couldn't tell what. "After you get the flash drive, we may be able to help you locate the children. It's a long shot, but it could work."

"How?" My voice caught, sharper than I meant.

"Not something for right now. Let's focus on getting the flash drive first."

He knew more than he was letting on, but I needed him to get me out of here tonight, so I let it go–for now. We all had our games to play, and if Kai wanted to join mine, I would allow it.

"I need to go back to my room, check in on an attendant, and get some different clothes. Should I plan on being back by dinner? Would that look less suspicious, in case anyone is watching you?"

"You'll be fine. I can set the parameters to have you be out until six, then come back here, do dinner, then sneak you out."

"Can you just take me, or anyone else, out of here at any time?"

"Yes. Among other perks. The main issue with you is your identity. You're Sarah King in here, and I assume you have someone on the tech side manipulating facial recognition software. Cameras all over this city, and West Borough, would be able to identify you immediately, though. My team can manipulate the cameras for a little bit, but too much makes it obvious, and I'd rather save most of that for another time. I think the best thing we can do is cover your face as much as possible, and then have you lie down in the back of the car until we reach the neighborhood. The windows are dark tinted for my privacy, and the only time you'd end up on cameras before West Borough would be right outside your house and I'll take care of that."

I thought of Morgan, Samara, and my plan to leave on my own. "I have a hoodie, some sunglasses, and I can wear my hair down, covering as much as possible."

"I'll see if I can get anything else from the girls downstairs. Okay, so you're going back to your room, getting ready, checking in on your friend. I am going to schmooze with some folks in the bar–"

"There's a bar here?"

"Yep."

"Let me guess, you go every time?"

"Yep. The Director likes to check in, and I like to find out new intel from his time with Thomas."

My body constricted at the sound of 'Director' and 'Thomas'. The shifting moments between presence and disconnection were taking their toll. Still, I had to compartmentalize until I brought my children home. I drew in a breath. *I'm getting out. I'm going to get my children. I'm going to take Thomas and the Nation down.*

"You okay?" Kai pulled me back to the present.

"Yeah. It's just a lot still."

"I can only imagine." Kai placed his hand on mine and a spark shot through me like a match was about to be lit. I pulled away.

Kai's eyes flicked down, and he withdrew his hand. "Sorry, I didn't mean to touch you."

"It's fine. I'm just–it's fine. I'm going to head back to my room. I will see you later tonight."

"Okay, Olivia. See you soon."

"See you soon."

When I reached the attendant's floor, I went straight to Samara's room. Knocking softly, I pushed the door open. She sat in a chair by the window, a light blanket wrapped around her shoulders, oblivious to my presence.

"Samara?"

She turned, her eyes like ghosts as they met mine. "Hi."

"Hey. How are you doing?"

"Fine." Her voice was quiet. "How was last night?"

"Good, actually. That's why I'm here. He gave me a break to come down here."

"You're staying with him another night? And with a break? That's highly unusual, even at Central." She snapped back into the Samara I remembered from before–in charge, focused, calculating.

"The citizen I'm with is going to help me leave tonight to get the flash drive and, I think, get me into the data system."

"And you trust this man because...?"

Samara had a point. I'd just met Kai and was ready to trust him with something as important as what she and I were doing. "He's our only option right now and I have full access to him when I'm in the room. He told me a few things that I want to look into when we get out of here, but, from what I can tell, he seems legitimate."

"Does he know who you are?"

"Yes."

"Olivia! How could you tell him and put the entire mission, the team, at risk?" Samara shot up from her chair, the blanket slipping from her shoulders.

"I didn't tell him, Samara. He figured it out, and then tested my DNA."

"How would a regular citizen be able to test DNA in a Challenge Center? That doesn't make any sense. Only people who are high up, or work for the Nation, can do that." She connected the dots. "What tier is he?"

"Tier-four, like us."

Her head tilted, "Why is he here, Olivia?" Her quick mind was an asset to me.

I leaned in and whispered, "He's here trying to get information to take the Nation down, just like us. He, and the people he works with, have been looking for me."

"Why, Olivia? This sounds like you're being lured int-"

"I know what you think, but you're wrong," I cut in quickly. "They need me to help them and I need him to help me. I'm not being lured into anything."

"You're kidding, right?"

"No." I stood firm.

"So, you're telling me that this man just happened to be here, at the same time as us? And was also looking specifically for you–the Director's wife–at a Center? And now he's going to help you, an attendant, out of a center, to get a flash drive. Olivia, use your head here. This can't be true. Think about it."

She was right. How could all of this be falling into place so easily? The odds of all of this to be happening at the same time, in a random place like Rose Bay, seemed off.

"Liv, do you think it might be that you want so badly to be back with the kids and out of here, that you're willing to believe him? That you're not seeing that maybe this is some trap being set for you, by Thomas? Think about it. Why is this mysterious flash drive we need at *your* house? Why would Thomas just happen to be on the phone with...that man...when we were there? It's too easy, Olivia."

"Too easy, Samara? We've been in here for weeks with nothing. No information. No leads. Nothing. This is one of the first things we get, and you're saying be cautious about it? This is exactly why we're here, so what if it seems to be falling into place too easily? So what if this guy that I just met says he wants the same things as us? We are here to find *him*. Someone to help us get my kids, and take the Nation down." I continued to raise my voice, "I know what I'm doing, Samara. I'm not going to be a victim anymore. This is right. I can feel it. Kai feels right, and I believe him."

"You also believed Thomas for ten years."

The sting from Samara's words lit a fire in me.

"How dare you use that against me now! I thought you were my friend–that we were in this together. Now you're weaponizing my past against me because I'm choosing to trust this person?"

"It's just...you haven't had the best judgment. There's so much on the line, and if you get caught, we can't do anything."

"So much on the line for who, Sam? You? Ethan? The Resistance? Remember, it's my life and my children's lives on the line. You and the rest of them will still survive whether or not this works. You still get your wife and your children. You still get your little war. I'm the one taking a risk here. And I believe it's right."

Samara shifted, pulling her shoulders back and sticking her chin out toward me. Her voice softened, cooling the fire between us. "Ask more questions, Olivia. And be careful with him. There's something about this I don't like for the Resistance, and for *you*." She walked over, opening the door. "When will you be back?"

"Tonight, after I get the flash drive, then back to my room tomorrow."

"Remember, don't trust anyone–especially someone you don't even know. He definitely hasn't told you everything, including the real reason he's here. What's his name? Did he even give you his real name?"

"Yes, he did. Kai Acosta."

A flicker of knowing crossed her eyes–brief, uncertain–but I couldn't be sure if she knew who he was, or if I was just reading too much into it.

"If I'm not back by tomorrow morning, let Morgan and the compound know."

Samara looked worried. "I will, but let's make sure that doesn't happen, okay?"

She put her hand on my arm, but we didn't hug. I left her room and headed to mine. The usual energy on the attendants' floor was in full force, and if you didn't know what this place really was, you might think it was totally normal. In some ways, it could have been mistaken for an adult summer camp: friends gathered around the television watching Nation-approved shows before their shift began, two people cooking in one of the small shared kitchens, and a woman curled up in a blanket by the long wall of windows with a book in her hands. But it wasn't a summer camp, or anything like it. The people who wandered these halls were still trying to make sense of the traumas they endured inflicted by both the Nation and its high level citizens. They coped however they could, escaping into the same distractions that people outside these walls relied on. The difference was that those on the outside didn't always need to escape, because they had the freedom to truly live. In here, attendants remained bound, surviving under the Nation's grip until their service, or their time in this world, was done.

When I arrived back in Kai's room, I found him standing at the island with a pile of papers.

"What are those?" I asked, as I stood across the island.

"Old maps of the tunnel systems in Central."

"Why are you looking at those?"

"I like to be prepared for anything. Finding you has given me new hope that we can finally take back Northern California. I was just looking through these in case they prove useful."

"I've been through that part." I pointed to the connection before the center and what used to be Old Sacramento.

"Well, good–you're already familiar with them if it needs to happen again."

"Not familiar at all. Just walked through that section on my way to a required massage, during my Challenge Pass stay."

"Required?"

"Yeah, Thomas had it orchestrated, I guess."

"Well, wasn't that just the worst thing ever?" He laughed.

"I guess you could say that, since I didn't know anything about him or my life at that point."

"That had to be quite a shock for you."

"Yeah it was." I picked up the old parchment paper. "We won't need these in West Borough. I will be in and out."

"Like I said, I like to be prepared for everything, but I also have a feeling that Thomas and the other leaders use these tunnels. I told my father I think they're connected to different buildings all over the capital, but there has to be a bunker somewhere too–we just haven't found it yet. When you lived with him, did he ever talk about being unavailable by phone or anything like that? Or did you ever go underground with him somewhere?"

I paused as I thought back to our ten years. "No, I was only at his office and the kids' school. We had fundraising events, galas–you know the norm for someone who was high up in his office–but that's about it."

"And you never suspected anything?"

"No. Never. There were moments I felt it...like a small tug inside my mind whenever he told me stories about where he'd been or why I couldn't reach him at the office. He was just so good at having answers without even thinking about it–looking back, it's as if he rehearsed it all. I would ask questions, he would give answers, and then place something shiny in front of me, or tell me something horrific that had happened to someone we knew. Thomas always knew how to pull me back to our world, *his* world."

"Sounds like my father. He has that way about him too. He commands everyone around him, making us all forget where we were before and where we wanted to go. It's always about him and the next thing he wants. They're good at distracting everyone around them to get what they want."

"What do you mean?"

"People like Thomas. People like my father. They're great illusionists. When people are distracted, they're easier to manipulate, to control." He paused and his tone shifted. "You know, when I was a kid...I hated magic."

"Magic? Like wizards and witches?"

Kai laughed. "No, like magic shows. You know, the ones in Vegas or the hustlers on the streets?"

"I never went to Las Vegas before I was married, and Thomas refused to allow us to go there once we were married."

"Gotcha. Well, my father loved to go to shows in DC, Vegas, anywhere we traveled. It was as if he was studying them and learning their misdirections so he could enact them upon everyone else. The magicians would draw our eyes to one side of the stage while the real trick was happening somewhere else. Their tricks weren't what they showed you, but really, what they hid. My father, he wants the highest office in the country and performs in all the right ways, says the right things, smiles at the right times. In reality, it's all happening backstage, in rooms with seedy people who want their piece of power too. While we watch them smile and say the right things, they're rewriting laws and sending people into wars that no one will ever talk about. While we're focused on the chaos of the calculated drama, they're seizing more power and making their circle that much smaller, tighter, keeping others out. While we're busy watching them reveal the trick, or waving to us, we're never noticing that our pockets are now empty." Kai leaned over the island and folded his hands together. "One of the best tricks he ever pulled was convincing me to focus on his words rather than his hands. And now, I'm part of that misdirection too."

"What do you mean?" My heart raced slightly wondering if

I had just walked back into another web of lies that I wouldn't be able to find myself out of.

"This. Me being here. Looking for you. You're a magician's assistant–the one who is required to make the trick happen. Without you, his illusion will never work and I will never be free."

I stood, observing Kai's demeanor. He was part of the show, just like I was, enhancing the performance and making their act more believable. We contorted our bodies, from inside the illusion, to make it work for someone other than ourselves. We stood in this in-between space waiting for it to become real, but it never would. For years, I had been on Thomas's playbill. For years, I had unknowingly been part of his trick; his assistant to the countless people who committed their lives to the Nation. But I wouldn't do that any longer. I was breaking free, stepping off the stage to start my own show.

I would rescue the children, then set fire to his stage, and the Nation's, burning it all to the ground. A part of me felt Kai was at this precipice too, no longer wanting to be part of his father's tricks. He felt trustworthy because of the truth he just spoke; maybe still lost, like me, in some ways, but perhaps the most genuine person in my world right now. I would still need to keep my guard up, but something about Kai Acosta felt right to me–as if we were reflections of the same story, that called for a better ending.

"When I get the flash drive, how will I be able to access it?" I changed the subject.

"My HoloTab will be able to get a good amount of the information. We can always see about getting my computer too, if we need it. But I'm guessing the tablet will be enough."

"Where's your computer?"

"A safe house in Central."

"Where in Central?"

"That's classified, Ms. Embers." A glint of charm sparkled in his eye.

"Whatever, *Mr. Acosta.*" I paused to wonder how many times Kai Acosta and I had unknowingly crossed paths over the years he'd been working for the United States while living as a citizen in the Nation. Had Thomas and I been at the same parties as him? Had we sat in the same cafe on opposite sides of the room, taking in Nation propaganda on the 24-hour news feeds? The world felt smaller to me, and even though we had just met, something tied us together more than we would probably ever understand. I was here to help him, just as much as he was here to help me.

20

OLIVIA

During dinner Kai and I talked through the plan and how I'd get in and out of the house unnoticed. We'd leave Rose Bay and drive to my neighborhood, where he'd drop me off nearby. I would slip into the house while he stayed out of sight at the children's favorite park, a giant pirate ship with musical instruments and a swaying flag they loved in summer. When I was done, I'd meet him there, and we would head back to Rose Bay to access the flash drive, hopefully opening doors that would let the Resistance and me get my children back.

"How am I going to get out?"

"You'll just walk out with me once I check you out at the front desk."

"Check me out, like I'm a library book?"

"Basically, yeah. You're the property of the Nation, remember?"

I couldn't imagine living like this. How desperate did people have to be to commit to this sort of life? What kind of system did we live in where people felt they had to sacrifice their bodies and independence just to survive? What about the people who were here unwillingly? What power would they ever hold, if they were ever to get out? How could I have ever been part of this system?

"You okay?"

"Yeah."

"Here, put these on. Figured you wanted a pair that actually matches your tier status better than whatever you had in your room." He smiled as he handed me a pair of Chanel cream-and-black sunglasses. We left his room and took the elevator down to the first floor.

"How did you get these?"

"Please, have you not learned anything in the last 24 hours? I can get *whatever* I want, *whenever* I want." His arrogance was surprisingly charming to me.

"Thank you. I had a pair similar to these years ago."

"I know." His smile was caught in the reflection of the elevator doors and I smiled back, placing the Chanel glasses on my face and pulling the hoodie over my head.

Once on the main floor, we walked into the lobby where Girly stood behind her desk.

"Hello Mr. Acosta. I see you are heading out for a little bit. Don't you just look far too good for that car you drive." Girly's voice was honey-soaked. Was she flirting with Kai?

"Oh, Girly, you know I only look like this for you. I know you like me in the heather gray." Was Kai flirting with Girly?

I stood back and watched the exchange. It felt strange yet familiar–the way attendants seemed to exist in spaces the wealthy don't even notice. But Kai noticed. Was it sincerity, or just part of the bigger game he was playing?

"Mr. Acosta, what would your wife say if she knew you were wearing Heather Gray for me?"

"What she doesn't know, won't hurt her." He winked, and my stomach turned. "Speaking of never knowing...I'd like to take 844 out for a test-run."

"Does the Director know?"

"Of course. I told him today at the bar. He said it should be in my file, and that there may be a possibility of purchasing her too."

"Well, she's new...he agreed to that?" Girly raised her eyebrows.

"Girly, you know how it goes...what Mr. Acosta wants, Mr. Acosta gets."

I choked, and both Girly and Kai looked at me.

"Are you okay, my dear?" She asked.

"Yes, sorry. Just a dry throat."

"Here, have a mint." Girly handed me a mint, I popped it in my mouth and started walking away from the desk.

"Thanks Girly! See you soon!" Kai waved to her, following behind me at first before quickening his pace to grab my hand and lead us to his all-black luxury BMW waiting outside the private entrance.

"Electric model?" I asked.

"Of course, but with one of the new turbo engines. I have to play the part, right?"

"Such a hard life." I smirked and slid into the back, hiding myself from view, but I was not going to spend the whole ride to Central laying down. "Um, what was that?"

"What was what?"

"You were totally flirting with Girly."

"Oh, that. Yeah. Do you know nothing about diplomacy?" He laughed, then looked at me. "So, you're not going to lay down?"

"Nope. The tinting seems just fine."

Kai shook his head, which told me that if it was really serious, he would have made me stay completely out of view. I kept my hoodie and sunglasses on as Kai drove us out of Rose Bay.

"How often were you in Central?" I shifted the air conditioner vent in the center console.

"A lot, actually. I couldn't stay in Rose Bay all the time. I'd be in Central maybe once or twice a month when I wasn't traveling. I upgraded my status to Rose Bay, so if I want more passes each month, I just book them. I don't want to draw too much attention to myself or what I am doing, so I stay in Central at my safe house. Every so often, I'd go to the parties the Nation threw to stay connected and make it look like I was a good citizen."

"I bet we were at the same parties."

"I'm sure we were."

"Did you ever attend the fundraisers for the hospital?"

"Yep. I always bought a table and filled it with Nation friends." He said sarcastically.

"We had a table too. Thomas insisted on the ones up front saying that's where the important people sat."

"Didn't you get an award one year?"

Had he been at the banquet where I received recognition for nursing?

"You were there?"

"Yeah, pretty sure. I think it's the first time I told my dad we needed to start paying attention to you, too. He thinks you're in on everything, but after the bombing, he's slowly coming around."

"In on everything?" I blinked.

"Yeah, like you're behind the wheels too. Not just Thomas. If you think about it, your job is the perfect cover because it's a noble profession. No one would suspect a nurse and a lab assistant were running one of the most corrupt sects in the world."

"Is that what people think about me? That I'm a bad person?" My chest tightened as the words left me.

"Some, yes. Others just think you're one of those wives who had a job only to make it look like she was doing something, even though she didn't really need one, you know?"

"Do people...like a lot of people, know who I am?"

"Yes, Olivia. The entire country knows who you are."

"How?"

"The tabloids, mostly. News Stations that feed on the sensationalism of the Nation. The irony of it all is, you could have simply walked across the Nevada state line, and been bombarded like a movie star, because your face is everywhere."

How could this be? My life, my little life with my children had been on display over the last ten years because of a man I married? It felt similar to when I found out that Ethan had been watching footage of my life. How could someone have no power over whether or not they wanted to be known by the masses? I thought about what Kai said and how if I'd just walked across the state line I could have been free from the Nation.

"Do they know about my children?"

"Yes. There are still no laws protecting famous children from the media in the United States. My father says he wants to try and push one forward, but with him, you never know."

"Ethan?"

"There are fan sites for Ethan."

"Fan sites? Why?"

"Well...and I say this as not me, Kai Acosta....he's hot. They love that whole rebel-with-a-cause and wounded-soul vibe. It also helps that he isn't particular about what gender he sleeps with. His ratings are pretty high on the threads."

I couldn't believe it. "How do they even know any of this? If it's just tabloids and news? It's not like they're watching us like a television show, right?"

"Do you remember the royal family?"

"Yes."

"They don't have a reality television show, but yet they were, and still are, everywhere. It's what we do. We latch on to other lives that seem more glamorous, or more of a train wreck, than ours. People think they know the King and Queen, but they don't. They never will, but that doesn't stop them from becoming emotionally invested in their lives. It's hard for anyone, even me, to ever be fully focused on my life and not wonder about the lives of the rich and famous."

"But you are rich and famous, right?"

"My father is. I don't want that life. Not anymore."

A My Chemical Romance song came on Kai's playlist and he turned the volume up, drowning us out. As more songs came on, Kai sang horribly off key, offering no more conversation as we pulled into my West Borough neighborhood. Streets lined with full-leafed trees held memories of my family, made only weeks earlier. Memories I would never make with my family again because this was no longer my home. No longer my family. No longer me.

We circled around the last corner until my court came into view. Red lights still illuminated the front of each house. Kai drove past, stopping in front of the pirate ship park. He then pulled out his HoloTab, and with a few swipes, the red lights across the area disappeared.

"Remember the plan, okay? Get in, find the flash drive, and get back here. We have about thirty minutes or so before any alerts will go off with the cameras. My team is running a loop for us, but if there's an emergency, or a citizen calls their security company because the cameras are acting funny, we have to go. Here, give me your wrist."

"Why?"

"So I can sync it to my tablet and track you."

"You can track chips on your HoloTab?"

"Yes."

"Why didn't you tell me? We could have found my kids." My frustration bubbling up before I could rein it in.

"It's not that easy. I can sync them if they're near me, or if I have their identifier code. I don't have that for your children. I tried to get some information earlier today when I was downstairs. I asked the Director if I could get the access code for an attendant from awhile back. He said that, since the bombing, they've locked down all access. I'd only be able to find the kids if we had an idea of where they were in the first place."

He was telling me the truth.

"Let's hope I find something in the house to help us narrow that down."

"In and out–got it?"

"Yes, sir!" I laughed and saluted him, which he did not find funny at all.

Once on my street, I went around the back of the house and entered the code on the back door. Inside, my home welcomed me back with the soft glow from sunset–a daily reminder in the past that one more day with Thomas was behind me. The last time I was here, Lucas was nestled in the corner of the kitchen, his hands sticky with maple syrup. I could still smell it as I breathed in those final moments before saying goodbye, and Penny ushered him to school. The house stood still–a witness to a past long gone. Her walls still hummed with echoes of laughter, the floors worn by footsteps that had since walked away. She held the ghosts of holiday mornings, whispered arguments behind closed doors, and quiet reconciliations with fingers crossed behind backs. Her rooms knew the weight of what was once shared, and what had to be eventually shattered.

My fingers traced along the walls as I walked through the hallway to Lucas's room. The perfectly painted white cabinets, with their black hardware, stood out in the dappled light from the dusty shuttered window. The floors led me to the taupe carpet, layered with blues and dark furniture–Thomas's choice, because it was more masculine than the white I wanted. Stuffed animals scattered across his bed. His worn out teddy bear, from his first hospital stay years earlier, sat next to his favorite book,

Charlie and the Chocolate Factory. I picked them both up and walked into Rose's room.

Soft pinks and deep-plum peony wall art now covered the room that had once been adorned with princess decor from her childhood. She wanted to redo her room last summer, so we took down all of the 'baby princess stuff', as she called it. Thomas had custom decals made from a boutique in Central, sparing no expense. He didn't care. 'Anything for my little girl,' he touted anytime she asked for something more. Her Tiffany-blue jewelry box sat alone on her dresser. I opened it. Inside, the pearl earrings my mother had given her for her birthday lay like a left-behind treasure. As the only granddaughter my mother would ever have, it was important to pass them down to Rose. "Heirloom jewelry is important to keep families and their history together," she'd said when I argued Rose didn't need something like that at her age. I pulled them out and placed them in my pocket.

My chest felt heavy and my house knew. I was done looking at a childhood that no longer existed for my children. A piece of motherhood lost to the Nation. I left Rose's room, pearls in my pocket, a teddy bear and a book in my hand.

The main room came into view. The shelves held tight to the books and photos of our past. A past enshrouded in a plastic coating that allowed me to breathe through tiny slits in the sealed edges. The HoloPic frame still rotated images of the children, their smiles as real as the lingering tears in my eyes—but no one would ever know except me. I was no longer the Olivia that stood on those shelves, the haunted version of myself that I could see so clearly now. I remembered the words he'd said to me before each photo, or the pull I felt to Ethan when it was Thomas standing next to me. I flipped the frames face-down, hiding my lost world from myself. Wiping the tears from my face, I remembered the time constraints I was under.

I walked down the opposite hallway to our room, but it

wasn't our room anymore. It smelled different–like perfume I had never worn–unlike the fresh lemon Thomas insisted on diffusing in the house during the spring and summer months. What woman was that? Penny, maybe? She never smelled like that when I was around.

"Turn low lights on," I ordered and she listened, letting me see a montage of memories spent in the intimate space that caged me for ten years. The soft orange illuminated a perfectly made bed covered in black and white floral fabric, and crisp white accent pillows. Thomas wanted the room to look like a home out of the magazines his mother had on her coffee table, before she succumbed to her own grief. He spared no expense when directing me in what to buy, and our home thanked us for it. The fiddle-leaf fig I'd ordered for his birthday slumped beside the bed, its leaves withered and drooping like a heavy heart. It was small when I bought it and had grown over six-feet-tall by the day I left for the Challenge Center–another reminder of the delicate dance we lived in this house of lies.

I turned to the walk-in closet. My shoes from the last day sat untouched next to a large box. And it was there, carefully placed for me to find, vacuumsealed against the world I'd surrounded myself with for ten years.

My wedding dress, preserved in a box I never asked for.

I tore open the box and pulled out my dress. Soft cream-colored satin shimmered with embroidered flowers in champagne, brown, and gold. I clawed at the seal and released it from its plastic cage.

My hands set softly on the smooth satin fabric. It was cool to the touch, frozen in time, as if waiting for me to thaw it with my warm hands. I pulled the bodice out first, then the train, until the softly-colored fabric took up the space on my closet floor. I thumbed it first, then rubbed my hands against the smooth fabric, remembering how it felt against my hands when

I walked down the aisle pregnant with our child before I became his.

I undressed. My body slid effortlessly into it. Between the baby weight I'd lost over the years and my consistent training the last several weeks, the dress hung languidly on my frame. It felt as heavy as the first day I tried it on, in the high-end boutique Thomas had reserved for my sister, my mother, and me. Expensive champagne from his favorite winery bubbled freely in crystal modern flutes held precariously in my hand. I sipped at the bubbles, forcing my nerves to surrender to the liquid escape.

I gathered the wedding dress fabric near the pockets and lifted the graveyard skirt. I walked down the hallway into the living room, sitting idly in the middle of the mausoleum of my life. My eyes wandered, my eyelids heavy in an effort to numb the reality before me. Pictures and books of a time that never belonged to me. A life that never belonged in my hands. A life he controlled without me ever knowing it. Each picture that lay on the shelf, a falsely crafted chapter of a book that he wrote. Smiles, to the untrained eye, looked picture perfect–only I could see the fissures through the glass. The crease in my lip, the squinted eye, the tilt of my head, the tentative bent leg–all tells of a woman trapped by a life that was slowly killing her.

How had I given him that much power? His words were like bars to the cage he kept me in. The slot machine patterns of love kept me tethered to him. Kept me tentatively believing we could be the ideal Nation marriage. Once I got pregnant with Rose, I knew there was no other option but to marry Thomas. I told myself we could be the ideal Nation family. That we would be the perfect image of love they wanted to showcase. Even if I struggled to love Thomas, Ethan was gone, and I had no choice. Thomas said he loved me, and I made it work. I took part in the marriage system. I was the system.

But he was clear on the tarmac, the last night I saw him. He never loved me, it turned out. He could never love me. I was a means to an end, and my life with him was nothing more than a transaction. He got his children, the money, this house–and he took away my chance at a real life with Ethan.

It was never me he wanted.

Just the idea of me.

The idea of what I could give him. What he could have in the Nation. What the Nation would see him as, and then give him in return.

Financially stable.

Attentive father.

Supportive husband.

"But everyone likes Thomas," my girlfriends would say whenever I shared hiccups in our marriage. Moments when his devotion wouldn't feel like devotion at all. Moments when my own sense of self, my sanity, my very way of being was called into question. The Maldives. The drugging. The carefully calculated steps he made every day to control me with his words, his money, his strength. I was never safe, and wondered if I would ever be safe again.

I looked at the end table next to the couch. A pair of Rose's scissors lay next to long tangled strings meant for friendship bracelets. Another moment frozen in time, but this time, it was her tangled mess, or more likely, something Lucas had done that she was trying to undo. I picked up the pile and placed it on my lap, mindlessly undoing the threaded chaos. My fingers pulled and untied string by string until four separate colors sat idly on the ivory sheen dress.

I took one color each, replacing the pile on the end table, and began knotting them together in Rose's go-to pattern. After a few moments, a friendship bracelet found itself arranged in a kaleidoscope of sunset colors. I tied the end off and reached for the scissors, cutting the excess string.

I set the scissors in my lap, staring at the metal against the smooth fabric. As if guided by someone else, my fingers grasped the handle, and the cool blades snaked into the expensive bridal fabric. The slicing reminded me of Ethan's mother in the sewing room of their house. That crisp sound of fabric being separated from its original shape, with the purpose of being made into something new.

In a frenzy, I cut more sections of the dress, set the scissors down, and clawed at the slits, pulling the fabric apart–releasing it from its wedding cage. Cool blades found themselves tearing through embroidered silver, taupe, and gold flowers, strings falling like feathers onto the floor. I stood up and continued ripping the fabric, throwing it to the floor.

Tears streamed down my face. Anger? Sadness? Grief? All woven together like wires in a bomb. A bomb that I could feel was in the final moments before it exploded. I tore the dress off, letting its frayed shell fall to the floor.

My anger fired first, and I yanked book after book off the shelf. I opened each one and tore page after page out. The Art of War, perfectly placed next to a golden hourglass, found itself in my hands, and shredded like the other books. I picked up the hourglass and threw it to the ground, letting it crash; the red sand salting the expensive area rug Thomas had insisted on having before we first hosted a dinner in the new house.

I opened another one and read the dedication he had inscribed, 'To my Olivia. Happy First Anniversary. May we have many more to come. Always, my undying love.' My hands shook, the words blurring on the page until I finally slammed the book shut, fury burning hotter than my grief.

"Lies!" I screamed. "You fucking liar!"

Even though I was never truly in love with him, I found a way to love him that allowed me to survive, and try to create a happy life for my family in the Nation–to do what I was expected to do.

He never loved me. He loved the life I gave him. It was never going to be me.

Grief. Unyielding and debilitating grief consumed my body.

I sacrificed so much. Gave him everything. And he never loved me. He faked it for ten years while I struggled to make myself love him...this life...the Nation. He never tried. It was a job for him. A career choice that he could replace. A replaceable wife, mother, friend. Had he already lined up my replacement in Penny? Had she served as my surrogate, or was someone else waiting in the wings for me to walk out the door so she could pretend to be the mother of my children? A job I would never give her, or any other woman in this world, the right to claim. A fire burned inside me with the thought of another woman raising *my* children. Not his, *mine*.

I needed to get dressed, stay focused on why I was here, and return to the Challenge Center with Kai. I left the mess in the living room and walked back down the hall to my room. After pulling my clothes back on, I went to Thomas's nightstand, where the safe sat alone on the bottom shelf. He had left it here, and I wondered if it was on purpose or a mistake. Was he spinning another web I was knowingly walking into?

I set the safe on the bed and let the biometrics do their work. Once opened, I found his mother's wedding ring–a token he would have never left behind. When he left our home, he must have been in an unusual frame of mind. A picture of his mother and father's wedding day, and a letter from his father to his unborn son lay solemnly next to a gun, and a small black envelope with a red orchid covering a key. I opened it, and inside was a small thumb drive with a note. 'T–Here's the info you needed. All's gone now except this. -VL'. This is what I was looking for, the VL must be Mr. Lope. I picked up the key. A perfect "F" had been cut into its intricate black metal. I placed the key in my pocket and grabbed the gun. Its cool, smooth metal contrasted against its weight. I released the magazine, finding it fully loaded. I put the gun in the back of my pants and walked back into the kitchen.

My fingers dragged along the countertops as if saying goodbye to a life that had never been mine, one more time. Throat parched, I opened the cupboard, grabbed a glass, and filled it with cooled water from the refrigerator. My eyes roamed over the magnets and trinkets from false family trips, then stopped on a piece of paper held under a bright yellow Viva Mexico magnet, the handwriting one I would recognize anywhere.

My Olivia, Thought you would eventually show up. Predictable as always. Just remember, you'll never get them back because you don't know how to fight like I do. XOXO, Your Doting Husband.

Had I walked right into another one of his webs? Was it Kai? Did he bring me here because Thomas asked him to? My chest tightened, breath quickening as dread clawed up my throat. I needed to get out of here, but the anger inside me swallowed everything else.

I threw the glass down, shattering it into a million little pieces, and screamed. Fiery tears followed and everything inside of me exploded.

"I fucking hate you!" I yelled at the potential cameras he was watching me through. I opened the cupboards and started throwing everything at the walls, shrapnel from a life lived in lies. Sharp pieces exposed, cutting up a life that was never mine.

I pushed the pictures off the shelves, our fake smiles falling to the floor in shrouds of glass. I pulled the picture of Rose and Lucas down, freed it from the frame, and threw the frame to the ground, glass hitting my body.

I was standing in the mausoleum of my Nation marriage—each photograph still clinging for life, each drawer still half-full, like grief had unpacked but never moved out. The silence wasn't peaceful; it was thick with everything left unsaid. My

Challenge Pass had fractured time, leaving behind artifacts of a love that couldn't survive but didn't quite disappear either. My home–she didn't mourn for me, not exactly. But she remembered me. And the children. And a marriage that was never mine to hold. She wouldn't let me forget, not as long as she stood, holding on too tight to a life that would never return to her. She wanted to be free too.

No one prepares you for the aftermath of a broken marriage, especially in the Nation. No one speaks about the anger and devastation, because in this world–my world–it wasn't supposed to happen.

But it did.

And I was here now.

And everything around me needed to be set free. No memories left to linger in the corners of her kitchen. No pictures of children laughing, as she hugged them tighter when the day turned to night. No couches left bearing the imprint of Rose reading a book, or Lucas trailing his trucks up the side of the arm. No built-in shelves holding on to a life that she always knew wasn't real, but could never tell me, because she desperately wanted it to be real too. She wanted me to stay, and in so many ways begged me to. If I had only stayed, she and I could be forever, a house and its mother, the foundations for any child's life.

But she had to go. She had to be set free just like me. She needed to move on and become reborn, in order to heal from the tragedy of her empty and silent rooms.

My body knew before my mind did, and my feet carried me to the junk drawer next to the sink. My hands searched until they found the one thing that could make it all disappear, so there would be no more memories and the stage would cease to exist. The table would be gone. The couch would be left in ruins. The shelves, piles of ash to be swept away in the wind.

A long plastic lighter found its home in my hand.

Thomas's note served as the tinder for a life I was ready to say goodbye too. A home that I called my own, and heard me when I would cry myself to sleep at night, holding me tight every time I was reminded of a life that wasn't mine. I would set her free. His note would help set us both free. We would rebuild, once I found my children and unseated the Nation's power. I would rebuild, once I used this gun to end his life and reclaim mine.

I clicked the lighter and let the flames kiss the paper first, then I delicately moved it to the books that were never mine. Pictures that were faked. Artifacts that needed to melt into nothing–because they were nothing.

My body pulled me back to watch the ending of a movie I'd been acting in for the last ten years. Slowly creeping flames became my co-star, trailing along the perfectly whittled white bookshelves and remnants of a life never fully lived. My feet felt the crumpling of crinoline and satin as I stepped back further.

I looked down.

My wedding dress called to me and begged for her ending too. I would set her free along with everything else held under his power.

I clicked the lighter again, setting sections of the dress aflame, burning the fabric shell that had caged me as I walked down the aisle on that fateful day, into the hands of a monster. My grandfather guiding me, and telling me Thomas was the right choice. My dress, stained red by the afternoon sunlight reflected on my body, bleeding for my future. The suffocating bodice held me in, making sure I lacked just enough air to be awake, but not enough to be fully aware of the choice I was making. The shoes squeezing my feet into place for the perfect walk toward a prince charming that never existed.

It burned slowly at first, quickly upstaged by the custom built-ins roaring with anger. My house was angry too–angry at not being chosen, at being left behind, denied the promise we made to her when we signed the papers and opened her heart with keys that no longer existed.

Black smoke filled the room and brought me out of my trance.

I was in a burning house.

A fire I had started.

A fire that was taking her away from me, but one that could not take me away from my children.

"I'm sorry." I said to her as I picked up tokens from a life left in ashes. Out of instinct, I opened the front door, but stopped. Even though the cameras were off, I wondered if fire sensors would alert the Nation Fire Department, giving me less time to get away. I closed the door, and headed to the garage. I opened the side door, locking it behind me, and snuck out the back gate that exited to a small green space for a garden that was never meant to grow.

21

OLIVIA

I walked away from my house calmly, glancing back when I heard the roar of the flames, and screams from neighbors. The sirens followed next. I placed my hands in my pockets, and the hoodie over my head. My thumb found the key, and I rubbed it anxiously. There was no way I could go to the pirate park. I would have to find Kai some other way, and hoped he left the scene before emergency services got there.

I was almost out of the neighborhood, on my way toward Central, when blue and red lights illuminated behind me. I could feel the warmth of the car as it pulled up beside me, but I continued to walk slowly, as if I were out for my nightly walk.

"Excuse me, will you please stop?" The car stopped, and two NSP officers stepped out.

I turned around, my hands holding remnants from a life I had just burned to the ground.

"Hello, mam. I'm Officer Bixby, and this is Officer Sampson. Not sure if you saw, but there's a large fire and we're checking the neighborhood to see if anyone saw anything suspicious. Have you been out here for a while?"

"No," I said calmly. "I just started my walk."

The bigger one, Bixby, narrowed his eyes at me. "In a hoodie, with those?" He pointed to the bear, and the photo.

"The mosquitoes like me a little too much, and I was taking these to a friend," my charm kicked in, and the lies I knew how to speak spilled out like water from a hose. "This has bug repellant on it, and I have to wear it even on hot nights like tonight."

"You here alone, Mrs...?" The other officer, Sampson pried.

Shit. I couldn't use Sarah King or Olivia Embers or Smith.

"Acosta. I'm Sarah Acosta."

"And where do you live, Mrs. Acosta?"

"In Central."

"If you don't mind, can we scan your chip to confirm your identity?"

Shit.

My heartbeat quickened and I knew there was no way out. I could run, but they would either catch up to me, or tase me. I couldn't go into the NSP station and keep my cover. Just as I was about to say something, the hum from an electric BMW pulled in front of the NSP vehicle and Kai Acosta stepped out.

"Honey! Oh my gosh, I'm glad I caught you before you got any further on your walk. Your mom called, it's your sister. We need to get to the hospital right away." Kai feigned panic and pulled me in for a hug that I tensed inside of. "Sorry, officers. Is everything okay with my wife?"

"She's your wife, sir?"

"Yes."

"Can we confirm your identity, please?"

"Yes, of course," Kai lifted his forearm to Bixby's HoloTab, and a green light illuminated.

Officer Bixby's body shifted uncomfortably.

"Tier-four. Mr. Acosta, we're sorry for the inconvenience. We stopped your wife because there were reports of a suspicious person near the fire," he motioned over to my neighborhood.

"I saw the smoke as I was driving over the Tower Bridge. Is everyone okay?" Kai's acting skills, coupled with his charm, reminded me of who I was dealing with; a mirror image of me.

"Not sure yet, but thank you for your concern."

"Of course. If it's okay then, can my wife and I head to the hospital?"

"Yes. Thank you for your time and I hope your sister is okay." Sampson said as he and Bixby made their way back into their vehicle.

"Thank you." We said in unison.

I resisted Kai's hand on my arm, unsure if I was getting into a car leading me straight to Thomas. I said nothing as I tried to think of a plan for a quick escape if it turned out he was doing all of this for Thomas. He stayed silent until we hit the Tower Bridge.

"What the fuck, Olivia?!?" Kai yelled.

"What?" I snapped.

"You burned the fucking house down? What happened to 'I'll be in and out, no one will even know'?"

"Look, it just sort of happened." I said nonchalantly, trying to read where he may have aligned his loyalty to–me, or Thomas.

"No, Olivia. One night stands after being drunk at a bar just *sort of happen*. Burning a fucking house down and drawing attention to yourself, with the way you're dressed, and with what? A god-damn teddy bear outside of a crime scene...that doesn't just happen. You look like a crackhead tier-one who could have started that fire. You could have been arrested, and then what? What would you have done? They would have scanned your chip and seen you were Sarah King, but then they would have eventually identified you as Olivia Embers... Smith...and then what would you have done? Thomas would have found you–you understand that, right? You would have been done. No getting your kids back, no rebellion, no bye-bye

Nation. I mean, what the fuck, Olivia?!" He hit his hands on the steering wheel, and sighed in frustration.

I softened my shoulders at his level of concern with me being caught–if he was with Thomas, this would have been perfect. I had no intention of explaining myself to him, though. He had no idea what it was like to lose a life on the magnitude that I had. He was never married. Had no kids. Lived like a nomad under the thumb of his father. I was not going to give him the power of an answer to something he didn't deserve to know.

"Where are we going?" My curt tone implied he would get no answer from me.

"My place. The safe house."

"Why?"

"Um, because you just burned a fucking house down, and I'm sure that within the next hour your face is going to be everywhere. The images from your house alone, and that neighborhood, are probably being uploaded now."

"Your team took them offline."

"Yeah, until something like a *fire* happens, then the emergency services kick in and restore cameras, regardless of them being turned off. No one in your little circle of Resistance friends told you not to start a fire?" He said sarcastically.

I growled under my breath and looked out the window. "Why are we in Central?"

"I live here. My safehouse, it's here at The Frederic."

The Frederic–where Thomas's first apartment was–the apartments across the street from where we found my father's body. Although I had been in and out of Central over the last ten years, I avoided that area at all costs, even during school events. Thomas was sympathetic to me and would drive longer routes to avoid it too–maybe one of the only positive things he ever did for me.

I didn't say anything as we drove through Central streets

that were lined with lights and cameras. I tightened the hoodie around my face, put the sunglasses on, and looked down to avoid any more cameras that could find me.

"Don't worry, my team is already wiping the footage from when the officers stopped you, until we get into the garage—including their body cams."

"Why couldn't they wipe anything from the fire?"

"Not enough delay." He was quiet and then in a gruff tone. "You can't do shit like this, Olivia. If you want my help and you want to get your kids back, you have to follow the rules...the plan...otherwise it turns into a mess that I may not be able to fix."

"I thought you weren't about following the rules." I scoffed.

"Not starting fires in a suburban home owned by the Director...is sort of a rule I do follow." He said sardonically.

"I followed the rules for ten years and it was still a mess. Just one that no one noticed."

He sighed and his tone softened. "I'm sorry, Olivia, for what you went through. It couldn't have been easy, but you need to remember that we are not just playing some game here. There are lives on the line, not just yours and your children. Thousands of people are being controlled by this government. You need to put the past behind you and see what you're capable of when you're not being completely irrational."

This motherfucker didn't just say that, did he?

"You do realize that all of this just happened to me, right? I found out months ago that my life was not my own. That the love of my life was alive and imprisoned. That my mother had been lying to me, and knew I was marrying into a horrible life, and still let me. That I don't actually live in a government that is real, and my children are gone, and people are dead, and people will probably continue to die as I take the Nation down. I'm not being irrational."

"Yes, you are. You need to think things through and not let him, or any of this, get the best of you."

"Oh, that's rich coming from someone whose whole life has been handed to him."

"You need to figure out how to let things go."

"My life and what he did to me, and the children, isn't something that I can just let go." I was seething.

"If you focus on what you do have, maybe you could." Contempt filled his voice, and I couldn't tell if he was talking to me, or to himself.

It was fruitless to argue with Kai. He would never see things the way I did because he came from a world that insulated him from hard choices. He stayed in his ivory tower, even though it was controlled by his father, never knowing the true meaning of sacrifice because he only ever had to take care of himself.

I stayed quiet until we reached The Frederic and drove into the parking garage.

"You need to keep your sunglasses and hoodie on. Even though they know I'm here and will keep interaction to a minimum with other residents, there's still a chance we could run into someone."

"How is it possible that people live here and no one ever runs into each other?"

"That's what money's for—to never be seen or see anyone else. It's a premium for a very private life."

Another example of the life he lives on the other side of the invisible line. I paused for a moment, pulling myself out of the contempt I had for him. Had I lived on the other side of that line, profiting off of Thomas's power?

Before being able to put too much thought into it, Kai opened my car door, and ushered me into the elevator. He waved his wrist over the panel and the light illuminated, taking us to the floor just below "PH."

"Not the penthouse, huh?" I snarked, and he said nothing as we went up and into his apartment.

"I have everything set to a specific routine for when I come home. My days at the Center, or in the Nation, can sometimes be a lot. I need calm as soon as I come home," he explained as if he already knew I was questioning him. "You can be in that room over there. The bathroom should be cleaned, my lady comes once a week, whether I am here or not. There's probably some food in the fridge, but I'll put an order in to be delivered by tomorrow morning–just leave me a list of what you want."

I scanned the room. Floor-to-ceiling windows with views of the Tower Bridge and lights reflecting off the river caught my eye first. A warm glow illuminated the modern apartment and Louis Armstrong played softly in the background. Vintage travel posters adorned the walls next to space-themed movies and nostalgic rom com posters. Deep green plants held their own in corners and on shelves, softening the room's emptiness. A gold circle bar cart with glass shelves and wheels stood quietly in the corner, stocked with Laphroaig and ornate tumbler glasses.

"Towels are in the closet over there," he motioned to the hallway. "You need to shower, you smell like a campfire."

I would take offense, but something in his voice told me not to.

"Thank you."

"Put your clothes outside the bathroom so I can wash them. I'll set some of mine out for you, until yours are cleaned. I'll order clothes for you tomorrow, if you just let me know your size."

"Thanks. Um...six for pants, medium for tops."

"Uh, and other things?" He blushed.

"Right. Medium for underwear. Bra size 36B. Shoe size, 9."

"Okay, I'll order a few things that make sense."

"Thank you."

"You're welcome. I'll be in my room if you need anything." Kai left and closed the door behind him. The music turned off in the main area and the lights dimmed. I could hear classical music coming from his room, but couldn't make out who was playing.

When I stepped into my room, the lights shifted to a soft orange and meditation music began to play. A painting of a woman in a ballgown, with a deep teal background, hung above the bed. Gold and white geometric shaped plant holders sat on the shelves with bright green heart-shaped cascading plants. A cream chair sat in the corner under a gold multi-globe light, perfect for reading before bed. A small stack of books next to the window sat waiting to be picked up.

I went into the bathroom, stripped down, and placed my clothes outside the door on the floor. Kai was right, I did smell like smoke. I turned on the water, and a waterfall showerhead greeted me with instant heat at the perfect temperature. One thing I knew about Kai Acosta in that moment was that he liked his creature comforts, sparing no expense in ways that looked unassuming to the naked eye.

As I washed the black ash from my skin, the reality of what I had done set in. I burned it. Every poisoned memory of my life with Thomas. Every beautiful moment with my children. Every hope and dream of a future I would never have. It was all gone. My life with him was gone.

I laughed hysterically. What had I done? I just burned my house down. I just burned Thomas's house down. Who does that? The uncontrollable laughter shifted at a moment's notice. Echoes of laughter faded into muted sobs, too heavy to make a sound, until they became one: a wail so deep no part of my body could unhear it.

I collapsed against the shower floor, curling in on my body, while the hot water baptized me anew. The hollow chest, a space for the grief to find surrender. A thinned body hugged by the only person who could pull me out of the darkness I had lived in for ten years. A voice silenced when it cried for help, was now free to be as loud as it wanted to be.

The shell of my life kept growing around me, yet was always destined to be too small. A skin too tight for me to live the next part of my life, left in bridal dress pieces burned under a June sky. A chrysalis I stepped into that fateful April day, my body shaking inside, while Ethan's rebellion strengthened my wings to let me fly.

No longer bound to a life that shackled my ankles to the ground, I was going to be free.

Free from him.

Free from the Nation.

Free from Olivia Smith.

22

OLIVIA

When I finished my shower, I opened the door to find a set of clothes Kai had left for me. Back in my room, I saw he had emptied my pockets and laid the remnants on my dresser: pearl earrings, a key, and the flash drive.

I picked up the flash drive and pushed the slider up and down, freeing its information in a room that couldn't listen. What could be on here that Thomas was so afraid of getting out? Was he just setting a trap for me, or was there something actually there that we could use? Ethan already released the files about genetic compatibility to all the citizens. What else could Thomas and the Nation be hiding that was so important he didn't want it near Central or the servers? I wondered if he knew I had taken it, or burned our house down.

I smiled at the thought of me pulling something over on him, especially with the note he left. In the kitchen, I made some chamomile tea, and went back to my room. I would find a way to make peace with what I had done, and eventually, when this was all over, I would heal from the trauma. For now, I would take each moment, good or bad, and place it on a shelf to be read like a book when I had the time for it.

With nothing to read and nothing to do, I curled up in bed and drank the tea. It wasn't late, but I was exhausted and I knew Kai was done with me today too. I set the cup on the night-stand, voice-commanded the lights to turn off, and sank into a sleep I needed more desperately than any man or moment in my life.

FLAMES SURROUNDED me as I heard my children scream. I ripped the blindfold off and held it in my hand. Rose and Lucas' voices fought for attention against the flames growing down the halls of the building I didn't recognize. Boutique blue-veined wallpaper served as the tinder for the approaching fire, trailing perfectly up to the ceiling where sprinklers choked out drips of water. I covered my mouth with the blindfold and maneuvered down the hall.

"Rose! Lucas! Where are you?" I screamed, as I opened the apartment door.

"In here!" Rose's voice yelled. "Mom! Help us. We're stuck! Help us!"

"I'm coming Rose! I'm here. I'll find you. I'm here." I screamed through smoked-filled lungs.

"Help us!" another voice yelled.

I opened another door and a group of girls were sitting in the middle of a burning room, bound together with sashes. Red orchid embroidery stood out among the white silk.

"Help us! Please! Help us!" They screamed repeatedly.

"Mom! We're in here. Help us!" Rose screamed, but I couldn't tell what room she was in.

"We're in here," a young male voice yelled right after her. The boy from her school?

I ran to the other doors, but tripped on one of the little girl's feet. With the flames roaring and gaining power behind me, I turned to her, seeing the flames ready to devour all of them. I sat up and began untying the sashes.

"Shh, it will be okay. You'll be okay," never looking at their faces until the last one.

The familiarity came in an instant. Olive skin, soft eyes, brown hair, reminiscent of Jessica when she was younger. But as my vision sharpened, I saw they all wore my face.

"Mom! Help us. Find us, please!"

I stared at the group of girls in my image, flames now at our feet, with Rose's screams in the background. Two of the girls looked sad, one was angry, and another was completely indifferent. The fifth, oblivious to the room burning around her, reached out to touch the flames as they kissed down from the peeling wallpaper.

"Don't touch that!" I yelled. "You need to get out! Go! All of you! Go!" I grabbed the angry one first, pushing her out the door with the indifferent girl. The sad girls followed, as if on cue, pitying me with their facial expressions. The girl stood unaware, unmoving as flames reached her feet. "You need to move. Please." I pleaded. "You have to leave now. You need to get out. The room is burning. You're going to burn. Please, take my hand."

I reached out my hand, and she tilted her head.

"It's okay, you know? All of this. It had to burn. And still has to."

In a moment, she changed from a young me into the one standing in my place. A mirror image of the woman I was today. I looked at her shoulders, sturdier than the ones I remembered seeing in the Maldives, in Central. Her jawline was more pronounced. Her eyes were steady, filled with a determination and a knowing that kept her going.

"Walk with me, Olivia." She said.

I froze. Rose was still screaming. Lucas? Was it Lucas? Was he burning too?

"I can't. The children."

"No, Olivia. They will burn without you. Walk with me."

I took her hand and stepped inside the flaming circle, heat burning the clothes I was wearing. I dropped the blindfold and watched the white cloth char as it feathered toward the red orchid symbol.

"Let it burn, Olivia."

"We're going to burn alive." I pleaded with her.

"You've already done that. And you rose from the ashes. Touch the flames, Olivia. Go ahead, reach out your hand."

I did what she said. I touched the flames. They didn't burn me. My hand moved through the flames, as if it were gliding through water.

The children's screams subsided and eventually disappeared, but I knew they weren't dying anymore–that they wouldn't die, because I had lived. The building burned around us and I watched the outside world appear through a mass of smoke and charred wood and golden flames.

It was Central. We were downtown, but it felt different. People crowded the streets, and when I turned to the Capitol building, I saw that where a white orchid flag had once danced in the Delta Breeze, the red, white, and blue of a long-forgotten time now waved.

I turned to her, and she smiled, revealing crow lines on either side of her eyes. She was still young, but with a knowledge I did not yet understand had aged her. She was real in so many ways. Her smile was finally genuine. Although solid, her body possessed a softness, accepting life's changes. Her posture was strong but relaxed. I looked at her hands, weathered slightly and unaccompanied by any man-made adornment that tethered her to a world she didn't want.

She was free. The free version of me living in a free world.

"How did you...?" I whispered.

"We finally listened, Olivia."

"And the children?"

"They survived, because you put your mask on first." She smiled, and I laughed softly under my breath.

"So we all make it? All of us?"

Her eyes pitied me like the little girls before. "No, Olivia, we won't all make it."

I could feel my throat tighten.

"Who? Who doesn't make it? Jessica? Ethan? Jude?"

She looked away into the distance, toward the towering buildings that once housed the Nation's epicenter, and then back to me, then to the burning building around us. She started walking away from me, toward the exit where the other little girls left.

"Who doesn't make it? Please! Tell me, who doesn't make it?" I cried.

She didn't turn around, and I continued to plead with her to tell me what future was about to unfold before me. "Please!" I cried.

"Pleeeeeease..."

23

OLIVIA

hand shook my shoulder and my eyes jerked open. "Olivia? Are you okay? You were crying and yelling in your sleep. I had to come in."

"Kai?"

"Yes, Olivia, it's me. You're here in my apartment. We're in Central."

I sat up and looked at the teacup, half empty. I searched the room, trying to gain my bearings. "It was a dream. It was just a dream," I convinced myself.

"Are you okay?"

"Yeah. I'll be fine."

"You want to talk about it? You were pretty deep, it took me a few tries to wake you."

"No. There's nothing to talk about. Like I said, I'll be fine." I shuddered at the memory of my children screaming for help. Was Rose trying to beg me to find her? Or was it just a hope that she wanted to be with me, instead of Thomas? And the boy, the one from her school. Why was he there too? And where was Lucas?

Kai looked at the dresser where the key and flash drive sat.

"Are you going back to sleep?" He asked.

"I don't know. What time is it?"

"Late, but if you're up for it, we can check out the flash drive."

"Yeah. Let's look." I said without hesitation.

We sat at his table with the HoloTab and flash drive in hand. Kai turned the HoloTab toward me, so we could both see the information. "Ready?"

"Yes. Let's see what he has on there."

Kai opened the folder and multiple files fanned across the screen, each one with a name we didn't understand yet. It reminded me of the database Ethan had told me about when he'd learned about our DNA. Kai began opening them one by one, each containing documents–some redacted, some not–and images of people I didn't recognize.

"Is it what we thought?"

"Maybe?" Kai continued opening documents, flooding the screen with them, all organized by dates and initials. "Look at this–" There were details about shipments similar to what my mother was saying my father had found. There were names of people, their age, their state, and what contract length they signed with Centers. Next to their names were columns: *Lab Date, Location, Trial, Citizen Name, Tier, Viable Y/N, Sex*, and finally *Deceased Y/N*.

"My mom was right. This is what got my father killed." I pressed a hand to my mouth, the words tasting like ash in my mouth.

"That aligns with some of the things we knew were happening, but just not to this level. We knew there was trafficking, and we knew there was a genetics program, but to think they may be linked is new to me."

"Do you think attendants died during the experiments? It says 'deceased' and look–" I pointed at the column. "Almost all of these attendants are dead. We need to figure out what killed them."

"Or who?"

I looked at Kai. "It can't be like that, Kai. I mean, these people were not only taken, but then, you're insinuating, they were killed too?"

"When it comes to the Nation, I don't rule anything out."

"But why? What would be the point of killing them? They needed people for the Centers–attendants–if they trafficked them in, so why would they kill them?"

"I don't know." He moved his finger to the screen, "but look here. 'Citizen Name'. I bet that has something to do it with. These attendants are all linked to a specific citizen. Then look here where it says 'viable' and 'yes or no', most are yes. Next to that is 'sex'. Oh my god." Kai pushed back and put his hands on his head. "It *is* a breeding program, Olivia. It's a fucking breeding program!"

I looked at the screen. Most of the citizen names were female, with a handful being male, and the attendant names on the same line were the opposite sex. All of the female attendants were marked as 'yes' under the deceased column, where the males were marked as 'no' with an asterisk.

"What does the asterisk mean?" I asked.

Kai scrolled through, looking for any key that would give us meaning. He stopped when he found it, "Sterilized."

Another layer to a world that I had participated in. I was complicit in the lies. In bringing others in, and convincing lower-level tiers that they could rise up and become something more in the Nation. I stood in my plastic world, searching for something real, but the reality around me would have broken me. I woke up every single day and played in a game where I, and all the other higher level tiers, would win. Where trafficked attendants would lose. Where women would lose their lives before the game was over. Where men and women would never have a chance to win the game because Thomas and the Nation had already fixed it so they couldn't.

I stood up and paced Kai's kitchen. He went to the refrigerator and grabbed me a bottle of water.

"Thank you." I opened it and took a sip.

"Are you okay?"

That was a loaded question.

"No. Not at all. Just when I thought I had learned enough about him. It's never going to end. He's never going to stop... this," I pointed over to the screen.

"Unless we stop him, Olivia."

There was nothing more than Thomas's death that I wanted, but only because that meant freedom from him. I wanted my children to be free of him, too. But now, this was bigger. He and everyone else tied with the Nation had to go. Thomas's death was no longer just about my freedom; it was about the freedom of everyone who had ever signed their life over to the Nation. It was for the women in that file who were taken, raped, impregnated, then murdered. Their bodies and babies stolen for the 'brave new world' Thomas and the Nation were trying to build.

I sat back down. "I don't want to look at that anymore. Can we see what else is on there?"

Kai came back over, "Of course, Olivia."

We searched through a few other folders that had names and locations, some documents relating to the United States that Kai said he would look at later, and then financial records with a list of account numbers that would take forever to get through.

I yawned, "This is a lot."

"Want to stop?"

"No, let's do this a little longer. Can you open that?" I pointed to a file titled *Transfers*. Tabs were organized at the bottom by year, starting with 2028. "Can I see that, please?" Kai handed me the HoloTab, and I clicked on 2028. Dates, along with the names of women, filled the screen alphabetically. Either Central Clinic, South Burrough, or West Clinic were listed next to their names. Next to the clinic location was another name I recognized: Blythe, listed line after line after line. Then the name of a woman and her tier status. A column titled *Success: Yes or No* with a color code green for yes, and red for no. The final column M or F.

"It can't be," I whispered.

"What?"

Frantic, I scrolled through the tabs until I found 2031. I opened it, not breathing, my body rigid, and scrolled down until I saw it. Olivia Embers. South. Blythe. Alicia Jones-5E, and the last column was green. "It can't be." The HoloTab hit the floor.

"Olivia!" Kai yelled as he tried to grab me before my knees made their ultimate drop on the floor.

"He's alive. He's alive." I shook.

"Who, Olivia? Who's alive?" Kai searched my face.

"The baby."

"What baby?"

"My baby. The transfer. My transfer. Instead of aborting our child, Ethan and I agreed for it to be a transfer. The transfer took, and the baby lived."

Kai picked up the HoloTab and looked at the database. He saw my name. "They've been keeping track of transfers this whole time? They were so quiet about the program, we didn't know that it worked." He scrolled to the end of the file. "The last year is 2038, so they ran it for ten years." He maneuvered through the file, highlighting each tab and then typing in a formula. "And there are 1,462 children that were successfully transferred. Not as many in the first few years, but a lot more after 2034."

"It was a boy, and he's alive. Ethan's and my son is alive. Can you go back to 2031 and copy the person's name so we can search for who he is?"

"Yeah, no problem. One benefit of the Nation's surveillance system is that every citizen's information is in here. This system provides much more in-depth information than attendant profiles, including financial and tracking data. Give me just a second...found it. Alicia Jones-5E, 14 West Heron Ave, West Borough. Husband: Paul Jones. Children: Cooper Jones, Layla Jones. Occupation: Teacher, Bridge to the Nation. Want me to keep reading?"

"Cooper...can you look up Cooper Jones? His picture? I want to see what he looks like."

Kai held down his finger on Cooper's name, and a profile of a face I knew appeared on the screen. It was the boy with Rose, the one at school. Tan skin and corkscrew tendrils. Chestnut brown eyes and a smile that lit up the screen. Traces of Ethan lingered in his eyes, the eyelashes pronounced against his skin. His lips were like mine, but the smile was all Ethan. A boyhood ghost living a life we thought had disappeared into the ether. Our son–my child–was alive, and living just a few blocks from me, from his sister, his little brother, from Thomas.

"*He knew the entire time.*" I clutched my neck. "Thomas...he knew Cooper, the boy, was mine...Ethan's."

"How can you be sure?"

"Cooper, I met him briefly when we were trying to get Rose and Lucas out. He was her protector, in a way...he kept her from leaving with us. At the BTN ceremony in April, they mentioned his name as a lead for the age groups. Thomas probably assigned him to be Rose's lead. Cooper was also Thomas's intern. I didn't hear his name much because Thomas had interns coming and going. Thomas knew, and was keeping Cooper close to him...to me. But why?"

"You're kidding, right?"

I let out a breath. "Sometimes there are moments when I

struggle to see Thomas as the villain. It's like I am almost ready to accept who he really is, but then I can't. It's hard to untangle him as the father and husband he was from the Director and evil man we all know him to be. Even though I hate him, and want him dead, it doesn't mean I can fully untangle him, and this new reality, from pieces of the past."

"You're living in a hopeful fantasy, Olivia."

His hot and cold demeanor was driving me crazy.

"And you're not?"

"What's that supposed to mean?" His head jerked back.

"This situation with your dad...Do you really think he's going to just let you go once the Nation is defeated? How would that look for his supporters?"

Kai looked at me and drew a deep sigh. "There's always been too many expectations in my world. Living up to them, and most of the time, failing to. No one else lived up to them either. He never told anyone to their face what he really thought about them, because it might risk his political movement. Everyone loves him. If you ever meet him, you'll see. I once saw him get an entire room to donate an enormous sum of money to get the Nation taken down. That was the first fundraiser. Since then, he's raised billions of dollars, and gained political support, to bring Northern California back into the union. It's the way he's trying to secure his place at the table. No one knows who he really is, except for those who've lived with him at home. So, yes, in some ways I may be too hopeful about my freedom, but I still see him for who he is."

"Just because I can't see all of Thomas for who he is right now doesn't mean I never will. People live in pockets of denial all the time to help them make it through the day. It's not completely unhealthy to live like that. I convinced myself for ten years that I could love a man, so I could protect and maintain a certain lifestyle for my family. It got me through. It helped me raise my children, and have a career and friends– "

"That's the problem with the Nation system. It lets people live in a mirage. A fake world that will never last. A world where they lie to each other, and themselves, every day."

"You have no idea what it's like to live in this place. No idea what it's like to be married with no viable options. No idea what it means to be a woman here. No idea what commitment is. What sacrifice is, especially when it comes to a family." A small match lit inside an invisible matchbook I was holding.

"I don't agree. People have the choice...the freedom to leave a bad situation at any time. If they're selling their soul to keep a certain status, or way of life, that's not really living. It's hard to respect them. I know I couldn't be with anyone like that." His voice raised slightly, as if we were in a couple's argument.

"Um...isn't that the kettle calling the pot black?" My voice raised, mirroring his.

"Until your father gains more political power, he's in control of you. From my vantage point, I can't see you ever getting your freedom. How is what you're doing any different from what I did? What so many other people in this situation had to do? Also, it's not like women are lining up at your door to be with you in the first place."

"What you did, and are doing, is not the same as this. I am doing this for everyone else. I am trying to free people from a terrible sect that took over and controlled everything, down to who could, and could not, reproduce. You chose to live the Nation life. To be a martyr for your children, and the cause. You continue to choose to be in this life. I don't know...I think it's just hard to respect someone like that."

"You have a lot to learn, Kai. If you think you're not a pawn in someone else's plan, you're mistaken." Kai's arrogance angered my core. "If you think you actually have a choice in what you're doing, look around. You're here, in an apartment your father is paying for, gathering information for him so he can become the President of the United States. A man who, from what you've told me, has complete control over your life. You're no different from anyone else who's been bound to a marriage, a job, or some government system. We're all the same: if we aren't the ones pulling the strings, we're just puppets in another show, on a different stage, at a different time."

I stood up and walked outside onto his balcony. I could be alone out here with my anger, letting it burn with the hot Sacramento Valley air. Fanning the flames until they settled into a rhythmic dance, or grew legs and ran wildly back inside to burn him down.

I sat on the chaise lounge curling my feet under my legs. Tiny beads of sweat adorned my forehead like a crown, offsetting the far less elegant sweat pooling behind my knees. I looked out, past the buildings and lights, to a burned down Central Challenge Center.

I stewed on Kai's words about not respecting anyone who made the same choices I did. He had no experience or idea what my life was like. He had no children, had never been married, and lived for a man that controlled him. Why was I giving him, or his words, any energy? It didn't matter how he saw me because he didn't know me, no matter how much research he'd done. If Kai Acosta wanted to be an ally, he would ultimately serve one purpose: a mark, a means to an end, someone who would get me into the Nation system and return my family.

I drew in a deep breath, stood up, and braced myself against the balcony railing. Even if I hated this guy for everything he'd just said and the way he saw the world, I still needed him–for now. He had access to the system that would help me find my children. I pushed my anger down, opened the door, and walked back inside.

"You're kind of an asshole, you know that, right?"

"I've been told that a time or two." He smirked.

"And you're really arrogant. Not to mention judgmental toward people, and things, you know nothing about, and have no actual experience with."

"I'm listening."

"You have no idea what it's like to be in a relationship where, at every turn, you're being controlled or manipulated without even knowing. You have no idea what it's like to live in a world where you are bound to a relationship because you're responsible for two other people. You have no idea what it's like to hold a life in your hands and know that one step out of line could make the end that much closer."

"You chose to have children, Olivia. You chose to save your sister. You chose the life you're living. I chose a different one."

"Yes, I chose this life, but I also didn't have a choice."

"We all have choices…options."

His naivete bordered on arrogance.

"That's your privilege and lack of real-life experience talking. As a man in a world where women are still the lower class, you have choices, options. Your father's wealth provides you with options. You have the freedom to move around and even disappear for a moment, because you have nothing that tethers you to anyone else. You can come and go as you please, with no consequences or thoughts of another person. Mothers can't do that. Sisters can't do that. Daughters can't do that. We are bound to our family in ways that men like you will never understand…never try to understand. And that's the saddest part. Your level of judgment is so off-base and cruel. It's no wonder you're single."

"Ouch. Throwing another shot, huh?"

"You threw the first shot when you said what you said." I snapped back.

"Just because I haven't been married, or had kids, doesn't mean I can't show sympathy. I just don't want to. Just because I am bound, as you said, to my father right now, doesn't mean I always will be."

"How is what you're doing different from what I'm doing?"

"You stayed in your situation because of the kids, right?"

"Yes, and for my sister and mother."

"You stayed with a horrible man who would inevitably raise your children and watch you slowly die every day, instead of leaving him and showing your children what a real woman should be–what you're doing now, who you're trying to become. And they're not here to see it."

I thought about the me that didn't leave–the fear and hopelessness that hugged her like a straight-jacket. Why didn't I leave? What was wrong with her? Me? Why did she stay and live like that for so long? She could have escaped, gone back to the compound with Jessica and my mother. Knowing what I know now, all I had to do was cross the Nevada border, and I would have been free. Why did that version of me never leave? Anger boiled, and I couldn't hold back my tears any longer. I screamed.

Kai jumped up and came over to me. "Hey, hey, hey. I'm sorry, Olivia. I'm really sorry." He pulled me close. "I know I can get a little out of pocket sometimes, and yes, I know I'm judgmental. It's just how I am and it's made things complicated in my personal life. But right now I can't have a personal life anyway. I shouldn't have said those things, and I'm sorry–truly sorry."

"You don't have any idea what it's like to put someone's life before yours. Before your own freedom because you don't have access to the most basic things." I choked back my tears. "He had all the money. Yes, I had access to it and contributed because of my career, but it was never truly mine. He kept a close watch on the accounts, on everything I did with the children, and on everywhere I went. The tracking devices they put in us made escape impossible; you can't get away with those in your body. You belong to the Nation when you sign that contract. You belong to *him*."

"I know. I'm sorry."

"The worst part of this is that you don't even see how you belong to your father, too. Someone like you should have never said those things to someone like me."

"You're right. I'm sorry. I really, really, am sorry." He pulled me tighter as I cried uncontrollably into his shirt.

Moments passed before I could regain my sense of self. It had been months since someone made me feel as small as he did. I pulled away and wiped my face. Kai searched for what he had hoped was peace inside of me, but it wasn't there. It would never be there for him.

I pushed away from him. "I'll be back."

I left for the bathroom and closed the door. Splashing water on my face, I looked in the mirror. The woman before me was the one I had left months ago in a suburban borough. She was broken again. Sad. Gaslit. I remembered her eyes–the me that didn't leave–they were sad. I remembered those lines across her face–markers of hopelessness, not laughter. I remembered the vacancy–blurry-filled nights with a monster.

My hands gripped the countertop as I let out a hollow scream, only for me to hear. She wasn't who I was anymore–the me that didn't leave. I stared and saw the me that *did* leave. The one who was not broken, but rebuilt anew. The one who was not a victim, but a survivor. The woman who, instead of being hopeless and controlled, was now determined and *in control*. I wouldn't let Kai, or any person for that matter, tell me who I was ever again. My eyes were no longer vacant, but alive and ready to see me only as this: a woman who did leave, and was ready to take it all down. This was no longer just a rescue. It was a revolution, and I was at the helm of the ship that would launch a thousand faces to end Thomas and the Nation.

My body felt like stone as I walked back into the living

room, where Kai waited with two empty glasses and his Holo-Tab, glowing in his hands.

"Peace offering?"

One look at my face and he knew–something had shifted. I had returned not to who I was, but who I was fighting to become. Stronger. Steeled. And no one, not him or anyone else, would ever break through my armor again.

"Two things: One, is there any way you can track the children maybe with DNA samples from Lucas's bear? And two, I'd like to see if we can figure out where this key goes." My voice was solid, cold, unmoving.

"Sure." He said tentatively, as if walking carefully toward a predatory animal. "I can probably figure out the key with old photo recognition software, but finding the kids might be a little harder."

"You were able to identify me with the DNA, so why not theirs?"

"I can try, but there are probably multiple samples on here. Yours was easy because I had your glass–this will take longer, and I'll need my computer, so we can work on two devices at the same time."

Kai went to his office and returned with a laptop computer and a black flat case. He set it on the island next to his HoloTab, connecting all three devices.

"Can I have his bear, please?" I handed it to Kai as he opened the case, put Lucas's bear inside, and then closed it. He typed in commands on the computer and the screen glowed red with a clockwise ring moving slowly. "When the whole thing is green, we will have the sample. And then we can try to cross reference that with anything in the database. The only thing is, he still needs to be nearby for us to locate his tracker."

"We could go to his school and connect that way?"

"It's a great idea, but you couldn't go with me. Let's figure out the key thing first, then go from there. Okay?"

"Okay."

Kai's HoloTab was flat on the island, and opening an image app, he placed the key in the center. Another red ring illuminated under it.

"It'll just take a few minutes."

Time stretched for too long.

"I'll take that peace offering now." I smiled, and Kai filled his and my glass half-full.

I watched the device, and the ring was halfway to green when an alert popped up on his screen with my face hovering above.

"ALERT: Wanted highly dangerous fugitive for arson, murder, and attempted murder. Olivia Smith is assumed to be armed and dangerous. Do not engage. May go by the aliases: Olivia Embers, Olivia Conrad. If seen, call NSP immediately."

It flashed over and over, repeating the same message with an image of me from one of the cameras that caught me after the fire had started. Then an additional image appeared of me escaping the Challenge Center in April, along with my nurse's ID badge.

"Attempted murder? What the fuck is that about? I didn't kill anyone."

Without a beat, Kai answered, "They're pinning the bombing on you."

"The bombing? The Challenge Center? Oh my god, if my kids see this they're going to believe what their father told them. Anyone who knows me is going to think I did this... they're going to vilify me."

"They've already vilified you, Olivia. Thomas planted that seed, most likely when you left, which is why your daughter wouldn't leave with you. This is part of something much bigger than you've realized. The good news is that they don't have Sarah Acosta or Sarah King as an alias–that would have linked you to me, and Rose Bay."

"That's the good news?" I said standing up and rubbing my hands through my hair. "This is going to be everywhere."

"Yes. It will be." He said calm and matter-of-fact.

"I'm stuck here. How am I going to be able to do anything to find my children if I am here? I can't leave to sync their tracker to your HoloTab."

"I wouldn't have let you do that anyway."

"Wouldn't have let me?" I said admonishingly.

"Yes, like I said before, it would be too much of a liability. I have all the privacy I want here, but there is always a chance that someone else could be in the halls and if they noticed you, especially now with this, it'd all be over. For both of us. And for the Resistance and the United States."

I felt the walls around me grow tighter, and the air begin to thin. I wasn't sure if it was the wine or the shock, but I needed to ground myself again. I put my hands on the island and drew in a long breath.

You have this Olivia. You're in control of the things you can be. This is just a bump, nothing more. The children are yours. You have your freedom. You have left the Nation. You are free.

I repeated it over and over again in my mind to gain a foothold over the panic that was trying to sway my strength. Just as I found myself again, Kai's HoloTab beeped and a green light shone on his screen, waiting for both of us to reach out to it.

He removed the key from the screen, and my mouth dropped.

The Frederic.

Kai and I looked at each other, eyes wide with disbelief. The key in Thomas's safe belonged to an apartment in the same building where I was hiding after burning my house to the ground.

"It's for here. We don't use keys though. Everything is

through our chips or codes. Maybe it's a relic, or something with the Center?"

"It's his old apartment key–that bastard! Thomas had an apartment here when we first got together. He told me he sold it before we married, saying we didn't need it anymore and it was a reminder of my father's death. My father had died across the street, so Thomas promised he'd sell it and we'd find another home to raise the children. That's when we bought the house in West Borough because of the childr-" My mind quickly went to the most logical conclusion and I gasped. "They're here."

24

OLIVIA

"What do you mean they're here? The children?" Kai asked and then swiped out of the image identifier app. Tapping on a red orchid icon with a white background, he opened a map with tiny black dots moving around. "I'm going to isolate the trackers to just The Frederic to see if you're right. Give me just a second. There."

Kai started clicking on each dot with names of people I remembered from parties and meetings with Thomas. Names that would see the alert about me and would surely recognize me in the building if I ever left this apartment. I was trapped until I could figure something else out. I would need help, but from who? Kai? The Resistance?

He clicked on our names. "Fuck! I didn't think about that." Kai snatched a knife from the set on his counter, ran to me, and without hesitation cut the tracker out of my arm. He crushed it in his hand and put it in the sink. I grabbed a towel, wrapping my arm in it to stop the bleeding.

He returned to the HoloTab, and my little black dot was gone.

"I'm sorry. It's just that–"

"It's okay. Also not the first time it's happened. Do you think they know where I am?"

Kai pulled up a chat box and typed in a few things, then went back to the tracking app. "My team will wipe any trace of it and will put in the comms that it was a glitch. They'll have your tracker go up the freeway and then ping it somewhere else too. People should believe it because there is no way that you would be here, or this close to Central. Thomas, and whoever's with him, will think Ethan or the Resistance picked you up. My tracker will ping back at Rose Bay. We should be fine."

"Thank you."

"You're welcome. Let's see who else is here."

He hovered over the apartment next to us, and two names appeared that I didn't recognize. Then he moved to the floor above, where three dots appeared–two in separate rooms and one in the kitchen area, moving slightly back and forth.Kai hovered over the moving dot: *Penny MacDubhain.* Could that really be *our* Penny? I didn't think she earned enough to live somewhere like The Frederic.

"Go to the other two dots, please." My voice was desperate. *Rose Smith. Lucas Smith.*

My children were *here.* Just above me, within arms length if only the ceiling fell away. Instinctively, I ran to the door and flung it open. As I was about to run out, two giant arms surrounded my body and pulled me back inside.

"No!" I screamed.

Kai threw me to the couch and stood in between me and the door. "You can't go out there. Think this through. Be logical. He can't see you, or know you're here. You will lose everything. Every inch you've already gained. Every possible advantage. If you do this, it's over." He walked slowly toward me as my body shook and tears streamed down my face. "Olivia, breathe."

I stopped breathing and my vision blurred. I curled in on myself and screamed again. Kai's body wrapped around mine as I shook and rocked back and forth in disbelief. They were here. My children were here. But where was Thomas? Was he here too? It's so late–maybe he was out, and that was why Penny was here. She was watching the children. That must be it–she was their nanny–and with me gone he probably hired her full time. Or maybe he was out of town? It was so late at night, Penny was probably just cleaning up before sleeping on the couch. My mind continued to tell me stories to soothe my heart.

"Olivia?"

"What?" I said softly.

"We need to get back to the HoloTab and listen to the audio feed. Can you come back to the island or do you want me to bring it here?"

"Bring it here, please."

Kai grabbed the HoloTab and returned to the couch, sitting as close to me as possible. "Are you ready?" The gentleness in his voice soothed me.

"Yes."

"Do you know Penny?"

"Yes. She's been our nanny for years."

Kai's eyes caught mine; he knew something I didn't.

"What?"

"I don't want to make this bigger than it already is, but I don't think Penny's just the nanny."

"What do you mean?"

"Her last name, Olivia. MacDubhain. Did you know that her father is Jeffrey MacDubhain?"

"Who's that?"

"Thomas's boss."

"No, Jeffrey's last name is Mac. The kids always called him uncle Mac because I wanted them to use the proper Mr., but Thomas insisted they call him uncle. His name is Jeffrey Mac."

A tender sympathy met me and I saw it all–more lies. More

stories spun for me to believe in the world Thomas and Jeffrey created.

Kai grabbed my hand and held it. "Whatever happens, or whatever you hear, please remember that you're not alone. You've made it this far because of your strength. There are people who want to see you win, Olivia. If, and I say if, Penny is alone, this will probably not be a big deal. But if Thomas is there, you need to prepare yourself for the unexpected."

"Thomas isn't there, his tracker would illuminate."

"Not his, Olivia. Thomas's tracker is encrypted–the U.S. hasn't been able to access it, which has made it difficult to connect him to everything we've learned about him. We can only track him through the people that he's with–meetings we already know about, or other intel that gives us a good idea of where he is. But it's never 100%."

"Play the audio. I need to know." I suited back up, pulling a heavy invisible armor over my head to protect my chest.

"I will, but you have to stay here, no matter what you hear. You do understand that?"

I nodded.

"Okay, let's see if Thomas is there too."

We heard the sound of dishes being set in a sink, and silverware clanking against a countertop. Two glasses were set down, a cork popped, and liquid poured. Footsteps crossed into what must have been the living room above us, and Penny's dot followed before going still as we listened.

"Well, my sweet Pen, were you able to find the book for Rose?"

Glasses clinking together and the sound of a kiss burned my ears.

"Yes. It was the last one at Capital Books and they held it for her. I just love them so much–they take such good care of Rose, and order anything she wants."

"Well, I love how close it is to us. Makes me feel better

knowing you and the kids don't have to walk too far. Did they get a new cat yet?"

"No, but Fern was there today, so that made Lucas very happy. He asked if he could get a puppy, and I told him we needed to talk to daddy about that."

"A puppy, in an apartment?"

"We can just change one of the rooms into an outdoor space, can't we?"

Thomas took a sip, "Let me see what the contractors say."

"Thank you, love." They kissed, and bile filled my mouth.

"Are you okay?" Kai asked.

I nodded.

Penny's voice shifted from the sweet girl I knew to one laced with sophistication and calculation.

"Thomas, have you learned anything new about where they might be? I'd like to not worry about the children and me when we're out for our walks."

What the ever-living fuck.

"We've traced them to Cameron Park, but I can't get any AV through their blockers. They have something we don't, which is making it difficult for us to get in. Alerts have started, so we'll get a hit in no time. And then, my love, this will all be over."

"How is it possible they have something that we don't have? They're lowly rebels with shit-for-brains and no capabilities. I thought the Nation's technology surpassed everyone else's."

"Our technology surpasses theirs, and my team will find them in no time. Then, we will have the family we've been working toward and the children will finally be raised in a home that supports our Nation ideals."

"*Our* children, not *the* children. They are mine. You promised, remember? When you made her exit plan. It's the only reason I picked you."

"I know. I know."

"Your age, remember? I could have chosen someone else. You were old compared to my other prospects."

"I remember, love."

Penny laughed.

"What?"

"I still love that she saw none of this coming. You, but mostly me. She had no idea the rug was about to be ripped out from under her. And the best part? She did it to herself by taking that pass. If she hadn't, that vacation would've been pretty messy for you."

"I know. I hate to think about it."

"Why?" Her tone was clipped. "You *were* going to kill her, right? Not chicken out?"

Thomas's voice changed, as if he had to prove himself to this girl–as if somehow she held the power, and he didn't. She was leading him, not the other way around. She knew how to make him do what she wanted.

"Of course I was going to, Penny. It was all part of the plan from the beginning. We just needed her body. I honored my agreement with your father, and will continue to honor it until the day I die."

Honey coated her next set of words. "I'm so glad my daddy found you when he did. Growing up with you around was the best thing that ever happened to *you,* and to me."

"I know."

They began kissing and the couch creaked as their bodies moved. I swiped the audio feed away.

"Are you okay?" Kai asked.

"No. But I will be." My hands curled into fists at my sides.

"I know you will, Olivia."

"I just can't believe they were together this whole time? She's so young."

"She's actually not, Olivia. You two are the same age."

"No, that's impossible. Her skin, her body, the way she spoke."

"Technology of the Nation for the upper tiers can help blur the age lines better than anything else. She never had children, either. The vaccines made her sterile." He paused. "It was one of the things we learned in Jeffrey's file, but didn't think it was of much use. He was our target, not Penny. There were definitely blind spots in our research, and we may even encounter more, as things progress."

"What? She was sterile?"

"Yeah. When Jeffrey took Thomas in, Penny was slightly younger and they basically grew up together. I'm guessing once they discovered she couldn't have children, they started looking for bodies–and found you and Ethan." Kai paused and the expression on his face shifted. "I'm sorry for everything I've said to you about your choices...about how you had the power to decide what to do. You were right. You've had no choice in the life you've been living. They created everything to take it from you." He sighed. "And for a long time, they did take your life from you. But now it's yours again, and I will do whatever I can to help you dismantle this. I promise when the time comes, the United States and my father will help you take down Thomas and the Nation."

I studied Kai's expression. Did I want his or the United States' help? Did I need their help, or was this something Ethan, Samara, and I could do without them? Adding another group–another set of men–to this made me uneasy. How could I trust their intentions? At the same time, did it matter? As long as I got what I wanted, did it matter who was involved? I knew one thing for sure: I would need more help with this than I naively thought in the beginning. A little voice in the back of my mind spoke to me, *call her.*

"Thank you. I think it makes the most sense for us to work

together. When do you plan to share this information with your father?"

"I can send a message tonight, but he won't see it until tomorrow morning."

"Once you give him the information, you'll be one step closer to your freedom too, right? So you won't have to live in two worlds anymore."

"Yeah. It's nice to think of that possibility. I get to do whatever I want. Be whoever I want. I can't wait for that day to come." He stared off into the future unfolding before him–a life without his father, without this job, without the albatross around his neck.

"Samara could help."

"Wait, Samara Siraj, Ethan's Samara?"

The words were like acid in my ears. "Yes, that one. Thomas and Jeffrey trusted her with everything. She worked together with Ethan to organize what happened with the data breach and the bomb."

"One of our spies reported her connection to the Resistance, but they couldn't find proof of her loyalty to the Nation, or to the cause. I was never introduced to her when I was at Central. It would have been nice to know though...maybe give me a little more information to work with."

"I'm not sure what role others played in the data breach and bombing, but Samara and Ethan executed it with their team. Samara found information about how the Nation was manipulating the database to create a particular population based on the best DNA. She and Ethan became...friends, and took their time setting everything up for the right moment."

"I need to find her then."

"She's at Rose Bay."

"What? Why didn't you say anything?"

"It wasn't important until now."

"If she's at Rose Bay, then I need to get her too."

"How will you do that?"

"I'll buy her."

"You can purchase attendants?"

"Yes. Remember how you got out of the Center because I wanted to try you out? Purchasing is another perk of my tier-four male status, anyway. They assume when I try an attendant out I am interested in purchasing them, but I want to see how they'll do outside the Center. I can also purchase attendants that I have a night with. I can buy Samara."

"How will that work?"

"At the end of my stay, the Director meets with me for a post-visit schmoozing because he wants me to come back, specifically to this center. Tier-four male visitor stats help rank the centers, and there's a kind of competition over who gets the most in a quarter. Directors greet us when we first get there and usually send us home with something extra when we leave. I will tell him I'm looking to buy someone before I leave to accompany me on a trip. I will mention something that describes Samara, and he'll probably list a few different women and put them in my feed. I have to pretend to want other girls before selecting her, so it's not too obvious. He might protest because of her stats–do you know if they're good?"

I thought of the night with the couple, and swallowed back the bile in my throat. "I don't know."

"Well, I am guessing they're higher because she looks more exotic than the other girls. And depending on his inventory here, I may have to pay more for her. Or less if he has too many women who aren't white."

"It's really like that?"

"Yes. Skin color, especially for women, creates a different value system. Race and gender continue to be a way we rank people, regardless of societal status. It's the first thing people see–what they use to make sense of you. We can make progress on race relations and gender rights, but things never veer far from those lines of judgment. Depending on where in the country I am, I get ranked low because of my Asian side. People are still hung up about the pandemic and the wealth gap between the U.S. and China."

"Wait, are you Chinese? I thought you were–" I stumbled because his profile said Filipino, but that could have been a lie too.

"See? You don't even know. The whole *all of them look the same* mentality that still exists."

"I'm sorry. I just–"

"Don't be. It's fine. If I let that bother me, I wouldn't get very far in life. People are going to see and believe and speak the way they want to. I can only control how I react or respond to it."

"So, where is your family from?"

"My profile was accurate. Filipino and white. My mom is white, but pretty mixed at this point, so it's hard to say where she comes from–we claim Scottish and French. My dad is Filipino, but fully assimilated in the public eye. Promoters use him in advertisements to bolster the American Dream ideal, playing on his ambiguity and the way he represents the ability to be more than just one thing."

"How much will you pay for Samara?"

"As much as it costs."

"You have that kind of money?"

"Yes. At least, the United States does–it doesn't matter what I need as long as it suits their current agenda, they throw money at things like it's nothing. I'll send a message to the Director now, letting him know I want a list of girls for tomorrow. I will return to the Center early, and be back here by tomorrow afternoon."

"Will they be suspicious that we've been gone tonight?"

"They think we're there. My team, remember?" He winked at me.

"What about the alert? Rose Bay would have seen my face by now, and at least Girly would recognize me, right?"

"Yes, but facial recognition software won't. We believe what we're told, rather than what we see. Even if Girly thought you looked like Olivia Smith, she would run Sarah's name through the system and would confirm that you're Sarah, not Olivia. People like Girly or anyone else with too much to lose, won't pursue their own suspicions. It's just not worth it. If the computer says one thing, they will believe it in order to still get access to their privileges, even if they have doubts."

There was truth in what he said. I believed what I was told instead of seeing the Nation and my world for what it actually was. We were taught to stay in the confines of the Nation, and we did, instead of seeing if its borders were safe to cross into a different world.

"Do you plan to leave once you have the kids back, or are you staying to help?" Kai changed the subject.

"Both. I've been saying I want to end the Nation and Thomas, but that was my anger talking, and I told the Resistance I would help them. I want my children back, but after learning about Cooper and everything else, I can't walk away. Thomas can't come out of this alive. After that, I don't know where I'm going, but I'm not staying here, or anywhere near the people who helped keep me trapped for ten years."

I thought about my mother, Ethan's family, and Ethan to some extent. The only way for me to truly be free from my past was to erase it completely. Cutting my family out would be the only way the children and I would ever be able to fully move forward and live a better life. Once I took care of Thomas and the Nation, I would be gone.

"I understand that. There's a part of me that wants to leave, too. Just go somewhere completely new. Start over, with no ties to my father and his political bullshit."

"Wouldn't you be giving up a lot, though, if you left?"

"Power, yes. Money no. One benefit of this job is that I get paid a stupid amount and don't have the time or need to spend any of it. Over the years, I have accumulated enough money to set me up for whatever I do next. I did it that way so my dad couldn't use money to control me anymore. He couldn't pull the strings, and I wouldn't have to let him."

"How would that work if you disappeared then? Don't you think he's going to need you for his campaign or whatever future political plans he has?"

"He'll let me out. I would be a liability to him at that point. I'm a washed-up researcher; I'm unmarried, have no kids, and will probably lose my job once the Nation is gone and my role becomes obsolete. I want to be a leaf in the wind, waiting to go wherever it takes me."

We all tell ourselves stories to survive the lives we lead–the lives we're trying to live now. Kai was no different. He believed his father would let him go once the Nation was gone. I knew differently, though. When someone's roots run too deep inside of you, you can cut away as much as you like, but something always finds a way to grow back when you least expect it. Kai would never be free from that man, because the roots were too deep. I needed him to believe he would get his freedom, though, so I could find mine.

"I hope that it all works out the way you want. Before I go to bed, is there any way to get a visual feed of my children's rooms?"

"Probably not tonight. Let me see what we can do tomorrow though. Thomas has firewalls that are stronger than what I can do. Audio feeds are easy for me, but video is a little bit different. You'll need to stay here tomorrow, okay?"

"I know that."

"For now, let's just get some sleep. It's been a long night. We can come up with more of the plan tomorrow, after we take a break from all of this. Sound okay?"

Although I wanted to say no and keep working to get my children sooner, I knew running on no sleep and all adrenaline would get me nowhere.

"Sounds good."

We resigned to our rooms. As I lay in the dark, under the floor where my children slept, I couldn't help but wonder what their rooms looked like. If Lucas had his starry night light illuminating his ceiling, or if Rose had her swan night light plugged into the wall. I could feel them, almost breathe them in, and I wondered if they could feel me too–now that we were so close to one another.

"I love you. Mama loves you." I whispered into the dark nothingness of my room.

25

OLIVIA

I woke to the smell of coffee and the sound of bacon crackling in the kitchen. The automatic curtains transitioned to sheer, letting in sunlight soft enough to remind me I was in Kai Acosta's apartment.

I was a fugitive. My children were in the apartment above me. So were my ex-husband and his nanny girlfriend. I lay in bed trying to make sense of it all, but ended up tucking it away so I could get up and walk into the kitchen. I'd feel it later. Right now, I needed to plan.

I walked to the bathroom first, catching a glimpse of myself. Dark circles met me in the mirror first, and I looked away as I washed my face. In the kitchen, Kai wore loose athletic shorts, a small red iridescent orchid swaying with the fabric as he moved from the stove to the coffee pot.

"Mornin'. Did you sleep okay?"

"A little."

"Coffee?"

"Yes, please."

I sat at the high top barstool, waiting for Kai to serve me. This morning, his calm confidence and odd joviality were unlike anything I'd ever seen. He maneuvered through the kitchen, multitasking like no other man I'd known. He placed the coffee in front of me and I took a sip. It was the perfect mixture of cream and sugar, and the caramel notes of the Nation coffee I'd missed desperately while being at the Center and the compound.

"Have you checked on the kids?"

"Yes, their trackers are moving. So is Penny's."

I looked at the clock. "They're getting ready for summer session courses." We enrolled the children in classes every summer for enrichment and to keep them from being bored at home. Rose loved to take art classes when she was younger, but this summer, she planned to take a science course to give her an edge in the higher-level courses. "They'll be leaving soon for school."

"I'm still working on tapping into the visual feed in the apartment, but we can see them leave the building, if you want."

"Yes. I want to see them."

I watched the HoloTab obsessively as I drank my morning coffee. The children's dots moved around the screen, and I imagined hearing their footsteps above me. At 8:00 am, their dots left the apartment and trailed out the building. Kai took the tablet and tapped the screen, pulling up a live street view to see my children.

There they were–Rose on one side, Lucas on the other, and Penny in the middle. Bodyguards hovered like drones at a show, but Penny and the children paid no attention to them. Rose had braided hair and was carrying her lunchbox. Lucas's mess of a hair was just like it had been in April, just a little bit longer. Penny wore yoga pants, a long shirt adorned with necklaces, and a fedora hat. Her dark sunglasses made it look like she was the classic stay-at-home mom, soaked in money and time.

The camera feed followed them until right before the

school, when another person joined them. Kai looked down at the tracker. *Cooper Jones* hovered above the dot and I stared at the screen. My three children were together, and just a short distance from me. Cooper put his arm around Rose, and she smiled. Lucas skipped around Penny and nudged Cooper. It was as if the three of them already knew who they were to each other–siblings bound together by one mother, who would one day take them all home.

I watched, enraptured, until they passed through the school gates and Penny kissed them goodbye. Those were not her foreheads to kiss, and I would find a way to make her pay for the time she stole from me. I closed the feed and looked at Kai.

"How do they look?" He asked softly.

"Good. The same, but different."

"What about the boy? How was that?"

"I didn't expect to see him, but it was good. It felt right seeing the three of them together. I can't really say more about it. I want to be with them. I should have been the one walking them to school, but I'm not. I will find a way to accept that for now...to let it go for now."

"This can't be easy for you, but just know it's temporary."

"Thanks."

"More coffee?" He held the pot in his hand.

"Yes, please. Thank you."

"No problem."

"What does today look like? You getting Samara and all?"

"I'll leave soon to meet with the Director, and hopefully by mid-afternoon we'll be back. Once here, we can figure out what to do next. We'll need to get in touch with your friends today, to let them know you're okay. I'm sure they've seen the footage and are worried about you."

Make a call, yes, I need to make a call.

"Have you ever done this before? Bought someone?"

"Yes. But I've only done it once because a friend of mine

needed help. At Rose Bay, we get tokens–sort of like a rewards program. Most people I've spoken with at the bar have done it too, and they keep their attendant in an apartment or vacation home until they're done with them. Others save their tokens over the course of a couple of years, and then spend them at once so they can have multiple attendants at their disposal anytime."

My shoulders tensed.

"Sorry. I know that must sound terrible."

"Yeah it does. Buying people, or saving up to buy them, is disgusting. What happens when they're done with the attendants?"

He winced. "I actually don't know. I tried to track one woman I'd interviewed on my first night. I wanted to select her for night two, but someone had bought her. Her chip was active for the first month, but then completely disappeared."

"Maybe she escaped. Cut it out?"

"Maybe. Or maybe..."

"She's dead."

"Yeah, I think that may be more likely."

We both knew the reality of what happened to anyone who lost their value to the Nation: disposable bodies filling a landfill somewhere in South Burrough.

My curiosity piqued again.

"Have you ever slept with an attendant during your time at the Centers?"

He took a long sip. "Just once."

"How did it happen? I thought–"

"It's sort of complicated. Yes, she was gorgeous, but there was more to it."

"Complicated how?"

"You want to talk about this, instead of something else?" He smiled.

"Yep." I didn't want to think about my children being within reach yet untouchable. I didn't want to think about Thomas possibly being upstairs and me unable to kill him. I didn't want to think about Samara and being unable to tell her what was going on.

"Well, before I tell you about her, I need to tell you about my ex, Emily."

For the first time, it felt like Kai was opening up to me. He'd shared about his father, and his hopes to be free once the Nation was gone, but he struck me as someone who lived a lonely life, an isolated life–one painted with nights at a bar alone, and single-ticket movies. A part of me wanted to know more about him, not just because it was strategic, but because it felt right.

"Emily and I had been together for a few years–a home together, Sunday dinners with the families, shared vacations, the whole thing. I went through the motions of being in a relationship, drawing from what I'd seen in my world–on TV, in movies. Like so many young, dumb, and impressionable people shaped by their parents and society, we followed the same path: got engaged, planned a huge wedding, and eventually called it off."

"Really?" A pang of jealousy coursed through my veins, because he called his off.

"Yeah. I mean, we were both miserable. Emily and I were only together because we came from similar families. It was the classic expectation–political families date and marry other political families. She was unhappy too, but we both were so tied to our parents and what they wanted, we let it go on for longer than it should have. My traveling was pretty intense, even before I took this job, and it helped us both realize that we didn't love each other the way a long-term couple should. We used this as an excuse to our families to end it, right before we sent wedding invitations out."

"You were going to marry her–and then you just called it off?"

"Yep. We did it together. I got home from one of my trips, exhausted and totally disconnected from our relationship. By then, after interviewing so many people, I knew I didn't want to get married. Marriage felt like an antiquated social construction meant to keep people in line–sex somehow 'purified', children sheltered from the atrocities of the real world. With all of my traveling, Emily had actually fallen for someone at work, but he wasn't from a family that had a powerful name."

"Did she cheat on you?"

"Yeah, totally did. But I was completely okay with it. I secretly hoped she would–as fucked up as that sounds–so I could get out. I didn't know she wanted out too. After we talked, I realized we were both in a bad situation, and I decided we could blame my job for our breakup. We said the time apart was too hard...the classic *we'd grown apart* thing. We even said that our children would suffer without the presence of their father, if we ever had any."

"What did your family say?"

"Oh, our parents were furious. They said we would bring shame to our families, and that their PR reps would have to create a backstory that wouldn't completely rock my father's future plans for running for higher office. Of course, it was always about them. Emily and I initially bonded over our shared experience of having narcissistic parents."

"That had to be hard, even if you both wanted it."

"Yeah, I mean, it was sad. But it would have been worse to stay together and be miserable. She deserved to be with the guy she cheated on me with. They're actually married now and, last I heard, she was pregnant. Once kids enter the picture, parents move on and forgive because they're so obsessed with the idea of becoming grandparents."

"And your parents? Do they want you to get married?"

"Yes. They will always want that. I know my mom secretly hopes I'll meet someone and settle down, even though I never meet anyone with the way my schedule is."

Kai paused and shoved two slices of bacon into his mouth.

"So, to answer your questions now about the attendant...her name was Allison. It was at Rose Bay, and it happened last year." He said, smacking the bacon loudly between words.

"The first girl you slept with after your breakup was an attendant at Rose Bay?"

"Judgey much? I didn't say she was the first girl I slept with after Emily. I said she was the first and only attendant I've slept with."

"Oh, so you're quite the player, then?"

His blush and boyish, flirtatious smile were impossible to hide. "I've had my moments."

"Is casual sex allowed in the U.S.? Like it used to be?" I hadn't thought about sex outside of marriage or the Nation system in years. How people used to join dating apps and sleep with people, with no connection or consequence. It became part of twenties culture prior to the edicts coming into place. I was with Ethan, and only him before Thomas, so I didn't take part in that world. Before the ban on dating apps, my friends in the compound told me their secrets. A few single mothers would share their stories with the married moms over too many glasses of wine, giving the young women on the property more insight into the dating world.

"Olivia, it's permitted. And if anything, it's more prevalent because of screening systems. They haven't banned dating apps; in fact, better algorithms now serve users' needs. It doesn't matter what the purpose is for the user, and it can change day-to-day if they want it to. The apps are completely customizable. All apps now require a DNA scan, which uploads any medical history to the profile–all diseases, conditions, whatever."

"That sounds like a huge invasion of privacy."

"To some extent, it is. But also, it also cuts down on people lying just to get sex. And for those looking for the long-term, it helps weed out possible shared genetic risks like cancer genes, heart disease, or vaccination histories. People still want to have children, too. The population has declined since the vaccines, but having the information upfront helps users make better choices for the future they want, and the American dream they're still searching for."

"Have you ever been on the apps?"

"No. I wasn't allowed because of my father's political image. People in my world didn't need dating apps–we hooked up with each other either out of spite for our parents or because we needed to escape the world we lived in. When it was time to settle down and present the perfect family image, private matchmakers were hired to pair the best sons and daughters."

"What if you were gay?"

"Matchmakers would do that too. And then adoption coordinators, if it's two men. Politicians, just like here, can't leave anything to chance."

"It's so crazy to think about all the ways people try to interfere in other people's lives."

"Yeah, it is. I'm just so used to it at this point that I don't think twice about it. I'm focusing on the endgame, and that's it."

"So what happened with Allison?"

His body leaned against the counter top. "I went through a period of my life when I would sleep with anyone that looked my way. A lot of that was out of spite for my dad, and the image he was trying to make me uphold, but the other reasons were darker–which isn't relevant right now. Allison was my first."

"Right, your first attendant."

"No, my first, first. We knew each other when we were younger. Our parents were friends, and we didn't want to go away to college as virgins, so we made a deal to sleep with each other at her parents' beach house the summer before we left. We agreed when we were high school freshmen, just as a joke one night after we drank too many of my mom's seltzers. And in the last week of our senior year summer vacation, our parents went back to the capital for a meeting, and we had the house to ourselves. They never worried about either of us being alone together because they thought Allison was gay. For a short time after college, she did date a girl, who I thought was perfect for her. Anyway, we didn't plan it, but we opened a really expensive bottle of wine, then another, and we remembered the promise we'd made years before. We went upstairs to the master bedroom, which had these amazing French doors. It was a full moon, and the only light in the room came from the reflection on the water. I know this sounds super sappy, but it was the way everyone wants their first time to be. After that, she went her way, I went mine, and we didn't see each other again...until I was at Rose Bay last year."

"How is that even possible? She's a politician's daughter, with all the money in the world. How would she end up at a Center?"

"After she broke up with her college girlfriend, she met some guy and then just sort of disappeared. Rumors surfaced she was into drugs, or that she was trafficked somewhere. Other rumors spread about political tensions between her father and another leader in a different country, but again, they were rumors. I didn't think I would ever run into her, let alone as an attendant for the Nation."

"Wait, was she on the list we just saw?"

"No, but it does make me think she was taken for political reasons."

"It seems like it would make sense. What did you do when you saw her?"

"I chose her right away. I had to. I had to figure out what had happened. When we got to the room, I motioned for her to not say anything until I had the system disarmed. Once we could talk, she told me that someone had taken and trafficked her into the Nation. She didn't know it was happening initially, because they'd offered her this high-level job and said she wouldn't have to be aligned with the image of her father anymore. Like me, she wanted freedom from our politically tight world, and the Nation knew exactly how to lure her in.

Allison told me how she'd started work in a Central office, and then one day her employer moved her to a new data tech firm in Rose Bay. She said nothing indicated anything bad was about to happen before they moved her. One day, she was at work; the next, someone locked her in a cell. She had no memory of getting there, and when she asked to make a call, they refused. They accused her of stealing data and selling it back to the U.S. and said they had records of her doing it. Videos, emails, texts. They showed it all to her. When she asked what she could do, they told her the only way to pay off her debt to the Nation would be to enlist. Worn down and with no one else to reach out to, she signed a five-year contract."

"That is awful." I thought of Ethan, and how similar his story was to hers. "This sounds like what happened to Ethan."

"Doesn't surprise me at all."

"What ended up happening?"

"We talked for hours, her telling me about the good and bad in her life since our night together at the beach house. I told her about Emily, and how we'd figured out a way to call off the marriage without our parents being too upset. I shared details about my job with her–maybe too many–but it didn't matter, since we were old friends who shared a connection. People can go years without seeing each other, then bare their souls over a bottle of wine with no judgment, and still see each other in the same respectable light they did before reconnecting. It's a gift, and I had that with her.

At one point, she started to cry, and I moved to the couch to comfort her. As soon as we touched, I remembered her body and the way it felt in my arms. It was just so natural for me, and when she looked up at me, the only thing we could do was kiss."

"Didn't you feel like you were sort of a predator? I mean, people literally trafficked this girl for sex."

"I didn't, and I know she didn't either. It's difficult to explain. That night, we didn't have sex. It was something else. I wanted her to know that I would protect her. I wanted her to feel safe, and I think she wanted me to feel safe, too. She was a connection to my past that I wanted to keep because, for that one night, we didn't have to be anyone but ourselves. Two young lovers discovering a truth about life in the most innocent way. Sleeping with her again, in some ways, proved something to me I haven't quite figured out yet. Part of it was the ego of getting her again, but it was also about feeling eighteen again–untouched by the years of a life that was never really mine."

"It sounds like you just added another notch to your belt." I arched a brow, my tone sharper than I intended, daring him to deny it.

"I get how it looks that way. The way it sounds. In some ways I am very much someone who wants to believe in love, even though I haven't ever really experienced it. In reality, the hero role comes much more naturally to me. I can step into that role with no hesitation. Being a hero, and standing up for what's right, will always trump any sort of emotional attachment I have to someone. She needed saving, and I did just that."

"By sleeping with her?"

"No, not just that."

"So you saved her after you slept with her."

"Yes. I get that. But still."

"I get reconnecting with someone from your past, but she was vulnerable–and did it ever occur to you that maybe she'd been so conditioned to sleep with people that your touch alone would be an automatic response to her body?" I shifted and tightened my hands.

He peered at me, amber eyes beginning to disappear under black pupils. "I get what you're saying, and I know what it must look like, but it wasn't. She wanted to be with me just as much as I wanted to be with her."

I laughed, "I think that's what a lot of men would say."

"We were a connection to a past that would never be again. Sometimes people need that, you should understand. Living in the past, even if for a moment, and even in a situation like that, can still provide some level of comfort, no matter how complicated things are."

"Was she the one you got out? The old friend?"

"Yes."

"Where is she now?"

"Back in DC with her parents."

"How is she doing?"

"Okay. As expected. She has the best therapists money can buy, but her parents like to use her as propaganda when they talk about the Nation. After seeing those files, it makes me grateful she didn't end up like the other women. I know that sounds bad."

"It doesn't. She meant something to you, and when bad things happen, there's always a part of us that is glad it wasn't one of our own. Have you seen her since she's been home?" A creeping sting slowly crawled up my throat, shifting the tone of my voice from soft to almost accusatory. Where was this coming from?

Kai noticed, but didn't play into it. "I've seen her a few times at her parents' home. She's never alone, though, and heavily guarded. She doesn't go out much, without someone following right behind her–either a parent or her bodyguard. She'll be happy again at some point."

"Or she won't, and will spiral into a depressive oblivion and never return."

"You're certainly all over the place this morning aren't you?"

He was right. I couldn't regulate my anger, disgust, and jealousy at hearing people reconnect without them being destroyed. Ethan was my first, and our time together was like nothing I would have ever given up. The love we shared was electric, and our bodies found ways of loving each other that I wasn't sure I would ever find, or even want, again. It was painful to slowly let him go, and I knew the further I moved into the steel version of me, the more he would be left behind, with nothing either of us could do to return.

"I'm going to take a shower and get going. I need to be back at Rose Bay as soon as possible. Are you going to be alright here?" He asked with a pitched tone.

"Yes. I will. I'll follow your rules, stay inside, blah, blah, blah." I got up from the island and started making my way back to my room.

"Olivia, I'm not asking you to stay inside to control you, you know that right?"

"Yes. I know, but it still doesn't mean I have to like it."

We closed the doors to our bedrooms and I crawled back into my bed, closing my eyes and hoping sleep would take me away until Samara arrived.

26

ETHAN

Olivia hadn't appeared on camera for the last two days, and panic gnawed at me. I should have gone with her. I knew she couldn't survive the vile things that happened at the Center. To clear my head, I left the surveillance room and headed for the lake. A run in the crisp summer morning, before the heat kicked in, would do me well. Afterward, I could return, search through the other footage, and finally end her time at Rose Bay.

It felt good to be running outside instead of on the treadmill, like I usually did. Motivated by the sound of crunching gravel beneath my feet, I increased my speed. The slight breeze, soon to vanish with the rising sun, cooled my skin. Birds busied with their morning routines watched as I sped past.

How was I going to fix all of this? Jude and I were done, which was one less thing to worry about. I needed to check the footage right before Olivia went missing from surveillance, to see if that could help me put the pieces together. I also knew that I couldn't allow Olivia to kill Thomas; it was my job to end him—proof that I loved her, and would do anything for her. She could never live with herself if she killed him. Nightmares and guilt would eat her alive and tear her from her children. Still, if it had to be done, I would be the one to kill him, and I would do it when I rescued the children.

I could be the hero.

The one she could rely on to protect her.

The one who would do anything, and risk everything, for her.

As I rounded the last corner of the lake, I saw Rebecca walking slowly. I wanted to avoid talking to her, because she was so weird the last time we'd talked, but I knew there was no way around it. I slowed to a walking pace as we met on the trail.

"Hi, Rebecca. You're out early."

"Yeah, before it gets too hot."

"Right."

"You're out early too."

"The heat, like you said."

We stood awkwardly for a moment; her mouth opened slightly as if to say something, then she shook her head, forcing herself silent.

"Is everything okay?" I asked.

"Ethan, you need to know something. But you shouldn't know it. But you need to know it."

"Okay, what is it?"

"I can't." She fumbled her fingers together, rubbing them over and over again. "I'm supposed to keep it quiet. That was the deal, the pact. If I stayed quiet, then Jessica would be okay. Olivia too. Even you."

I cocked my head. "Rebecca, you know you're safe here, right?"

"I won't be safe anywhere. Neither will she, but she refuses to listen to me."

"Who, Olivia?"

"Yes."

"Rebecca, she's been through a lot. We just need to be

patient. She'll come home and everything will be okay–like it used to be." I attempted to convince myself once again, by saying it aloud.

"Ethan, you need to know...nothing will ever be like it used to be. When she learns what I've known this whole time about the...when you learn it too, nothing will ever be the same."

"Can you at least tell me what you're talking about? Maybe I can help?"

"The boy–he's not–" Rebecca looked around, as if she thought she was being watched. "Nevermind, I need to go. My walk needs to be finished."

Unsure of what she was saying, I shook my head and continued my run. Maybe the trauma from her own loss had finally taken its toll, and with Olivia back in the Nation, her mind had wandered past the point of no return. She showed strength in the meeting room with my dad, but slipped so easily back into the weaker version of herself. I didn't have time to figure her out though. Once Olivia was back, the two of us could try and get Rebecca help.

I ran through crunchy gravel until my feet hit the tarmac at the compound. Once back inside, I went to check the rest of the footage for any updates that might help me find Thomas and the children.

"Don't do it, Ethan." Vivan's voice lingered behind me.

"What?"

"You can't look at the footage anymore. It's going to make things so much harder for you when she returns. Trust me, you don't want to keep doing this."

"Have you heard from Morgan about why she's been off footage the last two nights?"

"Yes, and it sounds like whatever's going on is helping us. Don't mess with it."

"Where is she?"

"She's there, but with someone who's also trying to remove

the Nation from power. His technology is better than both ours and the Nation's. He's able to block surveillance."

He? A growing jealousy roared up from my stomach to my chest.

"Better than ours and the Nation's? How is that possible? Who could the citizen possibly be working with that has better tech than us?"

"Not sure. Maybe a foreign dignitary? A group who wants to remove the Nation for their own political gain? Whatever or whoever it is, we need to leave it alone. Promise me you won't look at any more footage."

"I can't do that, Viv, and you know it."

She sighed, "Can't say I didn't try. Remember, once you see what's been happening, you'll never be able to go back."

"I've already seen the worst, Vivian."

"Trust me, Ethan, you haven't." She touched my shoulder, gave it a squeeze, and left me.

I opened the HoloTab on the desk, searching the surveillance feed for the nights before she went off-grid. It was the same thing for several nights–men, short in conversation and long in the bedroom. I put the footage on faster replay, so I didn't have to see or hear any of the details. At some point over the last few weeks, I convinced myself it was the same guy each time, so I wouldn't have to think about her body count stacking up like mine had over the past ten years. I couldn't even remember the faces of the women I'd slept with, barely remembered their bodies. The only thing that would come back and haunt me–the smells. They all had distinct scents, either from their shampoo or perfume. When I walked through a cloud of yesterday, I could distinctly remember where I was and who I was with, but their faces never came fully into view. Lips, eyes, bodies–fragmented pieces that never joined to form an image I didn't want to remember anyway.

The footage was still rolling when I saw she had another

attendant in the room–Samara–and they were with a couple. There was a moment where I wondered if I was invading Sam's privacy by watching her too, but I put it out of my mind and played the footage with the sound on. I felt sick. The couple that selected them would make none of it easy, and I knew that from the first word out of the male's mouth. It was familiar, and I changed the lighting to get a better look at his face.

Victor Lope. What was that sick fuck and his wife doing in Rose Bay? They were one of the few couples that came to Central together. I never interacted with them, but Jude did and what he told me was beyond anything I thought the Center would allow. Their cruelty and violence toward attendants knew no bounds. One of the new females we had a few years back ended up in the medical bay for a week; our machines did the best they could to repair her after their torture. The trauma from the night put her in a catatonic state, forcing Thomas to decide to keep her in medical. He told Samara if the attendant didn't come out of it within a week, he would take care of her himself. She didn't last long after that. It wasn't clear if she got transferred or, like so many others who crossed Thomas's path, ended up dead.

They cycled through different things they would do to attendants, and rarely slept with any of the ones that I knew about. They enjoyed torturing, humiliating, and dominating. Because they had deep pockets, and were willing to use their money, Mr. and Mrs. Lope could do anything they desired.

I watched in horror as I saw Samara and Olivia chained in a room with wolves. Their bodies being beaten and violated in ways that they could've never imagined. Tears streaming down Sam's face, then later, Olivia's. This is why I didn't want her to go–them to go–because I couldn't protect them from animals like the Lopes. I threw up into the trash can by the desk. The girls were now on a couch, huddled under blankets while the Lopes had sex in the bedroom. There was nothing violent about their sex. It was pure love, as if displaying violence against others was the only way they could keep from being violent with each other. Cruelty ran in both their veins and they needed an outlet for it. The Centers gave them the perfect opportunity. I threw up again and stepped away from the desk.

How could I let this happen? Let them go? They would never come back from this. Laura's knowledge of this would devastate her. Jude's devastation would be immense, too, after what they did to him. We kept him off the schedule for two weeks, which fucked his ratings up, but I didn't care, and neither did Samara. We could protect him, and we did. Now, two of the most important people in my life were alone in a room, broken by two of the most evil people that came through Center doors.

I sat back down and fast forwarded the footage. In the morning, I saw Olivia peer toward the door, so I slowed the footage back to normal and turned the volume up. Victor was talking to Thomas. Something about a flash drive at Thomas's and Olivia's house. A flash drive I was sure we needed for the Resistance. I would get it for Olivia. I would leave for Olivia's house as soon as I could. My mind wandered and calculated the timing. I would be able to get to South, then sneak into West just after dark, avoiding the cameras so that no one here would know where I was.

I stopped the footage and bolted out the door, slamming chest first into Jude.

"Sorry, Ethan, I was just looking for Brandon. Have you seen him?"

"No. It's been a sort of busy morning already."

"Are you okay?"

"Yeah. I'm fine." I paused. "You need to know something. I just watched some footage from one of the selection nights at Rose Bay."

"You've been watching the footage? That's really wrong.

Olivia would never want you to do that. It's an invasion of privacy, Ethan."

"It doesn't matter, Jude, as long as it's helping me keep her safe. Besides, I'm trying to look for information that the girls may be missing." I went straight for it, even though I knew I should be more tender. "But, Jude...the one I just watched was bad. The Lopes were there."

His face went ghost white, and he caught his breath as he stepped back. "No. I thought they were only at Central."

"They have the power to go wherever they want, I guess, and they were at Rose Bay. It wasn't good. Olivia and Sam–it was pretty violent."

"I have to see it."

"No, Jude. Don't do it. It will bring you back to that night. It took you months to recover from them. From what they did to you."

He played with his fingers, shifting back and forth on his feet. I could feel his need for comfort, and although I was trying hard to put us behind me, I closed the distance between and wrapped my arms around him. Jude's hands stayed together for a moment, then found their way around my waist. I held him as he cried into my chest, fighting the love I had for him. I thumbed through his hair and rubbed his back, while his ghosts watched us from just behind him.

27

OLIVIA

After my nap, I moved to the living room, searching for something to do. I scanned Kai's overstuffed bookshelf, trying to decipher the order he kept his books in. From what I could tell, they were mostly sorted by genre, except for a stack that lay haphazardly sideways. Most of the books were banned in the Nation, and I wondered if there were book bans in the United States too. If it was as free as he said, I hoped we could read anything we wanted to.

My fingers traced the paper and hardback portals to a past I allowed myself to feel hopeful about. When this was all over and the Nation was gone, would I have the freedom to read whatever I wanted? Would I have the freedom to give my children books that weren't controlled by someone else's agenda?

I thought back to the audio feed from the night before, and the thought of Penny taking Rose to the bookstore–my bookstore. It wasn't hers to take Rose there. Bookstores belonged to me, not Penny. My mind drifted to a time long before, to a moment I hadn't realized I would need to hold onto until it was already gone.

MY TINY HAND found itself inside Jessica's as we walked through downtown Sacramento. The air was cool under the fall morning sky, and we were on our way to get hot chocolate, after picking up my book from Capital Books. We rounded K street, and the blue-and-white sign I loved met my gaze. We walked in, and the black tortoiseshell cat greeted me by rubbing in and out of my legs.

"Good morning, Mittens." I said, smiling and bending down to pet her.

"We don't have a lot of time, Olivia, so please just find your book so we can meet Mom at Starbucks," Jessica whined as she scanned the store for her bookstore crush, Jacob.

I had just turned nine, and my parents gave me a gift certificate to Capital Books, a recently opened bookstore just a short walk from our condo. I peeled away from my sister and walked to the children's section, looking for a new chapter book. She passed me, quickly feigning interest in the fantasy section where the older boy she liked worked on the weekends.

"Hello, Olivia." A soft voice from behind found me.

"Hi, Mr. Ross."

"Looking for a new book?"

"Yeah, my parents got me a gift certificate for my birthday."

"Oh! Well, happy birthday! Looking for anything in particular?"

"No, just a chapter book."

"Hmm...well, let's see what we can find." Mr. Ross thumbed through the shelves, pulling books off one by one. I was notorious for judging books by their cover; if I didn't like how it looked I would shake my head no, and Mr. Ross would smile and place it back on the shelf. After putting back *The Swan Princess*, he grinned at me, "I think I have one for you, but it might be too long. Maybe a bit too old for you."

A book was never too long or old for me. "I can read long books...and what do you mean by too old, like for old people?"

"No, for bigger kids."

"I can read big kid books. I've already read all of *The Chronicles of Narnia* books and those are supposed to be for big kids."

"Well, indeed. Okay, then I think this book will work for you." Mr. Ross thumbed over to another section where *Call of the Wild*, *The Tale of Despereaux*, and *Guardians of Ga'Hoole* sat waiting to be chosen by a young child. "This is *Watership Down*. It's about a group of brave rabbits who set out to find a new home, after theirs is destroyed by humans. The book has danger and adventure, some good ideas about friendship, and of course, the fight to build a better life."

"Bunnies? Fighting for a better life? That doesn't sound that good," I scoffed.

"Really? Not even with that sell? I promise you it's good. It's about friendship and standing up for what's right–you seem like you like things like that, right?"

"Yes."

"How 'bout this. If you read it and don't like it, bring it back," he bent down close to my ear and whispered, "just because it's your birthday." He winked at me, handing me the brown and straw-yellow book with a giant brown rabbit on the front.

"Okay, Mr. Ross, I'll try it. But if I don't like it I will be back next weekend for a new book."

"I would expect nothing less, Olivia." He smiled, and then trailed back up the creaky stairs to the office that overlooked the entire store.

Looking for my sister, I went to the basement and found her twirling her hair while she talked to Jacob about something I had no interest in. She saw me, blushed, and then dismissed me with her hand.

"Go buy your book, Olivia. I'll be right there." Her tone told me she had no time for her little sister.

I headed upstairs where Ms. Katie greeted me at the cash register. "Hi, Olivia, what did you find today? Oooh, *Watership Down*, great book, one of my faves." Her ginger-red hair curled perfectly to frame her face and her hazel eyes. Ms. Katie was one of my favorites in the store. She would sneak me candy when my mom or sister weren't looking.

"Mr. Ross says if I don't like it I can bring it back because it's my birthday."

"Well, happy birthday, Olivia! And yeah, just bring it back, but I bet you won't. Here, take this too," Ms. Katie handed me a bookmark with a copper-colored, long-haired dog on it. "I'm trying out new swag for the bookstore–this graphic of the puppy spoke to me and I figured it would be a good look for us." She smiled, and I handed her my gift certificate. She rang me up and put the book and bookmark in a bag.

Jessica walked out just as Ms. Katie was finishing up. They exchanged a set of looks I didn't quite understand, but it wasn't friendly. "Let's go, Olivia," she clipped, and pulled my body forward out the tile floored door.

"Bye, Ms. Katie. Bye, Mr. Ross!" I yelled, as my sister and I left for Starbucks.

Our mom was waiting at a table outside with three drinks–hot chocolate for us, and a pumpkin spice latte for her.

"Perfect timing, the order was just finished." My mom looked at my bag. "What book did you get?"

"*Watership Down*."

"Great choice. I like how they choose to leave, but become a stronger family because of it." She paused, "Girls, if we ever had to leave our home, like the rabbits in the book, you know that dad and I will always be there for you, right?"

Jessica rolled her eyes, "Yeah, Mom, we know."

I sat, studying my mom, wondering why she would say something like that. "Are we moving?" I asked.

"No, nothing like that. I just want you two to know that it doesn't matter where we are or where we live–we're a family. When you girls go to college and start your own lives, we are still a family. Your father and I will be there for you, no matter what. We could go months without talking, and I would still be there if you needed it."

"Why would we ever not talk to you, Mom?" Jessica's tone was in full force this morning.

My mom smiled patiently, "Sometimes things just happen between moms and daughters. It's little memories like these, and the ones we will continue to make, that help us remember we're all we have. I will always be here for you. No matter what."

It felt like one of our mother's old future-castings–once unsettling, now just something we smiled and nodded at.

"Okay, mom. Sounds good." I said, taking a sip of my hot chocolate.

We sat until we finished our drinks, exchanging conversation about our plans for the weekend, and what dad's travel schedule was going to look like. The leaves were changing and starting to fall, dancing around the sidewalk in tiny circles. The three of us threw our empty cups away, my mom stationing herself in the middle of Jessica and me, grabbing one hand each as we walked back to our downtown home.

MY HEART ACHED at the memory of a time when my sister, mother, and I were close. So much had happened over the last few months–so many truths uncovered–that I couldn't picture us ever being close again. In so many ways I blamed them for stealing my life away. If we had only known about the United

States, I could have had the life with Ethan that I deserved, the one I used to want.

A beep sounded at the door and I jumped, ready to face whatever intruder might be walking in.

"Olivia! Oh my god, you're okay."

"Samara!"

I ran and pulled her in, but her body didn't ease into mine like she had a million times before. I stood back and looked at her. She was dressed in a tight black skirt and crop top, her face covered in make up, and long dangling earrings hung on either side.

"Are you okay?" I asked.

"Yeah. Just a lot, you know."

"Why are you dressed like that?"

"Because she had to, in order for me to buy her." Kai chimed in.

Samara was dressed up to be on display for purchase. In a world where I thought we had come so far, there were reminders like this that told me we hadn't. We no longer chain bodies of color, but we still treat them as chattel consuming their pain as entertainment. Shifting their value based on who held power. How long would this continue? Would we ever be able to change the narrative engrained in our collective memory? My friend–a mother, a warrior, the strength of the rebellion–stood waiting to be purchased while a group of men exchanged stories, laughed, and determined her fate. Disgusting. How many other women had this happened to? How many times had this happened at Central under Thomas's reign? How many more women would it happen to if we didn't fight back?

"How the fuck are we ever going to win? To stop this? To stop him?" I yelled. "The people that were trafficked and then sold like this..the women who were used for their bodies and killed! How could I have ever turned a blind eye to it? How could I have not known? How could I have woken up day after day, raising children to be participants in a system that takes and takes and takes?" I was angry. So. Angry. "And now, my face is everywhere. I'm trapped again. I can't even walk upstairs and open his door to take them away. I have no merit, no credibility, no power…again."

Samara slipped off her black high heels and walked to me, the warm woman I grew to love returned. "Liv? This is going to stop. We're part of something bigger than we could've ever imagined. We do have the power to stop this, and I really, truly believe we will. Kai told me everything. I can't believe I didn't know. I should have been paying more attention, but I was looking at everything else. There's an entire nation that wants to help end what our world has created for all these people. Ethan, and everyone on the compound, has power to help too. Just because it's dark right now, doesn't mean that light isn't going to find us. We're just at a waystation. As soon as everything lines up, we're going to jump on that train and move so fast that Thomas, the Nation, and Jeffrey won't even know what to do."

Samara tilted my face to hers. "Olivia. You may not want to hear this, but you need to call your mom."

"What? Why?"

"She's been trying to reach you through comms, through Morgan. She needs to talk to you."

Call her. The voice I heard. The tether between mothers and children is never broken, no matter how many times one or the other tries.

"What does she need?"

"I don't know, but she was pretty insistent. Morgan says she's been hounding her for the past couple of days."

"How? We don't have HoloPhones."

"Morgan slipped this in Kai's car when he was finishing up with the purchase."

Samara handed me a HoloPhone with the communications app already open. Names of people from the compound, displayed in alphabetical order, lined the left side of the screen. I scrolled through, but didn't see my mother's name.

"She's not here."

"You need to tap on the main line, just right there." Samara pointed to it.

"Thanks." I looked at her and then Kai, "I'll be back." I walked to my room and sat on my bed with the phone in my lap. It was clear I needed to call her, but what would I say? What did she want to tell me? Was there any point in having a discussion at all? It's not like she would apologize for what happened. She wasn't going to take ownership over anything that wronged me, because she saw it all as right. My mother would cling to her role as the protector, even if what she did wasn't protection at all.

"Fuck it." I tapped on the phone and waited.

The line trilled until a voice sounded, "Hello?" It was Jude.

"Jude?"

"Olivia! Oh my god, are you okay?" His voice was soft and desperate, like he'd heard the voice of a ghost.

"Hi, Jude. Yes, I'm okay."

"Your face, Olivia, it's everywhere, even up here. Did you really burn your house down?"

"Yes."

"They said attempted murder–did you try to kill Thomas?"

"No. I think that's from the bombing. I just burned the house down."

"*Just burned the house down,*" he laughed. "Well, good for you. I mean it definitely complicated things up here. Ethan doesn't even know about it, but once he finds out, he's going to be pissed."

"Why doesn't Ethan know?"

"He left, Olivia. After he saw the footag-"

The footage.

"Did he see what happened? With me...and Samara?"

"He did."

How could he have watched that? How could he have invaded our privacy like that? My body felt uncontrollable shame, and then anger.

"Did you see it too? Jude, did you see it too?" My tone was sharp.

A silence waned between the invisible electric current we once shared. "Yes, Olivia. I watched it. And I'm sorry they did that to you, too."

Jude and I now sat on a similar plane. Not only did we love Ethan and lose him, but we experienced abuse at the hands of one of the most evil couples in the Nation. I could feel him, and the ache that pressed down on his chest–that ache was like mine, two mirrors reflecting an image neither of us wanted to see.

"They won't last long, Jude. After Thomas, I'm going to take care of them too."

"Thank you," Jude whispered, and I could hear him sniffle before clearing his voice. "Why did you call? Who do you need to talk to, Olivia?"

I hesitated. "My mother. Is she available?"

He hesitated too, "Yes. Give me a minute."

The line was quiet, except for the sound of children in the background playing a game in what seemed like the main gathering room. I couldn't wait to hear those sounds fill my room again–the giggles eclipsed by arguing, then settled once more with laughter.

"Hello?" My mother's voice tentatively showed up.

"It's me, Olivia."

"Olivia! Thank god you're okay. You burned it down?"

"Yes. There's nothing left."

"Good for you, honey."

I was taken aback by her response. She stayed in a system, and kept us in a system that required compliance. Burning down that home was the complete opposite of everything she had modeled for me over the last ten years.

"Good for me?"

"Yes. You needed to burn it. You needed to show him that you're more than what he thinks. You are a force—you've always been one. We tried to cage your wings, but they never forgot how to fly. He knows you're coming for him, and he's scared, Olivia."

"How do you know that?"

"I spent a lot of time with him, and he treated me like his own mother–more than you ever knew. When you have a relationship that isn't natural-born, you can see things a little bit clearer. He needed a mother, and I needed to protect you and Jessica. He's scared, and won't ever admit it, but just wait. He's going to make a mistake, and that's when you fly in and take those children back."

"Thank you, Mom." I paused. "This doesn't change anything...you need to understand that, okay? What you did, and what you're doing now, doesn't make it all go away."

"I know."

"Samara said you needed to tell me something. Was it about Thomas?"

"No. The boy, the one that's been around Rose and Lucas... he's not who you think he is."

"I know, Mother."

"How?"

"There was a flash drive that had the data you said dad had when he died. Thomas didn't want it on the Nation servers, so it was transferred. I found out about it, and that's why I was in my house. A guy from the Center helped me access the information."

"Who?"

"A man named Kai. He was a citizen from the Rose Bay Center, but he's not actually a citizen. It's confusing, and too much to go into over the phone. Anyway, I found a list of the transfers and Cooper was one of the ones that made it."

"I see."

"Wait, how did you know?" I paused, *"How long have you known, Mother?"*

She sighed. "I'm sorry, honey. I've known a few years. Thomas–he used it like everything else. After the Maldives, I told him I couldn't lie anymore, and that I was taking everything to you and we were leaving. That's when he told me about the boy. He showed me the files, and then pictures of him. Once I saw his face, it was clear he was your and Ethan's son. Thomas said that if I went through with it, he would kill the boy."

The secrets women carry are sometimes armor in the battles we face, and sometimes the very dagger that slowly carves us apart. I had no intention of absolving my mother from the secrets she held that kept me caged, but learning what he would've done to Cooper gave me hope that, at some point, I could absolve her from this.

"I need to go."

"Olivia, I'm sorry for everything and I need you to understand. We women have always been the lifeblood of this world–and we always will be, as long as we continue to remember each other. What I did for you and Jessica, you will one day do, in your own way, for someone else. You need to bring that boy home when you get Lucas and Rose, do you understand? Bring those babies home, and end this with Thomas."

"Goodbye, Mother."

"Goodbye, Olivia."

Bring Cooper home? How would I even do that? He had his own family. I would be kidnapping him. Why would she tell me to do that? Was there more she didn't tell me–again?? It was getting to the point where I needed to assume I didn't have all the information, but it didn't matter right now anyway. My focus was Rose and Lucas, not Cooper.

I walked back to the living room where Kai and Samara were sitting on stools by the island. Samara had changed into pants and a T-shirt, looking like she did on the compound. They both had devices on the counter, and seemed lost in a plan that I wasn't part of yet.

"Hey," I said, and stood on the other side of the island.

"How'd it go?" Kai asked.

"Fine. She knows–knew–about Cooper."

"Who's Cooper?" Samara asked.

"Ethan's and my son." Edges of hope filled my voice.

"What?"

"The transfer, it took and he's been living here in Central the whole time. Cooper Jones." I smiled.

"Alicia's son?" Samara's eyebrows narrowed.

"You know her? Him?"

"Briefly. Cooper was Thomas's intern, and Alicia would drop him off every now and then at the office. When I wasn't at the Center I was there, and we'd chat before Thomas was ready to see him." She tapped on the HoloTab a few times, then said, "Oh my god, it is Ethan, but you're there too, Olivia. How did I not ever see it? He looks so much like my–" Samara stopped and looked at me.

"It's okay, Samara. I thought the same thing. And a little bit of Rose and Lucas too. They're all there, in him."

"Well, then we need to bring Cooper home too."

"What?!" Kai yelled.

"What? That's Ethan and Olivia's son. He doesn't belong with the Jones. He doesn't belong in the Nation. He never would have been here had it not been for so many other things. We need to rescue him too." Samara stood unwavering.

"Absolutely not." Kai stammered. "We are here for Rose and

Lucas, and that's it. This Cooper kid has done fine here. He has two parents, a good gig with the Nation. There is no way we are taking him."

"Thomas will kill him. Or use him as bait for me." My chest tightened just saying it, but I forced myself to keep going. "Once he learns we have the flash drive, he'll know that I know about Cooper. We have to get him too."

Kai rolled his eyes. "Well, we can't do any of this alone. I can see about getting help from my side, but can you guys get help from yours?"

"Absolutely. I'll message Brandon right now." Samara said, as she tapped on the HoloTab.

"Jude said that Ethan was gone. They don't know where he went."

"I think it's safe to assume he's somewhere down here. Did Jude say what happened to make him leave?"

"No, just that he was watching the footage of–" I stopped.

"I knew he would," Samara said. "He watched everything with you when he was in Central. There was no way to prevent him from seeing what happened to us. If he saw that footage, then he heard the conversation between Thomas and Mr. Lope. I bet he's at your house."

"Well...it's burned down, so he isn't going to find anything," I let out a laugh. "You know, if someone would've told me six months ago that I would have left my husband, slept with a ton of men, and burned my house down in order to eventually kill my husband–I wouldn't have believed them. Who knew that this year was going to turn out the way it has, huh?" I gave a breathy, disbelieving laugh. Kai and Samara joined in, though none of us were really sure what we were laughing at.

It felt good to laugh. To look at the gravity of the situation and be okay with its unpredictable outcome. I knew in my heart that, at the very least, I would have my children back. But beyond that, I had no idea what would happen. At some point,

Thomas would die. At some point, the Nation would end. And at some point, I would leave with the kids. I was going to do my best to burn everything in my path and make a statement so everyone would know this could never happen again.

"I think we need to plan out what's next, and if we can, end this today." I spoke with authority.

"What time is school out?" Kai asked.

"Summer schedule is usually three."

"I'm guessing Thomas will be at work, and Penny will be the one who gets the kids from school. She's upstairs right now, but we need to assume that she knows how to take care of herself." Kai said.

Samara looked between the two of us. "What does he mean, Olivia?"

"Penny and Thomas have been together all along. She's the same age as me, but the vaccines made her sterile. Her father, Jeffrey, along with Thomas and her, were looking for someone like me so that Penny could have children. She tried transfers, but they didn't take to her body." A small pang hit me in the chest. I knew what it was like to feel loss, and even though my body birthed my children, I could still feel empathy for her body not being able to. We're conditioned at such a young age to become mothers. Our first toy is a doll, and we rock it to sleep after carrying it around all day in our arms. When we grow up, we realize that society intrinsically ties our self-worth to motherhood, and we feel like failures if we cannot meet its expectations. We crawl inside ourselves–meeting the ugly that didn't let them stay–begging our body to give us just one more chance. When it does, we lose again, proving our redundancy. And when the baby showers get thrown, around the same time yours was supposed to be, you're reminded again of your lack, your body's incompatibility within this world. When the birth announcements circulate in message threads, the faces of babies you'll never send stare back at you, calling like ghosts from their own graves–graves that you'll never be able to visit because their bodies never found a home inside you.

"We think Penny was helping Thomas before Olivia accepted her Challenge Pass. The plan was to kill her on their tenth wedding anniversary vacation. Penny wants the children. She sees them as her own."

"It makes sense...she's been there almost their entire lives. If not in person, at least in the background. I wouldn't have even known about it." Samara said.

"Okay, so Penny could be a problem, unless we can get to her before the kids are there. What if we just go upstairs right now? Take her out."

"You're something fierce, Olivia." Kai laughed. "But we have to consider what security is in place, and since we don't have Thomas's tracker, that adds another layer to all of it."

"Could we tap into the audio feed, or maybe the video feed, by now?" I asked.

"I'll check. But the other part of this is that I can't go with you. It could blow my cover. We may still need me down here."

"Okay. Well, then why don't I just shoot her? One less person to worry about. We can just hide her body before the kids get home, then take them and go." My tone stayed neutral like we were talking about whether to go to dinner first or the movies.

Kai and Samara stared at me in disbelief.

"Have you ever killed anyone, Olivia?" Kai asked. "Besides that near attempt on my life." He laughed.

"Ha. Ha." I smirked at him.

"What's he talking about, Olivia?"

"Nothing. It was a misunderstanding."

"Tell that to my arm."

"Anyway, to answer your question–no I haven't–but if I'm going to kill Thomas, I guess I should have a practice one, right? She seems perfect for it." I said convincing the three of us I could do it.

"Who are you right now?" Samara asked.

"If it takes killing the woman trying to replace me to get my children back, then it's justifiable. In the end, both of them have to go if we take the Nation down."

They didn't say anything. They knew I was right, but I think there was a part of them that wondered if I could do it; a part of me too that I refused to acknowledge. The oath I took to care for people–to save their lives, not take them–would it overshadow my ability to pull the trigger, not just on Penny, but on Thomas as well?

Samara reached for my hand and her eyes softened. "I know you want to do this, Olivia and I think there's a big part of you that can. For now, though, I'll take care of her. Focus on the children, then Thomas. I've got this one. "

I drew in a breath and the armor I tried on in front of Kai and Samara didn't quite fit.

"Thank you, Samara. Thank you." It was here where I was reminded of the bonds that women can hold between each other. Bonds that emerge out of a sense of common struggle, and a common enemy. The Nation was our captor, and anyone who stood with them was against us. Like soldiers preparing for war, we knew we'd protect each other no matter what.

"I have the video feed from the building to see when Thomas gets back. It doesn't seem like he's in the apartment right now, just Penny. She's taking a nap on the couch."

"It'd be easy to go in there right now." I said.

"Not yet. We need weapons, and we need back up." Samara replied.

"I have weapons. They're in a false room behind the office. Anything you want." Kai said.

I watched the video feed cycling on Kai's HoloTab. Downstairs, a man eased around the corner, face shadowed by a ball cap and dressed in tier-two clothes. But his stride was too self-assured for someone of that status, and he moved with a familiarity of the cameras that left no doubt–it was Ethan.

I gasped. "Samara!"

"Who's that?" Kai asked, peering over my shoulder.

Samara sighed and shook her head, "Ethan."

I started to run, with no sense of self-preservation for the cameras that would identify me.

"Stop! Olivia, Stop!" Kai grabbed my arm and pulled me back in.

"I'll go get him." Samara offered.

"Hold on," Kai said, as he walked over to a drawer, and pulled out a key fob. "You'll need this to get in the elevator. It's synced to my name, but be quick. Put this on too." He handed her an old San Francisco Giants hat hanging on the back of the door.

"Thank you." Samara said, pulling the hat down to cover her face as she quietly snuck out.

Moments later, Samara, and a poorly disguised Ethan, walked through the front door.

"Ethan?! What are you doing here?" I yelled, as I hit my hands against his chest.

"I'm here to get the kids." His voice was solid, unwavering against my hatred.

"We messaged the compound. They said they were sending Brandon's team. How did you even know they were here, if you didn't get the message?"

"I was watching the footage from Rose Bay and heard Vic–" He looked at me, then Samara.

"Jude told me. You had no right to do that!" I screamed.

"I'm sorry, but I had to know you were okay when you were in there." He closed the gap between us and I extended my arm to block him. "When did you talk to Jude?"

"Just before you got here."

"I understand it may seem wrong right now, but I got the information to be here, and find the children. I knew Victor Lope. Samara, you did too." Ethan's face hardened. "The Lopes were the ones that hurt Jude."

Her face went ashen.

"I remembered Thomas had an apartment near the Center. Tyler and I would escort him back and forth, sometimes in between meetings. Once I saw your house burned dow–"

"You went to my home?"

"Yes. I heard about the drive from the footage."

"You just don't know when to stop, do you?"

"Olivia, I will stop at nothing for you. Don't you understand? I'm here to get them back."

"They're not your concern."

"I know you think that, but you don't really feel that way."

"You don't know anything about my feelings."

"Let's all take a step back here. There's a lot going on, and emotions are running high." Kai interjected.

"I'm sorry. Who are you? And how do you fit into all of this?" Ethan placed his hands solidly on the countertop, taking up space with his solid 6'3 frame.

"I'm Kai Acosta. I met Olivia and Samara at the Rose Bay Challenge Center. I chose Olivia for my nights while I was there."

"Nights? Like back to back? Since when does the Nation not follow the standard Center rules of only one night, and then a break?"

"I have tier-four status," Kai puffed his chest out slightly. "So, I get to have as many nights as I want with the same attendant."

"As many nights? Like you can just choose how long you want to be there?"

"Yes. But I usually only stay two to three days."

"Is that where she's been the past few nights? With you?" Ethan's eyes narrowed.

"She has been with me, yes." The corner of Kai's mouth lifted in a smug curl.

"Were you watching my every move while I was there?" I snapped at Ethan.

"There was no footage, which worried me. That's why I watched other footage–to see if you or Samara had been discovered. If Thomas knew about you. I told you both before you left that I didn't like the idea."

I rolled my eyes. "It wasn't your decision to make."

Ethan shifted his attention back to Kai. "And what exactly do you do, Kai Acosta?"

Kai looked at me, and I nodded. "I work for the United States government as a spy to the Nation."

"What are you talking about, the United States government? They're non-existent. The Nation took them out years ago to make this new, shiny piece of shit that we all get to roll around in over and over again."

"Ethan, it's all been a lie. We were taught lies about everything. The U.S. still exists. The Nation only took Northern California, not the entire country like they told us...showed us."

"Like deep fakes? That's impossible to do at the scale that the Nation operates on. Also, Samara and I would have found out with everything we had access to. Right, Sam?"

I winced when he said her name like that, and flashed to a storyteller's scene of him saying her name while he made love to her and fathered her children.

"It's true, Ethan." Samara leaned in and squeezed his forearm.

"Proof like U.S. deep fakes too? C'mon, think about it. How could something like the Nation run and be all over the world and have all the connections, if it were just here?"

"The government allowed them to occupy Northern California as a containment strategy. When they started to rise up, we countered with aggressive measures and they backed down, staying only in this area. During the last five years, we've been trying to undo their systems to eventually regain California, because of its impact on us and the rest of the world. The economic impact, and the trafficking, has increased our problems tenfold over the last few years. Thomas, Jeffrey, and Valentin want to expand to Southern California, which would take the remaining agricultural land away from us. If they have that, they can charge the world anything they want for what they grow, and can control water resources outside the state lines."

"What part of the U.S. government do you work for again?"

"It's classified."

"Of course it is."

"Ethan, we're going to need him to end the Nation. The supplies alone that the U.S. has would give us a tremendous advantage." Samara moved to direct the conversation into more tactical terms.

"She's right. We can help support your cause, and get everything back to the American way of life. Once you let me know where the compound is, I can start planning. What are the coordinates for the compound?"

"It's classified." Ethan replied.

"Look, it doesn't matter what department he's in, or what the problems will be if the Nation takes over more sections of the state. What matters right now is we get the children out of here as soon as possible, and back home." I interrupted their whole 'whose dick is bigger' match. "Penny is upstairs right now. Samara, do you know when the compound team will be here?"

"Soon. They're still on Highway 50." She tapped the HoloTab.

"Kai, can you pull the layout of the apartment up?" I asked.

"I don't have the layout because it's his place. We can use the video feed, but it won't give us the details a schematic would. I can have my HoloTab do a visual search with the feed, and create one based off of that, though."

"Thank you."

"I think the best bet is to go in fast, and get out fast, too." Samara said.

Ethan chuckled, "Yeah, Sam, the basics of any plan."

"Shut up, Ethan," she bumped his side.

"When the kids get home from school, let's be ready to move in. We need to assume there are going to be bodyguards with the kids–there were when we tried to take them from school, so here won't be any different. Ethan, you take the bodyguards out. Samara, you secure Penny–shoot her if you have to, just make sure the kids don't see. Then, you and I grab the kids and head back to Kai's apartment," I said as the rest of them listened intently. "Kai, how will we get out?"

"My car or–"

"The SUV from our team will be here by then. We'll just go with them," Ethan interrupted.

"Okay. I think this could work, but there's one thing missing. Thomas. What if he comes home? We have no way of tracking him and where he is," Kai said.

"Why can't you track him?" Ethan sneered.

"Because his tracker is blocked from the system." I said and then it dawned on me, "Do you think he even has a chip?"

"He has to...I mean everyone has one in the Nation. How else would he get into buildings and access everything else?" Samara said.

"It was just a thought. The compound team will help us. I know it sounds a little loose, but I think this could totally work, and we can improvise if we need to–we've all had enough training. I really think this is going to work." I repeated aloud for all of us to hear.

"You know it never works that way, Olivia." Ethan said.

"Well, there's a first time for everything, right, Ethan?" I snapped.

"What's that supposed to mean?"

"I think you know what it means."

"Please explain."

"First time to have children with someone who isn't the love of your life. First time to sleep with, and fall in love with, a man. First time fully betraying your so-called love of your life by leaving her children with a psychopathic monster. Should I go on? I'm sure I can think of more *first times* since being at the compound."

Ethan slammed his fist down on the counter, got up, and stared at me. "What are we going to do for weapons? I only brought my gun, and the team won't have enough for the three of you."

"Two of us, Kai isn't going," Samara said,

"Oh, he isn't, is he? That's convenient, don't you think?"

"Easy, Ethan," Samara whispered, and then placed her hand on his arm.

My blood boiled at another reminder of their close friendship, and the years I lost with him. It simmered down when I remembered what a lifeline she had been to me, and how she'd pulled me out of the darkness, and into the dawn of possibilities. It would take time to untangle my hold on a life with him that would never be, and in moments like this I was reminded there was still a part of me that loved him. I would find peace for that love one day, in order to finally let go and move on. I also owed him the truth about our son, but not today, not here, not now. We needed to get the children first, we can figure out Cooper later.

"Let's take a look. I don't have a lot, but I think what's here will work. We can check Penny's and the children's trackers to see what our timeline looks like."

Kai walked into a spare bedroom adorned with green-and-blue tropical wallpaper, and a queen size bed with a black frame. A gold-framed picture of a volcano hung above a small black dresser. Where a closet should have been, stood a tall black cabinet with four doors. Kai placed his thumbprint on the panel of each one and the doors automatically opened, rolling inside the cabinet. Weapons ranged from small hand-held pistols, to semi-automatic guns, to two automatic guns in the right side cabinets. The left side held knives, tactical gear, and a grenade launcher.

"You don't have a lot of weapons, my ass, Kai." I teased him.

"Well, compared to other places, this is not a lot," he bumped into me playfully.

Ethan looked between us, then peered at Kai. He walked to the guns and started taking the ones he wanted, like he was at a candy store. Samara followed, which made me scramble to get the guns I wanted. I took two of the handguns. Samara took two as well, while Ethan grabbed a knife, a few grenades, and one of the semi-automatics.

"And who will take the grenade launcher?" I joked.

"I don't think that will be necessary, considering you are just going to get in and out. We definitely do not want to draw any attention to ourselves before leaving. Road closures are already problematic, especially if you're trying to get back to the compound," Kai said.

Samara finished by grabbing the last two grenades before I took the extra knife Ethan had left. Kai walked into the kitchen and opened the refrigerator.

"Want anything to drink? Eat?" Kai asked.

"I'm fine, thanks." I stood next to the bar, while Ethan sat on the overstuffed couch poking at the pillows like they were inconveniences to him.

Kai, Samara, and I made small talk discussing our options for getting in and out quickly. The AI finished a tentative schematic of Thomas's apartment, which had been redone since our marriage. He had taken multiple units and made them into one large unit, fitted with too many rooms to count. Even with the schematics, the bodyguards and Thomas were still our unknowns. But if the help from the compound was here, we would outnumber them anyway. Kai planned to maintain audio communication with us so he could alert us of anything from the visual feed while we were in the apartment.

I looked at the clock. "It's almost time for the children to be home from school. Samara, when is the team supposed to be here?"

"They should be here anytime, really."

"Kai, can you check their locations?"

"Sure. It looks like they're still in the school's courtyard, but are walking toward the entrance."

"And is Penny with them, or still upstairs?"

"Penny's in the apartment. We should assume the bodyguards from this morning are with the children." The idea lit in my eyes, and Samara saw it.

"No, Olivia, we need to wait for the team." She shook her head.

"Why? If the three of us go right now, we can get Penny, then hide and wait for Rose and Lucas to get home. Ethan and you can take out the bodyguards, make sure Penny is unconscious or dead, then we take the kids and head out. It's faster than the other plan I came up with. We would be done before the team even gets here."

"It's rash, not thought out at all." Ethan chimed in.

"They're *my* children. We need to do this now. It's the best opportunity."

"Although I don't agree with this, I understand you want to get it done now. So, I'll support it." Kai's support calmed me, and I mouthed 'thank you' to him. "Take this too," Kai handed me an earpiece. "I'll be your eyes while you're in there." Kai's hand squeezed mine before letting go.

"Samara, ETA on the team?" Ethan interrupted.

"Twenty minutes maybe."

"The children are about ten minutes away. Olivia, if you're going to do this, you need to leave now. Do you have the key?" Kai asked.

"Let me get it." I went back to my room and grabbed the metal key I'd found in the safe, before I burned my house. It made sense how Thomas used keys instead of technology to get access to the apartment. It was the one thing he could control, in a world as advanced as the Nation's. It was probably near impossible to have duplicates made of this key, making his apartment one of the safest places to hide the children, and himself, from anyone else.

"Ready?" Ethan asked impatiently when I returned.

"Yes." I replied, key and gun in hand.

"Let's go," Ethan commanded.

28

OLIVIA

Samara, Ethan, and I slipped out of Kai's apartment and took the emergency exit, guns in hand, making our way up to Thomas's. The white stairwell was quiet, the red lights of surveillance cameras blinking overhead. I could only hope Kai's team was handling those too. We stopped outside the penthouse floor and walked into the hallway.

"I'll take the lead. Olivia, hand me the key."

I handed Ethan the key, and he entered the apartment first. Samara and I stayed behind him, guns drawn. Penny's back was to the door, and she had headphones in, dancing around the kitchen. On her final spin, she turned, peering straight at us. Ethan took advantage of her surprise and rushed her body, wrapping his arms tightly around her. She screamed, and Ethan put his arm around her neck, holding her until her breath went to nothing and she went limp in his arms.

He dragged her into a bedroom just off the expansive living room. As I followed, the room couldn't help but suffocate me. Pictures of Penny and Thomas adorned the walls–images of my children with her, layered like a cake under the frosting of their life without me. Two copies of *Art of War* lay haphazardly next to *Macbeth,* and a board-book copy of *Three Little Kittens.* He lived another life under the veil of ours. How could I have been so stupid to believe anything he ever said? The vows at our wedding were a script he burned long ago. The ring he wore was a symbol of a life cycle that would never be complete.

My body betrayed my mind. My armor wasn't strong enough against this confirmation. In plain view, they lived a life I was never meant to notice. My throat began to tighten, and I gulped for air.

"It's okay, Olivia. Shhhh. It's going to be okay." Samara touched my arm. "Breathe. It's going to be okay. We're minutes away from getting the children back. This place will become nothing once we walk out that door. His world with her, with them, will be nothing in just a few minutes. You have won, Olivia. You have won."

"How could any of this be true? I gave him everything!"

"Is everything okay?" I heard Kai, and then muted the comms.

"We have Penny subdued in the bedroom. She's passed out. Just waiting on the children." Samara continued to hold me.

"I gave him everything, Samara. My entire life I was told to chase this, to become a wife, a mother, a good citizen. And he just stood there, day after day, secretly laughing at me. His wounded bird, taking any small breadcrumb of love he, or the Nation, would give me. He kept me, Samara. He kept me for himself. For her." I choked back a sob.

"I know, Olivia. I know."

"Was it all really a lie?"

"Most of it was, Olivia. A lie for you both. Thomas wanted, and needed, this life just as much as you did. The only difference is that he had an exit plan with her, and you didn't."

"I wanted out though, Samara. I just…"

"He wouldn't have let you out even if you'd asked Olivia. He kept you, just like you said. You were never getting out alive."

"I would never make it to the end with him. Penny..." I looked at the woman passed out on the floor under Ethan's watch. "She was his choice–his end game the whole time." How foolish was I to believe in the love of a man? I looked at Ethan and thought about the love I once believed in. I thought of our son, that I would eventually tell him about, and the lie I was keeping from him. I was starving for air, and in that moment I realized there was no such thing as love except for that between a parent and a child. All other love didn't exist–couldn't exist–because people were too selfish. There was just me and the love for my children that I could count on. Everything else didn't matter anymore.

I looked at Penny again and felt a pang of sorrow. Thomas's love for Penny was just as fake as his love for me. He loved Rose and Lucas, and would do anything for them. But Penny was a means to an end, just like me. And because I was too selfish to love again, I would take away the one thing Thomas loved most, leaving Penny as the leftovers from a life he would never be able to hold ever again.

Samara pressed her earpiece. "Okay, got it. Thanks. We'll be ready." Samara turned to me, "Kai says Rose, Lucas, *and* Cooper are together, and about to enter the building. Video feed shows two body guards as well."

My heart beat faster at the thought of seeing my children again.

"Cooper? Who's that?" Ethan asked.

"A friend of theirs." I said, and shook my head at Samara.

"Ethan, is she still out?" Samara asked.

"For now."

"Olivia, remember your strength. You are the force behind all of this. You made a choice that freed you, Ethan, me, and so many others. You will continue to do that once we get the children home. You are the revolution, Olivia. You're what the tier-ones and -twos need. It doesn't matter that Thomas didn't love you the way he promised, because soon enough he will have nothing...be nothing...and you will have your freedom, and the world. You did this, Olivia," she waved her gun, "...all of this. Don't let some stale photos on the wall of an apartment that needed too much work to become a home tell you any different."

I steeled myself and nodded. "What will we do with her?"

Samara kicked Penny. "She should be out for a few more minutes. As long as we get the kids immediately, we'll be fine. If I need to, I can always put her back out," Samara smiled.

"What about Cooper?" I asked.

"He's coming with us, Olivia. There's no other way."

"But that's kidnapping, Samara."

"Something we can sort out later. Right now, we need to get the children—all three of them—somewhere safe."

"You're right." I looked at the HoloTab. "We're so close—they're so close."

"The bodyguards are going to enter first, and when they don't see Penny right away, they'll probably move down the hall while the kids come inside. You take one, and I'll take the other." Ethan said.

"Got it." Samara replied.

"And me?"

"Stay hidden until the kids are inside. We need to do this fast, because if it's like the last time, Rose will not want to come with us. That Cooper kid could be a problem, too."

"You can't hurt him, Ethan!" I snapped.

He furrowed his brows. "I wasn't going to. If he became a problem, I'd just do the same thing to him," he nodded to Penny, still lifeless on the floor.

"No, he's coming with us," Samara commanded in a tone that no one—not even Ethan—would argue with.

We heard the door open and footsteps walking toward the

kitchen. "Ma'am, we're back with the kids." A gruff voice echoed down the halls. "Ma'am?"

"She probably has her headphones on again." Another deep voice sighed, as the door closed and softer steps walked into the kitchen.

Ethan held up his fingers and mouthed to Samara to get into position. One set of heavy footsteps made their way down the hall, and Ethan tapped his chest and mouthed 'Just me'. Ethan stood off to the side, knife in hand. The bodyguard entered the room and noticed Penny on the floor right before Ethan grabbed him from behind, and slit his throat. His body slumped against Ethan's as Ethan dragged him to the side of the bed, letting blood pool below him. The smell of iron choked me.

Ethan motioned for us to head out and down the hall toward the other guard. I looked at Penny, still asleep on the floor, but as we left the room, I could have sworn her eyes opened slightly. As I looked back again, she was still, eyes closed, and motionless.

Ethan took the lead as we ambled down the hall, all three of our guns drawn. The bodyguard was sitting with his back to us at the counter, while the children were both looking in the refrigerator and pantry for snacks. Ethan quickly wrapped his arm around the bodyguard, choking him out like he had done to Penny. A loud thud made the children spin around.

Cooper grabbed Rose, then Lucas, and pulled her in. "Leave us alone!" He yelled.

Ethan held one gun over the lifeless bodyguard, while pointing another at Cooper. "Let her go, kid. She's not your concern."

"Like hell she isn't!" Cooper retorted, and I saw the same fire in him as his father.

"Rose, Lucas, it's Mommy. We need to go." I put my gun in the hem of my pants.

"We can't go with you! You're the murderer whose face is blasted everywhere!" Cooper yelled.

"I'm not going with you, Mom! Dad said you would try to come back. That you would take me and Lucas. That you killed all those people in April."

"Honey, I didn't do any of that. They're all lies, and I will explain everything to you once we are safe. We have to go. We need to get away from your father." I tried to keep my voice as calm as possible.

"Daddy says you're not our mother. That Penny is." Lucas's soft voice pierced through tears.

A jolt hit my stomach, and the world tilted around me. Was this why Rose hesitated to leave with me last time, or had he just told her these lies afterward?

"Rose, Lucas, that's just not true." My voice pitched. "I can prove it to you once we're home with Grandma and Auntie." I unmuted the comms. "Kai, we're trying to get the children out now, but it's taking longer."

Kai's voice panicked over the airwaves. "Olivia! Olivia! It's Thomas, he's in the stairwell! Find a different way out now!"

29

OLIVIA

Samara, Ethan, and I exchanged stunned glances, then turned back to the children. "How is he even here?" I asked.

"Maybe the bodyguards alerted him somehow? Or the childr–" I looked at Cooper, holding a small black key fob. "Did you tell Thomas we were here?" I demanded.

"You bet your ass I did!" Cooper stood solid in his protection of the little sister he didn't know he even had.

"Kai, how much time do we have?" My voice was panicked.

"No time at all. He's almost there."

"We have to go, Thomas is almost here!" I yelled, and then moved toward the children.

Cooper pulled a knife from the counter butcher block and pointed it at us. "Come any closer to her and I'll kill you."

Ethan laughed. "Kid, no you won't."

"I will! I swear I will!" He yelled, while his hands shook.

"Cooper, that's your name, right?" Samara said in a soft voice.

"How do you know my name?"

"Because it's my job to know your name," she lied. "I'm here to bring Rose and Lucas home with their mother, and to the rest of their family. We can track anyone who is with Rose or Lucas on our HoloTab. Cooper Jones, right?"

Where was she going with this?

She walked around the bar just as Ethan was circling the other side, caging both Rose and Cooper in like a pack of lions, while Lucas stood to the side, almost within my reach. Ethan looked at Samara and then at me, like he knew something I didn't about Samara.

"Since I know who you are, and who your family is, do you think they're going to be safe if you don't let them go with us?" She opened her HoloTab and showed the screen to Cooper. "See that little dot right there, Cooper? That's your sister, right? Looks like she's at school right now. Were you supposed to be there with her, Cooper?"

He looked down, and lowered the knife. "Yes."

"And what would your parents say if they knew you were here with Rose instead of her? A sister who will definitely need your protection, if you don't let them go with us? And you won't get there in time to help her, because our people are on the school grounds right now."

"Oh Samara, are you spinning stories again with that spider's voice?"

The hair on the back of my neck raised and I pulled the gun out from behind me and pointed it at Thomas. His bodyguards responded the same.

"Cooper, put that knife back–that one won't hurt you. And that one," Thomas pointed toward Ethan, "would kill himself if he ever ended up hurting you, but you don't know why right now, do ya Conrad?" Thomas sneered his snake smile.

"What are you talking about?" Ethan spit back.

"Oh, I just love how much fun it continues to be to play with you." He turned to me. "Oh, my sweet Olivia. What do you plan on doing with that?"

I closed the gap between Thomas and me, gun drawn, my finger on the trigger ready to pull it. I'd pictured this moment so many times before. I'd pulled the trigger so many times before, with perfect accuracy.

"Olivia, no! Don't do it." Samara yelled.

"She won't do it, Samara. It's not in her nature." He walked to me, landing his chest against my gun.

"No, Mommy, don't!" Rose yelled, and I turned to her.

"Oh, sweet Rose, Mommy isn't going to do it. She's just playing, right, Olivia?"

I felt sick, and my hand started to shake. A sting burned behind my eyes. I wanted to pull the trigger so badly. I wanted this to be over–for him to be over. For this frozen-in-time space to thaw and be forever changed by my one action. But I couldn't. I wouldn't. I looked at my children, and lowered my gun.

"That's right, Mommy, do as Daddy says. You've always been so good at that."

It was as if the rope he had tied around me for the last ten years finally became too tight, and in that moment it snapped. I raised my hand and fired my gun twice, hitting both bodyguards behind him, their bodies dropping to the floor like large sacks of flour.

Thomas put his hands up. The children screamed, and Samara ran toward them, sheltering their eyes from whatever was coming next. Ethan rushed to my side, gun still drawn.

"So you do have what it takes. I was wrong." Thomas chuckled. "I'll be damned." He looked at the kids, "Look! Mommy had what it took the whole time, who knew?" Thomas looked past me, and I turned just in time to see Penny, gun in hand, drawn at me. "There you are, my darling." Thomas said with a soothed confidence that angered me even further.

"She was great to let me know that you three were here. And Cooper, good on you for using the alert button too–I knew

I could count on you to protect Rose. It worked out perfectly, really." The chill in his voice unnerved me. "I can finally put the three of you where you belong, and use you to find the rest of the traitors. I always love how things just fall into place for me. Samara, move away from the children."

"No." Her body shielded them.

"Penny, take care of her, please." Thomas directed.

Penny moved her gun from me to Samara, about to fire, when a loud sound came from behind me. Penny's body dropped to the ground, and Rose screamed, burying herself into Samara's body.

"Ethan! What have you done?" Samara yelled.

Everything slowed around me like a movie. I looked at Penny's dead body laying on the floor, and turned to Ethan. His eyes held no regret, but instead a sense of accomplished protection. The children were crying, Cooper was in shock, eyes wide like a deer on the road about to get hit by a car. I finally turned to Thomas, a small smile from the corner of his mouth staying hidden under the relief in his eyes.

She was a liability for him, just like I was, like we all were. Our children, at some point, would be a liability to him as well if they didn't play the game the way he wanted. The only thing that mattered to him was himself. I couldn't hold back anymore or let him breathe in the same room as the children and me ever again.

I raised my gun to Thomas again, looked to see if my children's eyes were shielded, and was about to pull the trigger when gunfire erupted outside the apartment.

The team was here.

The front door opened and a blinding white explosion of light, like lightning, filled the room. A loud skull-rattling boom hit my chest and I dropped my gun, covering my ears from the high-pitched whine that brought me to my knees. Shadows flickered as I tried to gain a sense of where I was in relation to the children. My eyes burned as I peered into the white smoke, grasping for anything that felt like them. I grabbed Rose and Lucas, pulling them out of the kitchen as they screamed. Cooper lay sprawled out on the floor next to Samara, confused. Thomas was slumped against the floor, trying to gain a foothold. A team of four rushed inside, guns drawn and pointing at anything that moved.

"Ethan? Ethan, where are you?" Brandon's voice echoed through the smoke.

"I'm here, Brandon. Who's with you?" Ethan shouted.

"Chris, Tyler, Vivian! We have the vehicles ready downstairs, but we got some heat coming, so we need to leave now." Brandon yelled.

Shots fired, and I knew Thomas had grabbed my gun and was firing at the team. I scrambled with the kids, pulling them away from the gunfire as best I could. Another loud boom blanketed the room and a burst of flames shot up from the stove. Samara crawled, stumbling to Cooper, and pulled him toward the children and me.

"We need to get out of here now! Grab the children. Brandon, help Samara and the kid!" Ethan barked.

"You're not taking them anywhere! They're mine." Thomas growled as he stood and walked toward us.

Ethan stepped in front of us as Brandon, Chris, and Samara walked backwards, pulling Cooper and Lucas out the door, smoke filling the room. I held tight to Rose's hand and slowly stepped toward the door, my eyes never leaving Thomas, and the gun he had pointed at us.

"Get out of the way, Conrad! I don't want you. Get out of the way!" He coughed.

Thomas wouldn't let me have them, not with Ethan. He wanted me. This was my sacrifice. My time to put myself in front of the gun for my children.

"Take her."

"Mama, no!" Rose screamed.

"Rose, it will be fine. You're going with Mommy's friend for a minute. Daddy and I need to talk. We'll be right behind you, I promise."

"Don't leave him, Mommy. Don't leave him." Rose was sobbing.

"Please, Ethan, take her. Leave." I begged.

"I can't. Not without you." His voice cracked as he covered his mouth from the smoke.

"Do this for me, please. Fix it."

I knew he wanted nothing more than to right the mistakes he'd made the first time he left my children in the hands of this monster. Whether I was making it home alive tonight or not, my children would be. Ethan moved behind me, took Rose's hand, and moved through the door. In a moment they were both gone, and I was alone with Thomas in a burning apartment.

"Guess we both get to die now, right, Olivia?" Thomas laughed. Blood from a head wound dripped down his face. He struggled to breathe. "I always wondered how it would end between the two of us." He continued to walk toward me. "I'll take this, I guess, instead. A little more Shakespearean tragedy, don't you think?" He looked at Penny's body on the floor. "When did you figure it out? After the fire?"

"Yes."

"All of it?"

"Yes."

He shook his head, nodding in assurance. "Burning the house down, that was something new, huh? Never thought you would've done that. Did you look at the files? So you know about him too?"

I straightened my spine, my voice deadly calm. "I do. And everything else."

"It was a good plan, the whole thing. I was on the verge of

something…so perfect. Cooper, Rose, Lucas—they were just the beginning. Samara's girls…they wer–" Thomas coughed and slumped forward slightly, lowering his gun. His hand moved to his side, and when he lifted it up, a deep red coated his fingers. He braced himself against the wall, dropped the gun, and then fell to the floor.

The smell of melting plastic hit my nose, burning the inside. The kitchen was fully engulfed in flames, like a ticking time bomb waiting for one more gas line to fulfill its purpose.

It can't end like this.

A part of me wanted to see him die in this building with his mistress. With the two people who had pulled the invisible strings that I only saw now. There was no use in pulling her body out of the fire–she could burn for all I cared. But then I heard Rose's voice, and even though I wanted to see him dead, she would know he died because of me. I couldn't live with that, because no matter how much I hated him–he was still the father of my children.

I scrambled to his unconscious bleeding body, grabbing an arm to pull him out of the apartment. His body painted streaks like a newly mopped floor and he was so much heavier than I remembered from when he would find himself on top of me. When we were almost to the door, a quick hand tightened around my ankle and pulled me down, falling away from our escape. Thomas found his strength one more time, and I was trapped under him as flames swirled around us. My eyes searched the room, looking for anything that could help me up, but I only found pictures from their life that stood as tinder to their lies.

His hands tightened around my wrists. "Hey this feels familiar, right?" He laughed, and then coughed violently, blood spraying me.

I flashed back to the time in front of the stairs, at the condo in South Lake Tahoe. His hands gripped around my wrists. The children were in the other room. I'd just wanted to go upstairs, because I'd had enough of him that day. I asked him to let me go, and he laughed, saying he was "only playing a game" and "just teasing me". I tried to fight back for release and he said, "If you relax, I'll let you go." I should have known then, but I didn't.

Crackling and pin-pricked popping continued in the kitchen. I looked over and knew what would come next—the gas line was ready to scream again.

I wasn't going to let him hold me back. No more. I writhed beneath him, twisting my wrists against his restraints until my skin burned. He pressed down harder with what little strength was left, but I bucked my hips, and yanked hard, freeing me from the shackles of a life no longer caging me. I pushed him off of me, just in time to see him cough again and slump to the side. I crawled along the floor, slipping in his blood as I stood up to run toward my freedom for the last time.

Boom!

My body was hurled like a cannonball away from the door, crashing against the glass window and shattering it into a million little pieces. The air from outside wasn't much cooler than the heat in the room. Penny and Thomas lay on the floor, flames marching slowly up their body like ants in a forest. Smoke and flames were everywhere, refusing to take refuge when the automatic sprinklers turned on. I moved away from the exposed window, dropping shards of glass to the eight stories below. I tried to stand up, but instead gave in to my body's desire to stay still for just a minute longer. Flames danced through the room like a dragon in the sky. I rested against the only solid part of the wall that was left—a tiny cubby made just for me. I closed my eyes and let the warmth of the room soothe me like a warm car.

I could stay for just a minute longer.

Yes, just...a...minute...longer.

30

ETHAN

Smoke rolled down the hallway as I ran back into the apartment to get Olivia. Brandon and Chris were close behind, covering my six as the security detail prepared to swarm us. I covered my mouth with my shirt and pushed through the smoke. Thomas lay unconscious, still bleeding, surrounded by flames. Penny's body was already partially consumed—paying another penance for the life she chose to live with Thomas.

"Olivia! Olivia! Where are you?" Water rained down on us from the sprinklers. "Brandon, do you see her?"

We scanned the room.

"Over there! By the window. Careful! She's so close to the edge. Grab her, Ethan!" Chris yelled.

I ran to her. She lay slumped against the wall like a rag doll. I felt for a pulse, and thank god she had one, because I don't know what I would do without her. She was the love of my life, even with everything that's been happening.

"Got her, let's go!" I shouted to Brandon and Chris. Walking out, I instinctively pointed my gun at Thomas.

"Don't do it. The fire will take him. He's not worth it, man," Chris said.

I yelled and fired my gun into the ceiling. Chris was right, a bullet to the head was too easy for him. I wanted Thomas to suffer, just like we all had since he came into power, and the fire would grant me that.

Gunfire erupted everywhere as soon as we entered the hall. A bullet immediately struck Chris, and Brandon returned fire, hitting Thomas's man directly in the head. Brandon dragged Chris down the hall to the emergency exit, where he braced Chris against him as the two surviving security guards ran into the apartment.

"Can you make it downstairs?" Brandon asked.

Chris looked down and pulled his crimson-soaked hand back. Brandon turned to me. I knew those panicked eyes.

"Yeah. Yeah, I can make it." Chris said.

"Chris, you're going to be okay. We'll wrap it until we get to a healing machine." He grabbed Chris's face and pulled it in. "You will not die here."

"I love you Brandon." Chris said.

"I love you," he said to Chris, a look in his eyes I knew all too well.

I looked at the trail of blood as I followed Brandon and Chris to the exit. It wasn't good. We didn't have a lot of time to get him to a machine before he bled out. I carried Olivia down the stairs, with Chris and Brandon in front of me. "Brandon, do we have access to a helicopter anywhere, or just the SUV?"

"Just the SUV."

"Okay. On our way out of the city we need to stop and get the healing machine. It will buy us time getting back up the hill." There was no way we could lose Chris tonight. He and Brandon were just getting their lives back. Brandon had been with me since the beginning, just like Tyler. I couldn't bear the thought of him losing his husband, or for me to lose one more person, to the Nation.

We made it to the first floor and ran through the door. Two SUVs, doors open, waited side by side for us to jump in. Brandon pulled Chris into one with Vivian waiting in the driver's seat.

"Ethan! Olivia! Oh my God, what happened?" Samara screamed as she jumped out of the second one.

"Mommy!" Rose and Lucas echoed after.

The new guy, Kai, or whatever his name was, stood outside the car. "Olivia! Is she okay? Was she shot? Get her in the car. I have something that can help." He yelled at me.

"Thanks, but I can handle it." He wasn't going anywhere near her.

"Ethan, no you can't. Get her in the car with Kai. Rose, take Lucas and crawl into the backseat with your friend, okay?" Samara softened into her natural mother role.

Rose was in shock and slid obediently into the backseat. The kid she was with was in shock too, and stared silently at all of us.

"We should just leave him here for the NSP." I directed.

"No! Ethan, we can't do that. He has to come with us," Samara yelled at me.

"Why?"

"Because he does."

I didn't have time to argue with her. The new guy piled into the middle seat with Olivia and me, crowding what little space we had with each other.

"Can't you ride in the front, man?"

"It's Kai, and you know that. No, I need to be back here."

I looked at Tyler who rolled his eyes and then back at the new guy.

"Whatever." I called out the window, "Brandon, follow us,

but stop once you get to Mid Clinic. See you at home. Brandon, you've got this. Love you, man."

"Love you too." He flashed a half-hearted smile and waved goodbye.

"What happened in Thomas's apartment?" New guy asked.

"Gunshots and an explosion." I replied dryly.

He looked at the kid, "They'll track him. We need to get his chip out right now."

"Good point." I took out my knife and pulled the kid's arm up to mine.

"You can't be serious!" New guy yelled.

"I am, and we need to take out all of their trackers, too."

"You can't do that with them awake, or without medication and sterilization."

"You've clearly never been in battle, have you?"

"I haven't, but that means nothing in this situation. Don't do anything yet. Let me get my bag."

New guy crawled over the seats to the back of the SUV and crawled back with a bag.

"What's that?"

"It's a HM, and medicine for when I am in the field."

"A HM? Shit, we needed that for Brandon's husband. Didn't you see him slump his way out of the building? Did it even occur to you that he could use this? Samara, do you have their location?"

She checked. "Yeah, they already stopped."

"Okay, they'll get help there, but still, man, pay attention."

New guy looked like I had chastised him for taking a toy from someone at the playground. Was this guy soft, or just that inexperienced? He opened the case where syringes and vials sat on a black foam casing. He filled them both, then looked to Samara.

"Do you want to inject them, or should I?" He asked.

"You take Lucas, I'll take Rose," Samara said.

"Sweetie, can you hear me?" Rose didn't respond. "Sweetie, I'm going to give you some medicine to help you fall asleep. You might feel a little pinch, okay?" Samara didn't wait. She injected Rose, then new guy did the same to Lucas. Within minutes, they were both asleep.

"Shit, that's strong. What is it?" I asked.

"A sedative we sometimes use when bringing trafficked victims back to the U.S. They don't always adjust when they're traveling with us, because they're not sure if we're just like the Nation and taking them to some new horrible place."

"Are you going to give it to the boy, too?" I asked.

"Yeah. Give me a second."

This guy was an idiot.

I took my knife and got Rose's tracker out first. She didn't wake up or even move. New guy placed her arm in the HM and the wound disappeared in a moment. Lucas's small arm was a little bit harder and my knife made a larger cut than I had hoped. The HM took care of it and, if anything, he'd have a small scar for the time being.

"I'll inject the kid, give that to me." When I moved, his arm tightened as I injected him. In an instant, his fist balled up and he swung at me, landing his hand square in my jaw. I restrained him, as he screamed, and Samara grabbed the dangling syringe in his arm and pushed the contents into his body.

"Maybe we shouldn't have waited, huh?" I sneered at new guy, and he laughed.

He looked at me. "You have no idea, do you?"

"What are you talking about?"

"Nothin'. You'll find out sooner than later, man," he said, shaking his head.

"Whatever, *New Guy*."

"The name's Kai, not *New Guy*."

"Right, okay–Kai."

I took the kid's tracker out, and Kai used the machine again to make it seem like nothing ever happened.

"Here, hand those to me," Kai said, pointing to the bloody trackers. He placed them in the HM, frying the chip inside. "We're safe. They can't track us anymore."

Olivia, the children, and the kid remained unconscious, even after we rode through the compound gates. I carried her out of the car to the medical wing, while Samara, Kai, and the medical team took Rose, Lucas, and the kid behind me. Jessica and my parents came running out.

"What happened? She's not dead, right Ethan? Tell me she's alive." Jessica's panic filled the air.

"She's okay, Jess. She inhaled a lot of smoke. We think she may have hit her head a little hard. She'll be fine in no time." I lied to her, but also wondering if I was lying to myself. Will she be okay? Would she be my Olivia again, now that both her children were here? Would she come back to me, and all of this could just be a nightmare from the past?

"Rose! Lucas! Are they okay?" Jessica's voice cracked as she ran to their sides.

Samara replied, "Yeah, we gave them each a sedative to get the tracker out. I'm going to take them in to get checked out by the doctor. Will you let your mom know so she can come see them?"

"Yes, we will both be there when they wake up. Who's the kid? Who's the guy?" Jessica asked.

"I'm Kai Acosta, and I work with the United States government. The kid is Cooper Jones, a citizen of the Nation."

"The United States government? Where did you find this guy, at the crazy station?" Jessica laughed.

"It's true, but we don't have time to talk about it now. We need to get them inside," Samara said.

Jessica left to find Rebecca, and we entered the medical unit, staff flooding to our arrival. Kai stayed with the kid, and

Samara stayed with Rose and Lucas until Jessica and her mom arrived. I told the doctor I wasn't leaving Olivia's side, and they didn't push. After the exam, they said she had hit something pretty hard, creating a large contusion on the back of her head. Smoke inhalation almost killed her. They put her in the large HM, like the one we had at the Center. When she was done with the treatment, they moved her into a recovery room.

I sat next to her bed, combing my fingers through her tangled hair. With all my being, I loved this woman. I had loved her since the day she first drove into the compound and got out of the car with her messy hair and chaotic family. There was no me without her. There couldn't be a me without her. Not in this lifetime or any other. I had to win her back. I had to prove to her I was worthy of her love. That I would fight for her every day, until my last dying breath. We could be together now, as a family. Once we took down the Nation, it could just be us. I could use the money from my time as an attendant to buy her a place in San Francisco...by Land's End...with a view...our view.

I took her hand in mine and pressed my face against it, resting it softly on the bed.

"I love you, Olivia. I'm sorry. I'm so sorry. It won't happen again. I promise. I won't ever betray you again. Please, please hear me...please." I couldn't hold back any longer. Tears flooded my eyes and drenched her soft, olive hand. My shoulders shook and a deep wailing came from within me.

"Son?"

I sat up and tried to compose myself.

"You know you don't have to do that for me. Pretend. Be the strong hero who doesn't feel, right?"

"What do you need, Dad?"

"How is she?"

"Fine. The HM repaired most of the damage. We just have to wait for her to wake up to see if there's any long term brain damage."

"That's good. And Thomas?"

"We left him in the apartment while it burned, but we saw NSPs run in, so who knows if he made it out."

"You know...when Olivia wakes up, she may be different."

"I know that, Dad."

"I've been watching her, Ethan. She's not the same girl you fell in love with. And you're not the same boy either."

"I would hope not."

He sighed. "I just...don't want to see you suffer, or lose time with someone, when maybe there's another person more right for you."

I jumped up and grabbed the collar of his shirt. "There is no one else besides Olivia who is right for me. It's her, and only her."

"You're right." He held his hands up in surrender, and I relaxed my hands, taking them off his shirt. "I'm sorry, Ethan. For everything."

I looked down at the woman I loved and felt a deep longing–for forgiveness, for a fresh start, for the chance to begin again. That's what I wanted with her: for her to forgive me, to let go, to rebuild something new. Was my father asking the same of me? How could I deny him what I was so desperately hoping she would give to me?

"I know, Dad. I know."

"It's been a long few months...Ethan...a long few years." Guilt swarmed his voice as he swallowed.

"It's been a long...ten years."

He nodded. "When you're ready, let's talk about what happened down there and anything new you learned about the Nation."

"Dad, there's so much more than you even realize. It's hard to wrap my mind around it."

"Okay, son. Let's not worry about that tonight then. Focus on Olivia, and we can catch up tomorrow."

"Thanks."

He walked out, but paused and turned around. "Oh, they said they brought a boy in too. What's his name?"

"Cooper, Cooper Jones. One of Rose's classmates, I guess. Have you seen him?"

"Briefly, as I passed on my way to your room. When I saw him, I could've sworn it was you lying in that hospital bed."

"Please, that kid? Did you see how scrawny he is? Although, I will say, he packs a powerful punch."

"He hit you?" My dad chuckled.

"Yeah, and I was helping the damn kid."

"Hmmm...sounds like another person I know."

He smiled at me, and I laughed. Once he was gone, I moved my chair closer to Olivia, wrapping my hand around hers and setting my head on her bed. I fell asleep as entangled as she would probably have allowed at the moment, grateful for each rise and fall of her chest. She was the only love I ever wanted, and I would spend the rest of my life proving that to her.

31

OLIVIA

I awoke a few days after we returned, confused about my surroundings and what happened at The Frederic. At first, I thought I was back at Elysium, the sounds and smells pulled me to a time before the Nation. Once I realized where I was, all I wanted was to be with my children. I became extremely agitated when they wouldn't let me get out of the hospital bed, and the medical staff had to sedate me again.

Voices talked around me, about me, and I tried to follow, but couldn't fully. In the beginning, scans showed my brain was healing, but at a slower rate than they hoped. It wasn't until September when I finally started piecing together the remnants of what happened in Rose Bay and The Frederic. Flashbacks from the ten years I spent with Thomas played like horror movies any time I closed my eyes–memories I had long buried, but walking freely like ghosts in my room.

Ethan kept his distance after I screamed at him to leave me alone. He blamed the concussion, and said I "wasn't in my right mind." But my love for him had ended, and the life I once wanted burned in The Frederic, despite him saving me and the children. While I was in the medical wing, Samara helped me piece details together about The Frederic. She told me she called Kai on her way downstairs to tell him to get out. He grabbed what he could before the fire took his apartment as well. She visited frequently, keeping me updated on the different plans to infiltrate the Nation. But I didn't see Laura once. I worried she may have seen the footage, like Ethan, and would never forgive me for what I did to her wife. My children stayed with my mother and sister while I recovered in the hospital. Lucas came to visit me after my scans started to show improvement, but Rose had told my sister she wasn't ready to see me yet.

We learned Morgan was caught in Rose Bay. Kai's people said Girly saw Morgan slip the phone in his car when he bought Samara. NSP watched her when she was in the Center's tech rooms and caught her stealing data for us. The day after we got back to the compound, Kai received a message saying that she had disappeared from their systems. We didn't know if she was dead or alive.

Kai became the harbinger for the U.S., sharing every detail they had on the Nation, Thomas, Jeffrey, and Governor Valentin. Dr. Conrad and Ethan drove across the Nevada border, deep within the Truckee River side, because they didn't believe him. Once across, they saw a life we'd all left behind when we joined the Nation. A sense of cloaked freedom held close to their chest, letting them breathe in an air that the Nation skies would never provide.

You had to hand it to the Nation's leaders. They knew how to keep us all in the same cage. Just like lab rats trained generation after generation. If they tried to escape, they were shocked. Eventually, the electricity wasn't even needed. The bars stayed cold, but the fear stayed warm, encoded in the offspring, spoken in whispers. The rats never left, because they'd been taught never to try. We, like the rats, fell in line and never tried to leave the Nation.

Kai's intel told him that Thomas made it out alive. The NSP that tried to kill us pulled him and Penny's body from the fire, saving his life and returning her to Jeffrey. A misstep for all of us—had I just pulled the trigger, we would be fighting a different fight with the Nation. Chris died on his way to Mid Clinic. When they arrived at Mid Clinic, other rebels had already raided it, and there wasn't anything Brandon or Vivian could do to stop the bleeding. Ethan held Kai partially responsible for Chris's death because he failed to mention the HM was in our car. Shortly after we all got back, Ethan punched Kai, Kai punched him back, and the two of them put on a show no one had the energy to watch.

Kai visited me often to bring updates, but mostly just read books to me he found in our library. I think it soothed him, bringing a sense of normalcy to his daily routine as an outsider within the Resistance.

When I could finally leave the medical wing, I saw Brandon and Jude nestled under a tree on a bench by the lake. Brandon's shoulders shuddered while Jude embraced him. A strange familiarity swept through me, reminding me of a day just months earlier with Samara, a day when I wanted to burn everything down–including her. I knew Jude and the love he was capable of...the love he needed and wanted in return. Brandon was heartbroken now, but it wouldn't always be that way.

The transition back to full-time motherhood, and reconnecting as a family, proved to be more challenging than I had expected. Rose, in her adolescent way, continued to isolate and shut me out. She spent most of her days with Cooper, or playing with Lucas. We moved to one of the houses because I had a family now. I invited Cooper to live with us at least until, as Ethan said, "we figured out what to do with him." I knew what would happen, though, as soon as I told Ethan that Cooper was our son. Telling Ethan would propel his mind to create something that could never be anymore—a family for us. He would try to relive the past, and repair a wall that was beyond mending. Ethan deserved to know the truth, and I wouldn't keep it from him too much longer. I decided, however, that I wouldn't say anything until I needed to...until I wanted to.

I sat on the bench by the lake every night around sunset, like I'd done many times in the past few months. My mind wandered from what was next, to what I still needed to do. Navigating all the changes in such a short time was proving to be more wearing for me than I liked. I was tired more often, quieter, more reflective. I had to ensure my next step provided a clear escape route for the children and me. For the Nation to be dismantled. For Thomas.

I worried about my children and their distance from me. Lucas asked me questions about the propaganda and I told him it wasn't true. There were days when he still looked at me like I was a criminal, and Rose would continue to struggle until she saw her father for what he really was. Luckily, I had my sister and for the time being, my mother in their lives. They helped bridge the gap, like so many other women do for one another when the fissures between a mother and daughter grow too wide.

I would always be their mother. The one to rescue them if they needed to. But they needed someone else right now, and something else needed me. The people trapped in the Nation needed someone to rescue them. They were still broken, burning, and waiting for a hand to pull them out. I knew I would need to lead now and be the face of the Resistance. It wasn't meant for Ethan anymore, because even though his life was touched by Thomas and the Nation, it wasn't scarred like mine was...like my children's lives were. I would rise and become what they needed, and I would finish what was started back in April once and for all.

"May I sit here?" Dr. Conrad interrupted my trailing thoughts.

"It's all yours." I pushed my body toward the opposite side away from Dr. Conrad.

"Nice evening. The sun is almost finally gone. The heat is changing these days, and I can't say I can complain."

"Yeah, it's nice when it cools down again." I feigned interest.

"Only to start back up again next year, right?"

"Yeah, I guess so."

"You know, Olivia. I need to tell you something."

"Of course you do."

He sighed. "You've outgrown us, Olivia." Dr. Conrad said, staring out at the lake.

I turned to him. "What?"

"You don't belong here. But you don't belong there either." He pointed west toward the Nation skies. "It's like when a child goes away to college, leaves home for the first time. The first summer they return they go back to their old job. Hang out with their old friends. Have family dinners. Move into their old room. But that's just the thing. It's all in their past. It's a reckoning every young adult has to come to terms with. They can't believe that anything has really changed that much. They don't want to believe that the person–they, their friends, and their family–became after leaving is any different from who they were a year ago. But it has changed. They have. Everyone has. We change when we leave our first home. We grow into ourselves when we walk out the door. You and Ethan left these hills years ago...well, at least you did. I think my son never really left Elysium, that way of life. What it represented to him. What you represented to him. And he's held onto that so tightly, for so long, that he may have missed a few things...signs that the world around him may have outgrown his own memories. It's going to be hard for him, you know."

"What will?"

"When you choose someone else. It's going to slap him across the face, because he doesn't see it coming. His head knows...but his heart doesn't. And if anything is true about my son, it is that he's always led with his heart, for better or for worse. When you choose someone else, it will be his turn to shed the Ethan of the past. Without you moving forward, he will never become the man he's supposed to be. It's a burden you're going to have to bear, Olivia. A burden and a blessing, because you've already outgrown that man. As sad as that makes me and his mother, you outgrew him the moment you and Samara left for Rose Bay, and you made all of this your own."

His words disarmed me like no other. "I...I don't know what to say, Dr. Conrad."

"That's the beauty of it, Olivia. You don't have to say anything at all. And you owe no one an explanation for anything ever again. You're free to make your choices, and you get to decide who gets access to the hows and whys of those choices. You're on a different path than my son...and...I'm incredibly grateful for that, no matter how contentious we have been to each other."

I smiled, and he smiled back.

"There's something else I want to say to you too, if that's alright."

"Sure."

"Thank you for giving me a grandson." His eyes wet from pride as he looked at my shock and laughed. "You know I know that boy is the baby that you transferred, right?"

"How did you know about the transfer?"

"Ethan was devastated, and when he thought he was about to lose you too, I came down and helped. You wouldn't remember because you were so out of it. But as soon as I saw Cooper laying in that bed, I knew. I've watched him over the last couple months and everything about that child is his father's."

"And Ethan, does he know?"

"Not yet. But it's something that you'll need to share with him, sooner rather than later. What's funny is the boy drives him crazy. I saw Ethan trying to get him to do some cleaning up after dinner. The boy flat out refused. They both stood there, like two roosters about to show down in some backyard cock fight. I laughed, and when Ethan turned to me in question, I just told him, 'just funny seeing you with him, is all.' It is funny and beautiful. And when he learns there's a piece of him that will always live on, it'll heal his heart just a little bit from the break you're going to give it. It's good, Olivia. This is all good."

"I wish I could love him in that way again. I'm just so angry, still so angry."

"And you should be. But not just at him. He didn't throw your lives into ruin. He was part of the broken pieces that came out of slamming that plate to the floor. Your mother, Thomas, Jeffrey, Valentin, Penny...Mrs. Conrad and me. Those are who you can hold responsible for what happened. It's a shame what your mother went through."

"What exactly?"

"All the things she couldn't share with anyone, not even us. There's more that she knows, I'm sure of it, and one day I hope she finds a way to release it. Because if she doesn't, only darkness will consume her. It's hard, once someone makes a pact with the devil, to find their way out. That darkness starts like a small little seed, and eventually grows roots that spread across the entire body, soul, mind. If there's no one strong enough to pull someone out of that place, or if that person doesn't want to face the devil again and strike him down–he wins."

"I just don't think I can ever forgive her."

"She loves you, Olivia. She loves you, like all parents love their children, and sometimes that love can make us do some blurry things."

I knew she loved me, and at some point, I'd have to find a way out of my anger before it consumed me. My forgiveness, if that's what I would call it, would have to be for me, not her. She would never be able to atone for what she did, or for how she shaped the worst part of my life, but I didn't have to give her so much power over it either. When the Nation was gone and I had time to breathe in a new world, I would deal with her then. For now, I would focus on what she could give me, with the children, and keep her at arm's length to protect myself.

Dr. Conrad continued, "How do you think Mr. Acosta will fit into all of this?"

"What do you mean?"

"Well, he seems to pay attention to you more than he pays attention to other single women on this compound."

"Ha, ha Dr. Conrad. I'm really the only one he knows. He met Samara, but he and I spent some really intense days together when we first met, so he's just more comfortable with me. Maybe just a little bit of trauma bonding, too." I laughed, "Besides, apparently his father wants to know everything about me and what I know about the Nation, so they can speed things up with the takeover."

"Okay, whatever you say, Olivia. We need to make sure he and his father stay true to their word. The video calls I've had with his father make me question the United States and their intentions."

"I know. I told Kai to be careful, but he really believes Salvador is just going to let him go free when this is over."

"From what I've seen with Salvador Acosta, he's just like the rest of us trying to claim our seat at the table. We, you especially, need to be careful, just like you were with us. If you're not the one pulling the strings, Olivia, then it's your strings that are being pulled. And that man knows exactly what strings to pull–when, who, and where. Trust me."

I drew a deep sigh in and kicked a pebble across the dirt.

"Something else on your mind?"

"I just don't know what's next. What I should do next."

"You do what your 'I am' is telling you to do. You do what your children need you to do, if it's right for you. You do what that fire inside of you wants you to do. You're on your own, kid. And for the first time, I think we are all going to see who Olivia really is...and honestly, who she has always been. You, Ethan, your mom, the Nation–all of us–never really gave that Olivia a chance, because we only saw who we wanted you to be. But now, it's your turn. Become the Olivia who's been screaming to come out...your Olivia. No one else's."

He was right. For the first time, freedom felt real and within reach. I could step into this newly shedded skin and rediscover myself.

The Olivia who was smart, kind, and fiercely determined. The Olivia who loved her children with an unshakable devotion. The Olivia who could be a fighter, a mother, and, when the time came, a killer. The Olivia who would burn the Nation to the ground so others could taste the freedom it had denied them for so long. The Olivia who no longer needed anyone's permission to simply exist. To be.

Our voices stayed quiet as the sun dipped below the horizon, leaving its last golden kiss on the lake. It was on its way to say farewell to Thomas and the Nation, and we sat as silent witnesses to its journey. Another fight loomed ahead, another uncertain future, but for this moment, the stillness held our unlikely alliance.

A flock of geese broke the silence, their cries echoing as they skimmed the water and made their resting place on the dry, yellowed land. The air carried the crisp promise of autumn, the seasonal shift we had all been waiting for–a shift we desperately needed. The leaves would soon let go, surrendering their hold to the pull of time, and in their fall, they would blanket the earth in quiet preparation for what lay ahead: a war I would bring to the Nation's doorstep.

When the sun was gone, cool air greeted me like an old friend, unpredictable and bracing, a reminder that change was both inevitable and necessary. The winter would come with its unknown heartbreak, but beyond it lay the hope of a spring yet to bloom—cycles we all craved.

Change was coming. And with it, the time to let go of what no longer served me had arrived. The Nation had taken too much, and given too little. We would remain something to each other until I dismantled it, and the people held within its invisible borders finally knew the truth. I had my children. I had my life. And when the dust settled, when the sun rose again on a world reshaped by this fight, I would have my freedom.

And maybe, just maybe, that would be enough.

THOMAS

I kept my eyes shut, grimacing at the pain from my newly burned skin. If it hadn't been for the banging air conditioner in this tier-three apartment, I might have been able to sleep a little bit more, even with the burns. My gunshot wound had already healed, thanks to Jeffrey and the HM at his private hospital.

A part of me felt bad for him because of Penny. He was so angry that she was gone, and that Ethan, of all people, was the one to take her life. I liked Penny. She served her purpose. In my bed, but more importantly, in the mission of the Nation. Her strong sense of ambition, coupled with her father's power, helped me create the life I have today. She helped me drug Olivia throughout our marriage, and patiently waited until her time would come to reign in the seat of the Director's wife.

Her father had chosen me, not only for the Nation's needs, but for the needs of his daughter. I didn't mind though. I fucked her for months after he told me of his plan, and when we realized she couldn't get pregnant, our future changed forever. I kept our affair secret for the entire time Penny was in our service. I was good at so many things. Penny's and my affair was one I was particularly proud of.

But at some point I knew I would need to dispose of her too. Like all women, she was a liability—too emotional and never thinking things through with logical purpose. Her need for escaping when she was with the children worried me too. She started to dabble in experimental mommy pill's—what the other tier-four mothers called them. That didn't sit well with me considering my own mother's addiction. I wanted a wife, and a mother who was fully present with our children, especially in the most important years. Her death would have been an accident on a family vacation, that Jeffrey would've never been able to solve.

I shifted slightly. The burning tightness of my skin against the sheets angered me.

"Fuck." I turned and looked at the full bottle of pain killers. I never touched them, I never would. I could never end up like my mother, especially now, when my focus was on being a father again. I got up and went to the bathroom. The scars on my back were disgusting, but the skin grafting process would require anesthesia, and I didn't want to mess with any of that stuff.

I thought about Olivia's c-section scar. I hated seeing that imperfection on her. It never reminded me of my children, just hers with Ethan. He got her first. The perfect example of genetics wasted on him. When I first learned about his genetics, I refused to believe his superiority to me. How could someone like him have such a high score? He had to be removed so I could have her, and further the plans of the Nation.

But then, in an act of brilliance, I tracked down their transfer and started bringing him into my world. First, with his father, folding him into the company to keep an eye on how Cooper grew. Then, with a phony internship. Finally, as the friend to my sweet Rose. The plan was to keep Cooper around long enough to get the genetics results I needed and then let Olivia find out. After that, I would take care of him once and for all. A tragic accident, of course. It was going to be perfect. I had the information on the flash drive and I was going to conveniently leave the file open one day. She would see it and be destroyed. Still thinking Ethan was dead, she would try to find Cooper and seek him out. See if he looked like Ethan and the dumb fuck looked so much like Ethan. And then, Cooper would be killed in a car accident or school shooting or something else so loud and dramatic and grotesque that it would break her. She wouldn't have anyone to talk to; to tell about her pain. It was one of the best laid plans yet, even if it did wipe out a perfect specimen.

Unlike her c-section scar, the burns were reminders of how far I had come. I was so close to getting everything I wanted. I thought back to how all of this started, with Penny expecting me to kill Olivia on our tenth wedding anniversary vacation, but I was never going to do that. I wanted Olivia to suffer, just a bit longer. I needed her, and was planning on taking her to the lab, instead of killing her on our wedding anniversary.

Once I saw the feed from her time with Jude, however, I knew I wanted her to suffer even more. Giving her body to him like a common whore. I could choose to have an affair, to be with other women, but she couldn't. No matter how much I believed in this system, I was never okay with women sleeping with other men. It goes against everything we stand for–the purity of our wives' bodies for us. When they slip that ring on their finger, they are bound to us for eternity, their bodies especially. Olivia's body belonged to me until I was done with it.

I wondered if she would have ended up at Rose Bay. If Samara had suggested it because she knew the secrets kept there. I was sure Ethan had tried everything to keep her from going because he held a claim to her body, just like I did. The difference was, I actually had the power all along. I figured she would end up back at home, thinking there was something there that could help her find the children and me. The note was another little feather in my cap. I loved the footage–seeing her read the note and then burn it all down. The insurance money was better to me than selling it and having someone live in my home. I wished I had seen *that* Olivia when we were married–she would have been more fun than the one I had.

I went back into my room, my phone buzzing on the nightstand.

"Hello? Yeah, I see it. Send it over. Thanks."

I swiped the call away and clicked on the link in my message. Floating above my HoloPhone was a 3-D image of the Resistance's compound in Cameron Park. I knew where they were now. I wouldn't be here that much longer. Once I got the kids back, I would move us closer to the capital in one of the new high-end apartments made for people like me, then I would find a place for Olivia and Ethan. Some new lab, where they could see what I was doing to other one every day.

I smiled at the thought of seeing their tears day after day, and the anguish on Ethan's face.

For now, I would have to wait, bide my time until I faced Olivia and Ethan. They had no idea what force was coming for them. And when I thought of this, nothing made me happier, not even the first cry after my children's birth.

The downfall of Ethan and Olivia would be my greatest accomplishment yet.

ACKNOWLEDGMENTS

What an amazing place to be in, publishing my second book in a series that feels like my own becoming. Thank you to everyone who helped this project become a reality. Thank you even more for the countless number of people who pulled me out of the water when I wasn't sure I could do it on my own.

First, to my boys. I look back and think about so many things in our lives and how the last three years have shaped us. We are our own three little birds - the image inked on my side over ten years ago foreshadowed our world. I knew it then, that they were us, even though I tried to think they were something else. It's us against the world my loves. You two have been my light, the humor that has filled the room, the love that found me in the closet with my sippy cup full of wine. You continue to make me proud everyday and not once regret my decision to leave because you are turning into the men I always hoped you would be. And that's because you're living with a mother who is happy, healthy, and free. Love you to the moon, back, and maybe a quick trip to Jupiter too.

Jason, thank you for being the pull into my new life. I've lived a thousand lives with you in the last two years and I am grateful for the timing of our lives. Thank you for the late nights and life experiences across the world. For catching the huge plot hole that could have tanked the book. For the endless edits, the moments I was too deep in my own head, and the times I questioned why I was doing this at all. Your love and support have shaped not just this work, but the person I've become through writing it. Here's to what's next and the writing that will inevitably follow. I love you.

Jessica, I'm so sorry I gave you cancer. I will fix that in the last book and somehow make you a millionaire so we can go on Disney cruises. You've been my rock through all of this - my number one fan - my spicy voice of reason when I wanted to burn it all down. Thank you for being the best sister a girl could ever have. I couldn't do this life without you.

To my family that saw me through it all, the ups, downs and in-betweens, thank you Andrew, Mom, Steven, Aunt Steph, Uncle Dan, and Kathie. In the darkest and most challenging moments, when life tests us the most, it is true love and family that reveal their strength. I am deeply thankful for you showing up when it mattered, offering support and care that helped light my path.

Natalie and Matt, thank you for letting me write at your cabin–my major breakthrough happened drinking champagne at your table and watching the snow fall while Jason played a scary video game. I remember thinking how it wouldn't be the last time at your place, even though it was only my first. I love the place we have in each other's lives and look forward to everything else that comes with you and your beautiful family. All my love.

Nicole, whenever I hear Counting Crows and their line "Nicole's my oldest friend..." I think of how that line was always meant for you and me. Every year, our friendship grows stronger and more authentic. We've met in lifetimes before, finally getting to a place where we can cry-laugh at the things that make our hearts ache while also saying thank you for the pennies, swans, and whispers from the other side. Love you. Always.

Kelley, you're it girl. Stars aligned and gave us our second chance and it's the kind of story novels are written about. Let's book the trips, find our bars, and love our babies fiercely. Love you sis.

Ashleigh, thank you for being the foundation every, single, day. Whether during tea time, cry time, or fun time, you've been the most supportive human. My mornings have started with you for the last five years and I can't wait for the next ten. Heart you.

Gretchen, girrrrlllllll...thank you. The mom bestie award goes to you - forever and ever. Thank you and Jen for helping me burn my photos and keeping logic that maybe some should be saved for the kids. You two are amazing and I am grateful for you! G -Thank you for going with me when I had to put Cooper down. Thank you for pulling me out of the pit and keeping me safe while watching my little icon drive to make fun, poor life decisions. Love your family. Love you. Love our friendship.

Megan, my work wife. Thank you for being there every day and seeing me in the highs and lows and telling me it will be okay. You've cheered me on and supported me beyond what I could ever ask for. Our sushi dates and birthday dates have been one of the best parts of my life. I love you and am so grateful for our friendship.

Laura, sista queen! Love you and the time we've grown together over the years. Thank you for reading my stories and believing in them. For the questions about Olivia and Ethan's motivation and for being there in the moments when I needed someone to say "fuck that guy." You're incredible and I love you.

Jason G., thank you for the very day shenanigans, talks about life and dumbness and humor, and giving me a logical way to think every time I was going to burn it all down. You've saved a lot of lives, mainly mine.

Michele, thank you for our talks and hilariously healing moments at Streets. For checking in, for being my fire-sign Leo, for being fun and loving and one of the most amazing and strongest women in my life. Thank you for always being willing to read drafts and listen to the playlists. Heart you so.

Cory, thank you so much for everything over the years, especially the last few. Your words, texts, church sermons, and humor are so important to me. You've helped me in more ways than you will ever know. Love you - PHS sistas 4-eva.

Brittony, you were a pivotal part of my coming out of the dark, not to mention the words you spoke to me on a plane ride back from San Diego "Maybe she's outgrown him." I had terrible writer's block and that one phrase opened up Olivia's world to new possibilities outside of Ethan. Your texts, talks, wine nights, and constant support were the backbone of where I am today.

Amanda, I love our friendship, humor, and wit. Like, there isn't a single time when we're together and we don't laugh. Your support with including me in your book clubs to dedicating part of your birthday night to celebrate *my* book is just incredible - I love that you gave people homework for your birthday. Your kindness and generosity have meant more than words can say. I'm endlessly grateful for your friendship.

Susan, thank you for telling me to go, to jump, and to cry and be angry. Thank you for the texts, IG videos, and music that ended up on this playlist. We need to really work on making shirts for all the things.

Amy, thank you for your writing and it constantly inspiring me. You trust me with words so precious to you and it means so much to me. There's an Easter Egg in this book for you.

Laura L., thank you for being a ray of sunshine every time I see you. Your feedback and edits in the first draft were so helpful and your love for this world I built means everything to me. Keep writing. I want to have your book on my shelf one day.

To my favorite people in the most crazy job ever: Betsy, Tyler, Laurie, Angela, Jenn, Jenna, Jerry, John, Franny, Jason,

Prasad, Q, Ben, Jaime, Jamie, Jake, Kristie, Sarah, Russell, Melissa, Kuester, Porter, Patty, Megan, Doug and the amazing teachers and staff who make coming to work easy. Thank you.

Sarah B., thank you for getting me into Capital Books on K and being my fave hype girl! I love your Sagittarian fire and am so grateful for you!

Capital Books on K: Jacob, Katie, Hilarie, Julie, Ross, Faith, and the rest of the team - Thank you a million times over. I think back over the last three years and how serendipitous it was for our paths to cross. My writing career and love for the local book community has you threaded into it like it was always supposed to be. Thank you for your support and constant love to the Indie authors and community.

Jacob, thank you for the headshots and that little bit of liquid courage during our Knotty Con greatness. You're amazing and I'm so glad you and J are friends...but also annoyed he's the store winner because you feed his nerd addiction.

To my ARC readers: Laura L, Danielle H., Robin P., Kaitlyn C., Kandice S., Sarah B., Mari G., Haley L., Kimberly G., Kendra S., Lily O., Ana S., Jenny B., Ashley B., Stefani B., Tanishque S., Allana V., Amber A., Katrina S., Megan H., Lauren R., Ashley H., Alana C., Sonia R., Lizzie B, Michele M, Amanda D., Ashleigh P., Jessica M., Tammy I., John, Michael, and Jason A. THANK YOU so much! And Robin, thank you for the initial edits and feedback. Jessica, thank you for finding those last minute edits.

To my amazing Instagram community. The Bookish Crew, @madeleineeliotwrites @capitalbooksonk @knottynovels, @marissavanskike, and the amazing people and book clubs I met at Knotty Con - keep reading and keep showing up to their amazing events!

To the book clubs over the last two years! LitHappens,

Amanda's bday, and Suzanne's book club - thank you for the invitations, the conversations, and the love for these characters.

To the two people who helped bring this creation to life:

Hannah Sol Marie, your developmental edits were incredible. Olivia's story is better because of you and I am so grateful you challenged me to push her even further. You've been my cheerleader, my thought partner, and an amazing human to work with thank you!

Dan Aguilar, who knew twenty-five years ago our D bldg. friendship would bring us to today. This book cover is so personal to me. When I saw what you created, I was blown away. I knew what I wanted and you captured it perfectly. I love how you told me it was a gusty image - that's exactly what I think this book is, gutsy. Thank you for the back and forth creative brainstorming and every time I asked for a change. You're amazing.

To my students: I can think of 6 or 7 reasons why you make my job amazing. You are the reason I love walking through those doors every day. Your humor, curiosity, intellect, crazy tea, and joy for life make me so proud to be your teacher. Keep reaching for the stars and following your dreams.

Finally, to the things that get me through my writing sessions...Beats, playlists, Kelly Clarkson, Taylor Swift, Miley Cyrus, Riopy, San Antonio Blend, chocolate chips, vanilla scented candles, MacBooks, and post it notes.

Shoot...the calicos will kill me if I don't mention them... Aurora and Rose thank you for knocking over my coffee, pushing my notes on the desk, and sitting in the window judging me as I play Wordle instead of write. Stay sassy my little kittens.

PLAYLIST

A key part of my writing process is building playlists that I listen to while writing. I create different ones depending on the character, chapter, or emotional tone of a scene. Music helps me access the emotional core of a moment–sometimes I'll play a single song on repeat until the feeling lands just right on the page. I had to do this for Chapters 14-15 as well as Chapter 20 when Olivia can no longer contain her fire.

In Book One, songs followed certain chapters or the flow of the book, but in this book I wanted to create something that could pair with a movie. My brain pictures the scenes and actors in every chapter and I think about what songs would accompany them. The playlist that follows is divided up into sections that follow Olivia's journey–a few on here are also Ethan's–but for the most part this book is all Olivia.

- **Songs 1–11** reflect where Olivia begins–uncertain, restrained, and navigating the world before she takes control and chooses to enter the Challenge Center.

- **Songs 12–19** mark her discovery of sexual autonomy and the power she finds within her own body.

- **Songs 20–23** accompany the most violent section of the book and its emotional aftermath. These songs also serve as a broader acknowledgment of the violence women face in our society and how none of us are alone.

- **Songs 24–26** chart the beginning of Olivia's transformation, and her physical act of dealing with the grief, anger, and loss of her previous life.

- **Songs 27-32** lead us toward the final songs–anthems of hope, resilience, and revolution. Here, we witness her becoming who she was always meant to be: the face of the Resistance.

PLAYLIST

1. Coma - Taylor Acorn, Cassandee Pope
2. July - Noah Cyrus
3. The Tradition - Halsey
4. The Manuscript - Taylor Swift
5. Colorblind - Counting Crows
6. Time And Time Again - Counting Crows
7. Start a Riot - Banners
8. Youth - Daughter
9. Bad Husband - Eminem
10. Lucid Dreams - Juice WRLD
11. skip this part - Kelly Clarkson
12. Mr. Sandman - SYML
13. Little Girl Gone - CHINCHILLA
14. Desire - Meg Myers
15. Watch Me Burn - Michele Monroe
16. Water - Jack Garratt
17. one night - Christina Perri
18. Power Over Me - Dermot Kennedy
19. Another Place - X Ambassadors
20. Way down We Go - Kaleo

21. hostage - Billie Eilish
22. Silent All These Years - Tori Amos
23. Breathe Me - Sia
24. Gaslighter - The Chicks
25. Reckoning - Whiskey Myers
26. Bridges - Generdyn (feat. Fjøra)
27. The Only Way Out - Danielle Ponder
28. Breakfast - Dove Cameron
29. It's My Life - No Doubt
30. Rise - Katy Perry
31. The Fear - The Score
32. Burn it Down - 717 Tapes - Warren Zeiders

ALSO BY MELISSA GOWDY BALDWIN

The Marriage Wars Book One

Available to purchase from Capital Books on K, Amazon, Barnes & Noble, and other online retailers.

Upcoming Titles

Meet Me In Buenos Aires

Jillian Swipes Right

The Nation is Burning The Marriage Wars Book Three

Meet Me In Waikiki

www.ingramcontent.com/pod-product-compliance
Lightning Source LLC
Chambersburg PA
CBHW021408310726

48971CB00005B/1243